THE HILL OF
EVIL COUNSEL

Amos Oz

THE HILL OF EVIL COUNSEL

THREE STORIES

*Translated from the Hebrew
by Nicholas de Lange
in collaboration with the author*

A Harvest/HBJ Book
A Helen and Kurt Wolff Book
Harcourt Brace Jovanovich, Publishers
San Diego   New York   London

Requests for permission to make copies
of any part of the work should be mailed to:
Permissions Department,
Harcourt Brace Jovanovich, Publishers,
Orlando, Florida 32887.

Library of Congress Cataloging in Publication Data
Oz, Amos.
The hill of evil counsel.
"A Helen and Kurt Wolff book."
Translation of Har ha-'etsah ha-ra 'ah.
CONTENTS: The hill of evil counsel.—Mr. Levi.
—Longing.
I. Title
PZ4.0989Hi |PJ5054| 892.4'3'6   77-92543
ISBN 0-15-640275-0 (pbk.)
Printed in the United States of America
First Harvest/HBJ edition 1991
A B C D E

CONTENTS

The Hill
of Evil
Counsel

1

It was dark. In the dark a woman said: I'm not afraid. A man replied: Oh, yes, you are. Another man said: Quiet.

Then dim lights came on at either side of the stage, the curtains parted, and all was quiet.

In May 1946, one year after the Allied victory, the Jewish Agency mounted a great celebration in the Edison Cinema. The walls were draped with the flags of Great Britain and the Zionist Movement. Vases of gladioli stood on the front of the stage. And a banner carried a quotation from the Bible: PEACE BE WITHIN THY WALLS AND PROSPERITY WITHIN THY PALACES.

The British Governor of Jerusalem strode up to the stage with a military gait and delivered a short address, in the course of which he cracked a subtle joke and read some lines of Byron. He was followed by the Zionist leader Moshe Shertok, who expressed in English and Hebrew the feelings of the Jewish community. In the corners of the auditorium, on either side of the stage, and by all the doors stood British soldiers wearing red berets and carrying submachine guns, to guard against the Underground. In the dress circle could be discerned the stiffly seated figure of the High Commissioner, Sir Alan Cunningham, with a small party of ladies and army officers. The ladies were holding opera glasses. A choir of pioneers in blue shirts sang some work songs. The songs were Russian, and, like the audience, they were wistful, rather than happy.

After the singing there was a film of Montgomery's tanks

advancing across the Western Desert. The tanks raised columns
of dust, crushed trenches and barbed-wire fences under their
tracks, and stabbed the gray desert sky with their antennas. The
auditorium was filled with the thunder of guns and the noise
of marching songs.

In the middle of the film, there was a slight disturbance in
the dress circle.

The film stopped suddenly. The lights came on. A voice was
raised in a reproach or a curt command: Is there a doctor in
the house?

In row 29, Father immediately got to his feet. He fastened
the top button of his white shirt, whispered to Hillel to take
care of Mother and keep her calm until things were sorted out,
and, like a man plunging into a burning building at the risk of
his life, turned and pushed his way to the staircase.

It transpired that Lady Bromley, the High Commissioner's
sister-in-law, had been taken suddenly faint.

She was wearing a long white dress, and her face, too, was
white. Father hurriedly introduced himself to the heads of the
administration and proceeded to lay her limp arm across his
shoulders. Like a gentle knight carrying a sleeping beauty, he
helped Lady Bromley to the ladies' powder room. He seated her
on an upholstered stool and handed her a glass of cold water.
Three high-ranking British officials in evening dress hurried
after him, stood in a semicircle around the patient, and sup-
ported her head as she took a single, painful sip. An elderly
wing commander in uniform extracted her fan from her white
evening bag, opened it carefully, and fanned her face.

Her Ladyship opened her eyes wearily. She stared almost ironically for a moment at all the men who were bustling around
her. She was angular and wizened, and with her pursed lips,
her pointed nose, and her permanent sardonic scowl, she looked
like some thirsty bird.

"Well, doctor," the wing commander addressed Father in
acid tones, "what do you think?"

Father hesitated, apologized twice, and suddenly made up his mind. He leaned over, and with his fine, sensitive fingers he undid the laces of the tight corset. Lady Bromley felt immediately better. Her shriveled hand, which resembled a chicken leg, straightened the hem of the dress. A crease appeared in the tightly closed mouth, a kind of cracked smile. She crossed her old legs, and her voice when she spoke was tinny and piercing.

"It's just the climate."

"Ma'am——" one of the officials began politely.

But Lady Bromley was no longer with him. She turned impatiently to Father:

"Young man, would you be kind enough to open the windows. Yes, that one, too. I need air. What a charming boy."

She addressed him in this way because, in his white sports shirt worn outside his khaki trousers, and with his biblical sandals, he looked to her more like a young servant than like a doctor. She had passed her youth among gardens, apes, and fountains in Bombay.

Father silently obeyed and opened all the windows.

The evening air of Jerusalem came in, and with it smells of cabbage, pine trees, and garbage.

He produced from his pocket a Health Service pillbox, carefully opened it, and handed Lady Bromley an aspirin. He did not know the English for "migraine," and so he said it in German. Doubtless his eyes at that moment shone with a sympathetic optimism behind his round spectacles.

After a few minutes, Lady Bromley asked to be taken back to her seat. One of the high-ranking officials took down Father's name and address and dryly thanked him. They smiled. There was a moment's hesitation. Suddenly the official held out his hand. They shook hands.

Father went back to his seat in row 29, between his wife and his son. He said:

"It was nothing. It was just the climate."

The lights went out again. Once more General Montgomery pursued General Rommel mercilessly across the desert. Fire and dust clouds filled the screen. Rommel appeared in close-up, biting his lip, while in the background bagpipes skirled ecstatically.

Finally, the two anthems, British and Zionist, were played. The celebration was over. The people left the Edison Cinema and made for their homes. The evening twilight suddenly fell upon Jerusalem. In the distance, bald hills could be seen, with here and there a solitary tower. There was a sprinkling of stone huts on the faraway slopes. Shadows rustled in the side streets. The whole city was under the sway of a painful longing. Electric lights began to come on in the windows. There was a tense expectancy, as if at any moment a new sound might break out. But there were only the old sounds all around, a woman grumbling, a shutter squeaking, a lovesick cat screeching among the garbage cans in a backyard. And a very distant bell.

A handsome Bokharan barber in a white coat stood alone in the window of his empty shop and sang as he shaved himself. At that moment, a patrolling British jeep crossed the street, armed with a machine gun, brass bullets gleaming in its ammunition belt.

An old woman sat alone on a wooden stool beside the entrance of her basement shop. Her hands, wrinkled like a plasterer's, rested heavily on her knees. The last evening light caught her head, and her lips moved silently. From inside the basement, another woman spoke, in Yiddish:

"It's perfectly simple: it'll end badly."

The old woman made no reply. She did not move.

Outside Ernpreis the pants presser's, Father was accosted by a pious beggar, who demanded and received a two-mil piece, furiously thanked God, cursed the Jewish Agency twice, and swept an alley cat out of the way with the tip of his stick.

From the east, the bells rang out continuously, high bells and deep bells, Russian bells, Anglican bells, Greek bells, Abyssinian, Latin, Armenian bells, as if a plague or a fire were devastating the city. But all the bells were doing was to call the darkness dark. And a light breeze blew from the northwest, perhaps from the sea; it stirred the tops of the pale trees that the

City Council had planted up Malachi Street and ruffled the boy's curly hair. It was evening. An unseen bird gave a strange, persistent cry. Moss sprouted in the cracks in the stone walls. Rust spread over the old iron shutters and veranda railings. Jerusalem stood very quiet in the last of the light.

During the night, the boy woke up again with an attack of asthma. Father came in barefoot and sang him a soothing song:

> Night is reigning in the skies,
> Time for you to close your eyes.
> Lambs and kids have ceased from leaping,
> All the animals are sleeping.
> Every bird is in its nest,
> All Jerusalem's at rest.

Toward dawn, the jackals howled in the wadi below Tel Arza. Mitya the lodger began to cry out in his sleep on the other side of the wall: "Leave him alone! He's still alive! *Y-a ny-e zna-yu.*" And he fell silent. Then cocks crew far away in the quarter of Sanhedriya and the Arab village of Shu'afat. At the first light, Father put on his khaki trousers, sandals, and a neatly pressed blue shirt with wide pockets, and set off for work. Mother went on sleeping until the women in the neighboring houses started beating their pillows and mattresses with all their might. Then she got up and in her silk dressing gown gave the boy a breakfast of a soft-boiled egg, Quaker Oats, and cocoa with the skin taken off; and she combed his curly hair.

Hillel said:

"I can do it by myself. Stop it."

An old glazier passed down the street, shouting, "Perfessional glazing! America! Anything repaired!" And the children called after him, "Loonie!"

A few days later, Father was surprised to receive a gold-embossed invitation for two to the May Ball at the High Commissioner's palace on the Hill of Evil Counsel. On the back of the invitation, the secretary had written in English that Lady

Bromley wished to convey to Dr. Kipnis her gratitude and profound apology, and that Sir Alan himself had expressed his appreciation.

Father was not a real doctor. He was actually a vet.

2

He had been born and brought up in Silesia. Hans Walter Landauer the famous geographer was his mother's uncle. Father had studied at the Veterinary Institute in Leipzig, specializing in tropical and subtropical cattle diseases.

In 1932, he had emigrated to Palestine with the intention of establishing a cattle farm in the mountains. He was a polite young man, quiet, principled, and full of hopes. In his dreams he saw himself wandering with a stick and a haversack among the hills of Galilee, clearing a patch of forest, and building with his own hands a wooden house beside a stream, with a sloping roof, an attic, and a cellar. He meant to get together some herdsmen and a herd of cattle, roaming by day to new pastures and by night sitting surrounded by books in a room full of hunting trophies, composing a monograph or a great poem.

For three months he stayed in a guesthouse in the small town of Yesud-Hama'alah, and he spent whole days wandering alone from morning to night in eastern Galilee looking for water buffalo in the Huleh Swamps. His body grew lean and bronzed, and his blue eyes, behind his round spectacles, looked like lakes in a snowy northern land. He learned to love the desolation of the distant mountains and the smell of summer: scorched thistles, goat dung, wood ash, the dusty east wind.

In the Arab village of Halsa, he met a wandering Bavarian ornithologist, a lonely and fervently evangelical man who believed that the return of the Jews to their land heralded the salvation of the world, and was collecting material for a great work on the birds of the Holy Land. Together they roamed to the Marj-'Ayun Valley, into the Mountains of Naphtali and the Huleh Swamps. Occasionally, in their wanderings, they reached the remote sources of the Jordan. Here they would sit all day in the shade of the lush vegetation, reciting together from memory their favorite Schiller poems and calling every bird and beast by its proper name.

When Father began to worry what would happen when he came to the end of the money that his mother's uncle the famous geographer had given him, he decided to go to Jerusalem to look into certain practical possibilities. Accordingly, he took his leave of the wandering Bavarian ornithologist, gathered his few possessions, and appeared one fine autumn morning in the office of Dr. Arthur Ruppin at the Jewish Agency in Jerusalem.

Dr. Ruppin took at once to the quiet, bronzed boy who had come to him from Galilee. He also recalled that in his youth he had studied the tropical countries in Landauer's great *Atlas*. When Father began to describe the project of a cattle farm in the hills of Galilee, he took down some hasty notes. Father concluded with these words:

"It is a difficult plan to put into practice, but I believe it is not impossible."

Dr. Ruppin smiled sadly:

"Not impossible, but difficult to put into practice. Very difficult!"

And he proceeded to point out one or two awkward facts.

He persuaded Father to postpone the realization of his plan for the time being, and meanwhile to invest his money in the acquisition of a young orange grove near the settlement of Nes Tsiyona, and also to buy without delay a small house in the new suburb of Tel Arza, which was being built to the north of Jerusalem.

Father did not argue.

Within a few days, Dr. Ruppin had had Father appointed as a traveling government veterinary officer and had even invited him for coffee in his house in Rehavia.

For several years, Father would get up before sunrise and travel on sooty buses up to Bethlehem and Ramallah, down to Jericho, out to Lydda, to supervise the villagers' cattle on behalf of the government.

The orange grove near the settlement of Nes Tsiyona began to yield a modest income, which he deposited, along with part of his government salary, in the Anglo-Palestine Bank. He furnished his small house in Tel Arza with a bed, a desk, a wardrobe, and bookshelves. Above his desk he hung a large picture of his mother's uncle the famous geographer. Hans Walter Landauer looked down on Father with an expression of skepticism and mild surprise, particularly in the evenings.

As he traveled around the villages, Father collected rare thistles. He also gathered some fossils and pieces of ancient pottery. He arranged them all with great care. And he waited.

Meanwhile, silence cut him off from his mother and sisters in Silesia.

As the years went by, Father learned to speak a little Arabic. He also learned loneliness. He put off composing his great poem. Every day he learned something new about the land and its inhabitants, and occasionally even about himself. He still saw in his dreams the cattle farm in Galilee, although the cellar and attic now seemed to him unnecessary, perhaps even childish. One evening, he even said aloud to his granduncle's picture:

"We'll see. All in good time. I'm just as determined as you are. You may laugh, but I don't care. Laugh as much as you like."

At night, by the light of his desk lamp, Father kept a journal in which he recorded his fears for his mother and sisters, the oppressiveness of the dry desert wind, certain peculiarities of some of his acquaintances, and the flavor of his travels among Godforsaken villages. He set down in carefully chosen words various professional lessons he had learned in the course of his work. He committed to writing some optimistic reflections about the progress of the Jewish community in various spheres. He even formulated, after several revisions, a few arguments for and against loneliness, and an embarrassed hope for a love that might come to him, too, one day. Then he carefully tore out the page and ripped it into tiny pieces. He also published, in the weekly *The Young Worker,* an article in favor of drinking goats' milk.

Sometimes, in the evening, he would go to Dr. Ruppin's home in Rehavia, where he was received with coffee and cream cakes. Or else he would visit his fellow townsman the elderly Professor Julius Wertheimer, who also lived in Rehavia, not far from Dr. Ruppin. Occasionally there was a distant sound of faint, persistent piano music, like the supplications of a desperate pride. Every summer the rocks on the hillside roasted, and every winter Jerusalem was ringed with fog. Refugees and pioneers continued to arrive from various foreign parts, filling the city with sadness and bewilderment. Father bought books from the refugees, some of them musty books with leather bindings and gold tooling, and from time to time he exchanged books with Dr. Ruppin or with the elderly Professor Julius Wertheimer, who was in the habit of greeting him with a hurried, embarrassed hug.

The Arabs in the villages sometimes gave him cold pomegranate juice to drink. Occasionally they would kiss his hand. He learned to drink water from an upraised pitcher without letting the pitcher touch his lips. Once a woman directed a dark, smoldering glance at him from some way off, and he trembled all over and hurriedly looked away.

He wrote in his journal:

"I have been living in Jerusalem for three years, and I continue to yearn for it as though I were still a student in Leipzig.

Surely there is paradox here. And in general," Father continued
thoughtfully and rather vaguely, "in general there are all
sorts of contradictions. Yesterday morning, in Lifta, I was
obliged to put down a fine, healthy horse because some youngsters had blinded it in the night with a nail. Cruelty for its
own sake seems to me to be something sordid and thoroughly
unnecessary. The same evening, in Kibbutz Kiryat 'Anavim,
the pioneers played a Bach suite on the phonograph, which
aroused in me profound feelings of pity for the pioneers, for
the horse, for Bach, for myself. I almost cried. Tomorrow is the
King's birthday, and all the workers in the department are to
receive a special bonus. There are all sorts of contradictions.
And the climate is not kind, either."

3

Mother said:
"I shall wear my blue dress with the V-shaped neckline,
and I shall be the belle of the ball. We'll order a taxi, too."
Father said:
"Yes, and don't forget to lose a glass slipper."
Hillel said:
"Me, too."
But children are not taken to May Balls at the High Commissioner's palace. Even good children, even children who
are cleverer than is usual for their age. And the ball would
certainly not end before midnight. So Hillel would spend the
evening next door with Madame Yabrova the pianist and her
niece, Lyubov, who called herself Binyamina Even-Hen. They
would play the phonograph for him, give him his supper, let
him play a little with their collection of dolls of all nations, and
put him to bed.

Hillel tried to protest:

"But I still have to tell the High Commissioner who's right and who's wrong."

Father replied patiently:

"We are right, and I'm sure the High Commissioner knows it in his heart of hearts, but he has to carry out the wishes of the King."

"I don't envy that king because God is going to punish him and Uncle Mitya calls him King Chedorlaomer of Albion and he says the Underground will capture him and execute him because of what he's done to the Remnant of Israel," the boy said excitedly and all in one breath.

Father replied mildly, choosing his words with care:

"Uncle Mitya sometimes exaggerates a little. The King of England is not Chedorlaomer, but George the Sixth. He will probably be succeeded on the throne by one of his daughters, because he has no son. To kill a man except in self-defense is murder. And now, Your Majesty King Hillel the First, finish up your cocoa. And then go and brush your teeth."

Mother, with a hairpin between her teeth and holding a pair of amber earrings, remarked:

"King George is very thin and pale. And he always looks so sad."

When he reached the end of the third form, Hillel wrote a letter and typed it in triplicate on his father's typewriter. He sent two of the copies to the King in London and to the High Commissioner: "Our land belongs to us, both according to the Bible and according to justice. Please get out of the Land of Israel at once and go back to England before it is too late."

The third copy passed from hand to hand among the excited neighbors. Madame Yabrova the pianist said, "A child poet!" Her niece, Lyubov Binyamina, added: "And look at his curly hair! We ought to send a copy to Dr. Weizmann, to give him a little joy." Brzezinski the engineer said that it was no good exaggerating, you couldn't build a wall out of fine words. And from Gerald Lindley, Secretary, there came a brief reply on official government notepaper: "Thank you for your letter, the contents of which have been duly noted. We are always receptive to the opinions of the public. Yours faithfully."

And how the geraniums blazed in the garden in the blue summer light. How the pure light was caught by the fingers of the fig tree in the yard and shattered into nervous fragments. How the sun burst up early in the morning behind Mount Scopus to torment the whole city and suddenly turn the gold and silver domes to dazzling flames. How joyfully or desperately the throngs of birds shrilled.

The metal drainpipe absorbed the heat and was sweet to the touch in the morning. The clean gravel that Father had spread along the path that wound down from the veranda steps to the fence and to the fig tree to the bottom of the garden was white and pleasant under bare feet.

The garden was small, logically planned, uncompromisingly well kept: Father's dreams had laid out square and rectangular flower beds among the rocky gulleys, a lonely island of clear, sober sanity in the midst of a savage, rugged wasteland, of winding valleys, of desert winds.

And surrounding us was the estate of Tel Arza, a handful of new houses scattered haphazardly on a hilltop. The mountains might move in one night and silently enfold everything, the houses, the hesitant saplings, the hopes, the unpaved road. A herd of Arab goats would arrive to munch and trample chrysanthemums, narcissuses, snapdragons, sparse beginnings of lawn here and there. And the shepherd would stand silent and motionless, watching the ravaging goats and looking perhaps like a scorched cypress tree.

All day Hillel could see the ranges of bare mountains all around. At times he could sense in the bright-blue flood the autumn piling up in unseen valleys.

Autumn would come. The light would fade to gray. Low clouds would seize the mountains. He would climb to the top of the fig tree, and from there in the autumn light he might be able to see the sea and the desert, the islands in the tattered clouds, the mysterious continents that Father had told him about dryly and Mother with tears of longing.

Father used to say that the beautiful lands had vomited us up here in blind hatred, and that therefore we would build ourselves a land a thousand times as beautiful here. But Mother would call the land a backyard, and say that there would never be a river, a cathedral, or a forest here. Uncle Mitya the lodger used to chuckle through his rotten teeth and utter broken phrases about birth pangs, death throes, Jerusalem killing its prophets, God's curse on ruined Babylon. He was also a vegetarian.

Hillel could not make out from these words whether Mitya agreed with Father or with Mother. What Mother said seemed to him incongruous, and he would go down to the bottom of the garden to hide among the branches of the fig tree and sniff for the autumn. Autumn would come. Autumn sadness would accompany him to school, to his music lessons with Madame Yabrova, to the "Zion's Ransom" lending library, to his bed at night, into his dreams. While a rainstorm raged outside, he would compose an article for the class newspaper. The word "forest," which Mother had used when she wanted to denigrate the land, cast a strange, melancholy spell over him.

4

Hillel was a pudgy, awkward little boy. He had a hiding place at the end of the garden, behind the fig tree or up among its branches, which he called his "hideaway." He would hide himself away there and secretly eat sticky sweets that the women gave him, and dream of Africa, the sources of the Nile, the lions in the jungle.

At night he would wake up with attacks of asthma. Especially in the early summer. Feverish, suffocated, he would see the horrific smile of the terrifying white thing through the slats of the shutters and burst into tears. Until Father appeared holding a small flashlight, to sit on his bed and sing him a soothing song. Aunts, neighbors, and nursery-school teachers adored Hillel, with Russian kisses and Polish displays of affection. They called him "Little Cherry." Sometimes they would leave heavy lip marks on his cheeks or his mouth. These women were plump and excitable. Their faces wore an expression of bitter complaint: Life has not been as kind to me as I deserve.

Madame Yabrova the pianist and her niece, Lyubov, who called herself Binyamina Even-Hen, in the determined way they played the piano, seemed to be nobly refraining from repaying life for what it had done to them. Mrs. Vishniak the pharmacist would grumble to Hillel and say that little children were the only hope of the Jewish people, and particularly of herself. At times Hillel wrapped himself in introspection or sadness, and then he would delight them with a sweet phrase, such as:

"Life is a circle. Everyone goes around and around."

And stir ripples of emotion.

But the children of Tel Arza called him by the unpleasant nickname "Jelly." Unkind, skinny girls, vicious Oriental girls, enjoyed knocking him down on a heap of gravel and pulling his blond hair. Keys and amulets hung around their necks. They emitted a pungent smell of peanuts, sweat, soap, and halvah.

Hillel would always wait until they had had enough of him and his curls. Then he would get up and shake the dust off his gym shorts and his cotton undershirt; gasping for breath, his eyes full of tears, he would bite his lip and begin to forgive. How nobly forgiveness shone in his eyes: those girls did not know what they were doing; they probably had unhappy fathers and brothers who were high up in the underworld or in football; their mothers and sisters probably went out with British soldiers. It was a terrible thing to be born an Oriental girl. And one of them had even started to grow breasts under her sweaty vest. Hillel reflected, forgave, and was filled with love of himself for his ability to understand and to forgive.

Then he would run to Mrs. Vishniak's pharmacy to cry a little, not because of the scratches but because of the cruel lot of the girls and his own magnanimity. Mrs. Vishniak would kiss him, console him with sticky candy, tell him about the mill on the banks of the blue river, which no longer existed. He would tell her, in carefully chosen words, about a dream he had had the previous night, interpret the dream himself, and leave behind a delicate mood of poetry as he went off to practice the piano in the dark, airless house of Madame Yabrova and Binyamina. He returned the caresses he had received from Mrs. Vishniak to the haughty bronze Beethoven on top of the sideboard. After all, Herzl, in his youth, was called a madman in the street. And Bialik was always being beaten.

In the evening, before he went to bed, Hillel would be summoned to his father's room in his pajamas. This room was called the study. It contained bookshelves, a desk, and a glass-fronted showcase of fossils and ancient pots; the whole was skeptically surveyed from a sepia photograph by the famous geographer Hans Walter Landauer.

He had to utter an intelligent sentence or two for the benefit of the guests. Then he was kissed and sent off to bed. From across the corridor came the sounds of the grownups talking passionately, and Hillel in his bed caught their passion and began to pamper his tiny organ with his fingers through the opening of his pajama trousers.

Later, the forlorn sound of Lyubov Binyamina's cello came to him through the darkness, and he suddenly despised himself. He called himself "Jelly." He was filled with sorrow for all men and women. And fell asleep compassionately.

"He's a real *mensh,*" Mrs. Vishniak would say in Yiddish. "Clever. Witty. A little devil. Just like the whole family."

Beyond the low fence, which Father had made from iron

posts and old netting and painted in bright colors, began the
wasteland. Plots of scrap iron, dust, smelling of thistles, of
goat dung; and farther on, the wadi and the lairs of foxes and
jackals; and still farther down, the empty wood where the children once discovered the remains of a half-eaten Turkish soldier in the stinking tatters of a janissary's uniform. There
were desolate slopes teeming with darting lizards and snakes
and perhaps hyenas at night, and beyond this wadi, empty,
stony hills and more wadis, in which Arabs in desert robes
roamed with their flocks all day long. In the distance were
more and more strange mountains and strange villages stretch-
ing to the end of the world, minarets of mosques, Shu'afat, Nabi
Samwil, the outskirts of Ramallah, the wail of a muezzin borne
on the wind in the evening twilight, dark women, deadly-
sly, guttural youths. And a slight hint of brooding evil: distant, infinitely patient, forever observing you unobserved.

Mother said:
"While you, Hans, are dancing like a teddy bear with
that old lady you treated, I shall sit all alone in my blue dress
on a wickerwork chair at the end of the veranda, sipping a
martini and smiling to myself. But later on I, too, shall suddenly get up and dance, with the Governor of Jerusalem, or
even with Sir Alan himself. Then it will be your turn to sit
it out by yourself, and you won't feel at all like smiling."
Father said:
"The boy can hear you. He understands exactly what you're
saying."
And Hillel said:
"So what?"
For the occasion, Father borrowed from his neighbor Engineer Brzezinski an English evening suit made by the Szczupak textile factory in Lodz. Mother sat on the shady balcony all
morning altering it to fit him.
At lunchtime, Father tried the suit on at the mirror, shrugged
his shoulders, and remarked:

"It's ridiculous."

Mother, laughing, said:

"The boy can hear you. He understands everything."

Hillel said:

"So what? 'Ridiculous' isn't a dirty word."

Father said:

"No word is dirty in itself. In general, dirt lies either behind words or between them."

And Mother:

"There's dirt everywhere here. Even in the grand ideas you're always putting into Hillel's head. Even in your stray remarks. And that's also ridiculous."

Father said nothing.

That morning the newspaper *Davar* said that the politics of the White Paper were leading up a blind alley. Hillel, with an effort of the imagination, could almost visualize the "blind alley."

Mitya the vegetarian lodger padded barefoot from his room to the kitchen to make himself a glass of tea. He was a tall, etiolated young man with thinning hair. His shoulders always drooped, and he walked with short, nervous steps. He had an odd habit of suddenly chewing the tip of his shirt collar, and also of angrily stroking every object he came across, table, banister, bookshelf, Mother's apron hanging on a hook in the kitchen. And he would whisper to himself. Engineer Brzezinski declared hotly that one day it would emerge that this Mitya was really a dangerous Communist in disguise. But Mother good-naturedly offered to launder his few clothes with the family wash.

As Mitya shuffled to the kitchen, he waved his hand in every direction in greeting, as though confronting a large crowd. Suddenly his glance fell on the words "blind alley" in the head-line on the center page of *Davar*, lying open on the oilcloth on the kitchen table. He bared his bad teeth and snarled furiously:

"What rubbish."

Then, clasping the hot glass in his large white hands, he strode stormily back to his room, locking his door behind him.

Mother said softly:

"He's just like a stray dog."

After a short pause, she added:

"He washes five times a day, and after each time he puts on scent, and even so he always smells. We ought to find him a girl friend. Perhaps a new immigrant from the Women's Labor Bureau, poor but charming. Now, Hans, you go and shave. And Hillel—go on with your homework. What am I doing in this madhouse?"

5

She had come from Warsaw as a young woman to study ancient history at the university on Mount Scopus. Before a year was up, she was in despair at the country and the language. Nyuta, her elder sister in New York, had sent her a ticket to go from Haifa to America aboard the *Aurora*. A few days before the date of her departure, Dr. Ruppin had introduced her to Father, shown him her beautiful water colors, and expressed in German his sadness that the young lady was also leaving us, that she, too, found the country unbearable and was sailing to America in disappointment.

Hans Kipnis looked at the water colors for a while and suddenly thought of the wandering German ornithologist with whom he had traveled to the remote sources of the Jordan. He traced the lines of one of the pictures delicately with his finger, hurriedly withdrew his hand, and uttered some remarks about loneliness and dreams in general and in Jerusalem in particular.

Mother smiled at him, as though he had accidentally broken a precious vase.

Father apologized and lapsed into an embarrassed silence.

Dr. Ruppin had a pair of tickets for a concert that night by a recently formed refugee chamber orchestra. He was glad to present the tickets to the young couple: he could not go anyway, because Menahem Ussishkin the Zionist leader had unexpectedly arrived from abroad a day or two earlier, and as usual had convened a frantic meeting for that evening.

After the concert, they strolled together along Princess Mary's Way. The shopwindows were brightly lit and decorated, and in one of them a small mechanical doll bobbed up and down. For a moment, Jerusalem looked like a real city. Ladies and gentlemen walked arm in arm, and some of the gentlemen were smoking cigarettes in short cigarette holders.

A bus stopped beside them, and the driver, who was wearing shorts, smiled at them invitingly, but they did not get on. An army jeep with a machine gun mounted on it rolled down the street. And in the distance a bell rang. They both agreed that Jerusalem was under some cruel spell. Then they agreed to meet again the next day to eat a strawberry ice cream together at Zichel's Café.

At a nearby table sat the philosopher Martin Buber and the writer S. Y. Agnon. In the course of a disagreement, Agnon jokingly suggested that they consult the younger generation. Father made some remark; it must have been perceptive and acute, because Buber and Agnon both smiled; they also addressed his companion gallantly. At that moment Father's blue eyes may perhaps have lit up behind his round spectacles, and his sadness may have shown around his mouth.

Nineteen days later, the Nazis publicly declared their intention of building up their armed forces. There was tension in Europe. The *Aurora* never reached Haifa; she changed her course and sailed instead to the West Indies.

Father arranged to see his fellow townsman Professor Julius Wertheimer, who had been his patron ever since he had arrived in Palestine. He said he wanted to consult him on a personal matter. He was confused, furtive, obstinate, and tongue-tied.

Professor Wertheimer listened in an anxious silence. Then he drove his cats out of the room and closed the door behind them. When they were alone, he warned Father obliquely not to complicate his private life unnecessarily. And it was precisely these words that brought Father to the certainty that he was finally in love.

Ruth and Hans were married in Jerusalem on the day that Hitler declared in Nuremberg that he was bent on peace and understanding and that he detested war. The guests consisted of the officials of the veterinary department, including two Christian Arabs from Bethlehem, the Ruppin family, some refugees and pioneers, a few neighbors from Tel Arza, and an emaciated revolutionary student from the university who could not take his blazing eyes off the beautiful bride. He it was who toasted the happy couple on behalf of all their friends and vowed that right would triumph and that we would see as much with our own eyes. But he spoiled the effect of his words by getting thoroughly drunk on one bottle of Nesher beer and calling the bridegroom and bride respectively *"burzhui"* and *"artistka."* The guests departed, and Father hired a taxi to convey Mother's few belongings from her simple room in Neve Sha'anan to the house he had been making ready for several years in the suburb of Tel Arza.

There, in Tel Arza, in the little stone-built house facing the rocky wadis, there was born to them a year later a fair-haired son.

When Mother and the baby came home from the hospital, Father indicated his diminutive estate with a sweep of his hand, gazed raptly at it, and pronounced these words:

"For the moment this is a remote suburb. There are only young saplings growing in our garden. The sun beats down all day on the shutters. But as the years pass, the trees will grow, and we shall have plenty of shade. Their boughs will shelter the house. Creepers will climb over the roof and all over the fence. And the flowers will bloom. This will be our pleasure garden when Hillel grows up and we grow old together. We shall make an arbor of vines where you can sit all day through the summer, painting beautiful water colors. We can even have a piano. They'll build a civic center, they'll pave the road, our suburb will be joined to a Jerusalem ruled by a Hebrew government with a Hebrew army. Dr. Ruppin will be a minister and Professor Buber will be president or perhaps even king. When the time comes, I may become director of the veterinary service. And immigrants will arrive from every country under the sun."

Suddenly he felt ashamed of his speech, and particularly regretted his choice of some of the words. A momentary sadness trembled around his mouth, and he added hastily, in a matter-of-fact tone:

"Poetry. Philosophizing. A pleasure garden with overhanging vines, all of a sudden. Now I'll go and fetch a block of ice, and you must lie down and rest, so that you won't have a migraine again tonight. It's so hot."

Mother turned to go indoors. By the veranda steps she stopped and looked at the miserable, rusty pots of geraniums. She said:

"There won't be any flowers. There'll be a flood. Or a war. They'll all die."

Father did not answer, because he sensed that these words were not directed at him and that they should never have been spoken.

His khaki shorts came down almost to his knees. Between his knees and his sandals his legs showed brown, thin, and smooth. Behind his round spectacles his face bore an expression of permanent gratitude, or of slight, pleased surprise. And in moments of embarrassment he was in the habit of saying:

"I don't know. It's just as well not to know everything. There are all sorts of things in the world that are better left alone."

6

Here is how Mother appeared as a girl in her old photograph album: a blonde schoolgirl with a kind of inner, autumnal beauty. Her fingers clasping a broad-brimmed white hat. Three doves on a fence behind her, and a mustached Polish student sitting on the same fence, smiling broadly.

She had been considered the best reader in her class at the high school. At the age of twelve, she had already attracted the enthusiastic attention of the elderly Polish literature teacher. The aging humanist, Mother would recall, was deeply moved by her charming recitations of gems of Polish poetry. "Ruth's voice," the pedagogue would exclaim with hoarse enthusiasm, "echoes the spirit of poetry, eternally playing among streams in a meadow." And because he secretly considered himself a poet, he would add, overcome by the force of his emotions, "If gazelles could sing, they would surely sing like little Ruth."

When Mother repeated this sentence she would laugh, because the comparison seemed to her absurd. Not because of the idea of gazelles singing, but because she simply couldn't sing. Her affections at that time were directed toward small pets, celebrated philosophers and artists, dancing, dresses trimmed with lace, and silk scarves, and also her poor friends who had neither lace-trimmed dresses nor silk scarves. She was fond of the unfortunates she came across, the milkman, the beggar, Grandma Gittel, the maids, and her nanny, even the local idiot. Provided that suffering had not disfigured their outward appearance, and provided that they carried themselves woefully, as if acknowledging their guilt and attempting to atone for it.

She translated from Polish a story she had written on her fifteenth birthday. She copied it out neatly and told Hillel to read it aloud:

"The blue sea allows the sun's rays to draw up its water, to make clouds that look like dirty cotton wool, to pour down rain on mountains, plains, and meadows—but not on the ugly desert—and eventually all the water collects and has to flow back once more into the sea. To return to it with a caress."

Suddenly she fell into a rage, snatched the paper out of the boy's hands, and tore it into shreds.

"All gone!" she cried with desperate pathos. "Dead and done for! Lost!"

Outside, a wintry Jerusalem Sabbath, windswept, lashed by dead leaves. Inside the little house in Tel Arza, the kerosene heater burned with a blue flame. On the table there was tea and oranges, and a vase of chrysanthemums. Two of the walls were lined with Father's books. Shadows fell on them. The wind howled from the wadi. Mists touched the outside of the window, and the panes rattled. With a kind of bitter mockery, Mother spoke of her childhood in Warsaw, rowing on the Wisla, playing tennis in white clothes, the Seventh Cavalry Regiment parading down the Avenue of the Republic every Sunday. Occasionally she turned abruptly to Father and called him Dr. Zichel instead of Dr. Kipnis, Hans, Hanan. Father would rest his fingers on his high brow, unperturbed, unsurprised, silently smiling at the recollection of the acute remark he had made in Zichel's Café to the writer Agnon and the philosopher Buber. They had both been delighted; they had consulted him about the strawberry ice cream, and even complimented his companion.

When Mother was sixteen, she allowed the handsome Tadeusz to kiss her at the bridge: first on the forehead, later on the lips, but she let him go no further. He was a year and a half younger than she, an elegant, handsome youth, without a trace of acne, who excelled at tennis and sprinting. Once he had promised her that he would love her forever. But forever at that time seemed to her like a small circle bathed in pleasant light, and love like a game of tennis on a clear blue Sunday morning.

Handsome Tadeusz's father had been killed in the Polish war of independence. Tadeusz also had a cute dimple when he smiled, and wore sports shirts all through the summer. Mother loved to kiss Hillel suddenly on his own dimple and say:

"Just like this one."

Every year, on the national holiday, Ruth and Tadeusz would both stand on a decorated stage in the school playground. Old chestnut trees spread their branches overhead like a rustling bridal canopy. Tadeusz's task was to light the Torch of Liberty—the same liberty for which his father had given his life. Pupils and teachers stood in serried ranks, frozen in a strained silence, while the wind toyed with the flags of the Republic—no, don't touch the photograph—and Ruth recited the immortal lines by the national poet. Bells rang out joyously from atop every church in Warsaw. And in the evening, at the ball at the home of the director of the opera house, her parents permitted her to dance one waltz with General Godzinski himself.

Then Zionism broke out. The handsome Tadeusz joined the National Youth Corps, and because she refused to spend a weekend with him at his aunt's in the country, he sent her a disgusting note: "*Zidowka*. Dirty Jewess." The old teacher who was fond of the phrase "singing gazelles" died suddenly of a liver disease. And both her parents, too, in a single month. The only memento she had left was the sepia photographs, printed on thick card stock with ornamental borders.

Nyuta, her elder sister, quickly found herself a widowed gynecologist named Adrian Staub. She married him and went with him to New York. Meanwhile, Mother came to Palestine to study ancient history on Mount Scopus. She took a small room at the end of the world, in the suburb of Neve Sha'anan. Nyuta Staub sent her a modest allowance every month. In that room she was loved by several wonderful men, including, one Hanukkah festival, the furious poet Alexander Pan.

After a year, she felt defeated by the country and the language, and decided to join her sister and brother-in-law in New York. Then Dr. Ruppin introduced her to Father, and he told her shyly about his dream of setting up a cattle farm in the hills of Galilee with his own hands. He had a fine Galilean smell. She was desperately tired. And the *Aurora* changed course, sailed to the West Indies, and never reached Haifa.

To the northeast, in the white summer light, one could see Mount Scopus from the window of the house in Tel Arza, crowned by a marble dome, a wood, and two towers. These lonely towers seemed from a distance to be shrouded in a kind of veil of solitude. At the end of the Sabbath the light faded slowly, hesitantly, poignantly:

As though forever. And as though there were no going back.

Father and Mother used to sit facing each other in the room that Father called his study. The celebrated geographer Hans Walter Landauer gazed down skeptically on them from his large portrait. And their pudgy son built complicated brick castles on the mat, demolishing each suddenly with a wave of his hand because he always wanted to build a new one. At times he would ask an intelligent question of his father, and he always received a considered reply. At other times he buried his face in his mother's dress, demanded to be cuddled, and then, embarrassed at seeing her eyes fill with tears, returned silently to his game.

Sometimes Mother asked:

"What's going to happen, Hans?"

And Father would answer:

"I confidently hope that things will take a turn for the better."

As Father uttered these words, Hillel recalled how last Pentecost he had gone out with his friends to hunt lions or discover the source of the Nile in the woods of Tel Arza. He recalled how a faded golden button had suddenly flashed at him, and blue cloth, how he had knelt down and dug with both hands, tearing away the pine needles, to uncover the treasure, and found a rotting military tunic, a terrible, sweet smell coming from the tarnished gold, and how as he went on digging he had discovered white ivory among disintegrating buckles, large and small white tusks, and all of a sudden the ivory was attached to an empty skull that smiled at him with a kind of chilling affection, and then the dead teeth and the eye sockets. Never, never again would he search for the source of the Nile anywhere. Never.

On weekdays Father traveled around the villages wearing khaki trousers, sandals, a neatly pressed blue shirt with wide pockets stuffed full of notebooks and writing pads. In winter he wore brown corduroy trousers, a jacket, a cap, and over his shoes he wore galoshes that looked like twin black warships.

But on Sabbath Eve, after his bath, he would appear in a white shirt and gray trousers, his damp hair combed and neatly parted, smelling of shaving lotion and almond-scented soap. Then Mother would kiss him on the nose and call him her great big child. And Hillel would laugh.

Every morning, a bib with a picture of a smiling rabbit was tied around Hillel's neck. He ate Quaker Oats, a soft-boiled egg, and yogurt. On the Quaker Oats package was a wonderful picture of an admiral with a bold and resolute look on his face, a three-cornered Napoleon hat on his head, and a telescope in his only hand.

In Europe at that time, there was a world war going on. But in the streets of Jerusalem, there were only singing bands of friendly soldiers, Australians, New Zealanders, Senegalese looking like chocolate-cream soldiers, lean Scots wallowing in beer and homesickness. The newspapers carried maps with arrows. Sometimes, at night, a long military convoy crossed Jerusalem from north to south with dimmed headlights, and a smothered roar seemed to sound in the darkness. The city was very still. The hills were hushed. The towers and domes looked thoughtful. The inhabitants followed the distant war with anxiety but without any passion. They exchanged conjectures and interpretations. They expected a change for the better that would surely come about soon and might even perhaps make itself felt in Jerusalem.

7

In Tel Arza no civic center was built, and the road was not paved. A stone quarry was started on one of the farther slopes. Mr. Cohen opened a small workshop producing modish furniture for the notables of Jericho and Bethlehem, the Governor of Jerusalem, and even for the palace of Emir Abdullah in Transjordan. Engineer Brzezinski climbed onto the roof of his house and rigged up an enormous radio antenna so as to be able to catch the signals of the farthest stations each night. He also built a telescope with his own hands, and installed it, too, on his roof, because he had promised himself that he would be the first to see them when they arrived.

At night the valleys all around were alive with sounds. The wildness of the rocks and mountains reached out to touch the house. Jackals howled nearby, and the blood froze at the thought of them padding softly, tensely, among the saplings, up to the shuttered windows, perhaps even onto the veranda. A single Mandatory street lamp, encased in small, square panes and topped with a green dome, cast a solitary light on the unpaved road. The fingers of the fig tree at the bottom of the garden were empty. There was nobody outside in the dark. The square-paned lamp cast its light in vain. All the residents were in the habit of shutting themselves up in their houses as soon as darkness fell. Every evening Madame Yabrova played the piano, and her niece, Lyubov Binyamina, the cello, with desolating sadness. Father's fellow townsman the elderly professor Julius Wertheimer collected clippings from foreign newspapers that mentioned anything to do with supernatural phenomena. He considered the laws of nature to be a practical joke, and he longed to find a loophole in them, perhaps some revealing formula that would enable him and the whole persecuted Jewish people to escape from the pull of gravity and to float up into spheres where the contagion had not yet spread.

Every night, far into the small hours, Engineer Brzezinski twiddled the tuning knob of his radio, seeking and finding and then abandoning different stations, Berlin, London, Milan, Vichy, Cairo, and Cyrenaica. Some of the neighbors said that he often brought bottles of arak back with him from his work on the northern shores of the Dead Sea, and that at night he got drunk on this frightful Oriental drink.

He would tell them how as a young man he had been the director of a gigantic engineering project in Russia, how he had set up the hydroelectric power station in Taganrog, "like writing an epic poem." Then he had fallen foul of Stalin; he was captured, imprisoned, tortured; he escaped by the skin of his teeth and finally reached Jerusalem via Afghanistan, Teheran, and Baghdad. But here, at the Dead Sea Works, he was given trifling little jobs to do: mending pumps, keeping an eye on the generator, repairing miserable fuse boxes, supervising some provincial transformer.

One night he suddenly shouted "Fire! Fire!" at the top of his voice. He had come across a broadcast of Beethoven's *Eroica* Symphony from some Nazi station in the Balkans.

Father immediately got out of bed, dressed, and bravely crossed the dirt road; he knocked on the door and called out politely, "Mr. Brzezinski, please, Mr. Brzezinski."

The door did not open. There was no fire, either. Only the smell of dying campfires borne on the wind from the depths of the wadi. And the wail of a distant muezzin, or perhaps it was a hungry jackal crying in the woods. On nights like these, Hillel would wake up with an attack of panic and asthma.

He could see through the slats of the shutters the skull of the Turkish janissary hovering in the dark air, grinning at him with its dead teeth. He would pull the sheet up over his head and burst into tears. Then his father would get up and come into his bedroom with bare feet, to straighten the bedclothes and sing him a soothing song:

> Night is reigning in the skies,
> Time for you to close your eyes.
> Lambs and kids have ceased from leaping,
> All the animals are sleeping.
> Every bird is in its nest,
> All Jerusalem's at rest.

Then, toward dawn, Mitya the lodger might suddenly cry out in his sleep on the other side of the wall: "Ruthless! Don't touch him! He's still alive! *Y-a ny-e zna-yu! Y-a ny-e po-ni-ma-yu!* Nothing!"

Then silence.

Outside in the fields, there was nothing but jackals and mist until morning.

8

Mitya addressed Father:

"In that evening suit, Dr. Kipnis, you look like the spit and image of the martyred Haim Arlosoroff. There is no peace for the wicked. So I shall ask you a small diplomatic favor. Could you pass along a short message from me to the foreign High Commissioner? Just one or two urgent sentences? It is a message the High Commissioner has been secretly waiting for for some time, and he probably cannot understand why it has not yet come."

Father said:

"If I do actually manage to have a private conversation with the High Commissioner, which I very much doubt."

Mitya suddenly grinned, baring his rotten teeth. He chewed his shirt collar, with an expression of pain and disgust on his bony face and a fire in his eyes.

"Give him this message, word for word: Our true Messiah will surely come, he will not tarry. He will come whirling a flaming sword in his hand. He will come from the east and lay all the mountains low. He will not leave any that pisseth against the wall. Do you think, Dr. Kipnis, that you can repeat this message word for word without making a mistake?"

Father said:

"I don't think I can undertake to convey that message. And certainly not in English."

And Mitya, frantically stroking the oilcloth on the kitchen table, replied in a hoarse voice:

"Jerusalem, which slayeth its prophets, shall burn the new Hellenizers in hellfire."

At once he added politely:

"Good evening, Mrs. Kipnis. *Pozhal'sta*, why are you staring at me so cruelly, I was simply making a small joke with your husband. I shall never forgive myself if, heaven forbid, I have accidentally frightened you. *Nikogda*. I must beg your pardon right away; there, I've done it. How magnificent you look, Mrs. Kipnis, in your blue evening dress, if I may make so bold. How magnificent, too, is the springtime in our Jerusalem on the eve of the great destruction. And the hot tap in the bathroom is dripping and dripping and knows no rest. Surely we ought to do something without further delay. How much time do we have left? There, I've apologized and I've gone. *Da.* Good night. May the name of the wicked rot, and the innocent shall see it and be glad. Now good night once again to you all. Happy is he who waits His coming."

He nearly knocked the child over as he dashed back to his room, panting, his arms hanging limply at his sides, his fists clenched. But he did not slam his door; he closed it gently behind him as if taking great care not to hurt the door or the doorpost or the sudden silence he had left behind him.

Mother said:

"The High Commissioner could never understand how a boy like Mitya suffers. Even the King couldn't help. Or the Messiah himself, not that I believe in him."

She closed her eyes and continued in a different tone of voice:

"But *I* could. I could easily rescue him from the madness and death that are building up inside him. Yes, me. That's loneliness, Hans, that's real exile, despair, depression, persecution. I could come to him in the middle of the night in my nightgown, sweetly perfumed, and touch him; or at least I could bring him another woman in the night and happily stand by and watch. I could put out the rising fires and give him peace and quiet. So what if he smells. To the forests and the sea, every man and woman in the world stinks. Even you, Hans. And then to hear him moaning between my hands, shouting in disjointed Russian, singing, grunting like a felled ox. Then resting peacefully. I'd close his eyes with my fingers and lull him to sleep. Even the stars and mountains would love me for it. Now, stop looking at me like that. I want you to know once and for all how much I loathe, yes, loathe, your Wertheimers and Bubers and Shertoks. I wish your terrorists would blow them all sky high. And stop looking at me like that."

Father said:

"That will do, Ruth. The boy can hear you; he understands almost everything."

She drew the child violently toward her, pressed his head against her, and covered his face with rough kisses. Then she said quietly:

"Yes, you're quite right. You've already forgiven me, Hans. The red taxi will be here soon, and we'll go to the ball. Stand still, Hans, while I tie your silly bow tie for you. I've really

got no complaint against Buber and the rest of them. There,
now you've remembered how to smile. At last. Why are you
smiling?"

Father said nothing.

9

Mitya had left his kibbutz in the Jezreel Valley because of
an ideological argument at the end of the week in which Hitler
had captured Warsaw. At the same time, he had also suddenly inherited some jewelry from his only relation, a forgotten
aunt who had died in Johannesburg.

He had hastily sold the jewelry to a crafty Armenian gold-
smith in the Old City and decided to settle in Jerusalem to
study, with the aim of proving once and for all that the natives
of Palestine were descended from the ancient Hebrews. He
tried to produce conclusive proof that all the Arabs, nomads
and peasants alike, were simply Israelites who had been forcibly converted to Islam and whom it was our duty now to
rescue. Their clothes, the shape of their skulls, the names of
their villages, their eating habits, and their forms of worship
all bore abundant witness, he claimed, to the truth that the
Jewish Agency was trying to hush up. But they could not pull
the wool over *his* eyes.

For a pioneer, he was a skinny lad, with drooping shoulders
and abrupt gestures. He was an uncompromising vegetarian,
who called meat eating "the source of all impurity." His hair
was thin, fair, almost white. When Mitya stood by himself in
the kitchen making tea in his glass with its ring of worn gold
paint, Hillel would sometimes observe a lonely, fanatical glint
in his eye. His birdlike profile looked as though he were

forever suppressing a sneeze. And he would chew the points of his shirt collar with his rotten teeth.

On his arrival, he had paid Father two years' rent in advance, and was given permission to look over the headlines in the daily newspaper and to use the typewriter occasionally. Once he typed out with two fingers an "Epistle to Those Who Are at Ease in Zion," in which he voiced various complaints and sounded a prophecy of doom. But the newspapers all either rejected his letter or simply ignored it. And once he hinted to Father that since the Babylonian Beasts had murdered the heroic Abraham Stern, code-named "Yair," he himself had become the secret commander of the Fighters for the Freedom of Israel. Father did not believe this any more than he believed Engineer Brzezinski, who said that Mitya was a dangerous Communist agent in disguise.

Mitya was ruthlessly clean and tidy.

Whenever he had finished in the lavatory, he would produce a small can inscribed in English, "Baby's Delight," and sprinkle the seat with perfumed talcum powder. When he had read the newspaper he would fold it neatly in four and place it carefully on the end of the bookshelf. If ever he met anyone as he came out of the bathroom or the lavatory (which he called "the throne room"), he would turn pale and mutter an embarrassed apology. He cleaned and scrubbed his own room twice a day.

Despite all this, a faint yet repulsive smell, like that of old cooking fat, always accompanied him in the corridor and escaped from under his door; it even clung to his glass with the worn gold ring.

No one was allowed into his room.

He had fitted a double Yale lock onto his door, and he always locked it even when he only went to wash. Sometimes he would cry out in his sleep in the early hours of the morning. In Russian.

*

During the summer months, Mitya would set off on foot in the direction of Mount Scopus, crossing hills and valleys with his disjointed gait, spurning roads and paths, advancing in a line straight as an arrow in flight. He would traverse the suburb of Sanhedriya like a hurricane, skirting the police training school, with his birdlike head thrust forward, a distant look in his eye, and finally, panting but undeterred, he would emerge into the district of Sheikh Jarrah, where he would always break his journey to drink his morning coffee among mustached, kaffiyeh-wrapped Arabs, with whom he attempted persistently to enter into conversation, but without success, since he could speak only classical Arabic, and that with a heavy Russian accent. The Arab coffee-drinkers nicknamed him al-Hudhud, "the hoopoe," perhaps because of his crest of thinning hair.

He would spend whole days on end in the basement of the national library on Mount Scopus, endlessly covering little cards with feverish notes. When he came home in the evening, he would sometimes bare his rotting teeth in a grin and pronounce some cryptic prophecy:

"I promise you that tonight a mighty explosion shall resound. The mountains shall drop sweet wine, and all the hills shall melt."

Because those were eventful days, his prophecies sometimes came true in a way. Then Mitya would smile modestly, like a humble artist who has won a prize with one of his works.

During the last year of the World War, Hillel peeped through the keyhole and discovered that Mitya had huge maps hanging on all the walls of his room, from the ceiling almost to the floor. He had other maps spread out on his desk, on his bed, and on the straw matting. These maps were covered with thick black and red arrows, flags, buttons, and matchsticks.

"Daddy, is Uncle Mitya a spy?"

"That sort of foolishness is beneath your dignity, Hillel."

"Then why is he like that? Why has he got maps in his room, and arrows?"

"You're the spy, Hillel. You spied on Uncle Mitya. That's not a nice thing to do, and you'll promise me right now that you won't do it again."

"I promise, but . . ."

"You've promised. Now that's the end of it. It's wrong to talk about people behind their backs."

One day in 1944, Mitya proposed to Father that the British fleet should storm up the Bosporus and through the Dardanelles "like a rod of anger," gain mastery over the Black Sea, ravage half of the Crimea with fire, land "myriads of armies" all along the Slavic coasts, knock the heads of the two tyrants together, "and grind to dust the dragon and the crocodile of Egypt." Father considered this utterance in silence, proffered a mild, sympathetic smile, and remarked that the Russians were now on the side of the Allies.

"You are the generation of the wilderness. You are the seed of slaves," Mitya replied vehemently. "You have all been stricken with blindness. Chamberlains. Arlosoroffs. Gandhis. Plebeians. Eunuchs. I don't mean you personally, Dr. Kipnis, heaven forbid! I was speaking in the plural; you in general. I can see from your wife's eyes that she agrees with me deep in her heart, but because she is wise and sensitive she prefers to remain silent, and of course she is quite right. Surely no remnant shall remain of all the eunuchs. When they cry with upraised voice and outstretched throat 'eternal people,' 'forever and ever,' 'Jerusalem, the eternal city,' surely every stone of Jerusalem bursts out laughing. Now I must beg your pardon and bid you good night. I'm sorry; good night."

Once, when Father was out working in the villages and Mother was at the hairdresser's, Mitya trapped Hillel at the dark end of the corridor and addressed his fevered utterances to him:

"We who have returned to Zion, and especially your generation, whose souls have not been perverted by exile, have an obligation to make children by force by the women of the fellahin. We must give them children who look like you.

Masses of fair-haired children. Strong and fair and fearless.
It's a matter of life and death. A new breed, thoroughbred,
lusty steppe-wolves instead of namby-pamby scholars. The old
eunuchs will die off. Blessed are you, for you shall inherit the
earth. Then a flame shall issue forth from Judah and consume
Perfidious Albion. What could be easier. We know how they
go out alone at night to gather firewood. They wear long dark
dresses down to their ankles, but underneath their dresses they
have nothing on at all. They must be conquered and mounted
by main force. With holy zeal. They have women who are
dark and hairy as goats, and we have rods of fire. We must spill
fresh blood, dark, warm blood. Your parents may call you
Hillel, but I shall call you Ithamar. Listen to me, young Ithamar.
You are a new recruit: I order you to learn to ride a horse, to
use a dagger, to toughen yourself up. Here, take a biscuit:
you can't refuse, I'm your commanding officer. This'll all be a
closely guarded secret between the two of us: the Underground
has no pity on traitors and informers. Who is this that cometh
from Seir, with dyed garments from Edom? It is you and the
rest of your generation. Nimrods, Gideons, Jephthahs, all of
them skilled men of war. You shall see and behold with your
own eyes, O new recruit Ithamar, the whole British Empire
brought down into the dust like a rag doll. The Inheritor shall
come marching from the east. He shall ascend the mountain
and discomfit the plain with an iron hand until those lascivious,
black hairy she-goats of the fellahin scream at us in terror and
delight. Lascivious she-goats! Now, take this shilling and run
and buy yourself a mountain of chewing gum. It's yours. Yes.
From me. Never disobey orders. Now, scram!"

Suddenly his blazing eyes fell on Mother's apron hanging
on a peg beside the mirror in the corridor. He bared his teeth
and hissed:

"Painted Jezebel, mother of whoredoms!"

And he shuffled furiously back to his room.

Hillel ran out into the garden. He climbed up into his hide-.
away among the boughs of the fig tree, the sweaty shilling

tightly clasped in his hand. He was tormented by ugly yet persistent images. Jezebel. Fellahin women. Lascivious she-goats. Long dresses with nothing on underneath. Thoroughbreds. And the sweaty word "mounted." His free hand felt for the fly of his trousers, but there were tears in his eyes. He knew that the asthma would start mercilessly as soon as he dared to touch his taut organ. Iron hand. Ithamar. Rag doll. Marching from the east.

If the old days of the Bible suddenly came back, I could be a judge in Israel. Or a king. Mitya could be a prophet in a hair mantle, and the bears would eat him like the wicked Turkish soldier. Daddy would pasture the royal flocks in the fields of Bethlehem. And Mommy wouldn't be a Jezebel.

Among the flower beds, Dr. Kipnis appeared. His hair was still wet from the shower, his khaki shorts came down almost to his knees, and between his shorts and his sandals his legs showed brown, thin, and smooth. He was wearing nothing over his vest. His eyes, behind his glasses, looked like blue lakes in a snowy landscape.

Father carefully connected the rubber hose to the garden tap. He made sure it was well attached, and he regulated the flow of water precisely. He stood alone, quietly watering his garden in the early-afternoon sunshine, humming to himself the song "Between the Euphrates and the Tigris."

The water carved out branching and interlacing furrows. From time to time, Father bent down to block its path and direct it where it was needed.

Hillel suddenly felt an ecstatic, overwhelming love for his father. He scrambled out of his hideaway in the fig tree, ran up the path through the summer bird song through the breeze laden with the scent of the distant sea through the streaming afternoon sunlight, flung his arms around his father's waist, and hugged him with all his might.

Hans Kipnis passed the hose from his right to his left hand, stroked his son's head tenderly, and said, "Hillel."

The boy did not reply.

"Here, Hillel. Take it. If you want to water the garden for a bit, take the hose, and I'll go and clip the hedge. You can. Only be very careful not to aim the water at the plants themselves."

"Daddy, what does 'Perfidious Albion' mean?"

"It's what the fanatics call England when they want to be rude about it."

"What does 'fanatics' mean?"

"They're people who are always sure that they know best what's right and what's wrong and what ought to be done, and try their hardest to make everybody else think and act the same way."

"Is Uncle Mitya a fanatic?"

"Uncle Mitya is a sensitive man who reads a lot of books and spends a lot of time studying the Bible. Because he worries a great deal about our plight, and also perhaps because of his personal sufferings, he sometimes uses words that are not quite the words I myself would choose to use."

"What about Mommy?"

"She's having a rest."

"No, I mean, is she also a fanatic."

"Mommy grew up surrounded by wealth and luxury. Sometimes it's hard for her to get used to conditions here; you were born here, and perhaps you are sometimes surprised by her moods. But you're a clever boy, and I'm sure you're not angry with Mommy when she's sad or when she longs to be somewhere completely different."

"Daddy, I've got something to tell you."

"What is it, son?"

"I've got a shilling that I don't want at all. And I don't want you to start asking me who gave it to me, 'cause I won't say. I just want you to take it."

"All right. I'll look after your shilling for you, and I won't ask any questions. Only mind you don't get your new sandals wet when you're watering the grapes. Now I'm going to fetch the shears. Bye-bye. You ought to be wearing a hat in this heat."

10

Toward sunset, when the mountains were shrouded and the wind swept knowingly through the woods and the valleys and the bell of the Schneller Barracks resounded forlornly, the preparations were complete.

All that remained was to wait for the taxi, say good-bye, and go. Nothing had been overlooked. Hans Kipnis, in his borrowed dress suit and impeccably polished black shoes, with his hair neatly parted and smoothed down with water, with his round glasses, looked like a mild, good-natured Evangelical minister setting out with a pounding heart for his wedding.

"My own Dr. Zichel," Mother said with a laugh, and bent over to straighten the white handkerchief in his top pocket.

She was a little taller than he, and her scent was the scent of autumn. She was wearing her blue evening dress with its daring neckline. The light shone in her drop earrings. Ruth was erect and sensuous as she walked with a slow, rounded motion, like a large cat, to wait outside on the veranda. She turned her bare back on the house and looked out into the desolate twilight. Her blond plait had settled on the arch of her left shoulder. Her hip rubbed slowly, with a dreamy rhythm, against the cool stone parapet.

And how the bells had rung throughout Warsaw at the national festival. How all the marble horsemen had reared up in every square. How her warm voice had carried over the playground of the school as she had read the searing lines of the Polish national poet:

Slain cavalrymen never die,
They fly high through the air like the wind,
Their horses' hoofs no longer touching the ground.
At night in the storm in the snow you can hear them
    flying past,
Foam-flecked winged steeds and valiant horsemen,
Forever flying over forests and meadows and plains,
Ghost warriors eternally riding into battle.
At night in the storm in the snow they wing their way
    high over Poland.
Cavalrymen never die, they become transparent and
    powerful as tears. . . .

Ruth's voice conveyed a melancholy echo of violins, the tempestuous thunder of war drums, the roar and sigh of the organ. How they had all loved her. The handsome Tadeusz had stood stiffly at attention half a pace behind her on the platform, holding aloft the blazing Torch of Liberty. Elderly teachers who had themselves fought as cavalry officers in the great war for the liberation of Poland, and who still relived it in their dreams on happy nights, wept to hear her reciting. They stood with their eyes closed and strained toward her with all the force of their longing. She received their love and desire in her heart, and her heart was ready to bestow love on all good men.

She had never throughout her school days encountered bad men until both her parents died within a month of each other, and her sister, Nyuta, suddenly married the widowed gynecologist and left with him for New York. She believed that if bad men really existed outside fairy stories, they must lurk in dark corners. They could never come near her, with her gleaming white tennis dress and her expensive racket. Hence she was inclined to feel a certain sympathy even for them, if they existed. Their lot must be a sad one. What a terrible thing it must be, to be a bad man.

*

By seven o'clock, the mountains were growing dark. The lights of Jerusalem came on. In every house the iron shutters were pulled closed and the curtains were drawn. The inhabitants sank into worry and longing. For an instant the hills of Jerusalem seemed to be heaving and swelling like a sea in the dark.

Hillel was left with Madame Yabrova the pianist and her niece, Binyamina. They would play the phonograph for him, give him supper, let him play for a little with their collection of dolls of all nations, and then put him to bed. Meanwhile the taxi arrived, with its yellow headlights, and gave a long horn blast that sounded like the cry of an animal.

The whole street came out to see Dr. and Mrs. Kipnis off to the May Ball at the High Commissioner's palace on the Hill of Evil Counsel.

Mitya the lodger stood grinning darkly on the doorstep of the house, his silhouette hunched with suffering, clasping a half-drunk glass of tea between his hands. He was chewing the point of his shirt collar, and his lips were mouthing something in the darkness, a curse or a premonition of disaster. The elderly professor Julius Wertheimer, keeping his place with his finger in a German edition of the New Testament, raised his hat slightly and said sadly, as if they were leaving on a long journey to another continent:

"Don't forget us."

Mrs. Vishniak the pharmacist waved them good-bye and good luck from where she sat on a wickerwork chair under the single Mandatory street lamp. Two tears hung from her painted eyelashes, because not long beforehand the announcer on "The Voice of Jerusalem" had said that times were changing and that things would never be the same again.

At the last minute, Engineer Brzezinski emerged on the other side of the road, slightly drunk and holding a huge electric lamp. He was a big-boned man with thick red hair and

freckles. He was panting like a woodcutter and trembling with
emotion. He thundered to them at the top of his voice:

"Just you tell them, doctor, tell them to their faces! Tell them
to leave us alone! Tell them to go away! Tell them the White
Paper is rotten! Tell them the whole country is getting more
and more rotten every day! Tell them once and for all! And tell
them that life as a whole is a rotten trick! Cheap! Miserable!
Provincial! You let them know! And tell them that we, *sam
chort znayet,* will never stop suffering and hoping until our last
breath! Tell them!"

Suddenly he fell silent and pointed his great lamp furiously
up at the dark sky, as if he were trying to dazzle the stars
themselves.

Then the taxi choked, roared, and moved off in a cloud of
dust.

The street was left to itself. Everyone had gone indoors. Only
the square-paned street lamp continued to shed its forlorn light
in vain. The wind blew. The fig tree ruffled its leaves and
settled down. Its fingers were still empty. Dogs barked in the
distance. It was night.

11

Lyubov Binyamina was a short, heavy girl with a swarthy
complexion and a pointed chin. She looked like a plump,
slow-moving, melancholy partridge. Only her lips were painted
a bright scarlet. Her heavy bust forced out the front of her dress
almost violently. There was always something slovenly about
her appearance: a dangling button, a bad cough, a yellow oil
stain on her Viennese-style dress. She wore clumsy brown
orthopedic shoes, even around the house. She had thick down
on her arms, and she wore a man's wristwatch. Hillel sud-

denly recalled the terrible things Mitya had said about the fell-ahin women going out alone at night to gather firewood, looking like hairy black she-goats. He bit his lip and tried hard to think of something else, but Binyamina kissed his ear lobe and called him "child poet," and he buried his face in the carpet and blushed to the roots of his curly hair.

Madame Yabrova, by contrast, displayed the somewhat threadbare remnants of a former grandeur. She spoke with a heavy emphasis, in long, emotional sentences, in a strong voice coarsened by the Simon Arzdt cigarettes she chain-smoked. She would rush around the room, furiously wiping her mouth, picking things up and putting them down again, and turning on her heel with a kind of clumsy agility, like an aging prima donna. She had a slight gray mustache and bushy black eyebrows. Hillel could not take his eyes off her double chin; it reminded him of the pelican in the zoo on Prophet Samuel Street.

Madame Yabrova had changed, as she did every evening, into a theatrical mauve velvet evening gown. She filled the room with a mingled smell of mothballs, baked fish, and eau de cologne.

After a few affectionate words, she suddenly released Hillel, silenced her niece with a hoarse reprimand, and exclaimed:

"Be quiet. We must both be quiet. The child has an inspiration."

They earned their living by giving private music lessons, one on the piano and the other on the cello. They sometimes traveled by bus to remote settlements to favor the pioneers with Friday-night recitals. Their playing was always precise and free from frills and graces, if a trifle academic.

Every available surface in their home was scattered with mementos: tiny ornaments, elaborately carved candlesticks, lumps of rock, handmade objects of wire and raffia, on the piano, the dining table, the coffee table, bronze busts including a glowering Beethoven, Oriental pots, plaster-of-Paris figurines, a china replica of Big Ben, dolls in motley national costumes, a copper Eiffel Tower, water-filled glass globes in which, when they were shaken or turned over, fake snow slowly fell on a rustic cottage or a village church.

One whole shelf was alive with woolly animals: polar bears, leopards, deer, centaurs, zebras, monkeys, elephants, all wandering hopelessly through a forest of green baize or dyed cotton wool. Every quarter of an hour a headless cuckoo popped out of the wall clock and emitted a sound resembling a hoarse bark.

Hillel was seated in a deep armchair surrounded by large philodendrons. Here he huddled in his gym shorts and cotton undershirt, with his legs tucked beneath him.

He thought about the fanatics, of whom Daddy had said that they thought they always knew best what was right and what was wrong and what ought to be done, and wondered in a panic whether Daddy and Mommy might not be secret fanatics, because they, too, always seemed to think they knew best.

Madame Yabrova said:

"If you promise me never to pick your nose, you may have a piece of marzipan after your supper. Lyubov, *krasavitsa,* put down that filthy novel of yours for a moment and pop into the kitchen to get some bread and butter and jam for our guest. *Spassibo.*"

Lyubov said:

"It's not a filthy novel, Auntie. It's nothing of the sort. It's true it's not exactly suitable for children, it's got all sorts of disasters and erotic scenes in it, but there's nothing dirty about it. And anyway, Hillel's almost a grown man. Just look at him."

Madame Yabrova snickered:

"*Bozhe moi,* Lyubov! Nothing dirty, indeed! Smut! Filth! That's all she has in her head. The body, Lyubov, is the purest thing there is in the whole world. Writers should write about love and suchlike with proper reticence. Not with all sorts of filth. Hillel is old enough, I can see, to know what is love and what is simply disgusting."

Hillel said:

"I don't like jam. I want some marzipan, please."

The room smelled dank and brown. In six vases of assorted shapes and sizes, last weekend's gladioli drooped and wilted. The windows were all closed to keep out the wind or the sounds of the night. Mommy and Daddy were far away. The shutters were closed, too. The curtains were drawn. Madame Yabrova was chain-smoking her Simon Arzdt cigarettes. The air was turning gray. She reached out to touch the child, who had glumly eaten half a buttered roll; she felt the muscles of his arm and exclaimed dramatically:

"Molodyetz! Soldatchik!"

Madame Yabrova put a record on the phonograph. Two suites for flute were followed without an interruption by an infectious dance tune. She kicked off her shoes and moved heavily around the room in her bare feet in time to the music.

Meanwhile, Hillel had consumed a soft-boiled egg from a chipped enamel mug, and rounded off his meal with a piece of marzipan. He played for a while with the glass globes with fake snowflakes. He was tired, drowsy, and miserable. He was suddenly seized with a vague apprehension.

Lyubov Binyamina Even-Hen came back into the room in a pink dressing gown. Her heavy, restless breasts were straining at the top button. Madame Yabrova switched on the lamp on the piano, which was carved in the form of a blue nymph, and turned off the overhead light. The elaborate glass chandelier went dark, and so did the room. Drowsily Hillel let himself be fed a spoonful of plum preserve that tasted like sticky-sweet glue. Shadows played on the walls and the furniture. The two women came and went, whispering, exchanging secret giggles in Russian. Through his drooping eyelids, through the haze of cigarette smoke, Hillel seemed to see Binyamina slowly, painstakingly unfastening all the hooks and catches of her aunt's velvet dress. The two women seemed to be floating on the smoke and mingling with the blocks of shadow. They were

seemingly dancing on the carpet, dancing and smoking in time
to the music of the phonograph among the ornaments and figurines, one in a pink dressing gown and the other in a black
petticoat.

Then, in the dark, they leaned over him from either side
of the deep armchair, stroked his curly hair and his cheeks
with honeyed fingers, felt his chest through his cotton shirt,
and carried him off to bed in their arms. His nostrils suddenly
caught a strange smell. His eyes were shut tight with tiredness, but some sudden stimulus, a throb of sly curiosity, made
him open them just a crack. The light was poor. The air in the
room was full of smoke and sweat and eau de cologne. He
caught a strange, heart-pinching glimpse of the waistband of
Binyamina's knickers through the opening in the front of her
dressing gown. And a faint sucking sound behind the bed. A
moist whisper. Russian. A vague, unfamiliar feeling thrust its
way up and down his spine. Not knowing what it was, he lay
motionless on his back and glimpsed a shoulder, a hip, unknown
curves, and his heart pounded and pounded like a frightened
rabbit's.

He went on breathing deeply, calmly, as if he were fast
asleep. Now even he was shocked at his slyness. Sleep had
deserted him completely. He could feel the blood throbbing
in his ankles. He smelled a blend of strong smells, and he knew
that a large woman was blowing on his cheek to see if he was
asleep. The sheet rustled. Fear and excitement clashed in his
breast, and he decided to go on pretending to be a little boy
fast asleep. He suddenly remembered the gleam in Uncle Mitya's eye as he spoke about she-goats. He also remembered the
words "Perfidious Albion," but he could not remember what
they meant. Hands were pulling at his gym shorts. His organ,
which was taut like a thin pencil, was being touched with
something like warm, sticky jam. He gritted his teeth, and
forced himself with all his might not to recoil, not to stop his
rhythmic breathing. Asleep. Feeling nothing. Not here. Far

away. Only don't let it stop now the feel of velvet she-goats silk jam pink transparent more more. And the naughty Oriental girls who knocked him down on piles of gravel and pulled and pulled his hair and one of them was beginning to grow breasts under her vest. Mommy. A wet, licking feeling up his spine. And pinching. Then the slender pencil began to sneeze convulsively between the fingers of the musical women. The boy stifled a moan. Madame Yabrova let out a low, fleshy laugh. And Lyubov Binyamina suddenly panted like a thirsty dog.

The lamp on the piano went out. The room was dark and still. He opened his eyes and saw nothing but darkness. There was not a sound to be heard. Nothing stirred. In that moment Hillel knew that Daddy and Mommy would never come back and girls would never fight with him again on the gravel heap and there would be no more Mitya or anyone, they had all gone away and would never return. He was alone in the house alone in the neighborhood there was no one in Tel Arza no one in Jerusalem no one in the whole country he was left all alone with the jackals and the woods and the nibbled skeleton of the Turkish janissary.

12

The guest of honor at the ball was the Hero of Malta, Admiral Sir Kenneth Horace Sutherland, V.C., K.B.E., Deputy First Sea Lord.

He was standing, tall, pink-faced, and broad-shouldered, on the edge of the illuminated fountain, resplendent in his spotless white uniform and gleaming medals. He was holding a cocktail in his right hand, while in his left he twirled a single magnificent rose. He was surrounded by officers and gentlemen, by red-fezzed Arab dignitaries with gold watch chains strung across their bellies, and by wistful, sparkling-eyed English ladies, while tall, pitch-black Sudanese servants moved everywhere brandishing silver salvers, with snow-white napkins draped over their hooked arms.

Admiral Sutherland was telling a slightly risqué story, in a dry delivery spiced with naval slang, about the American general George Patton, a performing monkey, and a hot-blooded Italian actress by the name of Silvana Lungo. When he got to the punch line, the men guffawed and the ladies let out shocked shrieks.

Colored lights shone under the water in the marble pool, more lights hung suspended in the air, paper lanterns glowed among the trees, and the light breeze ruffled the pines. The gently sloping lawns were dotted with rose beds and divided by impeccably kept gravel paths. The palace itself floated on the beams of concealed floodlights. Its arches of Jerusalem stone were delicately, almost tenderly, carved.

At the foot of the veranda clustered some prominent figures of the Jewish community, including many of the leading lights of the Jewish Agency, the two elderly bankers Shealtiel and Toledano, Mr. Rokeah, the mayor of Tel Aviv, and Mr. Agronski of the *Palestine Post*. They were gathered in an excited semicircle around Captain Archibald Chichester-Browne, the British government spokesman, with whom they were engaged in a good-natured altercation. But for once the captain was disinclined to be serious. He pronounced one or two uncharitable remarks about the Arab League, which the prominent Jews interpreted as a favorable sign. Moshe Shertok dropped a hint to the others that they should be satisfied with this achievement and change the subject immediately, so as not to overstep the mark.

And so the conversation turned to the potash works that were rapidly being developed beside the Dead Sea. Captain Chichester-Browne took the opportunity to compare the Jewish kibbutzim to the early Christian communities that had once existed in the same region, and while on the subject, he even saw fit to praise Professor Klausner's work on the origins of Christianity. His audience drew further encouragement from these remarks, and mentally noted with glee that he had voiced two favorable sentiments in rapid succession. The captain then took his leave of the Zionist gentlemen with a charming, carefully modulated smile; he gestured ironically with his chin toward a group of Arab dignitaries from Bethlehem, winked at Moshe Shertok, and remarked confidentially that the other gentlemen were also demanding their pound of flesh. With that, he turned on his heel and walked over to join them.

After advancing slowly in a procession with other guests, Dr. and Mrs. Kipnis were eventually presented to the Military Governor of Jerusalem, to Lady Cunningham, and finally to Sir Alan himself.

Old Lady Bromley was nowhere to be seen. Perhaps she had fainted again. Sir Alan and Lady Cunningham greeted Father: "Pleased to meet you," "So glad you could come." Sir Alan allowed his grave blue glance to rest searchingly for a moment on Mother's black eyes as he said, "If I may say so, dear lady, your beauty and that of Jerusalem were molded by the same divine inspiration. I dare to hope that you will not be bored by our modest entertainment."

Mother responded to the compliment with one of her beautiful autumnal smiles. It hovered on her lips, as fine and transparent as the tears of the slain cavalrymen in the Polish poem.

Then a steward showed them to the bar and handed them over to an Armenian barman. Father immediately opted for a tomato juice, while Mother, after a moment's hesitation, the smile still playing faintly around her lips, asked for a glass of cherry brandy. They were conducted to a pretty wicker table and seated between Mr. Tsipkin, the Citrus King, and Madame Josette al-Bishari, the headmistress of the Arab National High School for Girls. They exchanged polite remarks.

Presently, the Military Governor of Jerusalem delivered a short, witty address from the veranda of the palace. He began with a reference to the crushing defeat inflicted on the enemies of humanity by Great Britain and her allies in May of the previous year. He paid a tribute to the guest of honor, Admiral Sir Kenneth Horace Sutherland, the Hero of Malta, and declared that the world had not yet seen the German, Italian, or lady who could resist him. He also paid tribute to the holy character of Jerusalem. He delivered an impassioned plea for fellowship and understanding among the adherents of the various religions. He added jokingly that if love did suddenly spring up among the different religious groups, the first thing the lovers would do would be to kick out the British. It was well known, he said, that in a love affair there was no place for a third party. But we British had always believed in miracles, and the idea of a Trinity was not entirely unfamiliar to Jerusalem; so whatever happened we would continue to haunt Palestine in the role of Holy Spirit, for which, of course, we were uniquely suited. A toast to the Crown. A toast to the Hero of Malta. Another toast to Sir Alan and his charming lady. And, if they would kindly refill their glasses, a final toast to the spring and to amity among all the inhabitants of the Holy Land, Moslems, Christians, Jews, and Socialists.

Then the dancing began.

From among the trees, which were hung with colored lights, the musicians of the police and military bands advanced in threes, their buckles gleaming. The whole hill resounded with the sound of percussion and brass. From behind the palace, fireworks lit up the sky over the city and the desert. The admiral, flushed and tipsy, roared, "Heave ho, me hearties! Splice the main brace! All guns fire!"

How colorfully the ladies' ball gowns blossomed by the light of the lanterns and fireworks. How riotously the music flowed into the heart of the night. How joyfully, how frenziedly, the couples whirled, the ladies twined like young vines, the men whispering sweet words into their ears. The Sudanese servants, coal-black faces atop white tunics, stared in amazement.

The last days of Rome must have been like this, Father thought to himself. As the idea flashed through his mind, his optimistic blue eyes may have reflected a momentary sadness behind his round glasses.

Mother was immediately snatched up by Mr. Tsipkin, the Citrus King. Then she could be seen, blond and radiant, in the arms of the Swedish consul. Then again resting lightly against the shoulder of a dark giant sporting a pair of Latin mustachios. With hardly a pause to draw breath, she was swept up by a one-eyed, battle-scarred colonel with predatory yellow teeth.

Father looked away. He struck up a desultory conversation with his neighbor, Madame Josette al-Bishari. No doubt he was telling her all about the cattle he inspected, or perhaps preaching with ill-suppressed zeal about the benefits of drinking goats' milk.

The High Commissioner himself was wandering, lost in thought, among the guests. He paused for a moment at the table where Madame al-Bishari and Dr. Kipnis sat; abstractedly he picked up a cocktail biscuit, eyed it cautiously, and returned it to the dish. He smiled faintly at Madame Josette or Dr. Kipnis or perhaps toward the lights of Jerusalem behind their shoulders, and eventually he spoke:

"Well, well. I see you are both sitting it out. Why aren't you dancing? I expect you're secretly hatching some sort of intrigue; but I've caught you red-handed, in the name of the Crown. Just my little joke. Good evening to you both."

He turned and moved away, a slim, erect figure, to continue his tour of the tables.

Father said, in English with a heavy German accent:

"I know a man who superficially resembles Sir Alan but hates him bitterly."

Madame Josette answered at once, in fluent German, with a kind of strangled fervor:

"Anyway, there's no hope."

"I am unable to agree with you on that point, madame," Father said.

Madame Josette smiled patiently. "I shall try to explain my-

self by means of a small illustration. Take yourselves, for
example. You have been leaving Europe for Palestine for forty
years now. You will never arrive. At the same time, we are
moving away from the desert toward Europe, and we shall
never arrive, either. There is not even the ghost of a chance that
we shall meet one another halfway. I suppose, sir, that you
consider yourself a social democrat?"

Father expressed surprise. "Surely we are meeting at this
very moment?"

To these words he received no reply.

The headmistress of the National High School for Girls
slowly gathered up her belongings from the table, her silk
handkerchief, her Virginia cigarettes, her fan with its picture of
Notre Dame; she apologized in French, which Father could not
understand, and a feminine slyness glimmered for an instant
in her eyes. She moved slowly away from the table, an elegant
yet unremarkable woman, thickening slightly around the hips,
in a long Marlene Dietrich dress. Then she was gone.

He followed her with his eyes until she had vanished in the
throng. Then he caught sight of his wife, thrown high above the
lawn, with her mouth gaping open in a soundless exclamation
of pleasure, then landing gently in the broad hands of the
Hero of Malta. She was disheveled and excited, her lips parted,
her blue dress lifted above her knees.

Admiral Sutherland laughed hoarsely and gave an exaggerated
bow. He seized her hand and raised the palm to his lips, kissing, blowing, nuzzling. She touched his cheek quickly. Then the
music changed, and they started dancing again, pressed tightly
together, with her head on his shoulder and his arm around her
waist.

The fireworks had finished. The music was dying away.
Guests were already leaving, and still she whirled with the
Hero of Malta on the dance floor on the lawn toward the wood,
until the darkness and the trees hid them from Father's sight.

Meanwhile the High Commissioner had withdrawn. The
Military Governor had left, in a convoy of armored cars and

armed jeeps, for the King David Hotel. The last guests had taken their leave and disappeared toward the parking lot. Captain Chichester-Browne and even the Sudanese servants had deserted the lawns and vanished into the inner recesses of the palace.

Darkness fell on the Hill of Evil Counsel. The paper lanterns went out one by one. Only the searchlights continued to claw the gentle slope and the bushes that were gradually sinking into ever-deeper shadows. A dry coldness rose from the Judean Desert, which bounded the palace on the east. And groups of palace guards armed with Bren guns began to patrol the grounds.

Father stood alone beside the deserted fountain, which was still pouring out jets of light and water. Now he spotted a single goldfish in the marble pool. He was cold, and desperately tired. His mother and sisters had probably been murdered in Silesia or somewhere else. The cattle farm in Galilee would never exist, the monograph or poem would never be written. Hillel would have to be sent to a boarding school in one of the kibbutzim. He will hate me for it all his life. Dr. Ruppin is dead. Buber and Agnon will also die. If a Hebrew state is ever established, I shall not be running its veterinary service. If only the Underground would come this very minute and blow the whole place sky high. But that's not a nice thought. And I—

In his borrowed dress suit, with a white handkerchief peeping out of his top pocket, with the strange bow tie and his comical glasses, Hans Kipnis looked like a pathetic suitor in a silent film.

He closed his eyes. He suddenly remembered the wandering Bavarian ornithologist with whom he had cut a virgin path many years before to the remote sources of the Jordan in the farthest corner of the country. He recalled the coldness of the water and the snowy peaks of Mount Hermon. When he opened his eyes again, he saw Lady Bromley. She appeared like a wizened ghost from among the bushy oleanders, old, spoiled, seething with venomous zeal, in a dark shawl, doubled up with malicious glee.

"What you have lost tonight, sir, you will never find again. If you like, you can leave a message with me for the head gardener. But even he cannot save you, because he is a drunken Greek and a pathetic queer. Go home, my dear doctor. The party's over. Life nowadays is just like a stupid party. A little light, a little music, a little dancing, and then darkness. Look. The lights have been turned out. The leftovers have been thrown to the dogs. Go home, my dear doctor. Or must I wake up poor Lieutenant Grady and tell him to drive you?"

"I am waiting for my wife," said Father.

Lady Bromley let out a loud, ribald guffaw. "I have had four husbands, and none of them, I repeat, none of them ever said anything as fantastic as that. In all my life I've never heard a man talk like that, except perhaps in vulgar farces."

"I should be deeply grateful, madam, if you could give me some assistance, or direct me to someone who can help me. My wife has been dancing all evening, and she may have had a drop too much to drink. She must be around somewhere. Perhaps she has dozed off."

Lady Bromley's eyes suddenly flashed, and she growled wickedly:

"You are the native doctor who poked his fingers into my corset ten days ago. How rotten and charming. Come here and let me give you a big kiss. Come. Don't be afraid of me."

Father rallied his last resources. "Please, madam, please help me. I can't go home without her."

"That's rich," gloated Lady Bromley. "Listen to that. That's wonderful. He can't go home without his wife. He needs to have his wife next to him every night. And these, ladies and gentlemen, are the Jews. The People of the Book. The spiritual people. Huh! How much?"

"How much what?" Father asked, stunned.

"Really! How much will that rotten drunkard Kenneth have to pay you to calm down and keep your mouth shut? Huh! You may not believe it, but in the twelve months since the end of the war, that stupid young hothead has already sold three woods, two farms, and an autograph manuscript of Dickens, all for cash to silence the poor husbands. What a life. How rotten and charming. And to think that his poor father was once a gentleman in waiting to Queen Victoria!"

"I don't understand," said Father.

Lady Bromley gave a piercing, high-pitched laugh like a rusty saw and said, "Good night, my sweet doctor. I am really and truly grateful to you for your devoted attention. Jewish fingers inside my corset. That's rich! And how enchanting the nights are here in Palestine in springtime. Look around you: what nights! By the way, our beloved Alan also used to have a thriving sideline in other men's wives when he was a cadet. But that leech Trish soon sucked him dry. Poor Trish. Poor Alan. Poor Palestine. Poor doctor. Good night to you, my poor dear Othello. Good night to me, too. By the way, who was the raving lunatic who had the nerve to call this stinking hole Jerusalem? It's a travesty. *Au revoir*, doctor."

At three o'clock in the morning, Father left the palace on foot and headed in the direction of the German Colony. Outside the railway station, he was given a lift by two pale-faced rabbis in a hearse. They were on their way, they explained, from a big wedding in the suburb of Mekor Hayim to their work at the burial society in Sanhedriya. Hans Kipnis arrived home shortly before four, in the misty morning twilight. At the same time, the admiral, his lady friend, his driver, and his bodyguard crossed a sleeping Jericho with blazing headlights and with an armed jeep for escort, and turned off toward the Kaliah Hotel on the shore of the Dead Sea. A day or two later, the black-and-silver Rolls Royce set out eastward, racing deep into the desert, across mountains and valleys, and onward, to Baghdad, Bombay, Calcutta. All along the way, Mother soulfully recited poems by Mickiewicz in Polish. The admiral, belching high-spiritedly like a big, good-natured sheepdog, ripped open her blue dress and inserted a red, affectionate hand. She felt nothing, and never for an instant interrupted her gazelle song. Only her

black eyes shone with joy and tears. And when the admiral
forced his fingers between her knees, she turned to him and
told him that slain cavalrymen never die, they become transparent and powerful as tears.

13

The following day, a heat wave hit Jerusalem. Dust rose from
the desert and hung over the mountains. The sky turned deep
gray, a grotesque autumnal disguise. Jerusalem barred its shutters and closed in on itself. And the white boulders blazed
spitefully on every hillside.

All the neighborhood was gathered excitedly in the garden.
Father stood, in khaki shorts and a vest, staring tiredly and
blankly up into the fig tree. His face looked innocent and helpless without his round glasses.

Mrs. Vishniak clapped her hands together and muttered in
Yiddish, *"Gott in Himmel."* Madame Yabrova and her niece
tried angry words and gentle ones. They held out the threat of
the British police, the promise of marzipan, the final threat
of the kibbutz.

Engineer Brzezinski, red-faced and panting, tried unsuccess-
fully to join two ladders together. And Mitya the lodger took
advantage of the general confusion to trample the flower beds,
one after another, uprooting saplings and tearing out plants
and throwing them over his shoulder, chewing his shirt collar
and hissing continuously through his rotting teeth, "Lies, false-
hood, untruth, it's all lies."

Father attempted one last plea. "Come down, Hillel. Please,
son, get down. Mommy will come back and it'll all be like before. Those branches aren't very strong. Get down, there's a
good boy. We won't punish you. Just come down now and everything will be exactly the same as before."

But the boy would not hear. His eyes groped at the murky gray sky, and he went on climbing up, up to the top of the tree, as the scaly fingers of the leaves caressed him from all sides, up to where the branches became twigs and buds, and still on, up to the very summit, up into the gentle trembling, to the fine delicate heights where the branches became a high-pitched melody into the depths of the sky. Night is reigning in the skies, time for you to close your eyes. Every bird is in its nest, all Jerusalem's at rest. He saw nothing, no frantic people in the garden, no Daddy, no house and no mountains, no distant towers, no stone huts scattered among the boulders, no sun, no moon, no stars. Nothing at all. All Jerusalem's at rest. Only a dull-gray blaze. Overcome with pleasure and astonishment, the child said to himself, "There's nothing." Then he gathered himself and leaped on up to the last leaf, to the shore of the sky.

At that point the firemen arrived. But Engineer Brzezinski drove them away, roaring: "Go away! There's no fire here! Lunatics! Go to Taganrog! Go to Kherson, degenerates! That's where the fire is! In the Crimea! At Sebastopol! There's a great fire raging there! Get out of here! And in Odessa, too! Get out of here, the lot of you!"

And Mitya put his arms carefully around Father's shaking shoulders and led him slowly indoors, whispering gently and with great compassion, "Jerusalem, which slayeth its prophets, shall burn the new Hellenizers in hellfire."

In due course, the elderly Professor Julius Wertheimer, together with his cats, also moved into the little stone house in Tel Arza. An international commission of inquiry arrived in Jerusalem. There were predictions and hopes. One evening Mitya suddenly opened up his room and invited his friends in. The room was spotlessly clean, except for the slight persistent smell. The three scholars would spend hours on end here, drinking tea and contemplating an enormous military map, guessing wildly at the future borders of the emerging Hebrew state, marking with arrows ambitious campaigns of conquest all over the Middle East. Mitya began to address Father by his first name, Hanan. Only the famous geographer Hans Walter Landauer looked down on them with a look of skepticism and mild surprise from his picture.

Then the British left. A picture of the High Commissioner, Sir Alan Cunningham, appeared in the newspaper *Davar,* a slim, erect figure in a full general's uniform, saluting the last British flag to be run down, in the port of Haifa.

A Hebrew government was finally set up in Jerusalem. The road in Tel Arza was paved, and the suburb was joined to the city. The saplings grew. The trees looked very old. The creepers climbed over the roof of the house and all over the fence. Masses of flowers made a blaze of blue. Madame Yabrova was killed by a stray shell fired on Tel Arza from the battery of the Transjordanian Legion near Nabi Samwil. Lyubov Binyamina Even-Hen, disillusioned with the Hebrew state, sailed from Haifa aboard the *Moledet* to join her sister in New York. There she was run over by a train, or she may have thrown herself underneath it. Professor Buber also died, at a ripe old age. In due course Father and Mitya were appointed to teaching posts at the Hebrew University, each in his own subject. Every morning they packed rolls and hard-boiled eggs and a Thermos of tea and set off together by bus for the Ratisbone and Terra Sancta buildings, where some of the departments of the university were housed temporarily until the road to Mount Scopus could be reopened. The elderly Professor Julius Wertheimer, however, finally retired and devoted himself single-mindedly to keeping house for them. The whole house gleamed. He even discovered the secret of perfect ironing. Once a month Hanan and Mitya went to see the child at school in the kibbutz. He had grown lean and bronzed. They took him chocolate and chewing gum from Jerusalem. On the hills all around Jerusalem, the enemy set up concrete pillboxes, bunkers, gun sites.

And waited.

1974

Mr. Levi

1

Once upon a time, many years ago, there lived in Jerusalem an old poet by the name of Nehamkin. He had come from Vilna and settled in a low stone house with a tiled roof in a narrow alley off Zephaniah Street. Here he wrote his poems, and here every summer he sat in a deck chair in the garden counting the hours and the days.

This quarter of the city had been built in a large orchard on a hillside, with a view of the mountains that surround Jerusalem. Every passing breeze caused a shiver. Fig trees and mulberry trees, pomegranates and grapevines, were forever rustling and whispering as though asking us to be quiet. The poet Nehamkin was already slightly deaf, but he tried to capture the rustling of the trees in his poems, interpreting it in his own way. The whisper of the leaves in the breeze, the scent of the blossoms, the smell of dry thistles in the late summer, all seemed to him to be hinting at an important event that was imminent. His poems were always full of surmises.

One by one, simple stone-built houses sprang up among the trees of the orchard. They had balconies with rusty iron railings, low fences, and gates adorned with a Star of David or the word ZION.

Little by little the settlers neglected the trees. Shady pines gradually overwhelmed the vines and pomegranates. Occasional bursts of pomegranate blossom were snuffed out by the children before they ever bore fruit. Among the untended trees and the outcrops of rock, there were attempts at planting oleanders, violets, and geraniums. But the flower beds were quickly forgotten, trampled underfoot, filled with thorns and broken glass, and these plants, too, if they did not wither and die, grew wild. In the backyards of the houses, ramshackle sheds proliferated, built out of the packing cases in which the settlers had transported their belongings from Russia and Poland. Some of them nailed empty olive cans to wooden poles, called them dovecotes, and waited for the doves to come. In the meantime, the only birds to nest in the area were crows and swallows. Somewhere there lurked a persistent cuckoo.

The residents longed to leave Jerusalem and settle somewhere less extreme. Some of them fixed their sights on other suburbs, such as Beit ha-Kerem, Talpiyot, or Rehavia. They believed almost without exception that the hard times would soon be over, the Hebrew state would be set up, and everything would change for the better. Surely they had completed in full their term of suffering. Meanwhile, the first children were born and grew up in the neighborhood, and it was almost impossible to explain to them why and from where their parents had come here, and what it was they were waiting for.

The poet Nehamkin lived with his only son, Ephraim, who was an electrician and ideologist. Like most of the children of the district, I, too, believed that this Ephraim played some secret and terrible role in the Hebrew Underground. In outward appearance, he was short, dark, wiry-haired, a technician who almost always wore blue overalls and found it hard to keep his hands still. He repaired irons and radios, and even built transmitters with his own hands. He sometimes disappeared for days on end, to return, eventually, suntanned and withdrawn, with an expression of contempt or disgust on his face, as if in the course of his wanderings he had seen things that had filled him with despair. Ephraim and I shared a secret. At the end of the winter, he had made me his lieutenant. One of his lieutenants, that is.

What it was, however, that he had discovered in his wanderings, Ephraim did not see fit to disclose to me.

Despite his scornful expression, despite his low brow and rough hands, he had various girls who came to him, including a skinny student from the university on Mount Scopus. Sometimes they would stay with him until daybreak. These visitors seemed to me unnecessary; not one of them was pretty or gay. I hated them because they called Ephraim by the ugly pet name Froike, and because I was afraid that love or lust would make him give away to them at night secrets that belonged to the two of us alone; I had sometimes seen in the movies how love can make even heroes lose their wits, and then there is no going back.

Once I helped set a trap with the Grill boys from next door. We tied a rusty tin can full of muddy water to a branch of the mulberry tree, and ran a fine cord from it across the lane. Then we hid in the tree. The skinny girl from Mount Scopus came down the lane, carefully stepped over the cord, cast a reproachful look up into the tree, and remarked sadly:

"You should be ashamed of yourselves."

The Grill boys began to laugh. I laughed with them. Then we put broken glass into some mailboxes.

Later, I felt suddenly ashamed. I felt ashamed for most of the morning, and at lunchtime I went to the workshop and made a clean breast of it to Ephraim. I didn't mention the Grill boys. I took all the blame upon myself. Ephraim locked the door, made me call our trap a stupid, childish prank, and forgave me. He taught me how to fill a tin can with gasoline and use a fuse to ignite it, so that when the time came I could play my part in the final battle and not go as a lamb to the slaughter, like the Jewish children in Europe.

Then Ephraim turned to the dry, dusty-looking girl who was sitting silently on his bed sewing a button on for him, and who seemed to me to have no lips:

"Uriel is in on it," he said. "He's a serious boy. And in general," he added, "there's excellent human material here in the neighborhood. This is Ruhama. And she's not what you think."

Ruhama straightened her glasses with two fingers, still holding the needle. She said nothing. I did not speak, either. Secretly

I was convinced that it was this Ruhama who would betray us all to the British police. I thought it strange that Ephraim should be so irresponsible as to have her in his workshop and let her sit on his bed and even stay all night sometimes. Love, I thought to myself, could definitely wait until after the victory. She wasn't even pretty. She didn't even talk to me.

The old poet used to do everything in his power to stop the girls going to the workshop. Sometimes he would lie in wait for them at the gate. But the garden had two entrances, and in places the fence was broken down, and anyway Ephraim's room had a back entrance from the rocky garden, up three stone steps that were slippery with dead pine needles.

Sometimes the poet could not contain himself: he would intercept one of the girls and smile at her with extreme politeness:

"Excuse me, dear lady, but I think you must have made a mistake. I must inform you, with all due respect, that this is neither an alehouse nor a den of thieves. This is a private house. And anyway, the young man is not here, he is away on his travels, he has left no instructions—who am I to say when he will take it into his head to return?"

From the beginning of the summer holidays, there was a secret alliance between Mr. Nehamkin and me against these periodic incursions. He lay in wait in front of the house, while I lurked in the garden.

Ephraim, if he was not away on his wanderings, liked to sleep from after lunch until the evening twilight. He would sleep, soaked in sweat, on a mattress in his workshop. He would toss and groan in his sleep, ward something off with his fists, turn over suddenly with a moan. I would tiptoe in to listen in case he uttered secrets in his dreams, so that I could keep them from prying ears. Then I would tiptoe out again and resume my watch.

If ever one of the girls came to disturb Ephraim's slumbers, we would both, Mr. Nehamkin and I, waylay her at the gate. We were armed with uncompromising replies to the mincing question "Where's Froike?"

"I'm his lieutenant. He's not in," I would say darkly.

And Mr. Nehamkin would add softly:

"It is quite impossible to know when the young man will return from his wanderings. It may be tomorrow, or the day after, or it may not be for many days."

Sometimes the girl would ask us to pass along a note or a message. These we would always refuse. There was no need. There was no point. And in any case, in times like these, who accepts letters from strangers?

The girl would either protest or apologize, and promise to call again some other time. She would hesitantly employ some such word as "misunderstanding" or "regret" and be on her way.

The moment her back was turned, Mr. Nehamkin would begin to justify our action in carefully chosen words:

"We told no lie; nor did we mislead the young lady. After all, slumber is a kind of distant wandering to remote worlds. As for billets-doux and notes, it is explicitly forbidden for a man to make himself a messenger of sin."

On such occasions he would also add some cautious prognostication prompted by the sight of the girl disappearing down the lane:

"She will surely soon find herself another young man, or maybe even two, according to the desire of her heart, whereas we have only one Ephraim. Therefore we shall continue to stand as a bulwark and as one man, the wretched poet Nehamkin and the excellent child Uriel. We shall never allow strangers to lead us astray. The aged poet and the youth shall hold the fort and guard the truth. Now return in peace to your wonted sport, and I shall go on my weary way. Each to his allotted task. O, that it may be granted us to behold the deliverance of Jerusalem."

2

Mr. Nehamkin was round and cuddly like a teddy bear. He dragged his feet and always walked with the aid of a carved stick. He looked as though he found his body a tiresome burden, as though he was forced to drag it around with him from place to place against his will, like a man carrying a heavy bundle that was gradually coming undone. The poet had discovered in Holy Writ one or two vague hints that in the Judean Desert, below Jerusalem, a green sea was hidden that no eye had ever beheld, not the Dead Sea, not a sea at all, but springs or wells of water, where were the Essenes and dreamers whom not even the Roman legions had been able to discover, and that was where he meant to go one of these days to shrug off his burden and set off lightened and freed along his own unique road.

He would say:

"How sorry I am for them. I could weep for them. Eyes have they but they see not."

Or:

"Their mouths speak but their ears hear not. The decree has gone forth. Their time has expired. The sword is already flashing. But as for them, they eat and drink. To outward appearances they are fearlessly made, but in truth they are merely blinded. Sorrow and compassion rend my heart."

At times it seemed as though Mr. Nehamkin's prophecies were almost about to come true. Once, in the doorway of the grocer's, he bent over and whispered to me that the King of Israel would soon rise up from his hiding place in the clefts of the mountain and slay the High Commissioner and seize his throne in Jerusalem. Another time it was revealed to him in a dream that Hitler was not dead but had hidden himself away among the murderous Bedouins in the darkness of the tents of

Kedar. And in the middle of the summer holidays, a few days before the fast of Ab, he took me among the drought-smitten oleanders in the garden and urged me to water the plants because the feet of the Messenger were already standing at the gates of Jerusalem. At five o'clock on the following morning, the neighborhood was awakened by sounds of shouting and moaning. I leaped into my gym shorts and rushed outside with no shoes on. The three Grill boys, Boaz, Joab, and Abner, were standing in the middle of the lane beating furiously on a broken tar drum. Half-dressed women ran out of the houses. Somebody shouted a question, and other voices shouted back. The dogs were barking as though they were out of their minds. From the Faithful Remnant Synagogue, the Venerable Rabbi Zischa Lufban emerged, with a retinue of saints and scholars, and cried out repeatedly in an awe-inspiring voice:

"Come out, unclean! Come out in the name of G—d!"

But it was only excited neighbors who came out of every doorway, and many of them were in their pajamas. Helena Grill ran from one man to another, begging them at least to save the children. I caught sight of Mr. Nehamkin standing mildly and thoughtfully at the gate of his garden. He was wearing a dark-blue suit, a Polish tie, a flaming paper flower in his buttonhole, and a polite smile of forgiveness on his face; he was clasping his walking stick by its tiger's-head handle.

Mother chose to stay indoors. She sent father to wake up Mrs. Vishniak the pharmacist. Mother was always afraid that somebody might faint or that there might be an accident. But there was no accident. We saw a colorful procession wending its way toward us out of the east, from the direction of the Bokharan Quarter. At its head was a little old man with an unwashed air, riding on a little ass. He must have been ill, or perhaps only exhausted, because he was propped up on either side by Kurdish porters. They were lean and dark-bristled, with sacks tied around their waists.

Following close on the heels of the old man came the whole Bokharan Quarter, men, women, and children, just like the Exodus from Egypt we were learning about at school. Someone

was beating on an old tin can, others were chanting guttural
hymns, or mumbling prayers and incantations. The ass seemed
to me piteously meek and wretched. It was far from healthy,
and it wasn't even white. I looked around for Ephraim, but he
was nowhere to be seen. His old father beamed at me, touched
my hair, and said peacefully:

"Blessed are they that believe."

The procession, meanwhile, had turned off Zephaniah
Street onto Amos Street. It continued westward along the stone
wall of the Schneller Barracks and came to a halt outside the
main gate, opposite the clock tower.

All the children of the neighborhood, myself among them,
rushed from either flank of the procession up to the gate. Here
we stopped, because the British sentries had cocked their
Tommy guns and rested them, pointing at the crowd, on top
of the sandbag barricade.

The Schneller tower was crowned by an indecipherable inscription in Gothic characters. The clock itself had stopped
many years before. It chimed regularly every half hour, day and
night, but its hands were lifeless. They pointed immovably
to precisely three minutes past three. A rumor ran through the
crowd: the stranger who had arrived out of nowhere at midnight would work a miracle and make time run backward. He
would summon King David and all his horsemen out of the top
of the tower. The massed troops of the ten lost tribes would
come sweeping down from the mountains. The old Bokharan
women started beating their breasts with their wrinkled fists.
A cripple began to declaim, "This is the day which the Lord
hath made," then suddenly thought better of it and fell silent.
Together with Boaz, Joab, and Abner and all the other boys of
the neighborhood, I chanted ecstatically:

"Free immigra-tion, He-brew state!"

"Woe upon me," cried Rabbi Lufban, but nobody heard him.

The British blocked the road with an armored car. An
officer stood up in it holding a loudspeaker. He was presumably telling the crowd to disperse, but there must have been

some flaw, since we could only see his lips moving. The noise died down. There was a silence like the still, small voice we had learned about at school, and in the silence birds and a cockcrowing far away. It was just before the dawn. The light was gray and blue. The cypress trees and the great water tower on top of Romema Hill seemed to be receding into the gentle mist. Then the old man straightened himself up on his ass, drew a filthy handkerchief from the folds of his robe, and hawked and spat into it. The people were silent. He folded the handkerchief and put it away, raised his head, carefully put on a pair of spectacles, pointed to the clock or perhaps to the tower with a trembling finger, and mumbled some words that I did not catch; but I could see him swelling, reddening, coming to the boil, and suddenly he cried out in a clear, strong voice:

"Let the sun rise and let the deed be done. Now!"

At that very moment the sun rose, gigantic, yellow, dazzling the mountaintop to the east, blazing on the Paternoster and Augusta Victoria towers, shimmering on the Mount of Olives, flashing terribly on the wooded slopes, gleaming off the cisterns on all the roofs of Geula, Ahva, Kerem Avraham and Mekor Baruch. I felt like running away, because it looked as though the whole of Jerusalem were on fire.

Everybody, believers and skeptics alike, Mr. Nehamkin, Rabbi Lufban—all watched the sun rise and turned their eyes as one man toward the clock tower. Even the British officer in the armored car looked around.

But the clock had not moved: still three minutes past three.

Far away, in the Geran Colony, a train howled. Somebody lit a cigarette. There was whispering. A woman began to laugh or sob. Then the old man sighed, slipped off the back of the gray donkey, leaned trembling on the arms of his Kurdish bodyguard, and said sadly:

"Another time."

At once, in furious Yiddish, the Venerable Rabbi Zischa Lufban ordered his disciples to send the scoffers and workers of iniquity straight back to the dark holes they had crawled out of and put an end to this blasphemous charade. The British officer, too, finally managed to make his loudspeaker work and gave the crowd five minutes to disperse peacefully.

I elbowed my way through to Mr. Nehamkin.

"Please, Mr. Nehamkin, what's going to happen now?"

He transferred his carved walking stick to his other hand, touched my forehead tenderly, and smoothed my hair back from my eyes. His hand was cold and ancient, but his voice was like a caress:

"We, Uriel, we have stamina. We shall go on waiting."

After a while, the British police appeared from the direction of Romema and began to disperse the throng. But they were powerless to undo what had been done: under cover of the press and tumult, almost as though it had all been prearranged, Ephraim and his comrades had plastered the walls, shutters, telegraph poles, and shopwindows with subversive posters. They proclaimed in inflammatory slogans that the days of Nazi-British rule were numbered, that the Hebrew Underground had passed sentence of death on the High Commissioner and would soon execute the sentence, and that as Judea had fallen in blood and fire, so in blood and fire it would arise again.

Then the saints returned to their synagogue, the Bokharans went their various ways, the shops opened, the mountains gradually caught fire, and another cruel summer's day began in Jerusalem.

3

Whenever he came home from his wanderings, Ephraim would visit us in the late afternoon, to give me a clandestine examination in radio waves and frequencies, to play a game of chess with my father, and to gaze from a distance at my mother.

While my father and Ephraim were absorbed in their game of chess, my mother would sit at the piano, with her face toward the window and her back to the room. Ephraim looked at her not longingly, like the heroes in the pictures, but with an expression that resembled dismay. I myself was dismayed at their silence. At that time, distant sounds of firing could be heard almost every evening in Jerusalem. Father chewed mint leaves: he was always afraid of having bad breath. Ephraim smoked so much that sometimes his eyes watered. Mother played the same étude over and over again, as if she had made up her mind never to move on until she had received an answer. Outside the wind touched the trees as if pleading for silence. But there was silence anyway.

On the sill of the deep-set window that faced north, my battlefields were laid out. Corks, pushpins, silver foil, matchboxes, and empty cigarette packs were battleships, troops, and tanks. I conducted cunning mopping-up operations by the army of Bar Kochba and Marshal Budënny against the Nazi storm troopers. By the middle of the summer holidays my Maccabees had conquered Athens, breached the walls of Rome, burned its palaces and razed its towers, and raced on to besiege Berlin and London. By the time the winter rain and snow made the roads impassable, we would force them to surrender unconditionally.

It was Ephraim who had outlined the strategy.

"Always attack on the flank," he instructed me, "always from the desert, from the forest, from the mountains, always from where you are least expected."

His eyes glowed as he spoke, and he could not keep his hands still. He would add in a whisper, "Only don't trust them. Never trust them. They're all thirsting for our blood."

He it was, too, who hit on the idea of the dry-land submarines, which we called "X-ray subs"; they could travel underground through the sea of molten lava and demolish whole cities by torpedoing them from underneath.

"The earth shall tremble," he would say, "cities shall be

burned to ashes, towers shall totter, and only then shall we know rest."

How I loved to see him swell with rage and then subside into silence.

My heart went out to him as he promised me earthquakes, tottering towers, and rest.

I would plead, "But when, Ephraim?"

He would respond with one of his cold, practical smiles. And say nothing.

Worse still, he would suddenly abandon me and tease me mercilessly.

"Now, Uri, you just go on playing with your toys. I've got real work to do. Every detail has to be taken care of well in advance."

All night long, Ephraim would experiment with cosmic radio waves and frequencies, in an attempt to isolate the death ray. If I begged him to give me at least a hint of what the death ray was, he would burst out, with a desperate grin:

"Sting ray. Disarray. Hip-hip-hooray. Why don't you learn to keep your mouth shut and wait for orders like a proper soldier, or else go and play with marbles and tops and paper darts with the other kids. Go on. Scram. Why are you always following me around? What do you think I am, your nurse-maid? Go on, now, piss off."

I withdrew from the workshop with my tail between my legs, like a field marshal stripped of his decorations and insignia and ignominiously discharged. I sat down on the cracked stone steps. I tickled myself behind the knees with pine needles. I tried in vain to hypnotize a stupid cat on the garden fence. And repented.

Ephraim and his father the poet ran their small workshop jointly. Mr. Nehamkin received the radios and electrical implements for repair and kept a record of them, collected overdue payments, exchanged views and surmises about the political situation with the customers, adducing evidence from Holy Writ, and entered details of income and expenditure in his copperplate hand in a large ledger. He was empowered to authorize a discount or even credit in certain cases.

Ephraim sometimes allowed his father and me to wind galvanized copper wire onto wooden spools. Once he took advantage of his father's hardness of hearing to promise me in an undertone:

"When he's dead, I'll take you on instead. You can be the poet and cashier then."

At once he changed his mind.

"No, we'll die first, and he'll pronounce flowery orations over our graves. *They were lovely and pleasant in their lives, and in their death they were not divided. Surely each night they shall arise and continue to fight the great fight for their people.* Something like that. The war is going to be a tough and bloody one. Only the generations to come will enjoy rest."

When he was not away on his wanderings, Ephraim used to sit all morning daydreaming among the broken irons and phonographs and antiquated radios. Sometimes he would explode with rage and attack these useless gadgets with screwdriver and pliers. He dismantled them completely, combined parts from different sources, and succeeded in transforming a heap of worthless junk into a gleaming piece of modern equipment. His favorite word was "rejuvenation." His work, as he described it, was to rejuvenate antediluvian equipment whose owners had given it up as beyond repair. But when his fit of rage had passed, he lapsed once more into drowsiness. The gray summer dust settled everywhere. Flies buzzed busily, while a spider lay in wait for them in its thicket in the corner. Ephraim would yawn like a whining fox, stretch himself furiously, spit twice on the floor, and repair Mrs. Vishniak's iron almost as an afterthought. Then he would plunge back into his usual morning reverie.

At lunchtime, he would fry potatoes for us all and share some sausages with his father. Then he would strip off his overalls and collapse onto the sweaty mattress in his underwear, as if exhausted by a hard morning's work. He slept restlessly till the onset of twilight, while we guarded him from the girls.

But in the evenings, I saw Ephraim come to hidden life, and then I was truly his lieutenant. He shinned up the drainpipe like a shadowy cat, rigged up various antennas on the roof, and began experimenting with frequencies. My task was to sit in the dark workshop among the glowing receivers and write down what I heard. Until I was called home to bed, and he continued on his own to search relentlessly for the single elusive signal that he was trying to isolate from the stream of astral rays.

Once he condescended to favor me with a simplified explanation. Gravity is a form of radiation. Here, look: in my left hand a hammer, in my right a cigarette; they both hit the ground at exactly the same time, but not with the same impact. Nature always contrives to produce opposing pairs: life and death, fire and water, hope and despair. So there must be some contrary ray somewhere that counteracts the ray of gravity and once we've found it everything will be possible and now just you scram and forget everything you've heard.

I could not understand the scientific meaning of all this. But as a military man myself, I fully realized what fate lay in store for the British Empire once we had mastered this secret ray.

Once in a while, one of the girls would slip through our defenses and manage to reach Ephraim and spend the night with him. But even on these nights, Ephraim did not switch off the receivers that brought him the astral signals. Lovemaking must have taken place inside his room to the accompaniment of piercing bleeps and whistles from outer space. Or perhaps not love, but some other kind of union that was not ugly, not sweaty, something I would have given my life to share and once I even crept up behind the shuttered window in the dark and hid like an owl in the sticky pepper tree and strained with all my might to hear and I shivered at the sounds I heard in the darkness because I did not know if they were sobs or muffled laughs or radio signals from the stars, and suddenly I panicked and the pepper tree smeared me with a bitter stickiness and I thought that everything was about to shatter to smithereens and that Ephraim and the girl would die and Mr. Nehamkin and Mommy and Daddy would die and I would be left all alone in the ashes of Jerusalem and the smell of the pepper tree would give me away and bloodthirsty gangs would swoop down on Jerusalem out of the mountains and I would be all alone. So I slipped down from the tree and crept around the house in the dark. I was startled by a startled cat. I stood at the window of the old poet's room, pressed my face against the wire mesh, and shouted in a whisper:

"Mr. Nehamkin! Please! Mr. Nehamkin!"

But he did not hear me. He could not possibly hear me. He was sitting, as usual, building a model of the Temple out of used matchsticks, following the descriptions in Scripture and in other sources. It was a project that had been going on for years, and its completion was receding further and further into the distance, because, as he explained to me, the evidence of the various sources was inconsistent, and he was constantly obliged to dismantle and rebuild it, now according to one plan and now according to another.

With his large, pale fingers, he dipped matchstick after matchstick into a bowl of flour-and-water paste. He had a piece of twine gripped between his teeth, and all the time he hummed to himself:

> Our Father, our King,
> Have mercy upon us and answer us
> Although we deserve it not.

Afterward, lying in bed, scratched and smelling of pepper, I could hear the fervent worshipers in the Faithful Remnant Synagogue, gathered for the Midnight Vigil. The summer would soon be over, and the Days of Awe would be upon us.

And outside, in the warm darkness, something was enraging or terrifying the dogs of the neighborhood and making them hesitate between barking and howling.

4

Ephraim was a sharp-witted but impatient chess player. Father sometimes managed to beat him because he refused to take risks and always conducted a cautious defensive campaign.

"Slow but sure," Ephraim would say condescendingly when Father occasionally succeeded in capturing a defenseless pawn on the outskirts of the field of combat.

Father was not offended. He merely urged:

"Concentrate, Ephraim. Don't give up yet. I shouldn't mind changing places with you, even with your present setup."

Ephraim dismissed this offer with a single contemptuous word: "Today!" He suggested they quit chattering and get on with the real business:

"You're just trying to confuse me with your speechifying, Kolodny. But any moment now, you'll find yourself in a spot, and then you won't feel much like making speeches."

"We'll soon see," Father replied mildly. "Meanwhile I'm besieging your castle, and I've made a good meal of your pawn."

"Make the most of it," Ephraim said angrily. "Nibble the bait to your heart's content; I'm ready with my rod and line."

"We'll see," Father repeated affectionately.

They sat facing each other across the heavy brown living-room table: Ephraim short and dark, his head held forward as if ready to charge, his shirt deliberately unbuttoned to show off his curly-haired chest; Father in a vest and a pair of khaki shorts that were a bit too large for him, his cheeks pink and close-shaven, the corners of his eyes wrinkled in a smile that I secretly called his "schoolmasterly smile."

The chessboard lay on the table between them, surrounded by nuts, biscuits, apples, and pale-blue paper napkins printed with pictures of white-sailed fishing boats. There was also a

china ashtray in the form of a woman's cupped hand. Among
the various delicacies stood a yogurt pot containing some wilt-
ing white roses. From time to time, a yellowing petal landed
gently on the oilcloth that covered the table, and found a rejuvenating echo in the vividly colored roses that were printed all
over it. Father would instantly seize the dead petal, fix it with
a concentrated stare, and fold it skillfully into ever-smaller
squares.

Ephraim would pick up a knight or a bishop, tap it impatiently on the boards as if calling Father to order, and say:

"Why ponder, Kolodny? You've got no choice."

Father:

"Yes. You're right. I'm just trying to decide which is the
lesser of two evils."

Mother, from her perch on the piano stool, said:

"Calm down, you two. It's not worth getting worked up
over a game."

This remark seemed to me to be uncalled for: it was not
Father and Ephraim who were getting worked up.

The living room was simply and cheerfully furnished. The
curtains were bright and airy, the ceiling was painted pale-
blue, and the walls were patterned with tiny flowers, as if the
decorator had fancied himself a gardener, rather than a painter.
Behind the sliding glass doors of the sideboard, the dinner
service was neatly displayed in serried ranks, like troops ready
to be reviewed by a high-ranking officer. There was a chandelier
with four intertwining branches, each surmounted by a bud-
shaped light bulb.

On the other side of the room hung a bookshelf containing a
Bible with a modern commentary, the *Gazetteer of Palestine,*
a history of the Jews and a concise world history, the complete
poems of Bialik, selected poems of Chernikhovsky, and Gur's
Hebrew Dictionary. A volume entitled *Gems of Literature* lay
on its side on top of the other books, because there was no
room for it on the shelf. Above the sideboard hung a picture
of a pioneer pushing a plow through a field in the Jezreel

Valley, oblivious of the black crows hovering over Mount
Gilboa in the top corner of the picture. On top of Mother's
piano stood a plaster bust of Chopin, which I secretly called
Mr. Szczupak because it reminded me a little of the proprietor
of Riviera Fashions on King George Street. The bust bore a
legend in Polish that Mother translated for me as "With all the
warmth of my heart and until my dying breath." Next to my
window sill, the Jewish National Fund collection box hung from
a thick nail. It was adorned with a map of the country, with
the areas we had already won back filled in in brown. I could
not restrain myself: I took my box of paints and drew one arrow
from Jerusalem northward through Gilead and the Golan
toward Mount Lebanon, and another southeastward to the borders of Moab on the shores of the Dead Sea. As a result of this
pincer movement, it became possible to paint the whole map
brown, and so to gain possession of the whole country. At
first Father was angry, and insisted that I carefully wash and
dry the box and remove every trace of this piece of cleverness.
Then he changed his mind, his face broadened into one of
his schoolmasterly smiles, and he said:

"All right. Leave it as it is. You were carried away by a
flight of fancy. So be it."

Mother said:

"Every Friday we put two mils in the box, and yet it never
fills up. Perhaps even money evaporates in this heat. Instead
of talking, Kolodny, maybe you wouldn't mind going out and
buying a quarter-block of ice for the icebox. Or else send your
son. I don't mind which of you goes, only get cracking, before
all the vegetables perish."

If Ephraim won the game of chess, Father would take it in
good part and remark cheerfully:

"After all, it's only a game."

But if Ephraim's concentration was distracted by Mother's
presence or by some ideological brainstorm, so that he made
one crass mistake after another and lost the game, Father's face
would be covered with shame and confusion:

"Look, Ephraim," he would whisper anxiously, "look what a spot you've got yourself into. What shall we do now?"

Ephraim would respond with a short burst of silent fury. He would pick up a nut and crush it between his teeth, glance at Mother's shoulders or beyond, at the hillside, which was visible through the window, and hiss through pursed lips:

"So, Kolodny, so you've won. So what? Now let's play seriously, for once."

As if the game that had just finished had merely been for practice. As if his losing had merely been a small gesture to my ungrateful father, and now the time had come for the real game in which no quarter would be given.

Mother would generally prevent the outbreak of this real game by interrupting her playing, coming over to the table, laying one hand on Father's shoulder and the other on the back of Ephraim's chair, and saying:

"That's enough. Stop it, the pair of you. Now let's all have a nice glass of tea."

At once Father and his guest would exclaim in unison:

"No, really! There's no need. Honestly! Don't take the trouble!"

Mother would ignore their protests and turn to me.

"Will you give me a hand, Uri?"

I would immediately abandon the corks and silver foil, impose a cease-fire on all fronts, and follow Mother to the kitchen. I loved to arrange everything carefully on the black glass-topped trolley and wheel it into the living room: five tall glasses with glass saucers; five dessert plates; five pastry forks with one broad prong and two narrow ones; five long teaspoons; sugar; milk, lemon; reinforcements of nuts and biscuits. Soon the kettle would come to a boil, and Mother would pour the tea. Meanwhile my job was to go down the steps and across the lane and wake the old poet from his midsummer afternoon's dream. Approaching his deck chair in the corner of the untended garden among the parched oleanders and the beds of thistles, I would address him politely:

"Mr. Nehamkin! Please! Mr. Nehamkin! We're having tea, and they'd like to know if you would care to join us."

At first the old man would not move. He would simply open his blue eyes and stare at me in surprise. Then a tired, hopeless smile would spread on his tortoiselike face, and his hand would point gently toward the pepper tree, where unseen birds were shrilling ecstatically.

"What's the matter, child, what's happened? Is there a fire, heaven forbid?"

At once he would add:

"Young Uriel. Yes? Speak up and let's hear what you have to say for yourself."

"They're drinking tea, Mr. Nehamkin, and chatting, and they'd like you to join them."

"What. Oh. One might have thought there was a fire, heaven forbid. But I see there's nothing burning. I shall certainly come. Indeed I shall. Come, let us go together, as one man: the poet and the youth. We shall go forth and come again with rejoicing, and surely we shall not return empty."

As we proceeded across the lane, through the garden and up the steps, the old man would already have embarked on his gentle homily, his velvet voice kissing the rare, carefully chosen words and caressing the ends of his sentences, as if it were all one to him whether his audience consisted of all the people or of me alone, or if there were no one at all to hear him. He spoke about the shamefulness of ignoring the misery of others, the completion of the full term of suffering, the ironies of fate, and the need to withstand the test. He was still speaking when we arrived, and Ephraim and Father rose to greet him and take the walking stick with its carved tiger's head handle and seat him at the table between Mother and the window. While they were seating him at the table, Mother poured the tea, and still he did not interrupt his homily; nor did he see fit to recommence it, but he continued to unburden himself of the ideas that, as he put it, had been gathering in his heart during his lengthy meditations:

". . . There is no shepherd for the flock and no pillar of fire.

Only the pillar of smoke that obscures all eyes. All eyes are darkened. Surely a thousand years are as a day. O, that a heavenly voice might sound, or a consuming fire flash forth. O, that something might happen at long last to put an end to the lamentation of Zion. We can continue no longer. We are almost doomed. No, ladies and gentlemen, no, I shall not drink a second glass of tea. No power in the world will make me drink any more, lest I be in your eyes as a glutton and a drunkard. I am well satisfied with a single glass. On the other hand, how can I refuse you, dear lady? I shall gladly drink a second glass with you, provided it is no trouble. And after that, with your permission, I shall recite one or two humble verses, then take my leave of you and go on my weary way. My thanks and blessings be upon you: very pleasant have you been unto me."

A short silence followed this speech.

Ephraim looked at Mother, and Father looked at Ephraim.

I took advantage of the opportunity to slip away from the table and return to my battlefield, to the cigarette packs and pushpins, some of which represented Panzer divisions and others, bands of Maccabees lying in ambush in the pass of Beth Heron, the few against the many.

Through the window I could see the parade ground inside the Schneller Barracks. Antlike soldiers were sweeping the parade ground, whitewashing the trunks of the pines and eucalyptus trees, marking off areas with rope, piling up roof tiles. In the evening light they seemed pitifully tiny and lost, these soldiers needlessly risking their lives.

The whole city was surrounded by mountains, and as night fell they tightened their grip on us. They could discern no difference between man and man, man and woman, woman and child. Perhaps they had already discovered the death ray and were preparing to surge up and merge with the sunset clouds. Or silently waiting for the stars to come out. A distant melody seemed to charge the sky each evening. Who was singing, and who but me could hear?

Beyond the mountains begins the silence. Beyond the mountains lies the icy northern sea. Beyond the mountains there is nothing. One evening I shall leave them to nibble their nuts and set out on my own across Tel Arza and the valleys through the chariot-clouds and bear-clouds and crocodile-clouds and dragon-clouds, until I arrive beyond the mountains to see what is beyond the mountains. Without haversack or water bottle I shall set out to discover what it is that the mountains want of us all the time. I shall go to the caves. There I shall be a mountain boy all alone all day all summer long in the rocks and the sun and wind and they will never know how the earth quakes and why towers topple.

At the end of the short silence, Father might suddenly decide that the time had come to make a fresh start.

"Well," he would say, "good evening to you, Mr. Neham-kin, and to you, Ephraim. I believe one may hazard a guess that autumn will not be late this year, even though at present it seems as though the summer will never end. They have already started meeting at night in the synagogue to say the Penitential Prayers."

The old man's only reply was:

"Things are getting worse."

And Ephraim, looking like a man dying of thirst with his curls hanging wildly over his thrust-out forehead, would add:

"Everything's going to change here soon. Nothing will be the same."

There ensued a political discussion that filled me with a sense of panic, for I realized how little they all understood. The discussion developed into an argument. Father cited various examples from the distant and more recent past. Then he expressed reservations about them because he considered that history does not repeat itself. Ephraim, in a fit of impatience, called all these examples and reservations rubbish. He cut Father short and insisted vehemently that they consider general principles instead of boring details. Mr. Nehamkin rebuked Ephraim with these words:

"Arrogance is a deadly sin."

"You keep out of this, you and your deadly sins," Ephraim retorted.

"You seem to have forgotten," Mr. Nehamkin said, smiling as though relishing his son's wit, "the causes of the destruction of Jerusalem. Let me remind you, beloved son of mine, of the reasons why Jerusalem was destroyed: internecine strife, envy, and groundless hatred. I should have thought the moral was self-evident."

"That's totally muddled thinking," said Ephraim. And presently he added:

"You're also a bit muddled, Kolodny. Let's drop this subject. The only one who might be on the right track is your son, only he's slightly batty. Excuse me, Mrs. Kolodny. I've said nothing about you, and I won't say anything about you now. We've all said enough, anyway."

At this point, Mother suggested a change of mood. She promised Mr. Nehamkin that we would listen to his new poem. Afterward she could return to her piano, and try to get to the end of the étude she was practicing, and Father and Ephraim could play that return match they were so looking forward to. Twilight had begun, Mother said, and would continue for a while. Should we turn on the light or not. It would still be twilight in an hour's time. Uri could take his new ball and play outside until it got really dark. What was the point of people like us getting worked up over politics; after all, there was nothing we could do about it. So please would they calm down.

5

Outside, in the blue evening light, children were playing "I love my love with an *A*." Boaz and Abner Grill poured some kerosene on the sidewalk outside the house. When the evening light touched the pool of kerosene, a riot of color broke out, breathtaking rainbows of purple, orange, blue, fire, gray, turquoise. How I loved this time of day. Joab made fun of me as usual with his stupid rhyme, "Uri, Uri, sound and fury," but I couldn't have cared less. The evening light was on everything. Bat-Ammi, the Grill boys' sister, sat on the fence nibbling sunflower seeds. "Why don't you answer them back?" she asked, laughing. "Because I don't care," I said. "You do care, and how!" She laughed. And from all the houses from every radio came streaming into the evening light into the enchanted pool of colors the British marching song "It's a long way to Tipperary, it's a long way to go." I didn't know where that place was, and I didn't care. "Look at Kolodny, he's always staring at Bat-Ammi," said Abner.

Let them say what they like, I thought to myself. Who cares. Good-for-nothings. As if we didn't all know who chalked on the wall: URI LOVES BAT-AMMI. As if I didn't know who crossed out LOVES and started to write another word instead, but gave up in a funk. Coward.

Next evening, after tea, Ephraim expressed the opinion that this autumn was going to be a crucial one. Father disagreed; he suggested that the world had finally learned its lesson, and that from now on everything would be different. And we would benefit, he believed, from this change: Russia and America would pull together; the shattered British would not be able to oppose them. The moment of truth was approaching, and it was up to us to display both caution and determination. Ephraim needn't have sacrificed his pawn, he added with surprise: he could easily have moved his rook to cover it. If only we knew two things for certain, (A) what exactly we hoped to achieve and (B) the real limits of our strength, then he believed we could gain the upper hand. For the time being, at any rate. And as for the pawn, he was prepared to allow Ephraim to reconsider: let's put it back where it was, so, and move the rook here. Now we can proceed from a more or less reasonable position. But Ephraim swept the pawn off the board and expressed a total lack of concern at his fate. So what. He could win easily, even without the pawn. He didn't want any favors. Dithering disgusted him.

"Don't do me any favors, Kolodny. You're the defender, and I'm the attacker. So why are you suddenly feeling sorry for me. You ought to be feeling sorry for yourself."

Mother was sitting at the piano. This time she was not playing, but staring out of the window at the darkening mountains, or perhaps at the birds. Her sadness suddenly moved Mr. Nehamkin. He addressed her in a tender tone of voice, as if praying alone in the open air.

"Mrs. Kolodny, please, don't make fun of us. Don't be too hard on us. After all, it's only our misery that makes us exaggerate. Surely you can read us like an open book, and you can see how we are wearing ourselves out with waiting. How you must despise us all. You must be longing desperately to escape from us and our chatter. Once and for all. So you sit at the window and lift up your eyes to the hills. Will you not let the light of your countenance shine upon us?"

Mother said nothing.

"We shall continue to wait," Mr. Nehamkin pleaded, "and our ears will strain to catch the sound of His footsteps when He comes. I beg of you, will you not let the light of your countenance shine upon us?"

"Don't worry, Mr. Nehamkin," said Mother.

And after a while she added:

"It'll be dark soon. Don't worry."

I could not suppress a malicious smile at the words "our ears will strain"; after all, Mr. Nehamkin himself was growing more deaf day by day.

"Yes indeed, you are quite correct," the old man said with a start. "It is really growing dark. I must postpone reciting my modest verses till another day, and hasten on my way. The hour is growing late. Behold my stick, and behold the door. How great is the task that still awaits us."

Deep in the dark behind a loose stone in the wall of the

printing press in the basement was a box. I had hidden it there myself, wrapped it in a silk stocking, covered it with sawdust, and mixed crushed garlic with the dust to baffle the bloodhounds. When Ephraim finally managed to isolate his astral ray, we would hide it away in this box. What was the point of all their endless arguments: Jewish Agency, commissions of inquiry, Bevin and Henry Gurney, great powers. The autumn would come, and Ephraim and I would go up on the roof and burn the whole of England to ashes with one long-distance ray. A crucial autumn. The shattered British. A and B. What do I care about all their talk. I'm for the mountains.

Mr. Nehamkin took his leave. He shook hands with Father, bowed to Mother, and pinched my cheek. Then he went on his way, shuffling in his worn-out shoes westward after the sun where it was setting behind the tiled roofs of the German houses near Romema. And on the handle of his walking stick, the tiger bared its cruel fangs; as though primeval forests had sprung up in Jerusalem overnight.

Father and Ephraim concluded their return game, either jubilantly or shamefacedly, and went downstairs together to switch off the printing press in the basement.

Then Father came back alone. Mother turned on the light. She decided to postpone the ironing until the next day. And we had a simple supper of salad, omelette, yogurt, bread, and olives.

Father would put on Mother's apron and wash up. He would rinse the plates one by one in a bowl of cold water. I would stand next to him and dry them. Mother would put some of them away and lay the others out on the kitchen table, ready for tomorrow's breakfast. It would be calm. We might sit down together to sort through the collection of picture postcards. I would be sent off to wash and get into my pajamas, while they sat outside on the balcony inhaling the smells of the night. From my bedroom window I would be able to see the lights in the workshop and Ephraim's room: all night long he would experiment with radio waves and listen to the wailing of the stars, while the old man would add or remove a row of matchsticks in the wall of his Temple. If the left-hand shutter were to be closed, I would know that Ruhama or Esther the divorcee or some other girl had managed to force an entry. Things that I adamantly refused to think about were happening there, to the accompaniment of the wailing of the stars. I don't want to know. I don't even care. I think fighting men shouldn't indulge in love and suchlike. Love can wait till after the victory. Love can make you suddenly give away secrets, and then there is no going back. I remember that when they wrote URI LOVES BAT-AMMI on the wall I asked her if she thought we might ever get married. Of course, I added, only after the British have been driven out and the Hebrew state has been established.

Bat-Ammi thought that she could only fall in love with a man who knew exactly what he wanted and could never be deflected from his purpose. Someone determined but considerate, she said.

I promised to guard her secret, so that no one would take advantage of her.

That made her laugh.

"Calm down," she said. "Why are you shaking like that? What do you want to have secrets with me for? What's the matter with you?"

I said that nothing was the matter and I didn't need to calm down. Bat-Ammi let me count with my finger the flowers her mother had embroidered around the neck of her Russian blouse. "But don't start getting ideas," I said.

"What's the matter with you? Who's getting ideas about who? Calm down."

I was sorry for Bat-Ammi, and that was why I did not argue with her. Let her say what she liked. I was sorry for her because that summer she'd started growing breasts and, her big brothers said, hairs, too. I was sad because there was no way back, and Bat-Ammi could never stop these growths and be the same as she had been before. Even if she tried with all her might, she could never go back now. She was never consulted about it. She had to turn into a woman, and I was sorry for her. She would never ever be a little girl again. She would never be able to ride a boy's bike.

It's none of my business. I don't want to think about what Bat-Ammi's growing and things like that. I'm Ephraim's lieutenant. I'm going to live beyond the mountains all on my own in the sun in the wind without disgusting thoughts. I'm going to be tough.

Before getting into bed, I watched Bat-Ammi's big brothers roasting potatoes in a bonfire in the garden and burning a rag effigy. I expect they had called it Ernest Bevin, to get their revenge on the anti-Semitic British minister. Presently the moon appeared, sailing quickly between two water cisterns on the roof opposite. The Grill brothers peed into the fire onto their potatoes and they didn't know I was standing at my window watching. They scattered furtively, bubbling over with malicious glee, lying in wait for the girls coming back from their evening classes at the Lemel School. They were going to tempt the girls into eating the potatoes they had peed on. They would nudge one another, and they wouldn't be able to contain their snickers.

Even at night, by the light of the moon, the British soldiers did not stop bustling about their parade ground inside the Schneller Barracks. They seemed to me to be dropping with fatigue as I watched from my window. What a long way to Tipperary. People were saying that next week the High Commissioner might be coming to review the garrison. They were also saying that the commander of the Underground was hiding somewhere in Jerusalem, planning the last details of the Revolt.

Half asleep, I could catch snatches of my parents' conversation from the rear balcony. Father said:

"Tomorrow or the day after, we'll start printing New Year's cards. The beginning of August is only two days off."

Mother said:

"Your Ephraim will end up electrocuting himself or blowing himself up. If he's not working all night, he's away for days on end. I think he's making mines and bombs and things for the boys. He's already turned Uri's mind. I've got a feeling it's all going to end in trouble."

Father said:

"Ephraim's in love with you, or something."

He gave a quick little laugh, as if he had accidentally said a dirty word.

Mother answered seriously:

"What a mistake."

But she did not specify whether it was Father or Ephraim who was making the mistake.

Then they fell silent. Father was probably quietly chewing his mint leaves, while Mother was deep in thought. The moon had left my window and crossed the lane. Perhaps it had stopped over our roof and was feeling the sheets and vests on the clothesline. I put my light out. I hid my head under the pillow and made myself a cellar. It's going to be a crucial autumn. What does crucial autumn mean. Where does Ephraim go on his wanderings. Printing New Year's cards seemed to me boring, pathetic, and shameful. There are those dogs barking again. And then the usual shouts. Comrade Grill, who was a driver in the Hammekasher bus cooperative and always came home after ten o'clock, had presumably awakened his four children as usual, lined them up in the passage, and given them a good hiding for all the day's pranks. In the middle of the beating Boaz suddenly cursed his father with the words "I wish you were dead." A moment later there was a rumbling, grating sound, like barrels being rolled. Helena Grill let out a piercing scream that must have roused the whole neighborhood:

"Murderer! Cossack! Help! He's murdering the child!"

At once there was silence.

It was my duty to get up right away and rescue Bat-Ammi. Too late. The Grill household was in blackest silence. The Cossacks had come and butchered them and their children.

A thick stream of blood was pouring down the stairs and would soon reach the street. I'll stay awake all night, I decided, I'll hear with my own ears once and for all whether there are spies abroad, whether Mother sneaks out before dawn, or Ephraim comes creeping to our house, whether the commander of the Underground rides through the night on his horse. I'll stay awake till I've found out. But as soon as I had made the decision I fell asleep, because yet another blazing blue summer's day had come to an end and I was very tired.

6

The soil in the backyards had turned to khaki in the summer heat; the parched oleanders had gone gray. The geranium stems were taking on a coppery tinge. Dry thistles stood waiting for the fire.

There was junk scattered everywhere, broken crockery, rusty cans, flattened cartons, remains of mattresses, fragments of the foreign packing cases in which the settlers had transported their belongings from Poland and Russia.

One morning I made up my mind to rejuvenate it all. To make a garden.

I made a furious start by attacking the rude words that the Grill boys had scratched on the rusty gate. I scrubbed at them with a damp cloth. In vain. I covered them with mud. In vain. I found a broken bottle and tried to scrape the writing off. I did not notice the cut until my gym shorts and vest and even my hair were covered with blood. So I abandoned the operation. After the victory, when the British had been driven out, a new era would begin. Then we would plant the whole country with beautiful gardens. Meanwhile, I went indoors, bleeding like a hero in the pictures, and Mother had a terrible fright.

Mother used to spend most of the morning lying with her feet up on the sofa. She covered her eyes with a damp dish towel. A jug of iced lemonade and a package of aspirin stood close at hand. Every hour or two, she made up her mind to ignore the climate and get up, put on her blue housecoat, and tackle the mounting piles of ironing. Sometimes the broom froze in her hands and she stood leaning on it as if in despair. She would suddenly close all the windows and shutters to keep the terrible light out of the house, then change her mind abruptly and throw them wide open because she felt suffocated. At times she would rush through the kitchen and bathroom turning all the faucets full on, so as to fill the house with the sound of running water. If I tried to follow her and surreptitiously turn them off, she would scream at me to stop, let her hear the water, stop tormenting her, all of us. Sometimes she went so far as to call us all savages.

But she would soon come to herself, turn off the faucets, laugh at the heat, put on some make-up, and dress in a low-cut blouse and white slacks, and then she put me in mind of one of the beautiful girls that the heroes in the pictures were always falling in love with, Esther Williams, Yvonne de Carlo.

One morning, Ephraim came and fitted her a special bedside lamp that strained the light and cast a dim blue glow like starlight. Mother was afraid of the dark and hated the light.

At lunchtime, when Father came up from the printing press, his nostrils twitched, and he said blankly, "Who's been here this morning? Whose smell is this?"

Mother laughed. Ephraim Nehamkin, she said, had dropped in to play chess with her. What was wrong with that. And he had also put up a marvelous lamp by her bedside.

"Ephraim again," Father said politely, and he smiled his schoolmasterly smile.

A few days earlier, Mother had asked Ephraim to invite her to his workshop to see how the bombs were loaded with dynamite. Ephraim had apologized, muttered an embarrassed denial, reaffirmed his friendship, groped for the right words, and finally managed to promise that everything would turn out all right. Mother had burst out and called him a charlatan.

I didn't know this word. All that I could get out of Father was that the word "charlatan" was a gross insult that did not fit an openhearted lad like Ephraim.

On reconsideration, Mother withdrew what she had said, agreed that the word "charlatan" did not suit Ephraim, but implored Father to stop talking: didn't he know that her head always ached in the summer, why did he always have to contradict her and torment her all day long with his arguments?

In the workshop I found old newspapers, silence, and dust. No bleeps or whistles. No frequencies. Ephraim had disappeared once again on his wanderings. There was only the old poet, dipping his matchsticks in paste; suddenly he seized a nail file and started demolishing layer after layer of his Temple to remove some tower or other for which there was insufficient evidence in the sources.

The three Grill boys went out to the Tel Arza woods to hunt a leopard whose spoor they had come across some days earlier. It had probably come up at night from the ravines of the Judean Desert, and perhaps it was hiding even in the daytime in a cave in the woods. Or perhaps it was not a leopard but a hyena, which we called by its Arabic name, *dhaba'*. If the *dhaba'* finds you alone at night it comes out and blocks your path with its hunched back and bristles like an enormous hedgehog and starts laughing at you hideously to make you go mad with fright until in a panic you start running in the wrong direction toward the mountains and the wilderness and you go on running till you drop dead and then the hyena comes and rips you to shreds.

"Bat-Ammi," I said, "I've got a secret I can't tell you."

"Stop showing off. You haven't got any secret except the same as all the other boys that come and want me to touch them and feel it."

"No, not that. I meant something else."

"If you meant something else, why are you shivering like a rabbit? Calm down, little rabbit. You've got nothing to shiver about."

"I can kill the High Commissioner if I feel like it. I can destroy the whole of England with a single blow."

"Yes, and I can turn myself into a bat. Or into Shirley Temple."

"Do you want me to share my secret with you on condition that you let me give you a kiss just on the forehead just once and I can talk to you for a long time?" I asked without pausing to draw breath.

"I can pee standing up. Like a boy. But I'm not going to show you."

"Bat-Ammi, listen to me, cross my heart it's not because of that, you may think I'm one of those but I'm not, with me it's something different, cross my heart, just let me talk to you for a moment and give me a chance to explain."

"You're no different," said Bat-Ammi sadly, "you're just the same as the others. Just take a look at yourself, you're shaking like a leaf. You're a boy, Kolodny, and you're just the same as all the other boys and you want the same thing as them only you're too scared to say. Look, you've even got pimples on your face. What's the matter, why are you running away? What's wrong? What are you running away for, what have I said? You're nuts!"

Beyond the mountains. To be all alone there. To be a mountain boy.

A few days later, Ephraim came back from his wanderings. He was sun-tanned and withdrawn, and as usual his face wore an expression of contempt or disgust, as if in the course of his wanderings he had seen things that had filled him with despair. Mr. Nehamkin and I took up our positions in the garden so that he would be able to rest for a day or two at least. Every hour

or so, we patrolled the broken-down fence together, toward
the gate, and occasionally we permitted ourselves a sally into
the lane. And we did manage to repel the young divorcee
Esther, who taught crafts in the Lemel Girls' School.

We told her that Ephraim was far away, and she believed
us, apologized, and promised to call again tomorrow.

"You must never use the word 'tomorrow' lightly," Mr.
Nehamkin said to her reproachfully, in his velvet voice. "It is
impossible to know what the day may bring forth. And particularly in days such as these."

I added maliciously:

"He doesn't need visitors. He's got enough to do."

But we did not succeed in stopping Ruhama, the lipless
student from Mount Scopus. At the hottest time of the afternoon, when the shutters were all closed and the streets were
deserted and the whole city was swept by gray fire from the
desert, I came and found her sitting in a blue *sarafan* on the
stone steps, which were covered with dead pine needles. Her
hair was full of dust. She was twisting a piece of galvanized
wire between her fingers. Perhaps she was passing the time by
making some sort of model. She seemed to be immune to the
heat, as if she herself were a heat wave.

"Hello," I said. "I'm his lieutenant. He doesn't need any visitors."

"You're just the neighbors' little boy at your games again.
You ought to be ashamed of yourself," Ruhama said sadly.
"There's no reason for you to wait for him, any of you. He'll
never marry any of you. You'd be better off forgetting him. He
doesn't need all this."

"You're still little," her glasses laughed at me, "and you don't
understand anything. He does need it. And how. Everybody
does. You can sit here for a bit, if you like. You'll grow up
yourself soon, and then you'll need it, too. You'll be dying for
it. And then you won't be such a little hero. What are you
staring at my knees for? Do you want me to give you a box
on the ear?"

When Ruhama raised her voice and threatened to give me a box on the ear, she looked as though she was choking back a sob, and I, too, suddenly started shaking and I could feel the tears coming and I turned and ran as fast as my legs would carry me to the front yard into the blinding sunshine. The Grill boys were struggling sweatily among the thistles with a kitten they were trying to hang from a low bough of the mulberry tree. I started throwing stones at them from a distance. Then they caught me and hit me on the back, in the stomach, in the face, but the kitten managed to escape among the pitch barrels. I, too, hid behind the barrels so that they would not see me crying. From there I saw Mr. Nehamkin showing Ruhama out and shuffling after her to the gate and down the lane, trying to comfort her. I could not hear the words; I could only sense his gentleness and compassion, until she was comforted and went on her way.

When she was gone I emerged.

"What's going to happen, please, Mr. Nehamkin?"

"We shall continue to suffer and to wait, Uriel. I am very sorry for us all. Eyes have we but we see not. To outward appearances we are fearlessly made, but in truth we are consumed by our afflictions. From now on, my boy, we shall redouble our vigilance, you and I: the versifier and the youth shall hold the fort and guard the truth. Do not weep, young Uriel; surely we have shed tears enough already in our long years of exile."

Ephraim woke up toward evening. He thrust his curly head under the faucet and returned, dripping and silent, to his work. He lit a cigarette with wet hands. He did not utter a word. For an hour and a half or so, until Mother came out onto the balcony to call me home, I sat on the floor in my gym shorts and "Young Maccabeans" T-shirt, with my hands clasped around my knees, and watched him dismantle and reassemble a complicated switchboard full of knobs, switches, and buttons. Ephraim was doggedly silent. I did not interrupt him. Once he looked up, chuckled sourly at the sight of me, and said with surprise:

"You still here?"

I smiled at him. I wanted to be big and helpful, but at the same time I wanted to stay little so that he would go on loving me. I was afraid to tell Ephraim how we watched over him while he slept, and how we had driven Esther and Ruhama away from the house. I was ashamed at the thought of how Ruhama and I had made each other miserable to the point of tears, and how we had almost broken down and cried together.

Ephraim said:

"We're making progress, despite everything."

"But when will we be able to start?" I asked.

He stood up and bent over me and cupped my head roughly in his hands; his lips touched my forehead and my cheeks and he could see close up where I had lost one of my front teeth and maybe even the new one that was beginning to grow there.

"Be patient, Uri. The fire will break out at the proper moment, all over the country at once. We're making progress, despite everything."

7

At half past five one Friday afternoon, when the white-hot light was beginning to fade and a different, more passive light was descending on the lane, a curfew was imposed and house-to-house searches began.

The wistfulness of Sabbath Eve, the hesitant rustle of the breeze in the leaves, which the poet was forever trying to decipher in his verses, the uneasy marriage of tin and stone, the closing in of the slowly moving mountains all around, the scents of Sabbath, had all been crudely shattered. Police cars with loudspeakers dispelled the silence of the streets. A metallic voice warned the populace in Hebrew and English that the searches might continue all night. No one was to go outside. Not even onto the balconies. Obey orders. No hoarding. Co-operate. Anyone found out of doors would be risking his own life. We were hereby warned.

As soon as the car had vanished and the metallic voice faded away to other streets, Helena Grill rushed onto her balcony and tried to muster her children. She stood, disheveled and frantic, among the tubs of cactus and asparagus fern, cursing her children and her husband, sobbing in Yiddish, and when she caught sight of me crossing the yard, she called after me, "Idiot!"

Other neighbors went running to the grocer's, which had reopened, to snatch up eggs, milk, canned food, and bread. There were some who feared that the curfew would last for several days. Others repeated various rumors.

Still, this was by no means the first time. In those days, the authorities were in the habit of suddenly cordoning off one district or another and searching the houses for Underground cells or illegal arms.

At the sound of Helena Grill's shouts, Father hurried out of the kitchen, where he had been meticulously dicing onions. He took off Mother's apron, which he had been wearing, carefully folded it, and put it away. He wiped his brow with the back of his hand and went downstairs into the yard. Extracting the Grill boys one by one from the disused garden shed, he dispatched them to their home. Then he shut himself up for a while with his printing press in the basement. Eventually he came back upstairs, smelling of onions and printer's ink. He washed his hands and face and started to chew his mint leaves. His eyes were still streaming from the onions as he assured Mother that we had nothing to worry about. They wouldn't find anything, even if they dismantled the printing press down to its last screw.

e sure," Mother said. Father inquired whether this was a question, a compliment, or a complaint.

"I'm not sure," Mother replied, and Father responded politely:

"Of course."

I knew perfectly well that Father was right: we had nothing to worry about. They would never find the subversive leaflets, which had originated with Ephraim, then been put into prophetic language by Mr. Nehamkin, and finally printed on yellow paper by Father and his two assistants. Nor would they find my box, which was hidden behind the loose stone, because I had wrapped it in a silk stocking stuffed with sawdust sprinkled with crushed garlic to baffle the bloodhounds.

They were bound to fail: after all, we were the righteous few, and they were the tyrants.

It was six o'clock in the evening when the neighborhood was sealed off. The streets were deserted. Armored cars converged on us from three directions and drew up arrogantly, perpendicular to the road, with two wheels on the sidewalk. Machine guns were trained on our windows and rooftops. Gleaming brass ammunition belts hung down from the guns. There was even a light gun mounted on a carriage, stationed halfway down Zephaniah Street, pointing toward the glimmering mountains, as if it were from the mountains that the legions of the Underground would emerge to burst into Jerusalem.

Four truckloads of troops arrived from the Schneller Barracks. From the living-room window I watched the soldiers jump down and fan out at a run along the garden walls, covering one another as they went. Each soldier was armed with a submachine gun and a commando knife in a black sheath, and equipped with a rectangular haversack, a water bottle, and ammunition pouches; they were wearing gaiters. Despite all this, those British troops did not look in the least like the soldiers in the pictures. Most of them looked etiolated; the Judean sun that bronzed us was not kind to them.

The soldier who stationed himself outside our gate reminded me, despite his uniform and kit, of the shy young cashier in the Chancellor Road branch of the Anglo-Palestine Bank. He was smiling timidly, tucking his shirt into the top of his shorts, and suddenly started to pick his nose furiously; apparently it never occurred to him that he might be under observation.

I felt sorry for him. And for the Underground fighters who had to be in hiding. I felt sorry for my mother. For Mr. Neham-kin, who was lying alone in his bed suffering from a bad attack of summer flu. And for Ephraim, who had vanished hurriedly on his wanderings as soon as the curfew was announced, to meet his fate in some Godforsaken place where the hyena might be lurking. I even felt sorry for Helena Grill, although she had called me an idiot for no reason at all. There was nothing but sorrow as far as the eye could see. The refugees who were being turned away daily from the shores of our country and being sent off to desert islands like Zanzibar or Mauritius. Bloodthirsty gangs were prowling in the villages. Maybe Jerusalem and the Promised Land of the Bible were not here after all, but in some other corner of the earth; surely in the course of thousands of years some mistake might have arisen. And it was there that the rose of Sharon and the lily of the valley bloomed, and there that rest and peace were to be found. Maybe the Hebrew state had already been established there, and only we had been forgotten among these mountains. For a moment I longed to pardon all the foes of Israel, to forgive them everything; the Maccabees would never live again, the lions had eaten Bar Kochba, Eleazar the Hasmonean had been crushed by an elephant, and Josef Trumpeldor had been murdered by brigands. Enough. How much longer would Ruhama sit and shrivel in the sun on the workshop steps, and how much longer would we have to drive her away?

I dispelled these thoughts. There was a biblical slogan pinned up on the wall of my classroom that said, THE ADVERSARY AND THE ENEMY SHALL NOT ENTER INTO THE GATES OF THIS CITY. But now the enemy was here in our midst and we were still powerless. It was I who had written

in red paint on the wall of the synagogue the words FREEDOM
OR DEATH: I could not suddenly give up. Let them come. Let
them search. We would withstand the test. And then we would
continue the struggle to our last gasp, because we had No Alternative.

Meanwhile, orders kept pouring out in English. The troops
invaded the gardens. A light evening breeze stirred, lost its
nerve, and retreated. Even the dogs had fallen silent. A reprimand sounded. Perhaps one of the soldiers had made a mistake
or been smitten with remorse. Their captain appeared at the
end of our lane. He was a stocky, harassed-looking man with
sloping shoulders. A short swagger stick danced in his hand.
He seemed to be splitting his men up into small teams, changing his mind, and starting all over again. I started preaching in-
wardly to the captain. Demonstrating what a terrible injustice
had been done to the Jewish people. Proving it from the Bible.
Telling him about the suffering of the Jews. After all, they were
lords of continents and islands, while we had only this tiny patch
of land, and we would never budge from it. In those days there
was a rumor that somewhere in or around Jerusalem was hiding the commander of the Hebrew Underground, the leader of
the Zealots, whom I secretly called the King of Israel. How little we all knew about the commander of the Underground.
Some said one thing, some another.
Once, when Ephraim had just returned from his wanderings,
he had deigned to hint to us that the commander could make
himself invisible at will by means of a secret scientific trick.
Comrade Grill, who was a driver in the Hammekasher bus
cooperative, had once testified on oath to the women that one
night, when his bus had broken down in the open country
south of Jerusalem, between the suburb of Arnona and the
kibbutz of Ramat Rahel, just as the bells of Bethlehem were
striking midnight a solitary horseman mounted on a magnificent steed had ridden up by the light of the full moon and
paused beside him for a moment before galloping off into the
distance toward the Hill of Evil Counsel and Mount Zion

beyond. He had even addressed Comrade Grill by his first name and said, "Zevulun, do not fear that you are alone tonight. The night is full of warriors."

There were those who maintained that the commander of the Underground was a Jewish general who had been the deputy of the Soviet Marshal Zhukov; he had commanded the successful tank offensive against the Nazi lines in the Rostov area in '44 and had later slipped into Palestine illegally, via the Caucasus and the Levant, to build up the secret Hebrew shadow army.

No one could persuade Mr. Nehamkin to abandon his firmly held opinion: for seven years a superman had been hiding in the ravines of the Judean Desert, herding goats and camels among the clefts in the rock, a seer of visions, swathed darkly in a desert robe like the chief of one of the tribes, sending his battle orders up to Jerusalem with barefoot urchins who were indistinguishable from the Bedouin children. Never, said Mr. Nehamkin, would the British be able to lay their hands on this superman, and he it was who, when the day came, would ascend the throne of the kings of Judah in Jerusalem. Mr. Nehamkin had dedicated some of his poems to him, including the cycle "A Waking Trance," the "Songs of War and Vision," an "Ode to Him That Cometh from Seir," and a short elegy entitled "Steel and Yearning."

Father used to listen politely to all this talk, Comrade Grill's story, Mr. Nehamkin's poems, Mother's playing. But he always suggested that it be treated with cautious skepticism. Who knew? It might be so, or then again it might not. However, in the absence of concrete facts we were entitled to indulge in guesses, and he himself would not withhold his own theory from us: there was no one commander. The old days, Father opined, were dead and buried. There was probably some sort of a committee, a small council, four or five clever Jews, not necessarily young ones, either, presumably planted here and there in perfectly innocent positions, as businessmen, school-teachers, or pharmacists, while secretly directing the Underground operations. Anybody could be one of them, Father said.

We had no means of identifying them. Even the fanciful story of our neighbor Comrade Grill, about the horseman, the broken-down bus, and the moonlight, might be not so much an innocent fantasy as a highly cunning piece of bluff. All in all, he thought, the results spoke for themselves: the British were finding Palestine about as comfortable as a bed of nails, as the saying went. Almost every night our windows rattled and tall flames could be seen in the strongholds of the British administration: Bevingrad, Schneller, Allenby Barracks, Russian Compound, King David Hotel, the secret-police headquarters on Mamillah Road. They were getting to be like a cat on hot bricks, as the saying went. He doubted if even the High Commissioner slept soundly at night in his palace. The main thing, he thought, was to maintain the right balance between Hebrew zeal and Jewish common sense; we should never lose sight of practicalities, and avoid premature action.

Mother would say:

"Instead of printing greeting cards, your father ought to be a minister in the government."

The poet Nehamkin would add:

"But the hands are the hands of Jacob. You are not very forbearing toward us, Mrs. Kolodny. Forgive us, it is only the misery speaking through our mouths. After all, we have only the best of intentions; why, then, do you judge us so severely?"

They won't get anything out of *me*, even if they drag me off to the interrogation cells in the Russian Compound. Not even if they burn me with lit cigarettes, just like the Grill boys did to Mrs. Vishniak's parrot. Even if they pull my fingernails out one by one I won't talk. I'll maintain a scornful silence. After all, I am Ephraim's lieutenant. At least, one of his lieutenants. The day before yesterday I spent three whole hours in the workshop, trembling with pride, drawing lines and arrows on a map of Jerusalem to plan the "John of Gischala" operation. Ephraim only gave me very general instructions, as usual:

"Always attack on the flank. Always from the forest. Always from the valleys. From the most unexpected quarter."

He inspected my plans silently, correcting, smiling, making slight changes, adding something here, removing something there, muttering "a brilliant solution," sadly pointing out some careless detail. All at once he was overcome with emotion: he hugged me and stroked my hair and my shoulders and breathed on me, and then suddenly he pushed me away.

Whenever I cried out in the night, Mommy and Daddy both used to get up and make me a glass of hot cocoa and sit on my bed and say, "There, there." Until I calmed down.

Maybe they thought that I should not have been allowed to read *The Hound of the Baskervilles*. Maybe they suspected that the Grill hooligans were having a bad effect on me. I said nothing, because I had sworn I'd never tell.

8

The twilight was dimming. Only on the windows of the house opposite, traces of blood and fire still blazed. The lane was drenched in shadows. We stood at the living-room window, with Mother leaning on Father's arm and me in the middle in front of them; we looked as though we were posing for a birthday picture for the photographer Mr. Kovacs. We looked out. We waited. We said nothing. Outside, the troops of the Sixth Airborne Regiment split up into small teams and started to enter the houses. Somewhere, far away, a single shot was fired. The Schneller clock began to strike seven. I knew that the clock was never to be trusted, because its hands always stood at three minutes past three. The patches of blood died away in the window opposite; it was dark, but the darkness was still gray, not black, and the sky still seemed to be reflecting distant fires. But we could see no fire, only the remains of the Grill boys' bonfire smoldering smokily.

It seemed as though darkness were falling on our stone

houses, on the dying orchard, on the rusty corrugated-iron balconies, falling on the broken fences and thistles, falling on the barking of the dogs and on the whole earth, not just for the night but forever. Mother broke the silence:

"This time they're not looking for pamphlets. They're not even looking for arms and explosives. They're looking for him."

Father said:

"Don't worry. If they do catch someone, someone else will take his place."

Mother said:

"They'll never catch him."

And I:

"Only there are all sorts of informers, and they might give him away."

"No informer can betray him to them, Uri," said Mother, "because he isn't there. I mean he isn't anywhere. He simply doesn't exist. He was invented by the Jewish Agency. By the Arabs. By us. The British invented him with their typical British madness, and now they're running after him with their Tommy guns and ransacking our houses and turning the whole country upside down, but they haven't got an earthly hope of catching him because he's like music, like longing. He's just their nightmare. He's everybody's nightmare. Let them search!" she suddenly exclaimed with almost desperate glee. "Let them search till they go right out of their minds. Don't you answer me back. Either of you. Keep quiet, the two of you. I'm the only one who can talk to them. Don't you interfere or they'll say to you, *'You bastard, you bloody Jew.'* Come in, please, Captain, come in and do your duty. There's a jug of iced lemonade in the icebox. Please help yourselves. And then do your duty. Nice evening isn't it."

They came inside and stood awkwardly in the passage, by the coat hooks where, in the summer months, there hung only Father's cap, a silk scarf, and the shopping basket. The captain apologized, returned Mother's greeting, explained politely that he and his men could not accept a drink when they were on duty, suddenly remembered to doff his cap in the presence of a lady, and asked for permission to glance around the other rooms. They would be as quick as possible, of course. He was so sorry.

We said nothing. Mother was our spokesman. She said, "Of course."

And she smiled.

The soldiers, three thin young men in khaki shorts and army socks up to their knees, stood pressed in the doorway as if ready to vanish at the slightest hint that they were not wanted. Meanwhile, the captain had managed to overcome his initial embarrassment. He was still behaving as though we and they were a group of well-mannered strangers stranded together by regrettable circumstances in a broken elevator. Even when he asked my father to stand with his hands up and his face to the wall, and my mother to be kind enough to sit down in the armchair with the dear little boy on her lap, the pleasant-faced captain still seemed to be merely volunteering helpful, boy-scout-like suggestions that would enable us all to make our escape from the elevator, perhaps by somewhat athletic methods, and thus reduce to a minimum the unpleasantness that had occurred to us all despite the good will and indisputable respectability of all parties involved.

Nevertheless, he did not remove his hand from the black holster. In recent times there had been some unbelievably nasty incidents in Palestine, always at unexpected moments and in apparently respectable places.

The three soldiers inspected the bookshelves one by one, carefully moving the complete poems of Bialik and the *Gems of Literature* aside to see what lurked behind them; they lifted the lid of the piano and sniffed among the strings; they took down the picture of the pioneer pushing the plow through a field in the Jezreel Valley oblivious of the crows, tapped on the wall behind, and listened intently to the sound. The bust of Chopin was lifted up and then reverently replaced. The captain apologized for his curiosity and wished to know who it was and what the inscription meant. Mother translated once more from Polish, "With all the warmth of my heart and until my dying breath."

"I am very sorry," the captain said in a tone of hushed awe, as if he had accidentally disturbed some religious ritual or defiled a holy object.

They proceeded methodically, searching the wardrobes, peering under the beds, hitting the walls gently with the butts of their Tommy guns, and listening for an echo. All the time I was sitting with Mommy on the armchair, and I kept my eyes averted so as not to have to see my father standing with his face to the wall and his hands raised in the air. Secretly I recited to myself the four cardinal rules for standing up to torture in interrogations. It was Ephraim who had taught them to me; perhaps he had invented them himself.

But there was no interrogation.

The captain only voiced a polite request: would Father kindly show them over the printing press that, according to their notes, was in the basement of the building.

When the search was concluded, they took with them various samples; since they could not read them, they were obliged to appropriate one copy of each item for examination. These were labels for matzoh packages, appeal forms for the Diskin Orphanage, receipts and counterfoils, and copies of a newsletter for thrifty housewives. With this the captain was satisfied. He regretted any unpleasantness we might have been caused. He expressed a hope for better times, which were bound to come soon. One of the soldiers called me a "boy scout." Another belched, and started at a stern look from the captain.

Then they left.

The lane was already in darkness. A solitary street lamp, swinging in the breeze, cast nervous circles of light on the asphalt. How unnecessary this yellow light was: the curfew still remained in force after the searches. There was not a soul in our lane. Besides the stray dogs. These dogs lived off our garbage cans. Nobody here wanted a pet dog. But nor would anybody volunteer to drive them away or put them down. Let them be.

Father said:

"They behaved perfectly correctly. You've got to admit it."

Mother said:

"What disgusting sycophants."

"What do you expect," Father rejoined. "That's just their manners. The iron fist in a velvet glove, as they say."

"Not them. You. Both of you. Don't answer me back. That's enough."

Outside, in the empty lane, the stray dogs raised their drooling muzzles to the moon and let out a howl.

Father said:

"Come along, Uri. Tonight you and I will fix supper. Mommy's not feeling very well."

9

The curfew was lifted on Saturday night.

The searches were now concentrated, according to rumor, in the southernmost suburbs: Bayit Vagan, Mekor Hayyim, Arnona, Talpiyot.

Father gave it as his opinion that everything Ephraim had said about a scientific trick that made the commander of the Underground invisible and so on was sheer fantasy. It was more reasonable to suppose that he followed a simple rule of moving from district to district on the heels of the hunt, always slipping into a neighborhood that had just been searched. This solution appeared to Father at least logical, if not necessarily conclusive.

Mother said:

"Which means that now he's here."

"If you choose to think so," Father said with a smile.

"It's Saturday night," Mother said, ignoring his smile. "If you stopped your constant yammering for a moment, we might be able to hear the church bells in the distance. Surely the bells are calling to somebody. The evening is calling to somebody. The birds are clamoring for attention. They've built bell towers on every hilltop in Jerusalem to ring out to the distance. When will they finally call to us? Perhaps they've already called, and we were so busy talking we didn't hear. Why can't we have some silence? Please, Kolodny, leave my arm alone. Leave me alone, too. Why do you keep pestering me?"

"Calm down," Father begged.

And as an afterthought he added:

"We haven't been out for ages. Why don't we go to the movies and sit in a café like civilized human beings. Life must go on, after all."

Early on Sunday morning, Mother went down into the garden carrying a tub of washing. I followed her downstairs without her noticing. The morning sky was grubby and overcast, as if autumn had arrived. But I knew these mornings; I told myself that it wasn't autumn yet, and that actually it was a sure sign of a blazing-hot day. I noticed a quick tremor run through her neck and shoulders. She stood all alone in the low gray light, which imparted a bluish, doubt-ridden hue to the stone, the trees, and the asphalt. It looked as though the light were a stream, and the houses on either side were its banks in a fog, and everything in between was being swept away by the leisurely current. The garbage cans, waiting along the sidewalk, were in the stream. A smell of fish. The smell of the oleanders. And a faint, almost pleasant reek was also in the stream. Not a stream. A ripple of light. A veil. Somewhere nearby there lived a persistent cuckoo that never stopped repeating a single urgent phrase as if it were impossible to remain silent. On the perches of the dovecote stood three lazy pigeons, exchanging views and opinions. They totally disregarded the cuckoo's interruptions.

My mother stood barefoot on the carpet of pine needles

in the shade of the restless trees, pegging the sheets up on the clothesline. There were moments, when she stood with her arms outstretched, when I had difficulty restraining myself from running and suddenly hugging her from behind and telling her secrets about Bat-Ammi and the John of Gischala plan. Far away, a radio was playing light morning music. My mother could sing, but she wasn't singing. The grocer, the greengrocer, and the barber had rolled up their shutters and opened their shops. Only Mrs. Vishniak the pharmacist was late getting up, as usual. The greengrocer was setting out boxes of apples, onions, eggplants, and pumpkins on the sidewalk. The wasps swooped down angrily. In the window of the grocer's shop was a flypaper covered with dead flies, and a jar of different-colored hard candies, two for a mil. There was an olive tree between the two shops. A flowering creeper clasped its branches with a blue flame. From a distance it looked as though the olive tree had gone out of its mind and set itself on fire. Women were draping their bedclothes over their balcony railings to get rid of the night smells. The quilts and pillowcases gave Zephaniah Street a poignant air of gaiety; it was impossible to banish thoughts about night and the neighbors' wives at night among the quilts.

On the deep window sills, among the asparagus ferns growing in old cans, stood sealed jars in which cucumbers were being pickled in a pale-green liquid with bay leaves and parsley and little cloves of garlic. When the Hebrew state was finally established, we would all get up and go to the valleys and the open fields. All summer long, we would live in watchmen's booths in the orchards. We would gallop on our horses to the springs and rivulets, lead our herds and flocks to pasture. We would leave Jerusalem to its fate at the hands of the pious.

I carved strips of pine bark with a penknife borrowed from Ephraim, to add another frigate to the fleet of warships that was riding at anchor on a shelf in my room, waiting for the great day.

Among the dead pine needles in the garden sprouted ears

of wild corn; they, too, were turning yellow, as if trying to assimilate to the dry thistles. There were broken bottles, scraps of newspaper, blackening boards under one of which I once found a tortoise withdrawn in terror and I waited for ages for it to calm down and put its head out until I couldn't wait any longer and picked it up and it turned out that there was no tortoise only an empty shell and the tortoise was long dead or else it had gone off in a huff.

My frigate snapped in two. I was bored with the fleet. I started to carve my name on a rusty can. The penknife made a grating sound on the tin, and Mother, the washtub clasped to her hip, turned to me in exasperation and begged me to stop driving her mad so early in the morning.

"I'm working," I said.

"You're a mad child, that's what you are, and you're trying to drive me mad, too."

"You're just working yourself up, Mrs. Kolodny," I said politely, like Father.

And to myself I added: We must always keep control of our temper. Not be drawn into unnecessary conflicts. We have the initiative and they are gradually losing their balance.

"I'm going to rest," Mother said. "I'm hot. If anybody calls, tell them I'm not at home."

After breakfast, one of the most decisive battles for Berlin was engaged on my window sill. The armored spearheads of the Hebrew, Russian, and American columns were penetrating the city from the forests and the lakes, snapping up the remains of the Nazi divisions, crushing the barricades under their tracks, shattering the buildings with their gunfire. Nine more days and the summer holidays would be over and the fifth form would begin. By then the foe must be vanquished. The monster must be bearded in its lair and made to surrender unconditionally.

Helena Grill appeared on the balcony opposite. She began collecting the bedding that was spread on the railing. Inside her nightdress, through the unbuttoned dressing gown, I could see her strong breasts. I struggled with all my might to ward off Ephraim's rough hands. The Grill boys must have gone down to the Tel Arza woods again, to see if the leopard had got caught in the clever trap they had set for it before the curfew. Comrade Grill was driving his green Fargo bus on the number 8 route toward Mekor Hayyim, picking up passengers at the bus stops and demanding that they step to the rear, please. He had a ticket punch in his bus and a set of little silvery Panpipes: you put the various coins in at the top and slipped the change out at the bottom with a flick of the finger. I was enchanted with the punch and the silver Panpipes. If Bat-Ammi agreed to marry me after the victory, I would let her feel me with her finger through my gym shorts on condition that I could play her father's Panpipes, feed different-sized coins in at the top, and take them out again at the bottom, punch star-shaped holes in the tickets. Helena Grill was still standing on the balcony. She was watering the geranium that grew in a rusty olive can. The water from the watering can looked like slivers of glass caught by the light. She was singing to herself in Polish; the song sounded to me full of longing and remorse.

Meanwhile, Father's two assistants, Abrasha and Lilienblum, arrived, bringing the morning paper. I declared a ceasefire in the suburbs of Berlin and ran to see what the headlines said. The newspaper told of the extensive searches mounted by the British all over the country and of bloodshed in one of the kibbutzim: the pioneers had forcibly resisted the confiscation of their defensive arms; two had been shot and wounded and many others had been interned in detention camps.

Father placed a glass of black coffee before Abrasha and handed Lilienblum a glass of *café au lait*. Meanwhile, he turned the newspaper over and scrutinized the obituary column minutely, sighing as he did so. Then he took off his glasses, suddenly thrust aside his accounts and the remains of his breakfast, caught a tottering yogurt pot just in time, and at once stood up and suggested that they get to work. It was nearly half past eight.

Unless, of course, he said, anyone wanted some more coffee.

I followed them down to the printing press in the basement. I knew that before the curfew Father had hidden the seditious pamphlets in a sealed can and sunk it to the bottom of a tub of printer's ink. I wanted to see with my own eyes how they would bring this submarine to the surface and where they would put it next. But Father reflected and decided not to change the hiding place, because it had not failed him. He switched on the electric motor. At once he switched it off again. He carefully checked the pivots and the rollers. He squeezed a few drops of oil onto the pistons. Then he started the motor again and turned to his composing desk.

"It's all over with Linda," Abrasha declared suddenly with the air of one resuming an interrupted conversation. "And good riddance, too."

"What, again?" Father asked, and I could sense his schoolmasterly smile.

"Finished. She's nabbed the son of Hamidoff from Barclay's Bank, and they're off to Paris next weekend. No wedding."

"There's no point in feeling bad about it," Father said reassuringly. "You were too good for her anyway."

Lilienblum suddenly exploded with a dull groan:

"To hell with them. They're all the same shit. Englishmen, Frenchmen, women. They ought to be kicked out, all of them. And Dr. Weizmann, too."

Abrasha was a taciturn albino, with no eyebrows and delicate white skin and hair, as if he were made of paper. He started the cutting machine. My private name for this machine was the Guillotine. When the High Commissioner was kidnapped, they'd bring him here and in this very basement Ephraim would execute the sentence mercilessly, without batting an eyelid. We must have no pity on the foes of Israel. Let alone plead with them, like Dr. Weizmann. A shy, unconscious smile played around Abrasha's lips as he guillotined the edges of the pamphlets. And I stuffed the wriggly snakes of paper down the front of my vest.

Lilienblum, who was an Orthodox Jew, was arranging the letters in the oblong frame, using steel forceps. His glasses were steel-framed, too. He always addressed me in Yiddish as "little devil." He would wheedle in his stentorian voice:

"A Yiddishe yingele mit a goyish punin. A pogromshchik mit a goldene neshome."

But for once he spoke not to me but to himself, as if unable to contain himself at this morning's sordid news:

"Barclay's Bank. Women," he grunted. *"Pfui.* Shit!"

At this I went out into the yard. The spell of the early light had worn off. There was no freshness left in the trees or around them. The air was beginning to glow white-hot, just as I had predicted. The Grill boys were not back from their leopard hunt yet. When they wanted to tease me, they would always chant their stupid rhymes at me: "Uri, Uri, sound and fury." Or: "Uri wants to play; frighten him away." And they made up dirty stories about Ephraim Nehamkin and my mother. They had written in yellow paint on the broken-down gate: KRAZY FROIKE FUKS URIS MOM.

Underneath this inscription, I suddenly discovered now a postscript that I could not begin to understand but which I started scratching out furiously with my fingernails:

AND URI TO.

At a quarter past nine, the van from the Angel Bakery turned into the lane. For some reason it pulled up outside our gate. I stopped scratching at the writing and watched to see what on earth. It was hot. Angry wasps were mustering under the dripping tap. A stray butterfly fluttered aimlessly among the thistles. There was a dusty smell in the air. Zaki, the baker's boy, leaped down from the driver's cab. He glanced quickly up and down the lane, opened up the rear door of the van, and drew out from among the baskets of bread a kind of surprised, blinking gentleman, a diminutive gentleman in a dark suit, clutching a tool bag. I couldn't understand why they had fetched the doctor. Perhaps ·Mommy had fainted again, or Helena Grill had had a fit of hysterics. But since when did doctors arrive in bakers' vans? As Zaki and the doctor ran past me toward the basement steps, I suddenly identified the man: it wasn't the doctor, it was Mr. Szczupak, the proprietor of Riviera Fashions on King George Street. I remembered how Mommy had taken me there to help her choose a summer dress. Perhaps she had been disappointed at the selection. She had changed her mind, and instead of buying a dress decided to go to another shop and put down a deposit on a phonograph. I recalled that Mr. Szczupak was not upset but invited her to come back to his shop after the holidays. In the autumn he would have a new stock in, he said. The fashions would have changed, too.

From somewhere or other Ephraim appeared, in a blue overall. He caught up with Zaki and Mr. Szczupak, gently took the visitor by the elbow, and escorted him downstairs to the printing press. Not a word passed between them. Zaki turned, slipped outside, scrutinized the rooftops and balconies briefly, sniffed the air, and made up his mind. He made a dash for the driver's cab and reversed the van up the lane and out into the road. A stench of gasoline mingled for a moment with the smell of dust. And then once more there was only dust and angry wasps around the dripping tap.

"Scram. Get out of here. This minute." Father ordered me out in an expressionless voice.

I had hardly ever heard him speak like that before.

I obeyed at once and left the press. But before I left I just had time to notice in a flash that it was not Mr. Szczupak after all, but another man who looked like him, an older man, a kind of faded, worn-out version of Mr. Szczupak. Perhaps his older brother. And I saw Ephraim and the visitor disappearing through a narrow passage between the piled-up rolls of paper. I felt an icy shiver down my spine. Even if they killed

me. Even if they pulled out all my fingernails one by one. Even
if they killed Bat-Ammi. I'd never tell.

10

At midday, the Grill boys came back from the hunt. I was
pleased to see that the leopard had been too cunning for them.
Still, they did not return empty-handed, and at that I was not so
pleased. They had brought back a cardboard box full of brass
cartridge-cases. Never mind. I didn't care. I knew, and they
didn't. In three places—in the back entrance to the staircase,
inside the door of the shed in the yard, and in another secret
place, in the mulberry tree—I had hidden explosive booby traps
the way I'd learned from Ephraim. They were cans full of kerosene with remote-control fuses. In the kerosene I had put live
matches, broken glass, slivers of brass, and electric wires.

Let them come.

They'll pay with their own blood.

Let them come, I say.

I decided for once to overlook the Grill boys' taunts. True,
their father was a cooperative bus driver, they had a sister and
I didn't, they had cartridge cases, they were on the tracks of a
leopard, and they hadn't taken me hunting with them. Never
mind. What I had seen that morning Boaz Grill would never
see, even in his wildest dreams.

Joab said:

"He's been trying to start something with Bat-Ammi. He
begged her to let him see and she laughed at him and wouldn't
let him and she told us all about it, how he cried and ran
away home. Little rabbit. He thought he could do to Bat-Ammi
what Froike Nehamkin does to his mom."

I said nothing.

"He doesn't know what to say. Look at him, turning his face away, as if we can't see that he's blubbering."

I said nothing.

I could have told them that I had seen their mom changing her dress the day before in the mirror through the window during the curfew. But I kept quiet and said nothing.

"Bat-Ammi says he's still a baby. She says he hasn't got a single hair down there yet," Abner shrilled.

Suddenly I turned and rushed up the stairs, taking them two at a time, running up, onto the roof, to my lookout, not hearing their laughter or the things they were saying about my parents. Let them talk. I've got no time for them. I'm on the lookout.

Carefully, thoughtfully, I had selected a concealed position on the roof, among the junk and the water cisterns, behind the clotheslines. From here I could survey the whole city. The Schneller Barracks were spread out at my feet. I even had a telescope, made from a Quaker Oats package and some disks of bluish glass. I could see the English soldiers busily preparing for the High Commissioner's visit. From here, if I only had a machine gun, I could pick off the High Commissioner, the Grill boys, everyone. And then escape to the mountains and be a mountain boy. Forever.

Meanwhile, I took careful stock of the situation in Jerusalem. I could see the roofs of Kerem Avraham, a corner of the Bokharan Quarter, and farther on I could see Mount Scopus and the Mount of Olives shimmering on the bright horizon, towers and church spires, minarets, Shu'afat, Nabi Samwil, a giant, trunkless tree hovering on the blazing air beside the minaret of Nabi Samwil—I would head for that tree when it was all over. I could see the Tel Arza woods, too. Secretly, I was on the side of the leopard who was hiding there. I knew that they would never be able to catch it because it was everybody's nightmare, as Mother put it. I would follow the leopard beyond the mountains to the forests of leopards, and I would live among them like Kipling's Kim.

I could see the German houses at the approach to the suburb of Romema, and the brown tower from which the water ran at night in underground pipes till it reached even us. I could see tiled roofs and pitch-covered roofs, and forest upon forest of washing all over the city, as if the Hebrew state had suddenly sprung up and the whole city were dressed in multicolored bunting. And I could see the midday sunlight growing brighter and brighter as if it would never stop and I would be absorbed in the sunshine and become invisible and pass through walls like a moonbeam and wreak revenge and go to Bat-Ammi at night and say: Don't be afraid Bat-Ammi you can't see me but feel me it's me I've come to take you away from here let's leave this place and go to the forests of leopards and there we shall be.

The city was turning white. White summer dust had settled on the treetops. The light of Jerusalem was a desert light. In the heart of the Judean Desert there was a sea, not a sea at all but springs of water, the home of the Essenes and the dreamers whom the Roman legions had not been able to discover. From there the wind blew bearing a smell of dry dust and a smell of salt. This would be the last time I'd cry. There would be no more tears, even when the English tore out my fingernails one by one, I wouldn't tell about the man disguised as the doctor, as Mr. Szczupak, in Daddy's printing press.

Through the dust and salt came another smell, faintly: I could not tell whether it came from far away, from the Mountains of Moab, from the springs of water, or whether it originated nearby, in the house or even inside me. If you tried to say to those mountains, "With all the warmth of my heart and until my dying breath," they would burst out laughing. They might not even deign to laugh, because they were mountains and we were none of their business and they couldn't care less what happened to us here. Theirs was a different language. If only I knew the language of the mountains I would also be at rest, I couldn't care less what.

I'd learn.

Meanwhile, I wouldn't budge from my lookout post on the roof, to sound the alarm if they came again to search from house to house. The city of Jerusalem was stricken with sea-longing through the blue glass of the telescope I had made. The pine trees were smoke. The stone and corrugated iron were burnished brass, and the forests of washing were flights of birds in the wind.

I stood on guard on the roof till two o'clock in the afternoon. At two my father came out of the basement, followed by Abrasha, Ephraim, and Lilienblum. He locked the iron door. They exchanged a few words and left. They had left Mr. Szczupak in the basement, unless there was a tunnel underneath the electric motor.

Not Mr. Szczupak. His brother. Someone else. A man who had arrived in the baker's van disguised as a doctor, but underneath the disguise there was no Mr. Szczupak but a wiry youth a leopard whose eyes flashed lightning.

We ate at three o'clock: bean soup, rissoles, potatoes, and raw carrots. Then I drank down two glasses of iced lemonade and hurried back to my lookout post, so that I could be the first to give warning of danger.

But there was no danger. Only the deepening evening, gathering force among the pine trees. At six o'clock, a railway engine hooted away in the German Colony. It's a long, long way. I could observe the scorching sun gradually swathed in soot above Sheikh Badr and then drifting away to Givat Shaul and beginning to sink in the violet clouds and touching the hills and the hills turning violet too till it was impossible to tell what was hill and what was cloud and what was troops of horses at the edge of the sky.

Finally the horizon darkened. Jerusalem was left alone, dotted here and there with spots of yellow light. The street lamp in our lane also started to glow weakly. Mother came out onto the balcony to call me indoors.

In the living room, my father and Ephraim were sitting

over the chessboard, one in a white vest and the other in a khaki shirt left unbuttoned on purpose to expose his dark chest.

The elderly poet dozed peacefully in the armchair.

He was deaf and tormented, his head withdrawn into his shoulders. I was suddenly reminded of the empty tortoise shell in the yard. I remembered how Ephraim had said that I would replace Mr. Nehamkin and be the poet and cashier. How he had regretted his words, and how he had reveled in the funeral oration his father would pronounce over the two of us when we had fallen side by side on the battlefield.

"Are we expecting a visitor?" I asked, and immediately was sorry I asked.

Ephraim pursed his lips.

"Did you say something?" he hissed venomously.

"Don't worry," Father put in anxiously. "Uri's all right."

Ephraim said:

"Don't talk so much, Kolodny. Every word is one word too many."

"That'll do now; stop it, the pair of you," Mother entreated. "Don't start quarreling."

Silence fell.

11

I could guess for myself what they had not told me. Underneath the printing press there was a steel trap door in the floor. From this trap door a winding staircase led down into an underground cavern under the house, an ancient catacomb or an Arab rock cave. Presumably Ephraim and his comrades were anxious to turn it into a bunker where we could shelter safely when the day of reckoning came. All along the cold rock walls, by lantern light, were ranged large cans of water and fuel, cans of provisions, ammunition crates, hand grenades, batteries and radio transmitters, maybe even some of Mr. Nehamkin's sacred books. And there, for the moment, Mr. Szczupak was resting till the heat was off; no, not Mr. Szczupak, the amazing lean leopard youth.

Perhaps he would come up tonight. Inside his doctor's bag he had a sniper's rifle, dismantled. The kitchen window commanded a view of the parade ground of the Schneller Barracks. The High Commissioner would come to review the troops, and suddenly a tiny flower would sprout on his forehead, and he would totter and fall. Then Ephraim and his comrades would emerge from their various hiding places and put the John of Gischala plan into operation. At a single stroke. I'll keep my clothes on tonight. I won't sleep. The earth will quake, cities will blaze, towers will topple to the ground. No more counting of the hours and days.

And when victory was ours, the Grill family would be carted off to the traitor's camps, but I would stand in the yard and say softly: All except Bat-Ammi. Let her be. She's all right. The commander would tell them to do as I said and release the girl at once.

"Where are you?" said Father. "Building castles in Spain?"

"The boy's miserable," said Mother.

"Nobody's miserable," I said. "I've come to give you a hand."

In the kitchen everything was carefully laid out on the black glass-topped trolley. Six teaspoons. Six cups. Six dessert plates. They'd brought out the best crockery tonight. Sugar, milk, lemon. Reinforcements of fruit and nuts. Paper napkins, each with a picture of a white-sailed fishing boat. The kettle began to whistle. Ephraim went out and came back with the visitor.

"Good evening," we all said.

He shrugged.

From close up, in the electric light, he was an immaculately dressed gentleman with woolly gray hair and wolflike jaws.

He took off his jacket, blew some specks of dust off it, and draped it over the back of his chair. Then he pinched both trouser seams a little way above the knee, lifted them slightly, and sat down. Only then did he speak.

"All right."

When the visitor took off his jacket, I could see that his trousers were held up by a pair of striped suspenders, but that he was also wearing a tightly fastened belt.

Father said:

"Now, look here, Uri. Listen carefully. This is Mr. Levi. He's our guest. Mr. Levi is going to stay with us for a little while, because where he lives there are certain difficulties. As far as the neighbors are concerned, and the same goes even for Mr. Lilienblum and Comrade Abrasha, Mr. Levi is your uncle; he has just arrived from abroad on an illegal immigrant ship, and we are seeing about his papers. I hope I need say no more."

" 'Course not," I said.

And Mother:

"Mr. Levi, you will stay for dinner, won't you? And in the meantime, how about a cup of tea?"

The visitor kept his doctor's bag on his lap. When Mother spoke, he scrutinized her with his slow, cold eyes; he eyed her bosom, inspected her hips and legs, and then transferred his gaze to Father and Ephraim in turn. His thumb stroked his bristly mustache for an instant, his head nodded up and down a few times as if he were coming to an inevitable conclusion, and he said:

"Everything's perfectly all right."

Father said:

"We do the best we can."

"But what's that child doing here?" the visitor suddenly exclaimed. "Admittedly children are our future, but they tend to be noisy."

So Mother and I went out to the kitchen. Mother started cutting thin slices of white bread, and I set to work making a salad in a wooden bowl. On cat's paws, like a thief, he followed us out. We didn't hear him coming, but suddenly he passed between us across the kitchen and stood at the window. "Perfect," he said as he turned back toward us. A hint of a smile spread on his wolflike jaws. And was suppressed.

"I was just making the tea," Mother said.

"I'm sorry, I've changed my mind. I won't be wanting any tea just yet. You can go now, and take the child with you. I'll stay here."

And he added emphatically:

"Alone."

We left everything in the kitchen and returned to the living room. The poet was expounding in carefully chosen words and a silken voice a new idea that had occurred to him in the course of his meditations.

"Night after night there are lights shining outside the city. Bonfires suspended, as it were, between heaven and earth. I am not speaking from my groaning heart but from what can be seen and observed. He was accounted as nothing and despised, but he is the expectation of the nations. I humbly request a glass of plain tap water, for the heart itself is weakened by yearning. Not fruit juice, not lemonade, but just plain tap water if you please. Provided it is not too much trouble. He will not tarry long, for we are surely wearied and our strength is failing. I shall just drink my water, and then I shall be on my way. Would that every heart were as innocent as a day-old babe's. Farewell to you all. I shall be on my way now; pray, do not despise me. The Capital has a Leader. Behold my stick, and behold the door. Farewell to those who remain from him who goes on his way."

But having spoken these words, the old man did not get to his feet. He simply sighed deeply and remained sitting where he was. At that instant the visitor floated in and sank into the vacant armchair. He still clung to his bag of tools.

"Can I offer you cigarettes, matches, an ashtray?" Father inquired.

"Everything's all right," said Mr. Szczupak's brother.

"Please go ahead if you wish to smoke, Mr. Levi."

"I heard you the first time," the man replied sharply, "and I also asked for silence. How can I concentrate with all this noise?"

We fell silent.

Father sank deep in thought, picked up a black knight from the chessboard, eyed it with a sad smile, and suddenly put it back in its place. He chose instead to advance a pawn. Quick as a flash, Ephraim slid a white bishop almost to the edge of the board and exclaimed furiously:

"There!"

"You're in trouble again," Father whispered.

Mother saw fit to remind them both that Mr. Levi had asked us to keep quiet.

In the ensuing silence, the visitor slipped across the room to the net curtain, with the doctor's bag in his hand and his back to the room, and inspected the yard, or perhaps my battlefield on the window sill. Then he returned to his chair and mouthed silently:

"The child, please."

"Uri," Father said with alarm, "you heard. Say good night. Mommy will bring you your supper. Good night."

"No arguments," said Mother.

Mr. Levi chuckled at her, showing his fine white teeth.

"Children," he exclaimed, "pictures, a piano! Games of chess! And flowers! What a way to live in times like these! A cozy nest, indeed! We must be out of our minds! I wouldn't say no to a small glass of vodka. What, no vodka? What have you got? Only tokay from Rishon Le-Tsiyon, I suppose. I might have guessed. Never mind. Everything's perfectly all right."

"The wind whirleth about continually." Mr. Nehamkin suddenly woke up and started speaking with passion. "And the wind returneth again in a circle. That is one side of the coin. But the other side, Mrs. Kolodny, you know what the other side of the coin is: the thing that hath been shall not be again, and that which shall be—no eye hath seen it. And you have a visitor. Good evening, Mr. Visitor. May you, too, be permitted to behold the deliverance of Jerusalem."

As he spoke, he struck the floor magisterially with his stick, as though he were trying to rouse the carved tiger from its wooden slumber.

"Do I have to put up with this decrepit imbecile as well?" asked Mr. Levi.

Father apologized:

"It's his age. It can't be helped."

And Ephraim added:

"We're doing the best we can, Mr. Levi."

Mother began to clear away the tea things and set the table for supper. Father noticed me and exploded shrilly:

"What are you doing here? Can't you understand what you're told?"

"Right," I said. And in a flash I swept away the pushpins and silver foil, smashed the battle lines, stuffed everything frantically into the toy box, troops, battleships, commanders, headquarters, artillery. Finished. That war was over.

And I fled from the room without saying good night.

I didn't even wash. I lay down on my bed fully dressed in the dark and whispered to myself: Quiet, calm down, relax, nothing's lost, even ordinary soldiers take part in the fighting and the victory, be calm.

But there was no calm and there could be none.

Night in the window. Night inside the room. Summer stars and barking dogs.

In the dark I stowed into my old haversack everything that my groping hand encountered: socks, water bottle, buckles, straps, a scout belt, an old sweater, a package of chewing gum, a pocket knife.

I was prepared.

12

Early in the morning, before five o'clock, I woke in a panic. The windowpanes were shaking. Masses of heavy aircraft were rumbling low over Jerusalem. Half-light flickering outside. Zevulun Grill was trying repeatedly to start up his bus. The engine groaned and struggled with a dull rattle. There were no aircraft. Comrade Grill set off. I left the window and sneaked into the kitchen.

Mommy and Daddy were sitting facing each other silently. They were still wearing yesterday's clothes. Dirty cups on the oilcloth. Dregs of coffee. Remains of biscuits and fruit. An ashtray full of cigarette butts and the air full of smoke. Daddy's eyes were tired and bloodshot:

"Hello, Uri. Do you realize it's only five o'clock?"

"Morning," I said. "Where is everybody?"

"Where's who, Uri?"

"Everybody. Mr. Levi. Ephraim. Mr. Nehamkin. Everybody."

"Go and wash your face, son, and comb your hair. That's no way to look."

"First tell me what happened."

"Nothing's happened. Relax."

"Where is everybody?"

Father hesitated. He hadn't shaved. Bristles on his neck. His brow furrowed:

"There's some bad news, Uri. Mr. Nehamkin got sick during the night. We had to get Mrs. Vishniak out of bed and ring for an ambulance. We took him to the Hadassah Hospital. Now he's resting and getting his strength back. They're going to examine him today."

"And where's Ephraim and Mr. Levi?"

"Ephraim has had to go away again for a few days. He has to travel occasionally. This time it may be a long while before he comes home again. Now go and get washed, and then come back and have a cup of cocoa."

"Where's Mr. Levi?"

Daddy looked at Mommy. Mommy said nothing. She was wearing summery white slacks and a low-cut, flower-patterned blouse. She looked as though she were going on a journey, too.

"Mr. Levi," I said. "The one who was here last night."

At the end of a silence Daddy spoke sadly:

"Mr. Nehamkin will get better, we hope. The doctor at Hadassah was optimistic. He's just had a slight stroke, and now he needs to rest."

"Did you take Mr. Levi to Hadassah, too?"

"Now go and wash, Uri," Daddy said, and he stressed the *sh* of "wash," as though telling me to be quiet.

"What have you both been up to?" I exclaimed with horror.

Mommy said nothing.

Daddy got up, emptied the ashtray, put the dirty cups in the sink, wiped the oilcloth with a damp rag, and dried it with a dish towel.

"If you like," he said, "you can come with us to visit Mr. Nehamkin in the hospital this afternoon. Provided they tell us on the phone that he's well enough to have visitors. Now go and wash. I've told you three times already."

"Not till you tell me where Mr. Levi is."

"Why does he keep tormenting me, this son of yours?"

Mommy said nothing.

Daddy made up his mind. He took me by the shoulders, then relaxed his grip; his lips touched my forehead.

"He's got a slight temperature," he said.

Suddenly he pulled me onto his lap and ran his hand over my hair, and his voice sounded sad but firm:

"Uri. You've been talking strangely ever since you got up. First of all, you wake up screaming in the night because you've had a bad dream, and then you get up before five o'clock and start to nag. All right. It's your age. It's understandable. We're not angry. But you must make an effort. Listen carefully. Last night we had two visitors: Ephraim Nehamkin and his father. The same as usual. In the middle of the night we had to call for an ambulance. I've already explained. Period. Now kindly go and get washed, if you don't mind. That's all."

I said:

"Mommy."

And suddenly, with a sob:

"You're both rotten."

I snatched a box of matches from beside the primus stove and rushed out of the kitchen and the house. I lit the fuses on all three bombs. None of them would light, even though I wasted one match after another. Ephraim had deceived me. I was nobody's lieutenant. The High Commissioner would never come to Schneller, and if he did come, I couldn't care less. Mr. Szczupak was selling dresses at Riviera Fashions. Mr. Nehamkin was going to die, and with him his springs of water. For all I cared, Ruhama could come and stay all night. There had never been a leopard in the Tel Arza woods. There would never be a Hebrew state. Even Abrasha's Linda had run away to Paris with the son of Barclay's Bank. You can watch me crying. Never mind. You'll cry, too, poor Bat-Ammi. You've also been thrown out of the house at half past five in the morning. Now there's just the two of us outside, and all the rest of Jerusalem's indoors. I'll take you somewhere far away the other side of the mountains and you'll teach me what my mother and Froike and the rest of them ... Come on, Bat-Ammi, let's go. We won't be sad.

Bat-Ammi is sitting on a stone. She has blue gym shorts like mine, only fastened with elastic. And she has an orange shirt, and her brothers are nowhere around. There's nobody around. The sun is beginning to come out. Light is shining again off the drainpipes and windows and corrugated-iron walls, and the clouds are blazing. Fiery horsemen can be seen galloping on mountains of fire above the Kedron Valley, transfixing the foes of Israel with lances of fire. The same as usual. Go away, horsemen, go to Tel Aviv even and to the sea. Without me. Bat-Ammi has a notebook open on her lap and she stops writing and doesn't ask me to tell her what and she doesn't tell me to calm down.

What is Bat-Ammi writing in her notebook on a big stone in the yard at half past five in the morning? She is making a note in her autograph book: *When snow is black and pigs can fly, only then will my memory die.*

Shall I write something, too?

I write:

> *Our little bear is feeling ill,*
> *He stayed up late and caught a chill.*

Soon the shops will start opening. The greengrocer will put crates of grapes out on the sidewalk. The wasps will come. Singsong sounds of Talmud study will come from the synagogue. Father and his two assistants will start printing New Year's greeting cards. There's a pile of shirts waiting for Mommy to iron. And there's a minor miracle here this morning: the bread hasn't come yet, but the air is full of the smell of fresh-baked bread. I remember: we've got to go on waiting. What has been has been, and a new day is beginning.

1975

Longing

FROM DR. EMANUEL NUSSBAUM TO DR. HERMINE OSWALD,
LATE OF KIBBUTZ TEL TOMER

Malachi Street, Jerusalem
September 2, 1947

Dear Mina,

There is not much time left. You are probably in Haifa by now, perhaps packing your brassbound black leather trunk; your lips are pursed, you have just reprimanded some waiter or obsequious clerk, you are throbbing all over with efficiency and moral indignation, repeating to yourself over and over again, perhaps even aloud, the word "disgusting."

Or maybe you are not in Haifa. Perhaps you are already on board the ship bound for New York, sitting in your second-class cabin, wearing your reading glasses, digesting some uninspired article in one of your learned journals, untroubled and unexcited by the swell of the waves and the salt smell of the sea air, undistracted by the seagulls, the darkening expanse of the sea, or the strains of the tango wafting down from the ballroom. You are completely absorbed in yourself, no doubt. As always. Up to your ears in work.

I am simply guessing.

I do not know where you are at this moment. How could I know? You never answered either of the letters I wrote you two months ago, and you left no forwarding address. So, you've made up your mind to turn over a new leaf. Your gray eyes are fixed firmly on the future and on the assignments you have undertaken. You will not look back, remember, feel longing, regret. You are striding purposefully forward. Naturally, you are not entirely unacquainted with weakness of mind: after all, that is the subject of your research. But who can rival your firm resolve to turn over a new leaf from time to time? And you didn't leave me any address. I even wasted my time trying at the Kibbutz Tel Tomer office. She's through. Gone away. She's been invited to lecture in America. She may have left already. Sorry.

It is possible that eventually you will be stirred by courtesy or curiosity, and I shall suddenly receive an American postcard with a picture of colorful towers or some grandiose steel bridge. I have still not entirely given up hope, as I said to myself this morning while shaving. However, the sight of my face in the mirror almost stirs feelings of curiosity and sadness in me myself. And disgust, too. My illness has made my cheeks collapse inward, it has made my eyes so prominent that they terrify little children, and it has especially emphasized my nose, like a Nazi caricature. Symptoms. And my hair, that artistic gray mop that you used to enjoy running your fingers through for the static electricity, is all faded and thin. No more sparks. If it went on falling out at that rate for a few more months, I shouldn't have a hair left on my head. As if I had deliberately set out to make fun of the appearance of my dear father, by exaggerating it.

What have I to do with exaggeration? What have I to do with fun? I have always been, and still am, a quiet man. The happy medium, a balanced choice of words—these were always my pride. Albeit a silent pride. There were times, in our nights of love, when I would let go and a savage, pulsating side of me would temporarily take over. Now our love is finished, and I am my usual self again. I have settled back and found nothing. A salty waste. An arid plain. A few stray longings scattered here and there like thornbushes. You know. After all, inside you, too—forgive me—there is a barren desert. A different kind of desert, though. Scorched earth, a phrase I came across this morning in the paper in connection with the termination of the British Mandate.

Well, then.

Dear Mina, as I have already said, there is not much time left. War will break out here soon; almost everybody admits it now.

This morning I had a few neighbors in for a kind of meeting in my study. Even my own Kerem Avraham is already forming a sort of civil-defense committee. That's how far things have gone.

What will come of this war I haven't the faintest idea. Only all sorts of hopes and fears. You will be in a safe place, far from Jerusalem, far from Galilee and the valleys you have explored so thoroughly during these last years. It goes without saying that I shall not be able to play an active part in the war, either as a doctor on the battlefield or in a hospital behind the lines. The illness is progressing toward its final phases. Not in a continuous straight line, though. It is toying with me, with cunning ploys, temporary concessions, feigned moderation, a brilliant strategy of deception and false hopes. I almost smile to myself: doesn't it realize it's dealing with a doctor, and not, say, an artist? It can't take me in. These arabesques, the alternating alarms and all-clears, the false hopes, the avoidance of a frontal assault, how unnecessary they all are when the designated target is a man like me, an experienced diagnostician, an educated man, with a modest medical library at my disposal and with German as my mother tongue.

In short, I am my usual self: in a state of calm despair. The terminal stage will begin in the winter and be over before the spring, or it may begin in the spring and continue at most until the first heat waves of 1948. I won't go into details. I trust, dear Mina, that there is no need to prove to you in writing that in the meantime I am quietly and confidently continuing with the routine of my daily life.

No news.

There's nothing much new that I can offer you in general. I don't have much time to spare, either.

I spend most of the hours of day and night on the lookout to see what is happening in Jerusalem. Now and again I still try to make my modest patriotic contribution, such as this morning, in the meeting of the local defense committee. And I still keep up certain friendly neighborly contacts. And I am continuing my chemical experiments in my private laboratory, which may eventually render some service to the community in connection with the war effort.

Meanwhile, my observations have yielded a definite conviction that here in Jerusalem the summer is gradually, almost from day to day, relaxing its hold. There are already a few unobtrusive indications of the approach of autumn. The leaves have not begun to fall yet, of course, but there are hints of a slight change of tint, in the foliage, or in the refracted light at dawn or dusk. Or in both together: no contradiction is involved.

There is a shadow of clouds over our backyards. People speak softly and seriously. The twilight is beginning earlier, and its glow is more subdued than usual, more fantastic, a poet might add more desperate, a kind of bitter enthusiasm like a last act of love, which is full of wild abandon because it is the last and there is no more to come. At the end of the twilight, you can see a column of gray light over the western mountains and splashes of fire on the windowpanes, the towers, and the domes, and some water tank or other on a rooftop may go crazy and flare up. After this fire, the mountains are swathed in smoke. And a miracle: suddenly there is even a smell of smoke in Jerusalem.

So the lazy summer sunsets are over and gone. There is a new seriousness in the air. It is even cool outside in the early evening. Occasionally I have the feeling that there are fewer birds around. I must check this latest detail carefully, though, because common sense would indicate that autumn brings back the migrating birds.

So here I am, Mina, writing this letter to you slowly, on these small, smooth sheets of paper with my name printed at the top in Hebrew and German, which I used to use for writing prescriptions. You used to call these letters of mine "schoolboy notes." The difference is that this time, apparently, I shall not be brief. Or witty, either.

I am sitting at a table on the balcony, wearing a gray pullover but still with the peasant sandals you bought me in the

Old City more than a year ago. Between the fingers that are writing to you and the toes in these sandals there seems to be a great distance now, not because I have suddenly grown taller, but because of the diseased organs in between. Dear Mina, the evening is still light enough for me to write, but I can sense the light beginning to fade. The whole city will be swathed, enfolded, district after district will attach itself to the cavalcade of night. The towers on top of the hills to the east will lead the procession, and the entire city will fall in behind, and march down into the enclosing desert. The nightly routine of Jerusalem. You have heard me say this before, and you called it all "poetic fantasy." There is nothing new. A particular pain has just started up and is almost tormenting me, as if a man like me is unlikely to take a mere hint. Very well. I shall swallow my pride and stifle the pain with an injection. Presently.

I should like to come back to the balcony and go on writing even when it is dark. The cool air is gentle and almost stimulating. I shall switch the lights on inside and try to bring the desk lamp out from the study. Will the extension cord reach? We shall see. I doubt it.

From the balcony opposite, across the neglected yard, my neighbor Mrs. Grill is questioning me:

"How are you feeling today, Dr. Emanuel, what does the radio say this evening, and when will your car be arriving?" My radio is the only one in the immediate neighborhood. Sometimes I serve as the link between the neighbors and what they call the outside world. The neighbors' boy Uri has taken to dropping in because I have permitted him to come and listen to the news, and so it was that he discovered my laboratory. As for the car, everyone here is saying that I shall soon have one of my own. The source of this rumor is apparently the boys, Uri's enemies. They know that I have stopped working as a doctor, they have somehow heard that I am doing some work for the Jewish Agency, and they have already invested me with a private car. I deny it gently. I apologize, as though I have been accused of doing something improper. Meanwhile, Mrs. Grill chuckles at me:

"Don't worry, Dr. Emanuel, we're used to keeping secrets. My husband's a veteran of the Trade Union, and as for me, I lost all my family in Lodz. You can count on us. We're not the sort to gossip."

"Perish the thought," I mutter. "It never entered my head to suggest that you . . . But the fact of the matter is that . . ." But she's already vanished: rushed back to her kitchen to save a pan of milk from boiling over or disappeared behind the linens she hangs out to dry on her balcony, among the crates and washtubs and suitcases. I am alone once more.

Let me tell you, in passing, about the Jewish Agency. I have a little cubbyhole tucked away behind my study, a storage room, a home laboratory, a darkroom. You complained once about the chemical smells that came from there and spread all over the apartment. I expect you remember. Well, I haven't given up my modest experiments. Some time ago I drew up a kind of memorandum about the possible military uses of a certain chemical of which we have relatively plentiful supplies. As a result, three weeks ago an engineer from the Jewish Agency or the Hagganah arrived in a great flurry to ask whether I would be willing to draw up an inventory of explosives that are legally stored in the Solel Boneh quarries in the mountains, and also of other explosives that are dispersed in various places in Jerusalem. And also to make a card index of useful chemicals held in Jewish factories in the city. And also to suggest all sorts of combinations and to work out what we have and what we would be short of in case of a prolonged war. We'd be short of everything, I replied; we wouldn't even have enough bread or water. My visitor smiled: he had decided I was possessed of a morbid sense of humor. "Dr. Nussbaum," he said, still smiling as he turned to leave, "everything will be all right. Just you compile the inventory. And leave the rest to us. We'll be prepared to try out any reasonable idea that occurs to you. Dushkin himself considers you one of the most brilliant minds in the field. We'll be in touch. Good-bye."

In short, I accepted. Anyway, the man didn't wait for an answer. As if he had given me an order. Ever since I had drawn up that memo, or perhaps since Dushkin had spoken to me in his usual effusive way at some meeting, someone must have been crediting me with magical powers, or expecting me to be a sort of alchemist for them. In brief, they would be very pleased but not at all surprised if I turned up tomorrow morning, tonight, clutching the formula for a powerful explosive that could be manufactured quickly, cheaply, in any kitchen, and of which a minute quantity would have a devastating effect. There is a slogan current here at the moment that is repeated every evening by the Underground on their short-wave broadcasts: "When your back's to the wall, even the incredible is possible." Admittedly, you or I could easily refute this slogan on a philosophical plane. But nevertheless, for the time being I accept it, both out of a sense of loyalty and because, with a little effort, I can discern a certain poetry in it. A crude poetry, it is true, but then, if I may so express myself, the state of affairs at the moment is crude.

A minor miracle has just occurred. I have managed despite everything to bring the desk lamp from my study out onto the balcony. The extension cord was almost long enough. A slight compromise: I moved the table a little nearer to the door. But I'm still outside, surrounded by a halo of electric light, with incredible shadows flickering on the stone wall behind me, and now what do I care if it's dark.

By the way, I have already numbered my little pages: I shall have to concentrate. On what? On the main point. Dear Mina, let me try to define just what the main point is at the moment. I shall put my empty cup down on the pages, because the wind is liable to blow up without warning, as usual here in the evening in the early autumn.

Well, then.

It has occurred to me to set down in writing various details about myself, about my immediate surroundings, certain observations about Jerusalem, and, in particular, my district, Kerem Avraham: things seen and heard. No doubt here and there cautious comparisons will emerge, and certain memories may find their way in. Don't worry, Mina: I don't intend to embellish or sully our shared memories in writing this. No chains around your new life. America, I have read, is a good and wonderful country where all eyes are constantly on the future, where even longing is directed to the future, and everybody agrees that the past is condemned to silence.

Have you arrived yet, Mina, have you discovered a quiet café among the towers and bridges where you can sit down, put on your glasses, and spread out your notes? Are you getting used to speaking Red Indian? Or are you still on the boat, on your way, just passing, say, the Azores? Does the name Sierra Madre mean something to you yet? Dear Mina, are you all right?

Perhaps it isn't too late yet.

Perhaps you are still in Haifa, packing, getting ready, and I could still catch the evening train, arrive before midnight, find you in some small boardinghouse on the Carmel, and sit with you in silence looking out over the dark water, the shadow of the Galilean hills, with British warships ablaze with lights in the bay, and one of them suddenly bursting into a plaintive moan.

I don't know.

My health isn't up to the journey, either.

And if I do come, and if I manage to find you, you're sure to say:

"Emanuel. Why have you come? And what a mess you look."

If I say that I've come to say good-bye, my voice will betray me. Or my lips will tremble. And you will remark with cold sorrow:

"That's not true."

I shall be forced into silence. There will be embarrassment, awkwardness, probably physical pains as well. I shall be a burden on you.

No journey. After all, I have no idea where you are.

I don't even know why I am writing you this long letter, what the subject is, what, as they say, is on the agenda, what I am writing to you about. I'm sorry.

It is evening now. I've already said that twice, but still the evening continues. Below me, on the sidewalk, some girls are playing hopscotch, and Uri, out of their sight, is following their skipping from his hiding place among the shrubs with a slow movement of the muzzle of his ray gun. Now he has stopped and is sunk in thought or in dreams. From where I am sitting, I can see his head and the silhouette of the gun. This child is always on guard and always seems to be asleep at his post. Soon the children will be going indoors. The cries will die away, but there will be no quiet. I have pains; one of them is particularly cruel, but I shall persist in ignoring it and concentrate on recording the place and the time. Dear Mina, please don't read these words with your patient, ironic smile; try for once to smile innocently or not at all. I hate your irony. Always effortlessly piercing the barrier of words, deciphering what lies behind them, always forgiving. How desolate. Are the birds really changing guard in the fig tree and the mulberry as the blaze of oleanders dies down in the garden? Evening has come. Barking of dogs far away, echo of bells, shooting, a raven's croak. Such simple, instant, trivial things—why do they all sound to me as though never again.

Now the moment is approaching when the light in Jerusalem is distorted. It is the light of the stone that is beginning to make itself felt, as if it were not the last traces of the sun setting behind the clouds but, rather, the walls, the ramparts, the distant towers projecting the inner light of their souls. At this point you may exhale your cigarette smoke through your nostrils, as usual, and say to yourself, "What, again."

You may, I said. Meaning, I can't prevent it.

I could never prevent anything. Whatever happened, happened because you wanted it.

You said to me once: Here we are, Emanuel and Mina, two educated people, two people with similar backgrounds, and yet there is no reason for them to establish a permanent relationship.

I agree. On the one hand, Dr. Nussbaum, a gentle man, a man beset by doubts: even when he wants something he always suspects his motives, and frequently his smile is confused, like that of a man who has finally dared to tell a story and immediately starts wondering: Is it funny, has it been understood, is it out of place. On the other, Dr. Oswald, a bitter, determined woman; ever her rare compromises are almost a matter of life and death. She stubs out her cigarettes as though she were trying to bore a hole in the bottom of the ashtray.

Surely we both knew in advance it would be a mistake.

Yet even so, you saw fit to be linked to me for a while. As for me—is it proper for a man like me, a man in my condition, to say so?—I loved you. I still do.

                                                              Jerusalem
                                                    September 3, 1947

Dear Mina,

In my dreams at night you come back to me in a gray-brown dress, with knowing fingers. Quiet. Even your voice in the dreams is different, calmer, warmer.

At midnight I had a snack: a roll with olives, tomato, cucumber. I gave myself my nightly injection and took two different pain-killing tablets. In bed I read a few pages of the journal of an acute English pilgrim who visited the Holy Land eighty years ago and saw Jerusalem in a dismal light. It was O'Leary who lent me the book. Then I turned off the light and heard the distant humming of engines, probably a British military convoy making its way to Ramallah and the mountains of Samaria. Drowsily, unconcernedly, I could see in my mind's eye the desolate valleys, the miserable stone-built villages, some sacred tree wrapped in darkness among the boulders, with perhaps a fox sniffing in its shadows, and farther on the caves, embers of bonfires, ancient olive trees, the sadness of the deserted goat tracks in the night, the rustling thistles in the scented, late-summer breeze, and the column of British jeeps with dimmed headlights winding up the mountain road. A very ancient land. Then there was a whispering on the steps of the house. My father and his lawyer in the passage, arguing, chuckling, I can hardly catch the words, but the subject is apparently some fraud, some investigation that threatens me, legal arguments that can still perhaps save me from some great disgrace. I lock the study door and rush to the kitchen. I must push my father almost roughly out of there, while the lawyer bows to me sadly and tactfully. In vain I search feverishly for the source of the damp smoke. I cough and almost choke. I must hurry. Any moment now, the British police may arrive, and Uri's parents would blame me for everything. And then your brown dress on the kitchen balcony, and suddenly you. I don't try to resist. I drape my jacket carefully over the back of the chair, roll up my vest, even guide you to the line of my diaphragm and almost enjoy the sight of your knowing fingers. Unerringly, painlessly, you rip open the skin, penetrate the rib cage, seek and find the affected gland, and extract the revolting fluid from it with forceps and a fine scalpel. There is no bleeding. No pain. The nerve endings are like white worms. The muscle tissue tears with the sound of ripping cloth. And I sit and watch your fingers operating inside my body as in an illustrated textbook. Look, Emanuel, you smile, it's all over. Thank you, I whisper. And I add: I'd like to get dressed. And then the gland itself, bloated and bluish-green, looking like a gigantic tick, swollen with pus, walking insectlike on thin, hairy legs slowly down my thigh, my calf, onto the floor; I throw the tin mug at it and miss, you crush it under the toe of your shoe, and a greasy jet squirts out. Now get dressed and we'll have a drink, you say, coffee, you say, but the shrewd light glints in your eye as you change your mind: You mustn't drink coffee, Emanuel, you must make do with fresh fruit until you are a little stronger. Your hands in my hair. I feel good. I say nothing. My child, you say, how cold you are. And how pale. Now close your eyes. Stop thinking. Sleep quietly. I obey. Inside my closed eyes the kitchen fades, and there is only the jam jar on the kitchen table, swarming with wormlike glands, hairy, damp, with insect antennae, and in the bread, too, in the fruit bowl, there is even one crawling up my pajama sleeve. Never mind. I am at rest. With my eyes closed I can hear your voice, a Russian song. Where did you get this Russian, from the kibbutz in the Jezreel Valley, from the fields, take me there when my strength returns, and there I shall follow you. Dear Mina. At three o'clock, the bell of the clock tower in the Schneller Barracks pierces my sleep. I switch on the light; with a shaking hand I clutch the cup of cold tea, remove the glass saucer that covers it, have a sip, take another pill, and return to the English pilgrim and argue with him in my mind about the line of the watershed, which he unhesitatingly locates along the ridge of Mount Scopus and the Mount of Olives. With the dawn, I fall asleep again in the twilight, without turning off the light, and I hear you say that now you can reveal that you have borne me a child and lodged it in one of the kibbutzim in the valley to spare me the trouble of looking after it in my present condition. Your lips in my hair. You have not gone, Mina. No, I haven't gone. I am here. Every night I shall come to you, Emanuel, but during the day I must hide because of the searches and the curfew, until we have outwitted the enemy and the Hebrew state has gained its freedom. I fall asleep with my head in your lap and wake up to the sound of repeated bursts of sharp firing. Tonight the Irgun or the Stern Group has raided the British barracks again. Perhaps the first tentative engagements of the new war have begun. I get up.

Pale light in the window. A cock is crowing furiously in the next-door yard. And the strange boy is already up and about, poking in the junk and dragging discarded packing cases hither and thither. Six o'clock in the morning. A new day, and I must put the kettle on for my shaving water and my early-morning coffee. For another half hour I can still keep the night-child alive, our son, the baby you bore me and hid from me. At half past six the newspaper arrived, and at a quarter past seven I heard on the news that the London *Times* has warned the Zionists against a reckless gamble that may prove fatal, and advised them to make a realistic revision of their aspirations and to understand once and for all that the idea of a Jewish state will lead to a blood bath. Another solution must be devised that may be acceptable to the Arabs, too, at least to their more moderate elements. However, the paper will in no way sanction handing over the achievements of the Zionist settlers to Moslem religious fanatics; the achievements themselves are admirable, but the inflated political aspirations of the leaders of the Jewish Agency verge on adventurism. After the news, while I made my bed and dusted the highboy and the bookshelves, David Zakkai gave a talk about the night sky in September. Then there was a program of morning music, while outside in the street the kerosene vendors and icemen rang the bells of their pushcarts. Over and over again I weighed the words in my heart: Recklessness. Gamble. Adventurism.

At eight o'clock, I decided to go to the Hadassah Hospital on Mount Scopus, to invade Professor Dushkin's office for a quarter of an hour and ask him again how my illness was developing and what he made of last week's tests. The piercing desert light had already engulfed Jerusalem. A dry wind was blowing among the hills. And in the dusty bus the students were joking, mimicking the German accents of their lecturers with a Polish twist of humor. Along the way, in the suburb of Sheikh Jarrah, there were wickerwork stools spilling over onto the sidewalk from a coffeehouse, and on one of them I saw a young, educated Arab in a pin-striped suit and horn-rimmed spectacles sitting in motionless contemplation, the tiny coffee cup seemingly frozen in his hand. He did not take the trouble to direct so much as a glance at the Jewish bus. In my mind I could not refrain from comparing his silence with the clamor of the students in the bus and the histrionic laughter of the girls. And I was filled with apprehension.

Professor Dushkin roared my name delightedly and immediately shooed out of his office a clucking, shriveled nurse who had been filling out index cards. He slammed the door after her, thumped me on the shoulder, and proclaimed in a Russian bellow:

"Out with it! Let's talk frankly, as usual."

I asked him four or five short questions concerning the results of last week's tests and received the expected replies.

"But look here, my dear Emanuel," he exclaimed rumbustiously, "you remember what happened in the summer of '44, with Rabbi Zweik, the mystic from Safed. Yes. We came to exactly the same conclusions with him, and yet his tumor dissolved and his condition was, how shall we say, arrested. And he's still alive and kicking. It's a fact."

I smiled. "So what are you suggesting, that I should settle down to study mysticism?"

Professor Dushkin poured out tea. He pressed me to accept a biscuit. Idiocy, he declared, was rampant on all sides. Even among his own faculty. Even in politics. The leaders of the Jewish Agency, he considered, were political infants, loud-mouthed amateurs, small-town autodidacts, illiterates, ignoramuses, and these were the people who had to pit their wits now against the sophisticated experts of Whitehall. It was enough to drive you crazy. Another glass of tea? What's the matter with you, of course you will. I've poured it out already, what do you want, have you only come here to irritate me? Drink! In a word, Shertok and Berl Locker. What more need I say: political Svidrigaïlovs everywhere. In December we'll have you in for some more tests, and if there's been no change for the worse by then, we'll be entitled to take it as an encouraging sign. No, more than a sign, a turning point! That's right. Meanwhile, how shall I put it, keep your spirits up, my friend. One cannot help admiring your composure.

As he spoke, I suddenly noticed a film of tears in his eyes. He was a heavily built, muscular, compact-looking man. He invariably wept at the first onset of emotion; he was always flushing and boiling over. I had secretly nicknamed him "Samovar."

I rose to take my leave.

So, no new tests just yet. And no treatment. Just as I had expected.

"Thanks, Dushkin," I said. "Thank you very much."

"Thanks?" he cried out as if I had wounded him. "What's the matter? What's got into you? Are you crazy? What have you got to thank me for all of a sudden?"

"You've been frank with me. And you've hardly uttered a single superfluous word."

"You're exaggerating, Emanuel," he said with sadness and emotion in his voice. "For once you're exaggerating. But of course," he added in his former tones, "of course when idiocy is on the rampage, any meeting like ours today is almost an occasion. Svidrigaïlovs, I say: political Svidrigaïlovs, and medical Svidrigaïlovs as well. Even here in our department there are all sorts of Shertoks and Berl Lockers living it up. Well. The bus into town leaves in ten minutes. Number nine as usual. No—don't run! There's no hurry, it'll be late. I swear it'll be late. After all, it's Hammekasher, not the Royal Navy. If you notice any change, come and see me at once. At two o'clock in the morning, even. You can be sure of a hot glass of tea. How I love you, Emanuel, how my heart weeps for you. Na! Enough. Since we were talking about that grubby saint Rabbi Zweik, who broke all the rules in our book and literally rose from the dead, let me repeat a little saying of his. He used to tell us that the Almighty sometimes plays a trick on His worshipers and shows them that if He wills He can save a life even by means of doctors and medicine. Now, fare you well, my friend. Be brave."

His eyes glistened again. He opened the door for me furiously and suddenly roared out in a terrible voice:

"Svidrigaïlov! Shmendrik! Come here at once! Run and clear the X-ray room for me immediately! Use force if necessary! Throw a bomb in, I don't care! But on the way show Dr. Nussbaum here to the elevator. No, to the bus stop. You're turning this Jerusalem of ours into a veritable Bedlam! As you see, gentlemen, at times I can be a terrible man. A cannibal. A tartar. That's what I am. Na! Be seeing you, Emanuel. And don't worry about me. You know me. I'll get over it. And also . . . Forget it. Good-bye, good-bye, good-bye."

Despite all this, I missed the bus. But I bore no grudge against Samovar. I waited on the bench at the bus stop for close to an

hour. The city and the mountains seemed amazingly quiet. Minarets and domes in the Old City, buildings overflowing down
the slopes of gray hills in the new town, here and there tiled
roofs, empty plots, olive trees, and apparently not a soul in
Jerusalem. Only the dry wind in the woods behind me, and birds
chattering calmly from the British military cemetery.

But on the other side lay the desert. It was literally at my
feet.

A neglected, rock-strewn terrain dotted with pieces of newspaper, thistles, and rusting iron, a wasteland of limestone or
chalk. In other words, from the scenic point of view Mount
Scopus is the threshold of the desert. I have a horror of this
propinquity between myself and the desert. Over there are
forsaken valleys, rocks baking in the sun, shrubs sculpted by the
wind, and there are scorpions in the crevices of the rocks,
strange stone huts, minarets on bald hilltops, the last villages.
On the opposite slopes and in the Jordan valley are traces of
ruined biblical towns, Sumieh, which my English pilgrim
identifies with Beth-jesimoth, Abel-shittim, Beth-haran, Nimrin,
which may be the ancient Beth-nimrah. And scattered among
these ruins are camps of Bedouin tribes, goatskin tents, and
dark shepherds armed with daggers. Justice through bloodshed. The simple law of the desert: love, honor, and death.
And there is a venomous biblical snake called the asp. How I
shudder, Mina, at this closeness to the desert.

Yes. Forgive me. You have already heard the gist of all this
from me, in Haifa, at the Lev Ha-Carmel Café, over strawberry
ice-cream sundaes. You remember. And you dismissed it all as
"Viennese *angst.*" I won't deny it: it is indeed *angst.* And
perhaps even Viennese *angst.*

Did I ever tell you this as well?

From my window as a child, I could see the canal. There
were barges. Sometimes at night a noisy holiday cruiser went
past, a riot of multicolored lights. The water was spanned by
two bridges, one arched and the other modern. Perhaps in your
student days you chanced to pass by these places. Perhaps we
passed each other in the street unawares. Night after night

I could see the consumptive sidewalk artist smoking and choking, smoking as though he reveled in the agony of coughing, vomiting in the gutter, and smoking again. I have not forgotten. The row of street lamps along the quay. The shivering reflections in the water. The smell of that gray water. The streetwalker on the corner of the old bridge. The boardinghouse whose ground floor was a tavern called the Weary Heart, where I could always see art students, all sorts of women; one of them stood there once and cried without a sound and stamped her foot. On warm evenings, gentlemen wandered around as if searching for inspiration, their faces either lost in thought or bereft of hope. The souvenir vendor wandered from shop to shop. "Like trying to sell ice to Eskimos," my father would jest. Every hour we could hear the bell of the local church, over whose door was inscribed the legend THERE IS A WAY BACK in four languages, Latin, German, Greek, and Hebrew (only the Hebrew was written in curious characters, and there was a slight spelling mistake). Next to the church was the antique shop run by two Jewish partners, the fakers Gips and Gutzi, whom I told you about when we went to Degania together on the valley train. Do you remember, Mina? You laughed. You accused me of "poetic license." And you forgave me.

But you were wrong. Gips existed, and so did Gutzi. I am putting this down in writing now because I have come to the point where I feel obliged to insist, even if it means contradicting you: the truth comes first. As I wrote the word "truth," I paused for a moment. Yes, a slight hesitation. For what is the truth, Mina? Perhaps this: I did not give up Vienna for Jerusalem; I was driven out, more or less, and even though at the time I thought of this expulsion almost as the destruction of the rest of my life, in fact it gained me eight or nine years of life, and it has enabled me to see Jerusalem and to meet you. All the way from there to Malachi Street. To Mount Scopus. Almost to the edge of the desert. If I were not afraid of making you lose your temper I would use the word "absurd." You and Jerusalem. Jerusalem and I. We and the heirs of prophets, kings, and heroes. We turn over a new leaf only to smudge it with ancient neuroses. My child, my neighbors' child, Uri, sometimes shows me his private poems. He trusts me, because I do not laugh at him, and because he thinks of me as a secret inventor who is lying low because of a conspiracy while perfecting wonderful secret weapons for the Hebrew state. He writes poems about the ten lost tribes, Hebrew cavalrymen, great conquests, and acts of vengeance. Doubtless some little teacher, some messianic madman, has captured the child's imagination with the usual Jerusalemite blend of apocalyptic visions and romantic fantasies of Polish or Cossack cavalrymen. Sometimes I try my hand at writing my own educational stories, about Albert Schweitzer in Africa, the life of Louis Pasteur, Edison, that wonderful man Janusz Korczak. All in vain.

In the laundry on the roof of his house, Uri has a rocket made from bits of an old icebox and parts from an abandoned bicycle. The rocket is aimed at the Houses of Parliament in London. And I alone am responsible for the delay, because it is up to me, Dr. Einstein, Dr. Faust, Dr. Gog-and-Magog, to develop in my laboratory the formula for the secret fuel and the Hebrew atomic bomb.

He spends hours on end immersed in my huge German atlas. He is quiet, polite, clean, and tidy. He listens respectfully to what I say but rebukes me for my slowness. He pins little flags in the atlas to trace the course of the advance (with my permission, naturally). He plans a mock landing of Hebrew paratroops on the Suez Canal and along the Red Sea coast. He captures the British fleet off Crete and Malta. Occasionally I am invited to join in this game that is more than a game, in the role of Perfidious Albion, hatching dark plots, conducting desperate rear-guard actions on land and sea, in the Dardanelles, Gibraltar, the Red Sea approaches. Eventually I am forced to capitulate graciously, to cede the whole of the East to the forces of the Hebrew Kingdom, to enter into negotiations, to pencil in lightly the limits of spheres of influence, and to admit sportingly that I have lost the diplomatic war of minds just as I have already been conclusively routed on the battlefield. Only then will the ground be prepared for a military alliance, and the two of us together, Kingdom of Israel and British Empire, will be able to operate against the desert tribesmen. We would advance eastward in a carefully coordinated pincer movement until we encountered a forward patrol of the forces of the ten lost tribes, right at the edge of the map. I have permitted Uri to sketch in in blue pencil a large but Godforsaken Israelite kingdom in Central Asia, somewhere among the Himalayan Mountains.

The game is not entirely to my taste, but I join in nonetheless, and at times I even experience a certain secret thrill: A child. A strange child. My child.

"Dr. Nussbaum," Uri says, "please, if you don't feel well again, I can give you your supper. And I can go to the greengrocer's for you and to Ziegel's and buy whatever you need. Just tell me what."

"Thank you, Uri. There's no need. On the contrary; there's some chocolate in the kitchen cupboard—help yourself, and you may find some almonds, too. And then you must go home, so they don't worry about you."

"They won't worry. I can even stay overnight and keep an eye on the laboratory so you can get some sleep. Mommy and Daddy have gone away to a sanatorium. There's no one at home except Auntie Natalia, and she won't make any trouble for us—she's too busy with her own business. I can even stay out of doors all night if I want to. Or just stay quietly here with you."

"What about your homework?"

"It's done. Dr. Emanuel—"

"Yes, Uri."

"Nothing. Only you . . ."

"What did you want to ask me, Uri? Don't be shy. Ask."

"Nothing. Are you always . . . alone?"

"Recently, yes."

"Haven't you got any brothers or sisters? Haven't you thought about . . . getting married?"

"No. Why do you ask?"

"No reason. Only I haven't, either."

"Haven't what?"

"Nothing. I haven't got any brothers or sisters. And I . . . I don't need anybody."

"It's not the same, Uri."

"Yes, it is. And you don't call me a crazy child. Am I a crazy child?"

"No, Uri, you're not."

"Just the opposite. I'm your assistant. And that's a secret between you and me."

"Naturally," I say without a smile. "Now you must go. Tomorrow, if you like, we'll spend some time in the lab. I'll show you how to reduce certain substances to their elements. It will be a chemistry lesson, and you tell them that at home, please, if they ask you about your visits to me."

"Sure. You can count on me not to talk. I'll say it was chemistry lessons like you said. Don't worry, Dr. Emanuel. Bye."

"Wait a minute, Uri." I hesitate. "Just a minute."

"Yes?"

"Here, your sweater. Good night."

He leaves the house. Slips away down the back stairs. From my balcony I can watch his furtive passage among the shrubs. Suddenly I feel a surge of regret. What have I done. Have I gone mad. I mustn't. Then again: he's the neighbors' child, not mine. And naturally my illness is not catching. But all this will end badly. I'm sorry, Mina. You will certainly view this strange relationship in a totally negative light. And you will be right, as usual. I'm very sorry.

September 5
Evening again

Dear Mina,

I should have told Professor Dushkin there and then on Mount Scopus that I could on no account accept his harsh

words about Moshe Shertok and Berl Locker. After all, these
poor delegates of a tiny, isolated community are almost empty-
handed. And I should have told the engineer from the Jewish
Agency that it would be better for them to give up their useless
fantasies about mysterious weapons and start making clear-
sighted preparations for the departure of the British army and
the impending war. And I should have tried to put up a fight
—forgive me for using such a hyperbolic expression—to put
up a fight for the soul of my child, my neighbors' child, to
put a firm stop to his games of conquest, to get him out of my
laboratory, to produce sensible arguments to counteract the
romantic dreams with which his Cossack Bible teacher has
apparently filled the boy's head.

But I cannot deny that these romantic dreams sometimes take
hold of me, too, at night, in between the attacks of pain. Last
night I helped Dr. Weizmann, disguised as a Catholic priest,
to make his way secretly in the dark to one of the bridges
over the Danube and empty phials of plague bacillus into the
water. After all, we are already infected, Dr. Weizmann said;
there's no hope for either of us, he said; if only we live long
enough to see that our death does not go unavenged. I tried
to remonstrate, I reminded him that we had both always
despised such language, but he turned a tortured, eyeless face
toward me and called me "Svidrigaïlov."

Early in the morning, I went out onto the balcony again. I
found the light on in my neighbors' window across the yard.
Zevulun Grill, who is a driver in the Hammekasher bus cooperative and a member of our local civil-defense committee,
was standing in his kitchen slicing a sausage. He was probably
making his sandwiches. I, too, put the kettle on for my shaving water and my morning coffee, and a strange, irrelevant
phrase kept grating in my mind like a trashy popular tune that
refuses to go away: a thorn in the flesh. I am a thorn in her flesh.
We are a thorn in their flesh.

Dear Mina, I must record that yet another bad sign has
joined all the others: for the first time I fell asleep fully
dressed on the sofa. I woke up rumpled and disheveled at

two o'clock and dragged myself to bed. So I shall have to hurry up.

"I went to the Tel Arza woods by myself after school," Uri said. "I've brought you a canful of that honey stuff that drips from pine trees when you break off a branch; hello, Dr. Nussbaum, I forgot to say it when I came in, and nobody followed me here because I was careful and made several detours on the way. This stuff smells a bit like turpentine, only different. My suggestion, which I thought of on the way back, is that we could try mixing it with a bit of gasoline and some acetone, then lighting it and seeing what the blast's like."

"Today, Uri, I suggest that we do something completely different. For a change. Let's close the windows, make ourselves comfortable, and listen to some classical music on the phonograph. Afterward, if you want to ask any questions, I may be able to explain some of the musical terms."

"Music," Uri said. "We get enough of that at home all day from my mother and her piano. Today you're not feeling well again, Dr. Emanuel, I can see, so maybe it's better if I come back tomorrow afternoon or Saturday morning to work by myself all alone on the experiments that are written in your notebook on the desk in the lab, with the sodium nitrate like you said, or the other thing, what's its name, nitric acid and nitrobenzine, does it say? Sorry to hurry you, only you're always saying that we must hurry up."

"I said that, Uri, I don't deny that I said it. But that was just in the game."

"You only call it a game because of the secrecy. Don't try to say you didn't really mean it 'cause I could see that you did. But never mind. I'll come back some other time."

"But Uri . . ."

"If it's one of your attacks, God forbid, then I'll run and call Dr. Kipnis, and if not, I'm ready to wash all the test tubes from the experiments in ten minutes and especially to fill the spirit lamp. Or if you like I'll go home now, and I'll report for duty the minute I see a slanting chink in your bathroom blinds like we arranged. Meanwhile, bye-bye, Dr. Emanuel, and be well, 'cause what'll I do if anything happens to you suddenly."

Do I have the strength, do I have the right, to try to influence his mind?

The education of children is totally outside my province.

Outside, in the yard, the Grill children ambush him and make fun of him. I can't hear the words, and even if I could I don't suppose I could understand them. I can hear their evil laughter. And Uri's heroic silence.

What can I do.

I sit at the table on the balcony, writing you an account that is incapable of yielding results or conclusions. Forgive me.

Meanwhile, it is almost dark outside. I have stretched the desk lamp out here again from my study so that I can write to you under this evening sky. Soon the first stars will appear. It is almost as if I could still expect some illumination. As if here in Jerusalem even a man like me could momentarily be chosen for the role of messenger.

Moths around the lamp. I have stopped writing for a moment to make myself some coffee by the most primitive method: boiling water poured on the black powder. No milk, no sugar. I had a biscuit, too. Then I had an attack of weakness and nausea; a sour taste rose in my throat. I took a pill and gave myself an injection. Forgive me, Mina, these physical complaints bore me and have nothing to do with the matter at hand.

But what *does* have to do with the matter at hand? What *is* the matter at hand?

That is the question.

Maybe this: that my neighbors' children have reduced Uri to despair outside, and he has climbed up the mulberry tree like a hounded cat. I ought to intervene to protect him, or call his parents. His parents are away. His aunt, then, that Natalia who has come from some kibbutz. Not now: late at night, when he is asleep, I should go and talk to her. Explain, warn, apologize.

How absurd. What can I say? And how can I, a total stranger, call on her late at night?

And I know nothing at all about the education of children. I shall go on watching. Now the boys who chased Uri have begun a sort of commando raid across the broken-down railings. Is it a hunt, from yard to yard, in the cellars, in the peeling entrance halls, and among the dusty shrubs that are dying here in the drought? They have Hebrew names that savor of the desert: Boaz, Joab, Gideon, Ehud, Jephthah. And because the darkness is still not complete, still touched by the last vestiges of light, I can manage from my balcony to make out the rules of the game: it is an air raid. They spread their arms wide, group themselves in spearhead formation, bend the top halves of their bodies forward, and stamp along pretending to be warplanes. Spread-eagle. Uttering sounds of explosions, drone of engines, and tattoo of machine guns. One of them happens to look up at my balcony, catches sight of me calmly writing by the light of the desk lamp, aims an invisible gun at me, and annihilates me with a single salvo. I accept it.

That is, I raise my hands in a gesture of surrender, and even spread a smile on my face, no doubt a Dutch uncle's smile, so as to reward him with a victorious thrill. But the dedicated warrior refuses to accept my surrender. He rejects it outright. He disregards my smile and my raised arms. The logic of war is pursued without favor or exception. I have been annihilated, and now I no longer exist. He goes on his way, surging forward to wipe out the last traces of the Jew-haters.

Friday night, and Jews in cheap suits are carrying prayer books under their arms as they go past my balcony on their way to the Faithful Remnant Synagogue to welcome the Sabbath. Probably they are secretly delighted at the sight of these child airplanes, muttering contentedly to themselves, "little pagans."

All through the summer the children have exposed their skin to the blazing rays of the sun. Needless to say, I have done my duty. I have warned my neighbors, their parents, time and again that excessive exposure is bad for the skin and can even harm their general development. In vain. The settlers here, Orthodox shopkeepers, municipal and Jewish Agency officials, refugees, thinkers and stamp collectors, former pioneers, teachers, and clerks—they all agree in elevating sunbathing almost to the level of a religion. Perhaps they imagine that Jewish children who take on a bronze color cease to be Jewish children and become Hebrews. A new, tough race, no longer timid and persecuted, no longer sparkling with gold and silver teeth, no longer with sweaty palms and eyes blinking through thick lenses. Total liberation from the fear of persecution by means of this colorful camouflage. But I must put in a word of reservation here: I am not at all well read in either zoology or anthropology, and hence the comparison between what is happening here and the mechanism of protective coloration that is found in a certain type of lizard whose name escapes me cannot be regarded as substantiated.

However, I shall record my own private observations.

Jerusalem, Kerem Avraham, mid-1940's: Bunem begat Zischa, and Zischa begat Myetek, and Myetek begat Giora. A new leaf.

Nevertheless, needless to say, I can see no benefit in this effort. At the close of a summer's day, Kerem Avraham exudes a smell of Eastern European immigrants. It is a sour smell. If I try to isolate its ingredients: Their sweat. Their fish. The cheap oil they use for frying. Nervous indigestion. Petty intrigues among neighbors motivated by repressed greed. Hopes and fears. Here and there a partially blocked drain. Their underwear, drying everywhere on clotheslines, especially the women's underwear, has a sanctimonious air. I am tempted to use the word "puritanical." And on every window sill here, cucumbers are pickling in old jam jars, cucumbers floating in liquid with garlic, dill, parsley, bay leaves. Is this also a place that in years to come someone will remember with longing? Can it be that when the time comes, someone will dream nostalgically of the rusting washtubs, the broken-down railings, the rough, cracked concrete, the peeling plaster, the coils of barbed

wire, the thistles, the immigrant smells? Indeed, will we sur-
vive the war that is coming? What will happen, Mina—perhaps
you have some suggestion, some consolation, to offer? No?
This morning, on the short-wave broadcast of the Underground
radio, they played a stirring song: "We shall climb together to
the mountains,/ Climb toward the light of breaking day:/
We have left our yesterdays behind us,/ But tomorrow is a
long, long way away." Here are the mountains, Mina, and here
we are among them. Jewish immigrants. Our last reserves of
strength. The tomorrow in the song is not for me, I know
that. But my love and fears are directed desperately—forgive
me—toward the darling child you bore me and hid away in a
kibbutz in the Jezreel Valley. What lies in store for him? I
imagine him lean and bronzed, barefoot, even his dreams
filled with taps, screws, and cogwheels.

Or Uri.

Look, just like Dushkin, I have a tear in my eye. Suddenly I, too, am a Samovar. It is not sadness at my death,
you know that, it's sadness for the people and their children
and for the mountains all around. What will happen? What
have we done, and what shall we do now? Yes. *Angst*. Don't
smile like that.

Friday night. In every kitchen now they are cooking chicken
necks stuffed with groats, stuffed intestines, stuffed peppers. The
poor people have cheap sausage with mustard. For me, of
course, only raw vegetables and fresh fruit. Even the quarrels,
the insults hurled every now and again from balcony to balcony, are in Yiddish: *Bist du a wilde chayye, Mister Menachem,
du herst mich, bist du a meshuggener?*

That is how it is in Jerusalem.

They say that in Galilee, in the valley, in Sharon, and in the
remote parts of the Negev a kind of mutation in taking place: A
new race of peasants is emerging. Laconic. Sarcastic. Single-
minded. Dedicated.

I don't know.

You're the one who knows.

For two and a half years now, you have been wandering

among the kibbutzim, dashing from place to place in their dusty trucks, making notes, interviewing, drawing comparisons, in khaki trousers and a man's shirt with large breast pockets, compiling statistics, sleeping in pioneer huts, sharing their frugal fare. Perhaps you can even speak to them in their own language. Perhaps you even love them.

A tough, spartan woman, uncompromising, strolling around those camps without the least embarrassment, collecting material for an original piece of social-psychological research. Stubbing out your cigarette as if you were pressing a push-pin into the table. Lighting up again at once, not blowing the match out but waving it almost violently to and fro. Entering the details of the dreams of the first native-born generation on little cards. "Patterns of Behavior and Normative Ideas Among the Products of a Collective Education." Mina, I am prepared to give my wholehearted admiration to those children, and to their pioneering parents, the enthusiasm, the silent heroism, the iron will, and the graceful manners.

And to you.

Mina, I take my hat off to you.

That is to say—forget it. A Viennese gesture. There, I've already regretted it.

As for me—what am I?

A weak Jew. Consumed by hesitations. Dedicated but apprehensive. And now, in addition to everything else, seriously ill. My modest contribution: here, in Jerusalem, in a neighborhood of lower-middle-class immigrants from Russia and Poland, I have put up a fight, as long as my strength lasted, without counting the hours, even working at night sometimes, against the dangers of diphtheria and dysentery.

Moreover, there are my chemical interests. Homemade explosives. It is possible that Uri can already see what I refuse to see. Perhaps a formula is really taking shape in my mind for the large-scale production of homemade explosives. Or at least I may be able to suggest a starting point to the Hagganah. In this area, at any rate. In the early hours of this morning, I devoted some thought to the salts we possess in relative abundance, such as potassium chlorate and barium nitrate. Any porous substance, such as chalk or charcoal, can be saturated with liquid oxygen. I must stop recording details like these. My heart is heavy because I do not want to devise formulas for explosives or to contribute to wars, but Uri is right, and so I am obliged to do so. But the sadness, Mina, how great it is. And the humiliation.

I have tried to resist this obligation. I have even taken certain steps. I refer to the poignant conversations I had at the beginning of the summer with an Arab friend, a colleague, a doctor from Katamon, Dr. Mahdi. Need I go into details? The abyss that divides two doctors of moderate views, who both abhor bloodshed. My pleas. His pleas. The historical argument. On the one hand and on the other. The moral argument. On the one hand and on the other. The practical argument. On the one hand and on the other. His certainty. My hesitations. I must try again. I must appeal to him at this late hour and ask him to arrange for me to meet the members of the Jerusalem Arab Committee and make them think again. I still have an argument or two left.

Only the heart says: It's all in vain. You must hurry up. Uri is right, and so is the Underground broadcast on the short waves: "To die—or to conquer the mountain."

I will not deny it, Mina: as usual I am very frightened.

And I am also ashamed of my fear. Let us not be halted by the corpses of the weak, as Bialik says, they died in servitude, may their dream be sweet to them, onions and garlic in plenty, bountiful fleshpots. I am quoting from memory. My copy of Bialik's poems is in the bookcase some five or six paces away, but I don't have the strength to get up. And anyway, I strenuously reject the line about the dream of onions and garlic. Insofar as it concerns me, you know full well what is in my dreams. Wild, even rough women—yes. Murderers and shepherdesses from the Bedouin—also. And my father's face with his lawyer, and sometimes longing for river and forest. But no onions and no garlic. There our national poet was mistaken, or perhaps he merely exaggerated so as to rouse the people's spirit. Forgive me. Once more I have trespassed on a domain in which I am no expert.

And you are in my dreams, too. You in New York, in a youthful dress, in some paved square that reminds me of Moshavot Square in Tel Aviv. There is a jetty there, and you are at the wheel of a dusty jeep, smoking, supervising Arab porters who are carrying cases of arms for the beleaguered Hebrew community. You are on duty. You are on a secret mission. You are throbbing with efficiency or moral indignation. "Shame on you," you reproach me. "How could you, and at a time like this? Disgusting." I admit it, fall silent, recoil, and retreat to the far end of the jetty. Reflected like a corpse in the water, I hear distant shots and suddenly agree with you in my heart. Yes, you are right. How could I. I must go at once, just as I am, without a suitcase, without an overcoat, this very minute.

The shame is more than I can bear. I wake up in pain and take three pills. I lie down again, wide awake and alarmed, and hear outside, just beyond the shutters, on a branch, at a distance of perhaps two feet from me, a night bird. It is uttering a bitter, piercing shriek, in a kind of frenzy of wounded self-righteousness, repeating its protest over and over again: Ahoo. Ahoohoo. Ahoo. Ahoooo.

> Jerusalem
> Saturday evening
> September 6, 1947

Dear Mina,

It will not be easy for me to wean myself from this child.

He spent the whole morning here, painstakingly copying facts out of the gazetteer and sketching a military plan for the capture of the mountain ranges that command Jerusalem from the north. Then he marked on his map the crossroads and the strategic points. On a separate sheet of paper, he allocated storm troops to each of the key buildings in Jerusalem, such as the central post office, the David Building, the radio station, the Russian Compound, the Schneller Barracks, the YMCA tower, and the railway station. And all the while he did not disturb me as I lay resting on the sofa. He is a thin, fair-haired child; his movements are abrupt, embarrassment and aspirations shine in his green eyes, but his manners are impeccable. Twice he interrupted his game and made me some coffee. He straightened my blanket and replaced the sweat-drenched pillow under my head with a fresh one. It was almost noon before he apologetically asked me my opinion of his work. Despite all my principles I praised it.

Uri said:

"I've got to go home soon and have my lunch. Please rest so you'll be strong enough to do the experiment tonight. I'm leaving a Matosian cigarette pack here, Dr. Emanuel; inside there are four live bullets we can take the gunpowder out of. And in my sock I've got the pin from a hand grenade. It's a bit rusty, but it's all there. I found it, and I've brought it for you. From our roof I counted nine British tanks in a shed in Schneller. Cromwells. Is it true, Dr. Emanuel, that a tank is finished if you put some sugar in the engine?"

Again the excited glint flickers in his eyes and dies down. He still trusts me, but his patience is beginning to wear thin: "How much more time will you need for the experiments? A fortnight? More? By about December the Irgun and the Stern Group will have started to blow up enemy districts in the city, because the English are already moving troops to Haifa."

I smile:

"There may still be an agreement, Uri. I read in the paper that America may yet agree to govern the country until the storm dies down and the Arabs start getting used to the idea of a Hebrew state. There is still some such possibility. Why must you be so enthusiastic for wars? I have already explained to you more than once that a war is a terrible thing, even if you win it. Perhaps we shall still manage to prevent it."

"You don't really mean that. It's just because I'm still a child and you think you've got to improve me, like my daddy. But nothing comes from words. I'm very sorry. Everything is war."

"And how, if you don't mind my asking, did you arrive at that rather sweeping conclusion?"

Now he stares at me in utter disbelief. He stands up. His hands are thrust deep into the pockets of his shorts. He comes over to the sofa, and as he leans over me his voice is trembling:

"I'm not an informer. You can speak frankly to me. Surely everything is war. That's how it is in history, in the Bible, in nature, and in real life, too. And love is all war. Friendship, too, even."

"Are you acquainted with love already, Uri?"

Silence.

And then:

"Dr. Emanuel, tell me, is it true that there's a Jewish professor in America who has invented a huge atomic bomb made from a drop of water?"

"You are referring apparently to the hydrogen bomb. That lies outside the range of my knowledge."

"All right. Don't tell me anything. There are military secrets that I'm not allowed to know. The main thing is that you do know all about it, and no one will ever get a word out of me."

"Uri. Listen. You are quite mistaken about that. Let me explain something to you. Listen carefully."

Silence.

I don't know what to explain to him, or in what words. It's not true:

The truth is that I am afraid of losing him. In his short trousers, with the buckle shining on his army belt, with his gentle hand once or twice on my forehead, am I still perspiring, have I got a slight temperature.

And so once again I give in. I start explaining to him what a chain reaction is and, in schematic terms, about the relationship between matter and energy. For a long while he listens to me in silent concentration, his eyes fixed on my mouth, his nostrils flaring as if they have caught a distant whiff of the fire storm in Hiroshima, which I am telling him about. Now he really worships me, he loves me with all his heart.

And now I feel better, too, as a result of his enthusiasm. Suddenly I feel strong enough to get up, to invite Uri into my little laboratory, I am suddenly animated by a kind of pedagogic enthusiasm, I light the spirit lamp and demonstrate a simple exercise to him: water, steam, energy, motor power.

"And that's the whole principle." I chuckle happily.

"My lips are sealed, Dr. Emanuel. I won't talk, even if the British arrest me and torture me, they won't get a word out of me, because I've got a way of keeping quiet that I learned from Ephraim Nehamkin. They won't get anything out of me about what you've told me, you can trust me a hundred percent."

Once more the beautiful rage flashes in his green eyes and dies away. My child.

Eventually he takes his leave and promises to come back tomorrow afternoon. And even in the middle of the night, if he sees a slanting crack of light at my bathroom window. In which case, he'll slip out and come to me at once. He'll be at my command, he says. Bye.

When he had gone, I suddenly began to argue with you in my mind. To apologize for it all. To justify myself about our first meeting. To re-examine how I went, two years ago, in the summer of '45, for a rest to the sanatorium at Arza. How I decided then, mistakenly, that my morning attacks of sickness were the result of general fatigue. How I made up my mind to relax completely, and how you came bursting into my solitary life, you and my illness. And as I reflected, I put the blame, if one can so express it, on you.

Dear Mina, if you mind my writing all this, then skip the next few lines.

Please. Try to see it like this: a bachelor, a doctor, with reasonable financial security, in receipt of an occasional mail remittance from his father, who is a confectioner in Ramat Gan. His expenditures are few: a moderate rent, simple clothing, and food in keeping with the times and his surroundings, the occasional expenses of his scientific hobby. He has a little put away.

Moreover, for some time now he has experienced a certain tiredness, and slight attacks of nausea early in the morning, before the first cup of coffee. A medical colleague diagnoses the first signs of ulcers and orders complete rest. Besides, certain European habits of his youth persist: summertime is holiday time.

And so, Arza, in the hills behind Jerusalem. A relaxed Dr. Nussbaum, dressed in a light summer suit and an open-necked blue shirt, sits in a deck chair under the whispering pines, half reading a novel by Jacob Wassermann. The paths are covered with fine white gravel. Every footstep produces a crisp crunching sound, which charms him and reminds him of other times. In the background, inside the building, the phonograph is playing work songs. Nearby, in a hammock, a prominent figure in the community and the Labor Movement is dozing, the gentle breeze ruffling the pages of the newspaper spread open on his stomach. Dr. Nussbaum does not admit even to himself that he is waiting for this public figure to wake up so that he can engage him in conversation and make an impression on him.

A Health Service nurse named Jasmine circulates among the reclining figures, distributing to each a glass of fresh orange juice and biscuits, a kind of mid-morning snack. This Jasmine is a robust, buxom girl. The fine black down that covers her arms and legs stirs a sudden lust in Dr. Nussbaum. The capricious physical attraction he feels for simple Oriental women. He politely declines the orange juice and tries to engage Jasmine in a lighthearted conversation, but the words come with difficulty, and his voice, as always happens to him in such situations, sounds false. Jasmine lingers to bend over him and smooth his shirt collar over the lapels of his jacket. A momentary glimpse of her breasts arouses a certain boldness in him: as in his student days in Vienna, when he would drain a glass of brandy at a single gulp and find the courage to utter a mild obscenity. So he gives voice to a false explanation of his refusal of the orange juice, a sort of ambiguous hint about forbidden as against permitted pleasures. She does not understand. However, it seems that she is in no hurry to move on: she must find him not unattractive, this gentleman in his light suit and his graying hair. She probably thinks him highly intelligent and respected, but modest. It is possible that she can detect his welling lust. She laughs and asks what she can offer him instead of the juice. He can have whatever he wants, says Jasmine. No, he replies, with a polite smile in his eyes, what he wants she may not be able to give him out here, surrounded by all these other convalescents. Jasmine shows her teeth. She blushes, and her dark skin takes on a darker hue. Even her shoulders participate in her laughter. "If that's the way you are, then have a glass of my juice anyway." And he, now caught up in sweet game-fever, suggests she try another temptation. Again she does not understand. She is slightly taken aback. "Coffee, for instance," he hastens to add, in case he has gone too far. Jasmine reflects for a moment; perhaps she is still not quite sure—does he really want a cup of coffee, or is the game still on? On the clear summer air there comes the buzzing of a bee, the caw of a crow, and a British airplane droning far to the south over the Bethlehem hills. "I'll see to some coffee for you," Jasmine says, "as a special favor. Just for you."

It was at that point that you came into the picture. Actually, you were there already: an intense woman on a nearby rocking chair, in a simple, severe summer dress. Sitting and judging.

"If I might be permitted to intrude in this exchange," you say.

And I, in a trice, return from the harems of Baghdad to my Viennese manners:

"By all means, dear lady. Need you ask? We were merely indulging in idle banter. Please."

And so you advise me to choose fresh orange juice, rather

than coffee, after all. From bitter experience that morning, you have discovered that the coffee here is ersatz, a kind of greasy black mud. Incidentally, I am not a total stranger to you: you once heard me lecture at a one-day conference at the Hadassah Hospital on Mount Scopus. I spoke about hygiene and the drinking water in Palestine, and impressed you with my sense of humor. Dr. Nussbaum, if you are not mistaken. No, you are surely not mistaken.

I hasten to reassure you, and you continue:

"Very pleased to meet you. Hermine Oswald. Mina for short. A pupil of pupils of Dr. Adler. Apparently we both share the same Viennese background. That is why I permitted myself to intervene and rescue you from the Health Service coffee. I have a bad habit of interfering without being asked. Yes. Nurse, please leave two glasses of grapefruit juice on the table here. Thank you. You may go now. What were we talking about? Ah, yes. Your lecture on the drinking water was entertaining, but quite out of place in that one-day conference."

You imagine I will agree with you on this point.

Dr. Nussbaum, naturally, hastens to agree wholeheartedly.

Meanwhile, Jasmine is receiving a noisy dressing down: the Trade Union official is grumbling, half an hour ago or more he asked her—or one of the other nurses, what's the difference —to put through an urgent telephone call for him to the office of Comrade Sprinzak. Has she forgotten? Is it possible?

You indicate him with your chin, smile, and explain to me *sotto voce:*

"Beginnings of egomania and overbearing behavior typical of short men. By the time he's seventy, he will be a positive monster."

We drift into lighthearted conversation. Jasmine, rebuked, has moved out of sight. You call her an *"enfant sauvage."* I ask myself whether you have overheard my foolish exchange with her, and find myself devoutly hoping that you have not.

"I react in exactly the same way as you," you are saying, "only in reverse. An Oriental taxi driver, or even a Yemenite newsboy, can throw me quite off balance. From a purely physi-

cal point of view, of course. These *'enfants sauvages'* still retain
—or so it would appear—some sort of sensual animal language
that we have long forgotten."

Dr. Nussbaum, as you will surely recall, does not blush to
hear all this. No. He blanches. He clears his throat. Hurriedly
he produces a freshly laundered handkerchief from his pocket
and wipes his lips. He begins to mumble something about the
flies, which he has just noticed are all around. And so, without further delay, he changes the subject. He has an anecdote
to relate about Professor Dushkin, who, you will recall, was in
the chair at that medical conference at the Hadassah. Dushkin called everyone—the doctors, the High Commissioner, the
leaders of the Jewish Agency, Stalin, everyone—Svidrigaïlovs.

"How unoriginal of him," you remark icily. "But Dr. Nussbaum, you may invoke whomsoever you will, Dushkin, Stalin,
Svidrigaïlov, to change the direction of our conversation. It
is not you but I who should apologize for the embarrassment
I have caused."

"Perish the thought, Dr. Oswald, perish the thought," Dr.
Nussbaum mutters like an idiot.

"Mina," you insist.

"Yes, with great pleasure. Emanuel," Dr. Nussbaum replies.

"You are uneasy in my company," you say with a smile.

"Heaven forbid."

"In that case, shall we take a little stroll together?"

You get up from your rocking chair. You never wait for
an answer. I get up and follow you. You take me for a leisurely
amble along the gravel path and beyond, down the wooded
slope, to the shade of the cypress trees, toward the smell of
resin and decay, until we come to the famous tree that was
planted by Dr. Herzl and was later felled by some Arabs.
And there we discovered, in the dry summer grass, a rusty earring with a Cyrillic inscription.

"It's mine!" you suddenly exclaim possessively, like a high-
spirited schoolgirl. "I saw it first!"

A tearful grimace played around your mouth for a moment,

as if I were really about to prize the earring from your fist by brute force.

"It's yours," I said, laughing, "even though I believe I saw it first. But have it anyway. As a gift."

Suddenly I added:

"Mina."

You looked at me. You did not speak. Perhaps for a full minute you looked at me and did not speak. Then you hurled the earring into the thistles and took hold of my arm.

"We are out for a stroll," you said.

"Yes, out for a stroll," I agreed happily.

What happened to us. What did you see in me.

No, I do not expect an answer. You are in New York. Up to your eyeballs in work, I expect. As usual. Who can rival your power of periodically turning over a new leaf.

If I were to try to examine myself through your eyes that day in Arza, I should not be much the wiser. You saw before you a withdrawn man with a pensive expression and a cautious way of moving. Rather a lonely man, to judge by outward appearances. Not lacking in sensuality, though, as you must have learned when you overheard him flirting with the girl Jasmine. Not bad looking, either, as I have already stated. A tall, thin man, inclined to turn pale in moments of emotion or embarrassment, his features angular and decidedly intellectual. Hair going slightly gray, but still falling luxuriantly over his forehead, enough perhaps to attract attention. He may have struck you as a rootless artist, he may have looked to you like an unconventional musician from the conservatoire of some German-speaking land, who had turned up here in Western Asia and now bore his degradation with silent, tight-lipped resignation: there is no way back. A melancholy man, yet capable nonetheless, in unusual circumstances, of whole-hearted enthusiasm.

In brief, an orphan and a dominating aunt, according to your definition. A definition, however, that you only voiced some time later.

By lunchtime, we were already sharing a table. Chatting about the poet Gottfried Benn. And putting our heads together like a couple of conspirators, trying to work out the order in which the various tables were served. It was Jasmine who served us. As she poured the mineral water I was splashed slightly, because she was not paying attention. I did not complain; on the contrary, as she leaned over me her firm breasts almost brushed my shoulder. At their base, glimpsed through the opening of her white overall, there showed a network of blue veins, such as one sometimes finds in marble from Galilee.

My lust did not escape your notice. You were amused and began to tease me. You started asking me certain questions about my bachelor life. All without batting an eyelid, as if you were inquiring where I bought my shirts. Apparently your practical experience as a psychologist (before you devoted yourself to research) enabled you to ask me questions of a sort not normally exchanged by new acquaintances.

As for me, I blanched as usual. But I made up my mind this time not to evade your questions. Only I found the choice of words very difficult.

"This time you have not changed the subject to Svidrigaïlov," you observed ruthlessly.

Again we went for a walk together, this time beyond the perimeter, toward the buildings of the small farming settlement of Motza. My loneliness, and perhaps my extreme caution in the choice of my words, aroused your sympathy. You liked me, and you said so in a matter-of-fact tone of voice. Afternoon light on the hills. The gentle cypresses. A blaze of geraniums among the houses of the settlement, red-tiled roofs, a poinciana flaming red like a greeting from Tel Aviv. A light, dry breeze. Our conversation now is impersonal, Viennese as it were, a sort of exchange of views on the question of sexual pleasures and their relation to the emotions. You are remarkably free in the way you speak about anatomical and physiological details. You find my hesitancy appealing perhaps, but definitely surprising nonetheless: After all, Emanuel, we are both doctors, we are both perfectly familiar with these mechanisms, so why are you so embarrassed, secretly praying for me finally to change the subject?

I apologize; my embarrassment springs from the fact that in Hebrew the intimate particulars of the anatomy—very well, the sexual organs—have newly invented names, which seem rather sterile and lifeless, and that is why, paradoxically, I find it hard to utter them. You describe this explanation as "pilpulistic." You do not believe me. When all is said and done, what is to prevent my switching to German, or making use of the Latin terms? No, you do not believe me. Unhesitatingly you identify psychological inhibitions. Latent puritanism.

"Mina," I protest, "forgive me, please, but I'm not one of your patients yet."

"No. But we are making each other's acquaintance. We are taking a walk together. Why don't you ask me questions about myself?"

"I haven't got any questions. Only one, perhaps: you have been humiliated by someone, a man, perhaps a cruel man, a long time ago perhaps, viciously humiliated."

"Is that a question?"

"I was . . . voicing an impression."

Suddenly, forcefully, you take my head between your hands. "Bend down."

I obey. Your lips. And a small discovery: tiny holes in the lobes of your ears. Is it possible that you once wore earrings? I do not ask.

Then you remark that I seem to you like a watch that has lost its glass. So vulnerable. So helpless. And so touching.

You touch my hair. I touch your shoulder. We walk on in silence. Darkness is falling. Overhead a bird of prey in the last rays of twilight. A vulture? A falcon? I do not know. And there is a hint of danger: outside the grounds of the sanatorium, Arab shepherds roam. Not far away is a notorious brigand village called Koloniyeh. We must be getting back. All around us the sadness of darkening rocks. Night is falling on an arid boulder-land. Far on the northern horizon, in the direction of Shu'afat and Beit Ikhsa, a star shell splits the sky, fades, shatters to shivers of light, and dies in the darkness.

After supper, a vulgar entertainer from the Broom Theater appeared in the dining room. He told jokes and made fun, in a heavy Russian accent, of the hypocrisy of the British government and the savagery of the Arab gangs. Finally, he even made faces at the audience. The Trade Union bigwig flushed, rose from his seat, and condemned such frivolity as being out of place in such critical times. The entertainer retired to a corner of the room and sat down, abashed, on the verge of tears. The audience was totally silent. When the speaker used the word "self-restraint," you suddenly burst into loud, resounding laughter, youthful laughter, which instantly provoked a reaction of astonished rage all around. At once people were laughing with you, or perhaps at you. We left the dining room. Darkness in the corridors and on the stairs. Almost immediately we were in each other's arms. Whispering, this time in German. You liked me, you said, you had a small volume of Rilke in your room, you said, and after all we were both adults and free agents.

In your room, almost without an exchange of words, rules were established at once. Orphan and dominating aunt. I must play the part of an ignorant, awkward, shy, but obedient pupil. But grateful. And very diligent. Yours to command in a whisper, and mine to obey in silence. You had all the details drawn up ready in your mind, as if you were carrying out an exotic program taken from an erotic handbook: Here. Now here. Slowly. Harder. More. Wait. Wait. Now. That's right.

Dear Mina, we both intended that night to be the first and the last. Adults, you said, free agents, you said, but, after all, who is an adult or a free agent, both of us were captured by a force that carried us away like twigs in a river. Perhaps because I was subjugated. Perhaps you had decided from the outset to subjugate me that night, and so I found myself a slave. But you, too, became a slaveowner, Mina, through my very subjugation. And again the following afternoon. And the next night. And again. And after the holidays you began sending postcards to me in Jerusalem with curt commands: Come to Haifa the day after tomorrow. Expect me on Saturday night. Come to Kate Graubert's *pension* in Talpiyot. I'll come to you for the festival. Tell Fritz that his fast is almost over. Hug Gips and Gutzi for me.

Until you finally taught me to call you Jasmine, to unleash the panting satyr, to conjure up a Baghdad harem in low-ceilinged boardinghouses. To torment and be tormented. To scream aloud. Again and again to grovel at your feet when it was all over, while you lit a cigarette, shook out the match, and studied our love-making in precise terms, like a general returning to a battlefield to analyze the fighting and learn lessons for the future.

No, Mina, there is no bitterness, no regret. On the contrary. Unbearable longing. Longing for your rare words of praise. And longing for your rebukes. For your mockery, too. And for your fingers. My own Jasmine, I am a sick man now, I don't have much time left. One might say I fell into your clutches. Or one might say I loved you out of humiliation.

New paragraph.

Let me return to my record of the place and the time. As I have already said, here I am, on the lookout.

Jerusalem, evening, summer's ending, signs of autumn, a man of thirty-nine, already retired for reasons of serious ill health, sitting on his balcony writing to a girl friend, or a former girl friend. He is telling her what he can see, and also what he is thinking. What the purpose is, what can be called the "subject," I have already said I do not know.

The daylight has been fading for an hour and a quarter now, and it is still not quite dark. I am at rest. On the face of it, this is a peaceful hour. Every Saturday evening there is a miracle of sound in Jerusalem: even the noises of the children playing, the cars, and the dogs, and in the distance a woman singing on the radio—all these sounds are assimilated into the silence. Even the shouting down the road. Even a stray burst of machine-gun

fire from the direction of Sanhedriya. The silence cloaks it all.
In other words, on Saturday evening total silence reigns in
Jerusalem.

Now the church and convent bells have started to ring out
from nearby and far away, and they, too, are inside the silence.
Tomorrow is Sunday. The color of the sky is dark-gray with a
segment of orange between the clouds. They are fast-moving
autumn clouds. And there is a flock of birds flying past. Larks,
perhaps. Various people pass below my balcony in Malachi
Street. A woman from next door with a basket. A student with
an armload of books. And now a boy and a girl walking past
rapidly, separated from each other by a good yard or so, not
exchanging a word, yet there is no doubt that they are together
and that their hearts are at rest.

Opposite, on the corner of Zechariah Street, an old Arab
woman is sitting on the sidewalk. A peasant woman. Cross-
legged and almost motionless. In front of her there is a large
brass tray full of figs for sale. At the edge of the tray, a little
pile of coins, no doubt milliemes and half-piasters, her day's
takings. She comes here all the way from Sheikh Badr, or perhaps even from Lifta or Malha. How calm she is, and what a
long journey she still has to make this evening. Meanwhile she is
waiting. Chewing something. Mint leaves? I do not know. Soon
she will get up, I almost said arise, balance the tray on her head,
and pick her way in the dark among the thistles and boulders.
Like a fine network of nerves, the footpaths stretch across the
fields, joining the suburbs to the villages all around Jerusalem.
A slow, sturdy old woman, at peace with her body and the
desolate mountains; my heart yearns for that peace. As she
goes on her way, the yellow lights of the street lamps will come
on all over the neighborhood. Then the ringing of the bells will
cease, and only the sadness of the evening will remain. Iron
shutters will be closed. All the doors will be locked. Jerusalem
will be in darkness, and I shall be alone in its midst. Suppose I
have an attack in the night. Will the child really watch out for
the slanting crack of light at my bathroom window, will he
really slip out and come to me, be at my command?

Panic seizes me at the very possibility of such a thought's occurring to me. No. Tonight, as usual, I shall be alone. Good night.

Sunday
September 7, 1947

Dear Mina,

I do not know what words one can use to describe to you a blue autumn morning such as we had here today, before the westerly wind blew up, bringing with it a cold, cloudy evening. The whole morning was flooded a deep sky-blue. Much more than a tone or a color: it was such a pure, concentrated blue that it felt like a potion. The buildings and plants responded with a general awakening, as though redoubling their hold on their own colors, or giving concrete expression to a national slogan that is current at the moment in the Hebrew newspapers and Underground broadcasts: To any provocation we shall react twofold; we are determined to stand by what is ours to the last.

That is to say, the blazing geraniums, for instance, in gardens, in backyards, in olive cans on verandas, in window boxes. Or the Jerusalem stone: this morning it is truly "shouting from the walls," in a powerful, concentrated gray. An unalloyed gray, like the color of your eyes. Or the flowering creeper climbing up the olive tree next to the grocer's, dotted all over with points of dark-blue brilliance. It all looked like a painting by an overenthusiastic amateur who has not learned, and has no wish to learn, the secret of understatement. I am almost tempted to use biblical Hebrew words, like sardius, beryl, carbuncle—even though the precise meaning of these words is unknown to me.

Should this miracle be attributed to the clarity of the desert air? To the breath of autumn? To my illness, perhaps? Or to some change that is impending? I have no answer to all these questions. I must try to define my feelings in words, and so I go back to writing: Today I feel painful longings for sights that are present, as though they were recollected images. As though they had already passed, perhaps as though they had passed beyond recall forever. Longings so powerful that I feel an urgent need to do something at once, something unusual, perhaps to put on a light jacket and go out for a walk. To the Tel Arza woods. Among the knitting mothers and their infants sprawled on rugs. To recall the Sunday outings of my child-hood to the Vienna woods, and suddenly to sense a smell of other autumns, elsewhere, a smell of lakes, mushrooms, drop-lets of dew on the branches of fir trees, the smell of *Lederhosen,* the smoke of holiday-makers' campfires, the aroma of freshly ground coffee. How strange I must have seemed this morning to the neighbors' wives in the Tel Arza woods: Look, there is Dr. Nussbaum out for a walk, tall and elegantly dressed, his hands clasped behind his back, smiling to himself as he treads the pine needles underfoot, as though he has just discovered an amusing solution.

"Good morning, Dr. Nussbaum, how are you this morning, and what are they saying at the Jewish Agency?"

"Good morning, a beautiful morning, Mrs. Litvak, I'm fairly well, thank you, and how your lovely little boy is growing. Lit-tle girl, I'm sorry. But still lovely."

"As you know, sir, happy are we who have been permitted to behold the light of Jerusalem with the eyes of the flesh and not merely with the eyes of the spirit, and surely what our eyes behold today is as nothing compared to the light that tomorrow will bring. Happy is he who waits."

"Yes indeed, Mr. Nehamkin, yes indeed. It's a wonderful day today, and I am very glad to see you so hale and hearty."

"Since you are also out for a stroll, sir, permit me to accom-pany you. Together we shall walk, and together our eyes shall behold, for, as it is written, the testimony of two witnesses is valid."

Only in this case the two witnesses were none too healthy. We were soon tired. My neighbor the poet Nehamkin apologized and turned for home, but not before assuring me that a mo-mentous change would soon take place in Jerusalem.

And I, as usual, turned into the Kapitanski brothers' milk bar for a vegetarian lunch: tomato soup, two fried eggs, eggplant salad, buttermilk, and a glass of tea. Then I came home, and, without any pill or injection, I fell into a deep afternoon sleep: as if I had been drinking wine.

At half past four there was another meeting of the local committee in my apartment. As I must have written to you already, even Kerem Avraham is setting up its own civil-defense council.

Four or five representatives of the neighbors came, including Mrs. Litvak, who qualified as a nurse before she married. She brought some homemade biscuits with her, and refused to allow me to help her serve the coffee; all I had to do was to tell her where I kept the sugar and the tray—no, no need, she'd already found them. She had found the lemon, too. And how wonderfully tidy my kitchen was! She would bring her husband, Litvak, here one day to let him see with his own eyes and learn a thing or two. The head of a school for workers' children, and he couldn't even wash a glass properly. Still, it was her fate. She mustn't complain.

And so the meeting began, while we were still being served coffee and shortcake, and I was being treated like a guest in my own home.

"Well," said Mrs. Litvak, "let's get down to business. Dr. Nussbaum, would you like to begin."

"Perhaps we might take up where we left off last week," I suggested. "There's no need to start from scratch every time."

"We were talking about the possibility of an apartment we could use as an HQ," Comrade Lustig said, "somewhere where the committee could organize itself, which could be manned day and night in an emergency. Or at least a room, or a basement."

He spoke standing up, and when he had finished he sat down. Lustig is a little man, with puffy bags under his brown eyes, and a perpetual look of silent amazement on his face, as though he has just been called some terrible name in the street for no reason. Zevulun Grill, a flaming redhead, whose two missing front teeth give him the look of a dangerous brawler, added:

"We were also talking about a radio transmitter. And, as usual, we did nothing about it."

Ephraim Nehamkin, the curly-haired radio technician, nodded his head twice, as if Grill's words corresponded precisely to what one might expect from him, and anyone who harbored any illusions about him had better wake up before it was too late.

"Ephraim," I said, "it might be better if we conducted our discussion by means of words, rather than dumb show. Perhaps you'd like to tell us all what has made you so angry?"

"We've got one," Ephraim growled. "It's always the same old story with us: we talk about the past instead of the present."

"What have we got?"

"A radio. Didn't I say last week that I was putting a battery transmitter together for you. Anyway," he suddenly exploded, "what the hell do we need a transmitter for? To beg the English to do us a favor and stay here to save us from the Arabs? To prick the conscience of the world with biblical quotations? To explain nicely to the Arabs that they mustn't kill us, otherwise there'll be no one to cure their ringworm and their trachoma? What's the point of this whole committee, with two doctors and a bus driver? What the hell do you think you're doing?"

"Don't get so steamed up," Nachtshe said, smiling. "Simmer down. Everything'll be all right."

Nachtshe is a slim, strongly built young man who is a sort of occasional leader in one of the Socialist youth movements. His short trousers displayed his muscular, hairy legs. His hair was tousled. You must have heard of his father, Professor Guttmacher, the expert on Oriental mysticism, a world-famous scholar who is semiparalyzed. Sometimes, in the evenings, Nachtshe and his young charges light campfires in the woods, carry out night exercises with quarterstaves, or make the neighborhood re-echo to songs of rage and longing sung to Russian tunes.

"Instead of poking fun, why don't you tell us what you suggest," Grill demanded of Ephraim Nehamkin.

"An attack," Ephraim erupted in a deep growl, as if his heart were hoarse with emotion. "Organize a raid. That's what I suggest. Take the initiative. Go out to the villages. Shu'afat. Sheikh Jarrah. Issawiya. Burn down the mufti's house in the middle of the night. Or blow up the Najjara HQ. Hoist the blue-and-white flag on the minaret of Nabi Samwil, or even on the Temple Mount. Why not. Let's make them tremble, at long last. Let *them* start sending *us* deputations. Let *them* plead. What's the matter with us all."

At this point, Dr. Kipnis, the vet from Tel Arza, intervened. He was standing with his back to the window, wearing a gray battle-dress blouse and neatly pressed long khaki trousers. As he spoke, he kneaded his brown cap between his fingers, and he looked not at Ephraim but at Mrs. Litvak, as though she—or her black coif—were giving him hints on some vital principle.

"It seems to me, ladies and gentlemen," he began cautiously, "that we are venturing along the wrong road. I may claim to have some acquaintance with the neighboring villages."

"Of course you have," Ephraim whispered venomously. "Only they know you, too, and other Jews like you, and that's what's whetted their appetite."

"Excuse me," said Dr. Kipnis, "I didn't mean to get into an argument with you about your principles. At any rate, not at this moment. All I wanted to do was to try to evaluate the present situation, to discover what the possible lines of development are, and to make one or two suggestions."

"Let's get organized!" Comrade Lustig suddenly exclaimed, and he even thumped on the table. "Quit chattering! Let's get organized!"

As for me, the chairman, it was only with some difficulty that I resisted the temptation to return Nachtshe's fleeting smile, which was apparently directed at me alone.

"Dr. Kipnis," I said, "please continue. And it would be better if we did not keep interrupting one another."

"Very well. We have three possibilities open to us," said Dr.

Kipnis, raising three piteously thin fingers and folding one of them back with each possibility he enumerated. "Firstly, the committee hands the whole country over to the Arabs, and we have to choose between a new Masada and a new Yavneh. Second, it recommends partition, and the Arabs either accept the verdict or have it imposed on them with the help of foreign powers. Not the British, naturally. In this eventuality, one of our tasks will be to be prepared for possible riots and—at the same time—to attempt to restore good relations with the Arab districts that surround us. To bury the hatchet, as they say."

"They must be driven out," Ephraim said wearily, "expelled, kicked out, what's the matter with you, let them go back to the desert where they belong. This is Jerusalem, Mr. Kipnis, the Land of Israel—maybe you've forgotten that, with your appeasement."

"Thirdly," the vet continued, apparently determined not to be deflected from his purpose by provocations, "total war. And in that case our local committee will not, of course, function independently, but will await orders from the national institutions."

"That's what I said," Lustig exclaimed delightedly, "we must get organized, organized, and again organized!"

"Dr. Kipnis," I insisted, "what exactly are you suggesting?"

"Yes, well. First of all, a delegation representing us, the Jewish districts of northwest Jerusalem, approaches the Jewish Agency, to explain the special difficulties arising from our geographical situation and to request instructions. I propose Dr. Nussbaum, Mrs. Litvak, and, naturally, Comrade Nachtshe. Second, a meeting with our neighbors. I mean the sheikhs and mukhtars. I am willing to volunteer myself for this assignment. We inform them that we, the inhabitants of the Jewish districts of northwest Jerusalem, will not take any hostile initiative, but will continue, no matter what happens to maintain neighborly relations. So that if they nevertheless choose the course of bloodshed, all the responsibility will fall on them, and they must accept the consequences and cannot complain that they have not been warned. And now I suggest that Comrade Nachtshe talk to us about the defense of our districts. He should at least outline the plans, on the assumption that we may have to withstand a local assault on our own for a while. That is all I have to say."

"Then I suggest that we start erecting barricades," said Lustig, and suddenly he burst out laughing. "Imagine— our Kerem Avraham as the Zionist Stalingrad."

"Let's be practical, please," I urged. "We still have to settle the allocation of tasks and so on."

"There's no risk," Ephraim remarked sadly, "of anyone here being practical. Forget it. Not here. Not in this *Judenrat.*"

"I must insist," I said, with unnecessary sharpness.

Meanwhile, Nachtshe had returned from the kitchen. He had clearly made himself at home. He was chewing vigorously on a thick sandwich. From his bloodstained chin I detected that, besides cheese and onion, he had put some slices of tomato in it.

"Sorry," he said with a grin. "I was famished, so I raided your icebox. I didn't want to ask permission, in case I interrupted your symposium." As he spoke, he dropped crumbs shamelessly on the armchair and the rug. More crumbs clung to his mustache.

"Feel free," I said.

"Good," said Nachtshe. "Have we got over the ideological stage yet? Right. Well, then."

Nobody spoke. Even Comrade Lustig was silent for once.

"The English are going to pull out soon. That much is certain. And we're going to have problems. But I don't want to talk about the problems now. I'm here to talk about solutions. Well, then. We've got arms in the neighborhood. Only light arms at the moment. And thank God we've got a few boys who know what to do with them. We needn't go into details now. Sonya. Mrs. Litvak, I mean. You get all the old dears together in your apartment tomorrow—as you were today—to sew bags. Never mind what from. That's instead of knitting balaclava helmets for the troops. Balaclava helmets you can knit us another time. I need a thousand, twelve hundred bags. The youngsters can fill them with sand and gravel. They'll be used firstly for armed positions, then for windows in general. Protection against bullets and

shells. Next. As of tomorrow morning, we keep a permanent
watch on Schneller from the Kolodnys' balcony. That's another
job for the youngsters. And another lookout post on Kapitanski's roof, toward Sheikh Jarrah and the police training school.
I want Litvak to release twenty or thirty boys from the school
for this, so that we know precisely what Tommy and Ahmed
are both up to. Next. In the event that the English do pull out,
or if we see that they're going to hand over the keys to King
Abdullah's Bedouins, my boys will chip in and take over Schneller. That's got nothing to do with your committee, of course, but
I wanted you to know, so that you can sleep soundly at night.
Next. Communications. Ephraim. Tonight we'll come and look
over what you've been putting together there, and if it's really
what you say it is, then we'll tune you into Hagganah HQ. You
and Lustig will take turns listening in, twenty-four hours a day.
You'll sit quietly with the earphones on, and you won't argue
with each other; you won't get up unless you need to take a piss
or you have something to report to me. Now you, Grill. Listen
carefully. There are two things. First, start collecting gardening tools from all over the district in your shed. Never mind
whether people like it or not—requisition them. Whatever you
can find, except watering cans. Spades, forks, hoes, everything. At a signal from me—as you were; at a signal from an
authorized person—you and a few other neighbors grab the
tools and get cracking, dig up the road at the bottom of
Zephaniah Street, at the corner of Amos and Geulah, and the
Tel Arza road. Dig in zigzags. Yes. Trenches. So they don't hit
us with armor. And another thing, Grill. The HQ will be in
your bedroom. That's because your house has three exits.
You've got two days to get your wife out before we move in.
Now, Kipnis. You, Kipnis, are not going to talk to the
sheikhs and mukhtars. We don't want to risk any of the boys to
go and rescue your mutilated corpse. Let's face it, doctor, after
the war—by all means, why not, you're welcome to go and
smoke the pipe of peace with them, and I'll even come with you
for a good shish kebab. But in the meantime, if you're so set on

your idea, why not send every sheikh a special-delivery registered letter proposing good neighborly relations. Go ahead. If it works, I shall personally beat my sword into a dagger. But till then, you just stay here and take charge of the grocer, the greengrocer, and the kerosene man for me. Make sure they bring in whatever they can get hold of. Only no black market and no panic. That's right, Sonya: hoarding. You heard. I want all the women to lay in supplies of canned food, biscuits, kerosene, sugar, as much as they can. Now let's talk about water. I want all the members of this committee—yes, all of you—to go from house to house and help move the water cisterns down from the roofs into the cellars. And then make sure they're full. And I want Almaliah to start making us tanks in his workshop. Water tanks, Ephraim, that's what I'm talking about, so don't jump off your chair. To begin with, anyway. Now our host. Nussbaum. You go to old Mrs. Vishniak's pharmacy tomorrow morning and check exactly what she's got and what she needs. Whatever she's short of, order it, at the committee's expense. And plenty of it. Your apartment here will be the first-aid station, with morphine and dressings and whatever else you need. Another thing: you, Grill, gradually start getting in supplies of gasoline for us. From your bus company or out of the rocks, I don't care where it comes from. Fifty gallons or so. The children are to collect several hundred bottles, and we— that's Ephraim and I—we'll start mixing cocktails. Nussbaum, you said you had something to suggest on this subject? Very good. But not now. It doesn't interest everyone. Now, is there anything else?"

"Yes," said Lustig, "we need to have some cyanide or something. If the Arabs do manage to get through despite everything, they'll butcher the children and violate the women. We need to be organized against even the worst eventualities."

"We're not in Warsaw now," said Nachtshe. "And if you come out with things like that outside this room, you'll be in trouble. And that's that."

"All right," muttered Comrade Lustig. "I've got the message."

"Any more questions?"

"Excuse me," I said. "What happens if the English don't pull out? Or if they hand over the whole of Jerusalem en bloc to King Abdullah?"

"If they don't go, they don't go. Don't ask me questions like that, ask Ben-Gurion. Who do you think I am? Right, then. Sonya, give these good people another cup of coffee. They're looking a bit pale all of a sudden. Dr. Nussbaum, thank you for your hospitality. I must be off now. As of lunchtime the day after tomorrow, anyone who wants me can find me or Akiva or Yigal in the Grills' bedroom. By the way, if the English come along to search or ask questions, don't forget that this district has a committee. Nobody knows me. I don't exist. Let the doctors talk to them. Nussbaum or Kipnis. That's all. Only don't worry, anybody: we haven't lost our hope, as the song says. Just one thing more: Ephraim, I want to say I'm sorry. If I've upset you at all, I didn't mean to. And now, good-bye."

He brushed the crumbs from his mustache, wiped the tomato juice off his chin, bared his perfect teeth in a broad grin, and left.

Hans Kipnis remarked softly:

"What can one say?"

Ephraim said:

"Don't you start all over again. You heard what you were told: you can write letters to all the sheikhs in the neighborhood."

Sonya Litvak said:

"Pray God he takes care of himself. What boys!"

Comrade Lustig:

"Like Cossacks. Always talking instead of getting organized. They'll end up by killing us, heaven forbid!"

And Dr. Nussbaum, dear Mina, your Dr. Nussbaum, said in an indulgent, ironic tone:

"With your permission, it seems to me that the meeting is over."

In my mind's eye I followed this angry, lissome youth as

he disappeared from my apartment into the evening shadows. Nachtshe, short for Menahem or Nahum, Guttmacher, in his shorts, with his tousled hair, his eyes the color of late-summer dust, his loneliness. No doubt he went back to his comrades, in the woods or the wadi. Dropping with fatigue, perhaps. Probably he hasn't eaten a proper meal in days. And I asked myself: Has he known a woman, and if so, was it the same way as he tore into the sandwich, or was he perhaps trembling, confused?

And what could I do, Mina? What would you have done in my place? Trusted him and said nothing? Rebuked him and made fun of his bravado? Tried to analyze his dreams? Or perhaps fallen in love and conquered him for yourself?

I feel at a loss. Perhaps I should have silenced him, squashed his arrogance, called him to order? But could I have done it? In my heart of hearts, as you must surely have guessed, I had made him into the secret child you bore me and hid from me in a kibbutz somewhere in Galilee, or in the valleys; he had grown up surrounded by horses and agricultural machinery, and now he had come up to Jerusalem to rescue us all. I must stop and conclude this letter at once.

Only this: when my visitors had left, while I was still washing the coffee cups and picking the crumbs off my rug, the sky suddenly altered. A damp, icy rage began to blow up from the northwest. Gone was the savage blue. Jerusalem darkened. Subsided. Then the first drops, and it was wintry night outside. I shall also start collecting empty bottles. At any rate, Nachtshe will have to come to me to learn what to put into a Molotov cocktail if he wants it to blow up an armored car. I shall stop now. I'll take a pill. I won't go to bed, I'll spend this rainy night in my laboratory. Time is short. Henry Gurney, the British administration secretary, is on the radio urging the members of all communities in Palestine to calm down and maintain law and order until the situation improves. The "Voice of Jerusalem" announcer translates into official Hebrew: It is strictly forbidden to congregate in the streets, it is forbidden to interfere with the normal course of life.

September 8, 1947

Dear Mina,

The rain was light. Not the autumn rains yet, but a slow night drizzle. This morning the city brightened again, and a damp, fresh smell rose from the gardens. Even the falling leaves today were washed clean of dust. I could not get to sleep until just before the dawn. I did not even want to. An idea for a formula kept running through my head after yesterday's meeting, a simple, fascinating chemical possibility, and I could not relax. From time to time the pain became so intense that the desk, the ceiling, and the walls went misty. I deliberately did without an injection, because it seemed to me that it was precisely in this mist that my hope of clarifying my idea lay. You are smiling. The notion of illumination or inspiration coming out of a fog of pain may strike you as immature romanticism. So be it. I even jotted down in the night various symbols and figures on a scrap of paper. Suddenly, long after midnight, as the Schneller clock struck three or two, with my tongue and palate parched from thirst and pain, in a mood of ecstatic longing, I had the feeling that I had discovered the way to produce a chain reaction by an amazingly simple means, with no need for fantastic temperatures. A way of releasing energy from the cheapest and commonest substances. It may be precisely thus that the elemental life force may erupt with holy dreadfulness in the mind of, say, a composer who hears in the night the strains of his final symphony, which is not yet his, and who knows that there is no way of capturing it in notes. Ecstasy and despair. I can decipher the meaning of all this: it is the rumor of approaching death. The bit of paper I scrawled on in the night is in front of me now, and it is all nonsense. Scientific ravings in the style of Jules Verne or H. G. Wells. It is worthless. What is more, at the time I was so feverish that I could see the Dead Sea blazing in the eastward-facing window, illuminating the night with a kind of mineral glare as of hellfire, and I did not doubt for a moment that my nocturnal discovery was already operating in the outside world. In a twilight. You and Uri were con-

cocting something in the laboratory. You and Jasmine and
Nachtshe on the rug, making love and calling me to join you.
And outside a mushroom of fire bursting into the heart of the
night sky, while I, with the help of a simple mirror, followed it
from here, from my room, over the mountains and across the
valleys. I fell asleep fully dressed again, toward dawn, on the
floor of my laboratory, and in my sleep I knew that the time
had come to send for Dushkin, and with him came Rabbi Zweik,
the sick mystic from Safed, and together they tried to talk you
into agreeing that the only way to arrest the tumor in my glands
was to operate and remove my head, while you maintained strenuously that a heavy concentration of X-rays directed at a mixture
of sodium and phosphorus would unleash a chain reaction that
would save my life and also radically alter the overall military
situation.

In the morning, after my coffee and a shave, I found I had a
slight temperature and also some blurring of vision. I could
read the newspaper, and I can still write. But when I reached
out to pick up a piece of buttered toast from the kitchen table,
I missed and upset a pot of yogurt. I may add, with no reference at all to this development, that a British reconnaissance
plane has been circling low over Jerusalem since the early hours
of this morning, perhaps because it was announced semioffi-
cially in this morning's paper that the commission of inquiry
will indeed recommend the partition of the country, and that
Jerusalem and Bethlehem will be under international control,
and will not be handed over either to the Jews or to the Arabs. It
was Uri who told me, on his way home from school, that without Jerusalem there would be no Hebrew state, or else a terrible
war would break out between the Hagganah and the Palmach, on
the one hand, and the Irgun and the Stern Group on the other,
and that that was precisely what the British were planning.

Incidentally, he is now in command of my laboratory. He
does whatever he likes. He made me comfortable on the sofa,
covered me with a woolen blanket, made me some lemon tea,
and even selected a record and put it on the phonograph to
please me. He also put a hot-water bottle on my feet. And

while I was lying there, too weak to object, the boy began un-
loading a crate of empty bottles. Then he went to the laboratory
to brew some concoction, chop off match heads, mix solutions.
I am gradually being driven out of my own home: Nachtshe
and Sonya Litvak in my kitchen, Uri in my laboratory, you in
my dreams. Soon I shall leave.

"Be careful there, Uri."

"I'm only doing what you showed me, Dr. Emanuel, don't
worry, I'm doing exactly what it says in your notes on the desk
here, and when you're better we'll work together again."

I am at peace. Mozart on the phonograph, and from the
laboratory sounds of test tubes, the spirit lamp, simmering.

Outside, at the window, another early-autumn evening.

The simple, searing, trivial things, what urgent information
are they straining to convey to me. The fading light, Mina,
the cawing of crows, a yelping dog, a ringing bell, these things
have been since time immemorial and will go on being forever.
I can even hear a train hooting in the distance, toward Emek
Refaim. And a baby crying. And the woman next door singing
a Polish song. The simple, familiar, trivial things—why do they
seem to be taking their leave of me tonight. And what am I to
do except turn to the wall and die at once. At once, too, like
an electric shock, this limpid certainty strikes me: there is a
meaning. There is a reason. Perhaps there is a way. And there
is still some time left for me to try to discover the meaning, the
purpose. Only a sadness continues to gnaw: I have lived some
forty years. I was banished, more or less, from one country to
another. Here I have even achieved something, to the best of my
modest ability. Here, too, I loved you. And now you are gone
and I am still here. But not for long. I am being rudely banished
from this place, too. And the conclusion, Mina, the moral, the
reason? What, as they say here, is the matter at hand?

Maybe this: Autumn outside, and everything is closing in.
Something needs to be done. It needs to be done immediately,
hopeless though it may be. What it is, I wish I knew. The present moment—is irrevocable. It has been, and it is no more.

I remember: A summer's day in Vienna. Early afternoon.

A nip in the air. Wispy clouds suspended in a pale, almost gray sky. In the street there is a subtle blend of smells, fried meat, garbage, and flowering gardens. Perhaps also the perfume of passing women. The cafés are crowded. Through their windows can be seen gentlemen in light suits, smoking, arguing, or doing business. Others are leafing through magazines or doing the crossword puzzle. Some are playing chess. I am on my habitual way home from the faculty library. My heart is empty. There is a slight temptation, not a real desire, to go and spend the evening with Charlotte or Margot on the first floor of the Weary Heart. As I pass the bridge, I pause for a moment. There, just by the bridge, stand a pair of Negro beggars. One is beating a drum while the other is wailing a kind of tune. There is a hat on the sidewalk with a few pennies in it. Neither of them is young. Neither of them is old, either. It is as if they are outside the European age scale, subject to another biological clock.

I stop and linger, watching them from a short distance away. Not long ago I took a course in anthropology, yet I believe these are the first Negroes I have ever seen. Outside the circus, of course. Yes, they are woolly-haired. Coffee-skinned, not cocoa-colored. A slight shudder ripples through me. I brush aside a fleeting mental image of the shape of their sexual organs. The taller of the two, the one who is wailing or singing, has a pierced nose but no nose ring. The other one's nose is so amazingly long and flat that it revives the suppressed image of their sexual organs. I can neither leave nor take my eyes off them. I am chained to the spot, as it were, by fear, fascination, and disgust. They are standing with their backs to the bridge and the water. One is wearing sandals held together with bits of string, the other a pair of large, worn-out shoes and no socks. I am suddenly overcome with shame, like the time when, as a child, I was caught gaping at the low neckline of my Aunt Grete's dress. Hurriedly I toss a coin into the hat.

Something is urging me, after all, to head for the Weary Heart, to spend the evening with Charlotte or Margot, or even both together for a change. But my feet are rooted to the

ground. I look at my watch, pretending to be waiting for someone. And I wait. In any case, without prior arrangement by
telephone there can be no Margot or Charlotte.

Just then a group of youngsters in the uniform of a national
youth movement draws to a halt beside the black beggars. I am
fixed to the spot. They are quiet-looking boys, handsome, thirsty
for knowledge, all with close-cropped hair, and from their
bronzed skin one senses that their prolonged hikes in the mountains and forests have instilled in them an element of military
toughness, although without undermining their fundamental
good manners. Then their leader steps forward. He is a short,
taut, athletic man of middle years, with ruthlessly cropped gray
hair and thin, molded lips. There is something about his gait
or the set of his shoulders that suggests that he would be
equally at home on a river, alone in the mountains, or in a
spacious mansion. The sort of man that my father longs for his
only son to resemble, at least in outward appearance. The
leader is wearing the same clean, neatly pressed uniform, dis-
tinguished only by his lanyard and by the colors of his badges
and epaulets. He starts to explain something to the youths. His
voice is clipped. Each short sentence ends in a bark. As he
speaks, he waves a finger in the air; he has no compunction
about pointing it an inch or two from the head of the nearer
of the two Negroes. He indicates the outline of the skull. He
emphasizes and demonstrates. I edge closer, to catch what he
is saying. He is expatiating in a Bavarian accent on the subject
of racial difference. His short lecture, as far as I can follow it,
is a blend of anthropology, history, and ideology. The rhythm:
staccato.

Some of his charges produce identical notebooks and pencils
from the pockets of their brown shirts and take eager notes.
The two Negroes, meanwhile, grin relaxedly from ear to ear.
They roll their eyes ingratiatingly. They are brimming with
good will, perhaps stupidity, innocent gaiety, respect, and gratitude. I must admit that at this moment they look to me like a
pair of stray dogs about to be taken in by a new master. And
all the while the leader is employing such words as evolution,

selection, degeneration. From time to time he snaps his fingers loudly, and the two Negroes respond as one man with high-pitched laughs and flashing, milk-white teeth.

The leader holds out his thumb and forefinger, measures their foreheads without touching them, then measures his own and says, *"Also."*

The short lecture concludes with the word *"Zivilisation."*

The boys put their pencils and notebooks back in their pockets. The spell is broken. Silently they go on their way. To me they look very worried as they march briskly away downstream, toward the city center and the museums. For an instant they resemble a military patrol, a forward-reconnaissance party that has stumbled on an outlying detachment of enemy troops, disengaged and retreated to seek reinforcements.

The spell was broken. I, too, resumed my homeward journey. On the way, ruminating, I was almost inclined to agree: Europe is indeed in danger. The jungle races are indeed on the threshold. Our music, our laws, our sophisticated system of commerce, our subtle irony, our sensitivity to double meanings and ambiguities—all are in mortal peril. The jungle races are on the threshold. And surely history teaches us that the Mongol hordes have already swept once out of the depths of Asia and reached the very banks of the Danube and the gates of Vienna.

At home, Lisel was silently serving dinner. Father was also silent. His face was overcast. Business was going from bad to worse. There was an ugly atmosphere in the city. Things would never be the same again. On the radio, a minister was vowing to crush Communism, cosmopolitanism, and other destructive elements. The government had displayed great forbearance toward the parasites, the minister declared, and had been repaid only with ingratitude. Father turned it off. Still he said nothing. Perhaps he privately blamed the Eastern Jews who were pouring in in droves, bringing us nothing but trouble. I, too, ate my dinner in silence, and retired to my room. Margot, her shoulders, her neck, was still at the edge of my thoughts. And what could I tell Father? He was always convinced that his only son was up to his neck in student flirtations and had no idea what was going on in the city and the world.

At midnight, I went downstairs to the kitchen for a glass of water and found him sitting there alone, in his dressing gown, silently smoking, with his eyes closed.

"Are you in pain again, Father?"

He opened an eye.

"What are you blathering about, Emanuel?"

And after a short silence:

"I got some Zionist prospectuses in the mail today. Brochures from Palestine. With pictures."

I shrugged, excused myself, said good night, and returned to my room.

Precisely a week later, the letter arrived.

It was anonymous. On the envelope Father's name was typed, in correct style, with the address of his factory. He opened it in the presence of his secretary, Inge, and suddenly his world went dark. Inside the envelope there was a small sheet of good-quality notepaper, with a watermark and gold-embossed edges, but with no heading, date, or signature. There was just a single word, inscribed in the very middle of the page, in a fine, rounded hand: *Jude*. And an exclamation point.

What do you think of that, Inge, Father asked as soon as he had recovered his voice. It's a fact, Inge replied politely, and she added: There's nothing to get upset about, Herr Doktor. It's just a plain fact.

Father muttered, with bloodless lips: Have I ever denied it, Inge, I have never attempted to deny it.

In less than a month, an eager buyer was found for the house with its beautiful garden. A partnership in Linz purchased the factory. Inge was frostily dismissed, while Lisel was packed off to her village in the mountains with an old suitcase full of Mother's clothes.

Father and I had no difficulty in getting immigration certificates for Palestine from the British consul himself: the privilege of wealth.

Father had already managed to collect information and draw up detailed plans for the establishment of a small factory in a new town not far from Tel Aviv. He had already learned something about conditions there and had even made certain calculations. But from time to time, he would talk about his longing to be speedily reunited with Mother in a world where there was no evil. Old family friends still tried to reason with him, arguing, pleading with him to reconsider. They were of the opinion that shock and humiliation had provoked a self-destructive impulse in him. The Viennese Jews firmly believed at that time that everything could be explained by psychology, and that the situation would soon improve because whole nations do not suddenly take leave of their senses.

Father was like a rock: gray and unshakable.

Nevertheless, he adamantly refused to admit that Dr. Herzl had foreseen all this. On the contrary, he argued, it was Dr. Herzl and his friends who had plunged us all into this mess.

But a year later, in Ramat Gan, he changed his mind completely. He even joined the General Zionist party.

I received my medical diploma four days before our departure, on the morning we got our visas. I was summoned to the rector's office. They explained politely that they did not think I would feel comfortable at the official graduation ceremony, they were bound to take into account the general mood of the students, and so they had decided to hand me my diploma informally, in a plain buff envelope. Wide vistas, they said, opened up for a young doctor in western Asia. The ignorance, dirt, and disease there were unbelievable. They even mentioned Albert Schweitzer, who was healing lepers in the middle of the jungle in Africa. They mistakenly stressed that Schweitzer, too, was of Jewish extraction. Then they turned to the bitter feelings I must be harboring in my heart, and begged me to remember, even when I was far away, how much Vienna had given me, and not only that she had humiliated me. They wished me *bon voyage* and, after a slight hesitation, shook hands.

I do indeed remember. And what I feel in my heart is neither bitterness nor humiliation but—how can I write it when I can see before me the expression of cold irony on your mouth and the cigarette smoke pouring contemptuously from your nostrils—Jewish sorrow and rage. No, not in my heart, in the marrow of my bones. I won't make homemade explosives for the Hagganah. I'll make them the ultimate explosive. I shall surprise Uri, Nachtshe, Ben-Gurion himself. If only my strength holds out. I myself shall be the jungle races on the threshold. I am the Mongol hordes.

I'm joking again, as usual, at the wrong time, as usual, joking without being funny, in my usual ludicrous way.

We reached Palestine by way of the Tirol, Trieste, Piraeus, and a French steamship. Father did indeed set up a candy factory in Ramat Gan that became well known. He even married again, a husky, bejeweled refugee from southern Poland. Perhaps it was his wife's influence that made him become an active member of the General Zionist Council and of several committees.

He occasionally sends me money. Unnecessarily. I have enough of my own.

Twice a year, at Passover and the New Year, I used to visit them and spend a few days among the vases, tea sets, and chandeliers. In the evenings there was a stream of visitors: middle-aged men of affairs, party workers and businessmen, middlemen who enjoyed *choolant* and snuff and cracked bawdy jokes in three languages with chesty, man-of-the-world laughter. "Felix," they would say as they winked at Father, "Reb Pinhasel, when are you going to marry off the boy? When are you going to initiate him into the mysteries of business? What are they saying about him, a Socialist you've got in your family?" While Father's wife, with a gold watch held between the jaws and tail of a gold snake wrapped around her freckled wrist, would leap to my defense: "What do you mean, business? Business nothing. Our Emanuel will soon be a professor at the Hadassah, and we'll all have to line up for three months before he'll so much as look at us, and even then only as a special favor."

I did indeed work at Hadassah for a while and put up uncomplainingly with Alexander Dushkin's rumbustious despotism. One evening he summoned me to his home in Kiryat Shemuel, and at the end of the tea, the jokes, and the gossip, I was informed: "Next week you're being handed over lock, stock, and barrel to the government of Palestine. To the bacteriological department. They've issued me an ultimatum to hand over to them some first-rate Svidrigaïlov who'll keep an eye on the whole water supply of Jerusalem and the surrounding area. So I sold you to them right away. Free, gratis, and for nothing. I didn't even claim my thirty pieces of silver. The pay's not bad, and you'll be able to travel around at His Majesty's expense, from Hebron to Jericho and from Ramallah to Rosh Ha'ayin. You'll have your own private empire. You'll like O'Leary. He's an educated, cultivated sort of chap. Not like me, a Tartar cannibal. You and I, Nussbaum, let's speak frankly, well, you're more the phlegmatic type, while I'm a madman—anyway, we're horses of a different color. I just want to say, Emanuel," Dushkin suddenly roared, as his eyes filled with tears "that you'll always find my door and my heart open to you. Day or night. I really love you. Only don't let me down. Now what's the matter with your tea? Drink it up!"

So I took my leave of Samovar and joined Edward O'Leary and my dear friend Dr. Antoine al-Mahdi. And I started my tours of the springs and wells.

Two or three times a week, we went out into the country. We passed beautiful gardens, olive groves and vineyards, and tiny vegetable-patches. We saw minarets reaching upward from the hilltops. The three of us together forced our way through thorn hedges and tramped for hours on end to inspect some far-flung spring or Godforsaken well. The smell of dung and ashes brought me a sensation of peace and calm. Occasionally Antoine would say apologetically: "The cattle are cattle and so are the fellahin. You can't tell the difference." If O'Leary jokingly asked him, "Do you enjoy the thought that one day every villager will wear a tweed jacket and tie like you?," he would reply, "That would be against nature." Edward would chuckle: "And what about the Jews? In the kibbutzim you can find lawyers milking cows and mucking out." Antoine would flash me an affectionate smile: "The Jews are a remarkable people. They always go against nature."

We used to go to King Solomon's Pools. To Nahal Arugot in the Judean Desert. To the Elah Valley. We collected specimens in glass phials and took them back to the laboratory in Julian's Way to examine them under the microscope. O'Leary would lend us books by English travelers from the last century who described the desolate state of the country in all its details.

"How does she do it?" O'Leary would ask in tones of amusement. "How does this worn-out, barren old girl make them all fall madly in love with her? I was once in southern Persia: exactly the same miserable hills, dotted with gray rocks, with a few olive trees and pieces of old pottery. Nobody crossed half the world to conquer *them*."

"Woman comes from the earth," Dr. Mahdi said in a velvety whisper, in careful English. "Man comes from the rain. And desire comes from the Devil. Look at the Jordan. For thousands of years it has flowed into the Dead Sea, where there is neither fish nor tree, and it never comes out again. There's nothing like that in Persia, Edward, and the moral of the story is: if it's hard to get in, then it's hard to get out."

I would contribute an occasional remark, such as:

"The Land of Israel is full of simple symbols. Not only the Jordan and the Dead Sea—even the malaria and bilharzia here take on a symbolic significance."

"You two use similar words to express totally different sentiments. We all three do, actually."

"Is that really so?" O'Leary would murmur politely. He would refrain from offering an explanation and would deftly change the subject.

*

Antoine ran a private practice in the afternoons and evenings in Katamon, and I had my home clinic in Kerem Avraham. I learned to cultivate polite relations with my neighbors
and to be a good listener in hard times. I lost track of the hours
I spent battling against diphtheria and dysentery. If I was called
out at night or over the weekend, when I was busy in my
amateur laboratory or listening to music, I never complained.
If the children made fun of me in the street for my German
ways, I never lost my temper. I fulfilled my obligations, more
or less.

Until you and I met in Arza, that is. And until my illness
appeared.

So there you have a résumé of the story of my life. Some of
it you knew already, and the rest you could probably have
deduced, in your usual way, from an analysis of my behavior.

Now I shall return to my observations.

Uri has gone off, probably on instructions from one of
Nachtshe's mysterious assistants, to stand on the Kapitanski
brothers' roof and keep watch on the Sheikh Jarrah district and
the traffic on the Ramallah road. And I, too, am on the lookout, sitting here on my balcony. The details I am amassing will
be of no military use: A Jerusalem street vendor, what he sells,
how he sells, who buys. My lower-middle-class Eastern European neighbors, and why they quarrel so much among themselves. And what, exactly, their communal ideal is. Their children, what is new about them and what is ancient. And the
youths, boys like Nachtshe, Yigal, and Akiva, how, and with
what measure of success, they all attempt to dress, talk, and
joke on the basis of some abstract archetype from Galilee, from
the Palmach, a venerated image of the pioneering hero.

And I myself: apart from my impending death and the code
of pains and symptoms, why do I sometimes abhor these brave
boys, and secretly call them "Asiatics," and sometimes feel a
powerful love for them as though I have an unidentified son
among them, a dark-skinned, barefoot, physically tough young
man, an expert with machines and weapons, contemptuous of
words, contemptuous of me and my worries? I don't know.

More rhetorical questions of an observer: What is regarded as funny here. What is considered embarrassing. What do they talk about and what do they pass over in silence. Who has come to Jerusalem, and where from, what did each of them hope to find here, and what has he actually found. Helena Grill compared to Sonya Litvak. The poet Nehamkin from the electrical and radio repair shop as contrasted with Comrade Lustig. What did they hope to find here and what have they actually found. And I don't exclude myself from the question.

Other questions: What is transitory in Jerusalem, and what is permanent. Why are the colors different here, the autumn colors and the evening colors. And on another level: What are the intentions of the British. Is there going to be a political vacuum. What are the real limits of our power, and how much is simply delusion and arrogance. Is Dr. Mahdi the real, deadly enemy. Is it weakness of will in me that I cannot desire his death, and that I keep trying to think up arguments that might convince him. Everything leads me on to the final point, to the single question: What is going to happen. What lies in store for us.

Because apart from this, what else have I got to think about? The sunsets, perhaps. The embers of my love for you. Doubts and hesitations. Pathetic preparations. Worries.

Mina. Where are you now, tonight. Come back.

These last words may seem to you like a cry for help. That was not what I meant. Forgive me. I'm sorry.

Tuesday, September 9

Dear Mina,

This morning I went to the Jewish Agency to hand in my report on readily available chemicals that may have military uses. On a separate sheet I offered some suggestions, even though it seemed to me that there was nothing new in them, and that any chemist in the university on Mount Scopus would have indicated precisely the same possibilities. My appointment was for nine o'clock, and I was a few minutes early. On the way, a fine drizzle lashed my cheeks. Later, the rain began to beat heavily on the windows of the office. They relieved me of the cardboard folder, thanked me, and then, to my great surprise, led me to Ben-Gurion's office. Somebody, apparently, had exaggerated and told him that there was a sick doctor here in Jerusalem who also happened to be an original chemist with daring ideas on the subject of explosives. In brief, he had asked to see me without further delay. Somebody had spun a meaningless myth about me.

Ben-Gurion began with an inquisition. I was asked about my origins, my family, was I related in any way to Nussbaum the well-known educationalist, were my views not close to those of the pacifist Brith Shalom movement. A volcanic man, with gestures reminiscent of Dushkin's, running backward and forward between the window and the bookcase, refusing to waste time on qualifications or reservations. He kept interrupting me almost before I had begun speaking, and goaded me on: The danger was imminent. A critical moment had been reached and we were almost without resources. What we lacked in materials we would make up in spirit and inventiveness. The Jewish genius, he said, would not let us down. We were up to our necks in it. Mr. Ben-Gurion, I tried to say, if you will permit me . . . But he did not permit me. On the contrary, on the contrary, he said, you will receive everything you need, and you will start work this very night. Make a note of that, Motke. Right. And now, out with it, doctor: tell us what you need.

And I stood there in confusion, with my arms held stiffly at my sides, and explained awkwardly that there appeared to be some misunderstanding. I was not a new Albert Einstein. I was simply a doctor with a modest competence in chemistry, who had volunteered a memorandum and some minor suggestions. The Jewish genius, by all means, but not me. A misunderstanding.

And so I came home, covered with shame and confusion. If only I could live up to their great expectations. Comrade Rubashov writes in the *Davar* newspaper that we will withstand the coming tests. My heart shuddered at these words. Tests. A real war is coming, we are without resources, and enthusiastic amateurs persist in using words like "tests." No doubt you will be smiling at this point, not at Comrade Rubashov's words but at mine: I wrote "a real war." I can imagine from far away the exhalation of smoke from your nostrils, the twist of your lips.

Last night I heard the drone of engines from the direction of Chancellor Street. Another British convoy on its way northward toward the port of Haifa, perhaps with blacked-out headlights. Is this the beginning of the evacuation? Are we being left to shift for ourselves? What if there is no truth in the image of the fearless fighter from the hills of Galilee? What if regular armies cross the Jordan and the deserts and we fail the test?

This morning from my balcony I watched Sarah Zeldin the kindergarten teacher, a little old Russian woman with a blue apron and a wrinkled face. It was immediately after I got back from the Agency. She was teaching the little children to sing:

> My pretty little village
> Set on the mountainside,
> With gardens, fields, and orchards
> Extending far and wide,

and I could see at that moment an image of the little village, the mountainside, the broad expanse. I was seized with terror. But the children, Samson and Arnon and Eitan and Mrs. Litvak's Meirab, made fun of their teacher and piped, "My silly little village."

What's going to happen, Mina.

"The Irgun and the Stern Group will blow up all the bridges and capture the mountain passes as soon as the English start pulling out," Uri said, "because the Hagganah can't make up their minds if they really want us to have a Hebrew state or if they want us to go on begging on our knees. Look I've got a khaki battle-dress, Dr. Emanuel, it's a present from Auntie Natalia because Mommy and Daddy are coming home today."

"Have you done your homework?"

"Yes, I did it at school during break. A drunk Australian soldier went into Kapitanski's to look for girls, and he left his jeep outside on the sidewalk. He took his pistol in with him, but he'll never see his magazines again. Look, I've brought them for you. Three full up and one only half. From a Tommy gun. Also, I found a small crack in the wall of Schneller, perhaps I can squeeze through it at nighttime, as soon as I get the order and some leaflets and dynamite. But don't breathe a word to Nachtshe because he always does whatever they tell him from the Hagganah, and nobody knows where Ephraim's disappeared to. So you decide."

"All right," I said. "No secret visits to Schneller. That's an order. And no more stealing from Australian soldiers. Otherwise I shall be very angry."

Uri gave me a look of amazement, nodded twice, came to a decision in his mind, and at the end of the silence requested permission to ask me a personal question.

"Go ahead," I said. And I added secretly: Little fool. Dear little idiot. If only I were your father. Only if I were your father I don't know what I would say or do to make you understand at last. Understand what. I don't know.

"Well," I said, "what's your question?"

"Never mind. You said no, so that's that."

"What I meant was, not without an order. Not before the time is right."

"Dr. Emanuel, is it the illness?"

"Is what the illness?"

"Is it the illness that makes your hands shake like that, and . . . one of your eyes is a bit closed, and it keeps blinking."

"I wasn't aware of that."

"Your illness . . . is it something very dangerous?"

"Why do you ask that, Uri?"

"Nothing. Only that if it is you ought to teach me about everything in the lab, so that if anything . . ."

"Anything what?"

"Nothing. Don't worry, Dr. Emanuel. Give me a list and a

shopping basket and I'll go to the greengrocer and to Ziegel's and get you anything you need."

"Why are you so concerned about me, child? Is it just because of the bomb I've still got to make?"

"No special reason. I don't know. That too, maybe."

"What too?"

"You're like an uncle to me. No, not an uncle, I mean some-one serious."

"What about your parents? And your Auntie Natalia?"

"They just laugh at me. They say my head's stuffed full of nonsense. You don't laugh."

"No. Why should I laugh?"

"You don't think my head's stuffed full of nonsense?"

"No, Uri, not nonsense. Or else we've both got the same sort of nonsense in our heads."

Silence.

And then:

"Dr. Emanuel, are you ever going to get better?"

"I don't think so, Uri."

"But I don't want you to die."

"Why me specially?"

"Because to you I'm not a crazy child, and because you never tell me lies."

"You must go now, child."

"But I don't want to."

"You must."

"All right. Whatever you say. But I'll come back again."

And from the doorway, from outside, a fraction of an instant before he closed the door behind him:

"Don't die."

His departure left behind a total silence. Inside the silence, the throbbing of the blood in my temples. What is there left for me to do now, Mina. Sit down, perhaps, and copy out for you a few items from this morning's paper, because in New York you probably lack details of what's going on here in Palestine. I shall skip the headlines. To judge from them, the British government is fed up with our bombs, our slogans, our delegations, our regular disgusted memorandums. One of these nights they will order a curfew, impose a deathly silence on Jerusalem, and in the morning we'll wake up to find that they have upped and gone.

And what then, Mina?

Hebrew traffic police have started to operate in Tel Aviv with the consent of the British governor. They have eight policemen working in two shifts. A thirteen-year-old Arab girl is to stand trial before a military court, accused of possessing a rifle in the village of Hawara, Nablus district. Some illegal immigrants from the *Exodus* are being deported to Hamburg, and they say they will fight to the last to resist disembarkation. Fourteen Gestapo men have been sentenced to death in Lübeck. Mr. Solomon Chmelnik of Rehovot has been kidnapped and badly beaten up by an extremist organization but has been returned safe and sound. The "Voice of Jerusalem" orchestra is going to be conducted by Hanan Schlesinger. Mahatma Gandhi's fast is in its second day. The singer Edith de Philippe will be unable to perform this week in Jerusalem, and the Chamber Theater has been obliged to postpone its performance of *You Can't Take It with You*. On the other hand, two days ago the new Colonnade Building on the Jaffa road was opened, containing, among others, the shops of Mikolinski and Freiman & Bein, and Dr. Scholl's chiropody. According to the Arab leader Musa Alami, the Arabs will never accept the partition of the country; after all, King Solomon ruled that the mother who was opposed to partition was the true mother, and the Jews ought to recognize the significance of this parable. And then again, Comrade Golda Myerson of the Jewish Agency Executive has proclaimed that the Jews will struggle for the inclusion of Jerusalem in the Hebrew state, because the Land of Israel and Jerusalem are synonymous in our hearts.

Late last night, an Arab set upon two Jewish girls in the vicinity of the Bernardiya Café, between Beit ha-Kerem and Bayit va-Gan. One of the girls escaped, and the other screamed for help until some of the local residents heard and succeeded in preventing the suspect's escape. In the course of investigations by Constable O'Connor, it emerged that the man is an employee of the Broadcasting Service and is distantly related to the influential Nashashibi family. Despite this, bail was denied, on account of the gravity of the alleged offense. In his defense, the prisoner declared that he had come out of the café drunk and had been under the impression that the two girls were prancing around naked in the dark.

One further item of news: Lieutenant Colonel Adderley, the presiding officer of the military court, hearing the case of Shlomo Mansoor Shalom, has found him guilty of distributing subversive pamphlets but found that he was of unsound mind. Mr. Gardewicz the probation officer requested that he not be sent to the lunatic asylum for fear of a deterioration in his condition, and pleaded with the judge that he be isolated in a private institution instead, so that his weak intellect might not be exploited by fanatics for their own criminal ends. Lieutenant Colonel Adderley regretted that he was unable to accede to Mr. Gardewicz's request since it was beyond his powers; he was obliged to commit the unfortunate man to custody pending a ruling by the High Commissioner, representing the Crown, on the possible exercise of lenience or clemency. I am copying out these tidbits of news to give you a clear idea of how things are here. No, that's not true: I am doing it to avoid sinking into all sorts of thoughts and emotions. On the radio, Cilla Leibowitz is giving a piano recital, and after the news we are promised a commentary by Gordus, and then some songs sung by Bracha Tsefira. I expect some of my neighbors will join me to listen to the news. Grill or Lustig, perhaps Litvak. Ephraim has not been seen around lately. Nachtshe has also disappeared. Only the poet Nehamkin strolls up and down Malachi Street, testing the substance of the stones of Jerusalem with the tip of his walking stick. Or perhaps he is tapping to discover a hollow spot, an ancient crevice in the rock on which we live, as is promised in his sacred scriptures. Happy is he who believes. My distant Jasmine, just as I was writing of a crevice in the rock a new pain came, unknown to me before, but resembling a certain piercing pleasure that you revealed to me not long before you left me. It appears that later in the autumn Dr. Nussbaum will begin to lose control of his bowel movements. He will have to be transferred to the Hadassah Hospital. From his window he may be able to watch the delusive desert light at dawn, and the shimmering skyline of the Mountains of Moab. Professor Dushkin will not stint on the morphine, nor will he try to spin out the death agonies unnecessarily; we have an unspoken agreement. Then there will be interference with breathing and vision. The heart will weaken. The consciousness will fade. From then on, the patient will only occasionally utter connected speech. He may ramble in German. He may whisper your name. How I hope he will not scream. His father and stepmother will come to take their leave of him, and he and his father will make a supreme effort and try to exchange an anecdote or two in German, even if it means speaking through clenched teeth. Afterward everything will go black, and he will struggle on for a few hours, a day or two at the most. It will be the rainy season. It is very likely that the January rain will already be falling on his grave on Sanhedriya or on the Mount of Olives. What is going to happen in Jerusalem he does not know. Nobody knows. It seems that Musa Alami and Golda Myerson will not budge from their positions. But in the end these hard times, too, will come to an end, and you will forget him and his troubles. Perhaps you have already forgotten. The one person who may remember as time goes by, with mixed feelings and perhaps even with longing, is Uri, the son of the printer Kolodny. I beg you, Mina, if Jerusalem survives and if these letters reach you and if you wish to dispose of them, please, in years to come, make an effort to find this Uri and to let him have them. I expect you are sick and tired of me now. Enough.

They are sitting on their balcony as I write, Kolodny the printer, his wife, his sister, Natalia, and our mutual neighbor the poet Nehamkin from the radio repair shop. They are surrounded by geraniums in cans and cacti growing in boxes of earth. Where is the child? I implore you to watch out for the child, in case he takes it into his head to sneak into the Schneller Barracks and launch a single-handed raid on the British army. I cannot see Uri. And they seem so unperturbed, sitting there chatting, talking about politics, I expect, apparently calm. I consider their calmness nothing short of outrageous. Above their heads there is a yellow light bulb around which the insects are swarming dementedly. Kolodny the printer is a pale-faced, equable man, yet even he for some reason chooses to dress in what is almost a military uniform: wide khaki shorts, a brass-buckled belt, long khaki socks held up just below the knees by garters. The poet Nehamkin, on the other hand, is wearing his habitual Polish suit and silk tie: ready at a moment's notice. It seems to me that with the exception of us two, everyone in the neighborhood is more or less a pioneering type. They are all positive, constructive characters, apparently incapable of panic. And death is not a possibility. They are chatting. Laughing, Mrs. Kolodny passes around a bowl of oranges, but nobody takes one, and she smiles distractedly. What is transitory in Jerusalem and what is permanent. What will Uri look back to nostalgically in times to come. Corrugated-iron sheds. Plywood partitions. Empty yogurt pots. European manners blended with a certain crude gaiety. A city of immigrants on the edge of the desert whose flat rooftops are all festooned with drying sheets. The inhabitants are always scurrying from place to place with sunglasses pushed up on their foreheads. A general expression of "I'm very busy but I'll stop a moment just for you." An expression of "Business calls." An expression of "Sorry, we'll have a nice long chat some other time, but right now I must dash, we all have to do our duty."

I am not complaining, Mina. These are crucial times, and soon there will be a war. Everybody, even a man like me, must do his best to make his modest contribution to the general effort. Perhaps it is true that this is the last generation to live in chains. But is it really the last generation. Is it true that different times will come that I shall not know.

Only the women, it seems to me, are not strong enough: lining up for rice, lining up for ice, waiting beside the kerosene cart, they seem to be on the point of fainting. And at times on summer afternoons, when Jerusalem is ablaze, swept by the desert light, I can hear Mrs. Kolodny playing her piano behind her shuttered windows, and it sounds like a desperate moan.

So the British will leave. The King David Hotel in Julian's Way will be emptied of its officers with their greased, neatly parted hair, emptied of its weary Englishwomen who sit on the hotel terrace looking out over the walls of the Old City as if fishing on the banks of the biblical past. No more morning sessions under the picture of the King in Edward O'Leary's office, where Dr. Mahdi from the Arab Council and Dr. Nussbaum from the Hadassah Hospital discuss ways of protecting the city's water supply from bacteria or destroying the breeding grounds of the mosquitoes in the Kedron Valley. Different times will come. "Excellent people like yourselves," says Dr. Mahdi, "such an intelligent, enlightened community, how have you all come to be captivated by such a terrible idea as Zionism?" I try my best: "For heaven's sake, Antoine, make an effort, just for once, try to see things from our point of view." And Edward, as always, firmly: "Gentlemen, perhaps we had better. Let's get back to the business at hand, if you don't mind."

What is the business at hand, Mina, my dear?

Perhaps you know?

Pitch-black outside. Crickets. Stars. Wind. I shall stop now.

Early hours of Wednesday morning
September 10

Dear Mina,

I shall not use the word "blame." You are not to blame for what you do to me in my dreams. But perhaps you are responsible, up to a point.

With a hint of a gray mustache, a smell of cigarette smoke

emanating even from your hair, wearing army trousers and a large man's shirt with several pockets, you stand beside my bed. Antoine is feeling my Adam's apple; he is clasping my chin in both hands, to keep me from wriggling during the operation. His polite face is so close to mine that I can see a yellow boil with a pink rim on his nose. A slight asymmetry between the two wings of his mustache. He is chubby and well mannered, and he smells of eau de cologne as he smiles at me. "There, there," he says in English; "let's both try together," he says. Two strong young men are holding my legs above the knees, but apparently their minds are not on the operation, because they are whispering to each other and chuckling. You are holding out a scalpel, or perhaps it is not a scalpel but a kitchen knife, a bread knife. Samovar thanks you in his usual way, with a slight bow, and takes it from you. "Slowly," you tell him. "With him there's no need for you to hurry." "There." "Now there." "And here." He does exactly what you say. He is wearing rubber gloves. He is a bright crimson. And he cuts amazingly gently. I must try to say something, at once, before my head is severed from my neck. Perhaps I shall remind Antoine how he came to see me late one night last winter, and begged me to cure him of a dose of gonorrhea that he had apparently contracted on his last trip to Beirut. And how I put him up here in my apartment for four days and gave him injections. But I promised Antoine to carry his secret with me to the grave. I shall remain silent. How strange is the deepening cut in my throat: no blood, no pain. On the contrary, Relief. "That is all, Dr. Oswald," says Ben-Gurion, as if he cannot believe his eyes. "It is a very simple operation, after all." And I indicate with a movement of the lips that the meeting is now over.

I am awakened by heavy rain. The light refuses to come on: it would seem that there is a power failure in Jerusalem. I strike a match. Look at my watch. One o'clock. I must get up. Wind and rain at the window. This time it is the autumn rain at last. The insects that have been dancing around the balcony light in the evenings have been swept away. The pine trees and the stone are what has endured, washed clean of dust, purified by wind and water.

I must get dressed. I must go at once. Go where, Mina. The dead praise not the Lord. In New York, you have said, a neo-Viennese school is reassembling. You must be there to report on the collective recovery that is taking place in the hills of Galilee and the Jezreel Valley. On the beginning of the eclipse of centuries-old ethnic neuroses. There is a way, ladies and gentlemen, you will proclaim to those scholarly refugees, there is a way, and it lies open.

Will you tell them about me, too? Will you be able to use me at least as an example, a curiosity, a detail that sheds a certain light or casts a shadow on the new pioneering reality among those ancient hills?

I must go. Tonight. At once. Perhaps to Katamon, to knock on Antoine's door and implore him by everything that's holy. To plead with him. To plead for the lives of our children, his and mine. Or perhaps not to Katamon but to Haifa and the kibbutzim in the valley. Is it already too late? Are the wind and rain meant for me this time? The Schneller bell rings once, twice, and is silent. I am sitting writing to you by the light of a kerosense lamp, in my gray flannel dressing gown. I ought to get dressed and go. There is a way and it lies open. Happy is he who waits, says Mr. Nehamkin; he will surely reach his goal. He who waits will never reach his goal, my dear fellow: only those who travel ever reach their goal. What is that goal. There is a way and I must get up and go. Which is the way, Mina, that is what I do not know, but we have a son and he will be able to travel it. The man who is writing to you is tired and ill. He must give himself an injection, take his pills, and go quietly back to bed. Enough. The inscription on the parish church was in four languages in the Vienna of my childhood; in four languages it promised every man and woman that there is a way back. It is a lie, I tell you, a bald-faced lie.

I must go. Not tonight, tomorrow morning. I must go to Mount Scopus and tell Dushkin, as I promised I would, that my condition has taken a turn for the worse. It is not for me to work a minor miracle in Jerusalem, to win over Dr. Mahdi or to make a discovery that may turn the military situation on its head. "Dew underfoot and the stars up above,/The Valley of Jezreel sparkles with love." So runs the song they are playing this early morning on the Hagganah short-wave broadcast. But here on Malachi Street, the trees are showing pale in the half-light of a murky dawn, and the rain has not stopped. As I wrote earlier, there is not much time left. You found me, used me, and set me aside. One of these days, you will come back to Jerusalem, a famous woman, a professor, the pioneer of a new discipline. You will bring fresh methods to the young Hebrew state. My death may even contribute to your fame. In the course of time they may mistakenly number me among the victims, and behind your back they will say that Professor Oswald lost her young fiancé in the war, an original scholar from Vienna. Jerusalem will overflow its boundaries and become a big city. Old men and old women shall dwell in her streets and rejoice therein, and no foe shall menace her gates. Just as my neighbor the poet promises us. There will be wide boulevards. There will be streetcars to link the various neighborhoods. Castles and towers will spring up. Perhaps they will make a river here and span it with bridges. It will be a beautiful, tranquil city. I shall close now, yours affectionately, and go back to bed. I have finished with recording time and place. This witness may stand down. He hopes that in due course, time, place, and witness will all be granted a kind of pardon. In Uri's longing, perhaps. Good night. Everything will be all right.

1975

New York's 50 Best

Places to Find Peace and Quiet

Completely revised and updated
6th Edition

Allan Ishac

Universe Publishing

Acknowledgments

For a book this little to last this long is a tribute not only to its value in helping New Yorkers find wonderful sanctuaries, but also to the many people who have worked to keep it alive and fresh. My publisher Charles Miers at Rizzoli/Universe has been a faithful champion of this book through four editions. My editor, Claire Gierczak, has been a guardian of its message through the last two. I am also grateful to the book's first publisher, Helene Silver, formerly of City and Company, who still treats this title like a pampered child. Finally, I appreciate the research and fact checking of Cari Jackson, as well as the location suggestions of Richard Siegel, Carol Fiorino, Dianne Stasi, and other knowledgeable New Yorkers who crave serene and silent places as much as I do.

First Universe edition published in the United States of America in 2003
by Universe Publishing
A Division of Rizzoli International Publishing, Inc.
300 Park Avenue South
New York, NY 10010
www.rizzoliusa.com

© 1991, 1995, 1997, 2001, 2003, 2011 by Allan Ishac
Previously published by City and Company
Interior Design by Don Wise & Co., based on an original design by Nancy Steiny
Cover Design: Paul Kepple and Jude Buffum @ Headcase Design
Cover Illustration by Mary Lynn Blasutta

2011 2012 2013 2014 / 10 9 8 7 6 5 4 3 2 1
Sixth Edition
Printed in the United States
Library of Congress Catalog Control Number: 2010939239
ISBN 13: 978-0-7893-2242-5

Publisher's Note: Neither Universe Publishing nor the author has any interest, financial or personal, in the locations listed in this book. While every effort was made to ensure that all data was accurate at the time of publication, we advise calling ahead or checking websites to confirm details.

Dedication

I dedicate this book to all those stewards of the city,
both public and private, who commit time and
energy to creating wonderful new places to find
refuge, retreat, and renewal in New York.
This may be the city that never sleeps, but thanks
to them, we're all able to rest for a while.

Contents

～

Preface

In the past year—perhaps due to increased
economic and environmental stress—more people
than ever have written and spoken to me about their
quest to find restful city sanctuaries. I responded
by creating an iPhone application called
TranquiliCity—an instant locator for peace and
quiet in New York City. Wherever they stood,
the app would point users to a refuge nearby.

It's a fine app, and many people are using
TranquiliCity. But I admit that I created it with
some reluctance. While I recognize that it fills
a need, it relies on smart-phone technology,
and all technology is fast. In my view, the use of
computers, mobile phones, and other digital devices
accelerates our nervous systems, and once activated,
it's hard to slow down and bring our bodies
back into balance.

That's why I love that you're holding this book.
Because, unless you're reading it on a Kindle or

iPad, this book is made of paper, and paper is wood pulp, and wood, like all natural materials, is grounding to your senses. The tactile experience of reading a paper book just might make you turn the pages a bit slower and read the words with more care and consideration. Perhaps you'll even use the location descriptions as a way to insulate yourself on a busy subway or soothe yourself in a bustling office.

That's what I intended. That the book itself would become a sanctuary of sorts, a place to pause during your day, a small gift of solace. After all, it's a book. No wires or microchips required. And that's still a slow and wonderful thing.

Allan Ishac

Introduction

This is the sixth edition of this
quiet little book—remarkable when you consider
that it has never made a best-seller list or
received a lot of publicity.

That suggests to me that peace and quiet
never go out of style, that sanctuaries are
a vital part of urban living, and that everyone,
native New Yorker and visitor alike, craves a
counterpoint to this fast-moving city. We all love
New York's energy and pace, but we also realize
that every hour of nonstop action calls for
a few minutes of sanity-restoring calm.

That's where this little book comes in. As with
every edition, I have selected the location entries
with care. I have visited them personally and
sampled the serenity they offer. I think you will find
this to be a reliable guide to relatively tranquil,
stress-free zones throughout the city—from
tension-relieving pocket parks and meditation

centers to quiet restaurants, rejuvenating day spas,
and much more. These are safe retreats that
will allow you to decompress from city stress
and immerse yourself in solitude.

Bring your desire for peace and quiet with you
when you visit these havens and hideaways and
they will remain vital places to renew the spirit,
while elevating the serene soul of our city.

Astor Court
at the Met

**Address: Metropolitan Museum of Art,
Fifth Ave. and 82nd St.**
Phone: 212-535-7710
**Hours: Tuesday through Thursday, Sunday,
9:30 A.M. to 5:30 P.M.; Friday and Saturday,
9:30 A.M. to 9 P.M.; closed Monday**
Admission: $20 suggested donation
Getting there: 4, 5, 6 to 86th St., walk west
Website: www.metmuseum.org

the wooden pillars were carved from rare *nan* trees in China, and the floor and ceiling tiles were also crafted traditionally in a former imperial kiln. In fact, when built in 1981, every detail of Astor Court was carefully considered to ensure that visitors had an authentic experience of a Ming Dynasty scholar's garden.

The story behind this gift to the Metropolitan Museum of Art is fascinating. Brooke Astor, one of the city's great philanthropists, spent part of her childhood in Beijing. Cherished memories of her time there inspired her to conceive and fund this flawlessly re-created garden, modeled after an existing courtyard in the city of Suzhou.

It is an unspoken rule of the Met that this refined environment retains its sanctuarylike qualities. Thus, voices are lowered, cameras are pocketed, and visitors wander the pillared walkways in a state of reverie and respect. Meant for contemplation of nature, the courtyard contains a rock garden, Chinese plantings, a trickling waterfall, and a goldfish pool. A tinted glass dome overhead simulates the sky and suggests its traditional use as an open-air moon-viewing terrace in its native setting. Even on the sunniest days, the installation is cast in a diffused, dreamy twilight.

Garden courtyards in China were often given poetic names by their scholar owners. This one, appropriately enough, is called "In Search of Quietude."

*Note: Two other Met destinations promise repose. The **Temple of Dendur** in the Egyptian wing, with its slanted 40-foot glass wall and black reflection pool, is almost eerily quiet. Seasonally, you can also enjoy the **Cantor Roof Garden** on the fifth floor. Part wood deck, part stone terrace, this perch offers memorable treetop views of Central Park.*

Bartow-Pell **Mansion Museum**

Address: 895 Shore Rd., Pelham Bay Park, Bronx
Phone: 718-885-1461
Hours: Museum open Wednesday, Saturday,
and Sunday, noon to 4 P.M.;
grounds open daily during daylight hours
Admission: $5 for museum tour; free to grounds
Getting there: 6 to Pelham Bay stop, then take
45 Westchester-Bee Line bus to gates
(no bus Sundays)
Website: www.bpmm.org

no matter how much you love our stimulating city, at some point you're going to contract a serious case of "urbanitis." But have no fear, while it's a nagging illness, there is a cure: trees, grass, and open space. On those days when even Central Park lacks adequate healing power, you will find ample doses of the much-needed antidotes at the lovingly restored Bartow-Pell Mansion in the Bronx.

Although located near the Westchester border, Bartow-Pell's quiet corner is surprisingly accessible by public transportation. Peering up the winding drive and wooded estate grounds from the mansion's massive entrance gates, I am always filled with a splendid anticipation of the country elegance lying just ahead.

The 1842 mansion, one of the finest examples of early Greek Revival architecture in America, is famous for its seashell-shaped, three-story hanging staircase, a gravity-defying marvel of construction. The self-guided tour includes a visit to a pleasant orangery—a French-style greenhouse room—where strong southern light warms the chilliest of winter days.

Outside, explore the mansion's nine-and-a-half rolling acres, including the walled formal gardens with lawns that spill seamlessly into nearby Long Island Sound. The cure for city claustrophobia reaches its full potency after you've walked the property's well-marked paths through unspoiled forests and marshlands, or ventured to the bordering Siwanoy Hiking Trail through more than two thousand acres of surrounding Pelham Bay Park.

Got an unshakable case of urbanitis? Take a two-hour hike in undisturbed wilderness and call me in the morning.

The **Chapel** of the
Good Shepherd in
St. Peter's Church

Address: Lexington Ave. at 54th St.
Phone: 212-935-2200
Hours: Daily, 8 A.M. to 8 P.M.
Admission: Free
Getting there: 6 to 51st St.
Website: www.saintpeters.org

I n the mid-seventies, the acclaimed American

sculptor Louise Nevelson was commissioned to

design "a place of purity" within the new Citicorp

complex. She proceeded to transform a sliver of

jutting architecture into a private corner of celestial

calm, a hushed and hopeful place called

The Chapel of the Good Shepherd.

As much an exuberant work of modern art as

a dulcet haven for heart and soul, the chapel is

Nevelson's only permanent sculptural environment

in New York. She wanted this unique prayer and

meditation space, tucked inside the north wall of

St. Peter's Church (the jagged granite appendage at

the base of the Citicorp building), to exude purity.

That's why almost everything in this 28-by-21-foot, five-sided chapel is white: white painted sculptural elements on white walls, white columns, a white sanctuary lamp, and white frosted windows. Even the floors, altar, and pews (with off-white cushions) are made of a light bleached ash.

Nevelson's *The Cross of the Good Shepherd*— a heavily stylized sculpture loosely suggestive of a traditional crucifix—sits against a field of gold leaf on the north wall, giving the eye a calming focal point from which the surroundings gently fall away. I am unable to pass within five blocks of this little pocket of peace without its enthralling gravity drawing me in. The stillness here is palpable. Just gaze into the solitary sanctuary lamp for a minute, and you'll return to the streets a more agreeable human being.

Cherry Walk at
the Hudson River

Address: 100th St. to 125th St.; enter
Riverside Park at 98th St., walk west to the river
Hours: Daily, 24 hours
Admission: Free
Getting there: 1 to 96th St.,
walk five minutes west

Consecrated by the feet of a hundred thousand serenity seekers: that's how I think of Cherry Walk, the narrow ribbon of land that meanders along the Hudson River between 100th and 125th Streets.

The ambling masses had been so devoted to this simple but seductive footpath for decades that the Parks Department finally decided to make it official. In 2001, the city tastefully and artistically paved the single track of dirt and christened it Cherry Walk, in honor of the pervasive cherry trees that explode with puffed blossoms and fragrance along both sides of the Henry Hudson Parkway in the spring (they even added 35 new trees).

Sensitive landscape architects have managed to preserve all the grace this shoulder of grass and trees has to offer. Not more than 30 feet wide in most places, the macadam walkway serpentines between trees and quarried granite boulders, which have been strategically placed for intermittent rest stops and riverside contemplation. At the shoreline, massive flat stones slope gently toward the water and provide an inviting place to remove your shoes or Rollerblades and lean back to face the sun, while the tidal surge licks and laps at your feet.

Despite its proximity to the highway, Cherry Walk seems remarkably insulated from the traffic— you can easily saunter along, almost oblivious to the passing cars. People who have loved this hospitable path since it was just a rutted trail have always known this. Now you can make that pleasant discovery yourself.

The Cloisters

Address: 99 Margaret Corbin Dr.,
northern tip of Fort Tryon Park
Phone: 212-923-3700
Hours: Tuesday through Sunday,
9:30 A.M. to 5:15 P.M.
Admission: $20 suggested donation
Getting there: A to 190th St.,
walk ten minutes north
Website: www.metmuseum.org

In medieval Europe, cloisters were central to monastic life. Protected from the outside world, monks were able to walk quietly in contemplation, meditate, read religious texts, and tend flower and medicinal herb gardens. Our own Cloisters in upper Manhattan is such an exquisite reconstruction of a medieval monastery—architecturally and atmospherically—that it has become a cherished urban sanctuary for many New Yorkers. The utter serenity of this hilltop structure is a rare gift that makes the ambitious trip worthwhile.

The Cloisters opened as a branch of the Metropolitan Museum of Art in 1938 on family property donated by John D. Rockefeller. To ensure that the arcadian views would be preserved, Rockefeller also purchased a tract of land directly across the river in New Jersey. He then shipped original architectural elements from five cloisters in France to be reconstructed as the centerpieces of this medieval world high above the Hudson.

Built to house the museum's 5,000-piece, medieval art collection dated from the ninth to fifteenth centuries, everything here is authentic—from the magnificent unicorn tapestries and Romanesque colonnades to the cobblestoned courtyards and grotesque stone gargoyles. Haunting Gregorian chanting fills the air as you pass through the vaulted passageways.

The three cloister gardens have been rigorously researched to ensure that the hundreds of plant and herb varieties were familiar to monks during the Middle Ages. There is a particularly beautiful, espaliered pear tree—now almost 80 years old—that grows in the Bonnefont herb garden. It should not be missed during your monastic meanderings.

Conservatory Garden

Address: 105th St. and Fifth Ave.
Phone: 212-860-1382
Hours: Daily, 8 A.M. to dusk
Admission: Free
Getting there: 6 to 103rd St., walk west
● Website: www.centralparknyc.org

1 have heralded the special joys of the Conservatory Garden in every edition of this book. Yet, despite all my pleading and prodding, lifelong New Yorkers still tell me they've never visited it, and the city's only formal garden remains one of the prettiest, most pristine secrets in Manhattan.

The six-acre Conservatory Garden has three distinct personalities—French, English, and Italian. The northernmost section has French influences, with elliptical beds surrounding the Three Dancing Maidens fountain. In springtime, the display of tens of thousands of tulips rivals that of any urban garden in the world.

The south end, also called "the Secret Garden" as a tribute to the Frances Hodgson Burnett children's classic, seems always to be filled with birdsong. Designed to resemble the intimate backyard of a stately English home, it has particular charm, with a whimsical fountain, trimmed hedges, hidden niches, and bountiful flowerbeds.

The central Italian-style garden is the real showcase. Romantic white and pink crab apple allées line a magnificently maintained lawn, and a huge wisteria pergola stands at the western end, towering above a 12-foot-high jet fountain.

Pampered and protected by a full-time staff, the elegant, four-season Conservatory Garden is as inviting in February, when the buttery hellebores come out, as it is in May, when delicate narcissus make their brilliant appearance.

*Note: Five blocks north through the park, the once-decaying **Harlem Meer** has been transformed into a lovely fishing pond with pristine wetlands, a charming waterfall, and sandy beach. It's worth the walk.*

D'Mai Urban Spa

Address: 157 Fifth Ave., bet. Lincoln and
St. Johns Sts., Brooklyn
Phone: 718-398-2100
Hours: Monday through Friday,
11 A.M. to 7:30 P.M.; Saturday and Sunday,
10 A.M. to 7 P.M.
Admission: Spa services from $85
Getting there: R to Union/Fourth Ave., walk east
● Website: www.dmaiurbanspa.com

In the past decade, day spas have invaded New York. This is not a bad thing. With rest and a rejuvenating back rub available on virtually every corner, our "calm quotient" inevitably goes up. The trick is in finding the best places to go.

Start with D'Mai Urban Spa in Brooklyn, where the Balinese themes reinforce the feeling that you've arrived at a faraway escape. The dominant design feature is a 70-foot interior boardwalk of white cedar, framed on both sides by a silent stream of smooth, gray river pebbles. By this planked path, spanning the length of the spa and dotted with lounge chairs, you could rest contentedly in your silk robe and slippers for hours . . . but skilled hands await you.

A good massage can drop tension like a stone,
and at D'Mai the stress-neutralizing benefits are
multiplied in settings like the Cabana room—
a tented, healing haven poised below a draped
skylight. During my deep tissue massage,
rain fell lightly, showering the room's ceiling
with a soporific pitter-patter. On the floor,
visible below my face cradle, was a bowl of fragrant
orchids. Later, I was handed a glass of cool spring
water with cucumber slices. Details like these
make D'Mai truly special.

For excellent spa treatments in subdued surroundings you can also try **Devachan (**425 Broome St.,
212-274-8686, www.devachansalon.com), where
the Deva Signature Facial evokes spasms of
contentment. The superheated sauna experience in
the Hwangto igloo at **Athena Spa** (32 East 31st St.,
212-683-4484, www.athenaspany31.com) proved to
be the perfect complement to my foot reflexology.
Feel confident beginning your plan of inaction
at any one of these healing destinations.

The Elevated Acre

Address: 55 Water St. at Old Slip Rd.
Phone: 212-747-9120
Hours: Open daily; May 1 through Sept. 30,
7 A.M. to 10 P.M.; Oct. 1 through April 30,
8 A.M. to 8 P.M.
Admission: Free
Getting there: N, R to Whitehall St., walk east
Website: www.elevatedacre.com

nothing pleases me more than discovering a bona fide urban oasis that has escaped the eyes of most passersby. This one was suggested to me by a downtown friend who visits the public plaza regularly to enjoy journal writing over morning coffee. Virtually invisible from the street, I realized how unique the Elevated Acre was when I walked by twice before locating the access escalator.

The rooftop plaza was featureless and uninviting until a $7 million renovation in 2005 transformed the nearly one acre of terrace into a rejuvenating park-like setting. Designed with a rising slope that crests onto a wide-plank boardwalk of Brazilian hardwood, it overlooks the East River, with fine views of the Brooklyn Bridge and Governor's Island.

Landscaped areas are planted with native species and beautiful dune grasses that gently swish in the breeze, the sound masking the drone from the FDR Drive, which passes below the plaza's eastern border. High grasses shield strategically placed teak benches, creating quiet recesses for reading or conversation. Facing north and west is an elaborate amphitheater of poured concrete steps offering more outdoor seating as it tiers down to a 7,000-square-foot grassy area.

The Elevated Acre's most striking feature is the rectangular Beacon of Progress light sculpture with a grid surface of glass, rising 50 feet above the street. This high-tech, LED lantern is lit nightly in themed color combinations (such as red and green for Christmas or red and pink for Valentine's Day) and anchors the relaxed setting.

*Patriot's Note: Follow the plaza's southeast steps to the **Vietnam Veterans Memorial** nearby. You'll be moved by the evocative, glass-brick "letter wall."*

Equitable Tower Atrium

**Address: 787 Seventh Ave.,
bet. 51st and 52nd Sts.
Hours: Daily, 10 A.M. to 6 P.M.
Admission: Free
Getting there: N, R to 49th St.; 1 to 50th St.**

he right atrium at the right time
can save your sanity. I consider this one to be
the eye of the hurricane in Midtown,
providing a dramatic cessation of sensory assaults
whenever I need it most.

The real gift of solitude at the Equitable Atrium is
tucked into a 40-foot, semicircular marble settee
located smack in the center of the building's lobby.
The curving bench is a sculptural, spatial, and
acoustical phenomenon. I will never understand
how it works, but take just a few steps inside this
skylit crescent and you have the distinct
sensation of being held firmly in a noise-muting,
marble cocoon. Add the flora-filled marble fountain
and dense screen of tropical conifers,

and it becomes nearly impossible to leave
this protective embrace.

You'll marvel at Roy Lichenstein's *Mural with Blue Brushstroke*, a monumental piece that dominates the wall behind the bench enclosure, painted on-site by the Pop artist in 1984. But, personally, I ask little more of this spotless atrium space than to rest my city weariness upon its cool surfaces.

*Note: Incentives to developers who provide public atriums and open spaces have resulted in a mixed bag of mall-like settings and truly splendid escapes. Here are some that make my list: the **Maiden Lane Atrium***'s *(Maiden Ln. and Front St.) intricate Tinkertoy interior is a playful place to relax; the **Deutsche Bank Building** (60 Wall St.) has palm trees and ample seating; the former **IBM Building** (590 Madison Ave. at 56th St.) soothes with its bamboo court and conservatory; the **Olympic Tower Atrium** (641 Fifth Ave. at 51st St.) has an appealing waterfall.*

Ford Foundation Building

Address: 320 East 43rd St.,
bet. First and Second Aves.
Phone: 212-573-5000
Hours: Monday through Friday,
10 A.M. to 4 P.M.
Admission: Free
Getting there: 4, 5, 6 to Grand Central,
walk east

In a stroke of architectural genius, the designer of the Ford Foundation, Kevin Roche, placed the building around the park, instead of the other way around. Here you can enjoy a 160-foot-high, glass-walled, one-third-acre terraced garden, lushly landscaped with exotic greenery.

Because there are no formal benches or chairs, and no food or drink allowed, Roche's towering greenhouse plaza does not draw the kind of crowds that other public spaces seem to attract. A busload of foreign tourists might disembark for a few minutes to study the building's impressive architecture, but frequently this rain-forestlike atrium is unoccupied.

You'll be most comfortable ascending to the east side of the top tier, where a low sun-drenched sitting wall provides a quiet vantage point from which to study the seventeen full-grown trees (including acacia, Norfolk pine, and eucalyptus), 1,000 shrubs, 150 vines, and nearly 22,000 ground-cover plants. The landscapers also rotate seasonal plantings, with tulips in spring, begonias in summer, chrysanthemums in fall, and poinsettias in winter. The three levels of garden court are lined with brick pathways descending to a still-water pool, into which you can drop your coins to benefit UNICEF. Rainwater is captured in cisterns on the roof to feed this pool and irrigate the garden during water shortages.

At the Ford Foundation, the air is dense with the earthy scent of bursting horticulture, a kind of intoxicating chlorophyll panacea guaranteed to calm the most hyperactive minds.

Fort Tryon Park

Address: 192nd St. at Ft. Washington Ave.
Hours: Dawn to dusk
Admission: Free
Getting there: A to 190th St.,
walk 100 yards north to entrance
Website: www.nycgovparks.org/
parks/forttryonpark

gazing out from the high terraces in Fort Tryon Park toward the Hudson River far below, it is easy to imagine what Manhattan Island must have felt like in simpler times during its unspoiled beginnings. The oak trees are ancient and huge, the raw and rocky Palisades Cliffs look much as they have for centuries, and the wooded slopes running down to the river are pocked with groundhog holes, the warning chirps of chipmunks perforating the air.

If you let it, the "old" quiet of Fort Tryon can be used to connect to the less hectic, more soothing places inside you. Taking conscious steps along more than eight miles of pedestrian paths, for instance, can center a restless spirit. In plentiful open areas with expansive river views, you can spread your arms and take long, slow breaths of healing, chlorophyll-suffused air. In pampered gardens, the colorful faces of giant dahlias will activate visual pleasure centers refreshed by the sight of beauty.

In the last few years, I started meeting a vintage childhood friend for seasonal lunches in the stone coolness of the nearby New Leaf Café (see page 105), which prompted regular sojourns to this uptown sanctuary. Now I love this 67-acre park, particularly three features that stand out for serenity-seekers: the lower-tiered grassy meadows where I have often sat alone on unoccupied benches for hours; the amiable, three-acre Heather Garden, constantly maintained by volunteers who keep it in bloom with vibrant surprises year round; the upper stone terraces with towering trees and rows and rows of park benches situated for maximum exposure to wide-open river views.

Fort Tryon seems like an older, wiser, slower park to me. And like a knowing sage, the gifts it imparts leave deep impressions.

Gantry Plaza
State Park

Address: 474 48th Ave., Queens
Phone: 718-786-6385
Hours: Daily, dawn to 1 A.M.
Admission: Free
Getting there: 7, one stop from Grand Central to
Vernon-Jackson Ave., Queens; walk west on
48th Ave. to the river

a rugged pier revisioned into a glittering park, Gantry Plaza is a jewel on the Long Island City waterfront. The four parallel piers, each with its own signature identity and distinct features, along with a quarter-mile esplanade, have turned this former blot along the East River into one of the city's finest examples of urban restoration.

Built to encompass two huge gantries—waterfront cranes used to load and unload floating rail cars during this area's industrial heyday—the 12-acre park has won awards for its striking design and sensitive use of the natural shoreline. And it keeps getting better. Future phases of the development plan call for 19 total acres of stress-relieving park, serving shoreline lovers, bird-watchers, ballplayers, picnickers, sunbathers, strollers, evening romantics, and moon gazers.

Just one stop on the 7 train from Grand Central Station, Gantry Plaza State Park is a quick and satisfying hop from Manhattan. At the center of the park complex are the looming black gantries emblazoned with the words "Long Island" in faded red letters. Fishing is permitted on the southernmost pier, where you'll find a wavelike 40-foot bench. The second pier has four wooden chaise lounges fixed in place to face the southern sun.

Farther north, you'll find dozens of big boulders shaved flat to accommodate loungers, as well as high-backed throne chairs and stationary recliners dotting the water's edge. Wide boardwalks, manicured gardens, additional creative seating, and a unique mist fountain are located closer to the famous neon Pepsi-Cola sign seen in LIC when looking east from Midtown. Just imagine the views looking back.

The General
Theological
Seminary

Address: 175 Ninth Ave., bet. 20th and 21st Sts.
Phone: 212-243-5150
Hours: June through August,
Monday through Saturday, 10 A.M. to 5 P.M.;
September through May, 10 A.M. to 3 P.M.;
closed Sunday
Admission: Free
Getting there: A, C, E to 23rd St.;
1 to 18th St.
Website: www.gts.edu

You will be utterly amazed that these pristine grounds are open to the public—they really are that idyllic. But this generous outdoor "peace offering," hidden in plain sight, is a simple way for the extraordinarily friendly seminarians here to contribute to their community.

Once an apple orchard donated to the Episcopal Church by Clement Clarke Moore (author of "'Twas the Night Before Christmas"), this shaded seminary enclosure has been a heavenly urban getaway since the mid-1800s. Here you'll find the pastoral serenity of a New England campus quad seamlessly combined with the cloistered formality of a collegiate English close.

The red-brick buildings that frame the seminary grounds were built beginning in 1836 and cover an entire city block. Recently restored, they are exquisite examples of nineteenth-century Gothic Revival architecture and one of the reasons this complex is registered as a National Historic Landmark.

Don't miss the Chapel of the Good Shepherd at the heart of the block-long quad. It's a charming, simple, countrylike chapel that emanates warmth with its beautiful stained glass and dark, rich woodcarvings. After strolling the landscaped pathways of the seminary's outer yard—dotted with mature and majestic oak, birch, elm, and linden trees—I've always found the chapel an ideal place to explore my own inner pathways.

Greenacre Park

**Address: 221 East 51st St.,
bet. Second and Third Aves.
Hours: Daily, 8 A.M. to 6 P.M.; in summer,
until 8 P.M.
Admission: Free
Getting there: E or F to 53rd St.;
6 to 51st St., walk east**

he brilliant landscape architect Hideo Sasaki created this vest-pocket park in the early 1970s. According to him, the primary design goal was "to provide a place for the general public to gain special repose from the increasing city experience of noise, concrete, and humdrum." His vision was certainly realized, as Greenacre Park has been named one of the top urban parks in the world by the Manhattan-based Project for Public Spaces.

This diminutive park in the heart of the east Midtown commercial and residential district is nowhere near an acre in size (it's just 110 feet deep by 60 feet wide), but perhaps because green space is such a rarity in this generic part of town, it seems to offer an acre's worth of tranquility. Like Paley Park, its smaller cousin a few blocks away (see page 74), Greenacre Park boasts a dramatic two-story waterfall, this one constructed of massive granite blocks. There's a babbling brook here, too, which ambles along the east wall and empties into a plunge pool. The intermingling sounds of gurgling, flowing, and cascading water, along with a curtain of dense, overhanging honey locust branches, significantly mask street noise, insulating this pleasant park from the incessant throb of the city.

You can also enjoy the park on rainy days, when it's possible to ponder the waterfalls alone, undisturbed, and comfortably dry under the trellis roof of the west terrace. While always a fine urban escape, be advised that in good weather, Greenacre Park is a magnet for local office workers, who enjoy the park's snack bar and chance to soak up some sun in relative quiet.

Green-Wood
Cemetery

Address: Fifth Ave. at 25th St., Brooklyn
Phone: 718-768-7300
Hours: Daily, 8 A.M. to 4 P.M.
Admission: Free
Getting there: N, R to 25th St., walk east
Website: www.green-wood.org

forget for a moment that there are 500,000 dead people here.

Consider instead that this urban cemetery was designed in 1838 by civil engineer David Bates Douglass as a pastoral park with rolling hills, five lakes, thirty miles of serpentine pathways, and some of the city's oldest trees— all in a bucolic setting half the size of Central Park.

Within this sepulchral masterpiece situated at the highest point in Brooklyn, you'll find no cars, no trucks, no subways, no sirens, no screaming kids, and virtually no (living) people. The stillness here is profound, much like you'd find at, well, a cemetery.

Green-Wood has the additional appeal of its celebrity occupants, among whom are stained-glass master Louis Comfort Tiffany, pencil man Eberhard Faber, piano maker Henry Steinway, sewing machine inventor Elias Howe (along with his dog, Fannie), soap magnate William Colgate, and composer Leonard Bernstein. As for why Green-Wood Cemetery has a particularly magical air, perhaps it's because this is also the eternal resting place of actor Frank Morgan. You know . . . *The Wizard of Oz.*

Designated a National Historic Landmark in the fall of 2006, Green-Wood encourages public visitation and is also a favorite destination for bird-watchers. For a guided tour of the famous monuments, conducted throughout the year, call ahead or check the website for schedules and gathering locations.

Note: If you find solace in the hushed and solitary expanse of cemeteries, visit the 400-acre **Woodlawn Cemetery** *in the Bronx (501 E. 233rd St., 718-920-0500, www.thewoodlawncemetery.org), with some of the grandest, most ornate crypts in the world.*

High Line Park

**Address: Ganesvoort St. to (eventually) 34th St.,
between 10th and 11th Aves.**
Phone: 212-500-6035
Hours: Daily, 7 A.M. to 10 P.M.
Admission: Free
**Getting there: A, C, E, 1, 3 to 14th St.;
access points every 4 or 5 blocks**
Website: www.thehighline.org

from the moment the High Line opened in June of 2009 it became one of the city's most celebrated urban parks. The elevated oasis is so masterfully designed, it has also become the template for similar reclamations of derelict industrial districts in cities worldwide, from Philadelphia to Rotterdam, Jersey City to Jerusalem.

The vision was inspired—take a mile-and-a-half section of abandoned, moldering railroad track suspended thirty feet above the street, and create a meandering, magical landscape. Forbid bicycles, Rollerblades or motorized vehicles of any kind, too, making the High Line "walking pace only" and fully compatible with long spells of relaxation, contemplation, and conversation.

There are highlights on the High Line, of course: the ingenious wood, stainless-steel, and concrete benches that seem to grow underfoot, springing up from the walkways; the wide wood recliners just north of 14th Street, movable on rusted tracks; the water feature between 14th and 15th streets ideal for toe dipping; the cluster of café chairs on the lower porch overlooking the river between 14th and 16th streets; the bank of tiered steps at 17th Street overlooking uptown traffic on 10th Avenue.

For me, the essential joy of the High Line is simply strolling alongside dense grasses, perennial flowers, and thriving birch trees that have a wild, self-seeded look growing between original 1930s track and concrete walkways. And while you will be sharing the High Line (its instant, iconic popularity put it on every tourist itinerary), any morning, and particularly in the evenings, the High Line rewards you with peace, nature, and plenty of uplifting places to sit in safety and solitude. It is brilliant and beautiful every step of the way.

Hudson River Pier
Parks

**Address: Pier 45 at 10th St.;
Pier 62–64 from 22nd to 24th Sts.; Pier 95–96
at 55th St.; more from Battery Park to 59th St.
Phone: 212-627-2020
Hours: Dawn to 1 A.M.
Admission: Free
Getting there: Various Westside locations
reachable by 1, 3, A, C, E
Website: www.hudsonriverpark.org**

rebuilding 550-acres of riverfront property into
a magnificent public park has taken more than a
decade and a massive infusion of city, state, and
federal funds (this is the largest park construction
in Manhattan since the building of Central Park).
Mostly completed in 2010, the results have exceeded
a city's worth of expectations and New Yorkers
have immersed themselves in the sprawling park's
sanity-saving grace with bikes, blankets, and picnic
baskets in tow. Here are some peak pier points:

At **Pier 45** at 10th Street, walk the tranquil long
pier out to the tip, where it's possible to converse
softly while in marvelous contact with the river.
An adjacent shorter pier has picnic benches under
shade trees that quench a thirst for quiet.

At **Pier 62** near 22nd Street, pass the imaginative
native animals carousel to reach the wide
boardwalk. Along concrete walls retaining
densely planted berms are comfortable, low-backed
benches. Few people venture out this far,
yet it's entirely peaceful and safe.

Pier 63 has a spectacular "great lawn" that forms
an inviting green bowl along the Chelsea Cove.
Fronted on the west by a wall of low-lying, granite
boulders, this is an ideal place to plunk a sarong
and close your eyes. A few steps north, a meditative
walk through "Stonefield"—a small field of craggy,
multicolored boulders—is rewarding.

Pier 64, with its sloping grass strip angled toward
the river, is my personal pick for
panoramic sunset views.

The rhythms of **Pier 95** at 55th Street coalesce seamlessly with the gentle rise and fall of the embayment
waters in Clinton Cove. Find solace on the well-
maintained lawns edged with pristine flowerbeds.

Share my joy in the transformation of these
neglected piers and find inspiring aesthetics and
quietude along the way.

Isamu Noguchi
Garden Museum

Address: 9-01 33rd Rd., bet. Vernon Blvd.
and 10th St., Queens
Phone: 718-204-7088
Hours: Wednesday through Friday, 10 A.M. to
5 P.M.; Saturday and Sunday, 11 A.M. to 6 P.M.;
closed Monday and Tuesday
Admission: $10
Getting there: N to Broadway (Long Island City),
walk west ten blocks to Vernon Blvd.,
south two blocks to the museum
Website: www.noguchi.org

We could all learn a lesson in contemplation and patience from Isamu Noguchi. The late Japanese American sculptor would sometimes study a piece of raw marble or granite for years before making his first strike. He called this process "discovering the stone's essence."

At the Isamu Noguchi Garden Museum, you can almost feel the master artist urging you to take up your own, inner sculpting tools—to thoughtfully split, cut, chisel, and polish your way to discovering the essence of self. Noguchi's sculptures always speak this personally and deeply.

This dignified, uncluttered gallery and garden is situated in the otherwise bustling heart of Long Island City's industrial waterfront—a site Noguchi chose for its proximity to the marble-cutting shops that were once located here. The museum, part raw cinderblock open to the elements, part former industrial plant, contains more than 250 Noguchi sculptures of stone, metal, wood, and clay. Each is placed with precision and sensitivity to elicit the most profound reaction. The peacefulness of the sculpture garden alone rewards your extra effort in getting here. A half-day trip is advisable, so you'll have time to absorb the illuminating messages Noguchi has chiseled into his oracular boulders.

Note: From the museum, walk two blocks north to **Socrates Sculpture Park**, *a rugged, unruly, riverfront creation that's home to outdoor sculpture on a towering scale, and very peaceful. You'll see.*

The Jacqueline Onassis Reservoir Running Path

**Address: Central Park; enter at 90th St.
and Fifth Ave.
Hours: Daily, 24 hours
Admission: Free
Getting there: 4, 5, 6 to 86th St.,
walk west to entrance**

Perhaps the most famous jogging track in the country, this historic reservoir running path has something unique going for it. If you stand by the South Gate House (86th Street, looking due north), you'll see one of the most unusual sights in Manhattan—a buildingless horizon. You can cast your gaze far out into the distance and behold only water, trees, and flocks of migrating birds. What a relief for skyscraped eyes.

Of course, this much-loved oval (famous location for city-centered films) is also where many New Yorkers begin their days and end their evenings, letting their rhythmic footfalls soothe the mind. They might even attain that state of quasi-euphoria that every serious aerobic athlete experiences, in this case called the "reservoir runner's high." It kicks in with sweet reliability after a lap or two.

This big (by Manhattan standards) body of water attracts a large variety of migrating waterfowl, along with the normal contingent of native mallards, loons, and seagulls. An unused bridle path runs parallel to the track for much of its length, with the effect of making a circuit of the elevated, 1.6-mile cinder path seem like jogging the perimeter of a country lake. You'll pass other runners along the way (path etiquette calls for counter-clockwise revolutions), but these are conscientious, quiet athletes. It's a civilized group.

The congenial reservoir path is more than a spot for furtive celebrity watching (the loop attracts many recognizable runners); it's a refreshing island of water in a big stone sea. Drink deeply.

Jacques Marchais
Museum of Tibetan Art

Address: 338 Lighthouse Ave., Staten Island
Phone: 718-987-3500
Hours: Wednesday through Sunday, 1 P.M. to
5 P.M., February through December; in January,
by appointment only
Admission: $6 adults, children free
Getting there: Check website for
detailed directions
Website: www.tibetanmuseum.com

Incorporated into the complex of fieldstone buildings at this cliff-clinging museum on Staten Island is a re-creation of a Tibetan mountain temple. Built in 1945, it was the first Himalayan-style architectural replica in the United States. It's also so authentic that Buddhist monks have come here to perform rituals and religious practices.

The brainchild of Jacqueline Klauber, an important American collector of Tibetan and Himalayan art (she used the name Jacques Marchais for professional purposes), the monastery museum holds one of the largest collections of Tibetan art outside of Tibet. The lamasery altar is so jam-packed with gilded Buddhas, ornate prayer wheels, and elaborate incense burners, you'll wonder how peaceful prayer ever happens here . . . until you let the transformative powers of these sacred objects envelop you.

While there are no Himalayan vistas, the museum is located at the highest point on the Eastern Seaboard, and the distant harbor views are a favorite local secret. On the patio is a tranquil meditation garden, which Klauber named the "Samadhi Garden" (the word *samadhi* suggests a point of deep stillness in the mind). Here you'll find huge baboons, trumpeting elephants, and prancing rabbits . . . all of the stone variety. The goldfish in the lotus pond, however, are real.

Look beyond the graceful altar and marble Buddha to the colorful prayer flags fluttering in the trees. It is believed that the wind carries their blessings and messages out to the world. I prayed for more places like this one.

Note: The museum has an extensive calendar of Far East–related events. Visit the website for listings.

Jamaica Bay
Wildlife Refuge

Address: Cross Bay Blvd., Broad Channel, Queens
Phone: 718-318-4340
Hours: Trails open daily, dawn to dusk;
Visitor Center open 8:30 A.M. to 5 P.M.
Admission: Free
Getting there: A to Broad Channel,
walk west to Cross Bay Blvd., turn right (north),
walk half a mile to the visitors center
Website: www.nyharborparks.org/visit/jaba.html

Watching shorebirds soar and swoop and float on invisible air currents is a passive activity that always leaves me better (and calmer) for the experience. At one urban wildlife sanctuary, you can get a year's worth of wings in one afternoon.

The Jamaica Bay Wildlife Refuge is located on the Atlantic Flyway—an important seasonal migration route—and provides a layover point for birds resting and feeding in the sanctuary's salt marshes, freshwater ponds, woods, and wetlands. Known nationally among birders as a hotspot for feathered friends, the wide cinder trails are clustered with bird-watchers toting cameras and binoculars, silently observing their subjects nesting, resting, fishing, and preening. Piping plovers, blue herons, snowy egrets, Canada geese, ospreys, barn owls, and about 300 other species have been spotted throughout the 9,155 acres.

Make your way around the 1.5-mile West Pond trail. Despite its close proximity to John F. Kennedy International Airport, the refuge is located far enough from the flight paths of those soaring metal birds to ensure water-washed solitude for your nature stroll. While easily walked in an hour, the restorative benefits of this shore-hugging trail increase if you take your time. Stop at viewing benches, turn at side trails (like the terrapin nesting path that leads to a beach), and read the informative flora-and-fauna guide markers.

On a recent trip, a friend and I wandered through the secluded upland trails, where we startled a quail in the scrub, spotted a cardinal perched on a pine bough, and watched ring-necked ducks waddle through the reeds. It was a fully gratifying wildlife afternoon—with the Manhattan skyline visible over our shoulders in the distance.

John Finley Walk at Carl Schurz Park

Address: Enter at 86th St. and East End Ave.
Hours: Daily, dawn to 1 A.M.
Admission: Free
Getting there: 4, 5, 6 to 86th St.
Website: www.carlschurzparknyc.org

the broad, sweeping, two-sided staircase that rises up to John Finley Walk from 86th Street portends something special lying just beyond. As you make your way to the top of those significant bluestone steps, the mystery reveals itself in exhilarating views of the East River from every point along this historic promenade.

John Finley Walk is encompassed by Carl Schurz Park—a gem of the Upper East Side lovingly maintained by a community group in conjunction with the Parks Department. This reliable, four-season refuge and its century-old esplanade run along the eastern property line of Gracie Mansion (Hizzoner's house) making it a safe place to amble at any time of the day or night.

Carl Schurz Park's 15 acres serve respite seekers of all ages—from young families to elderly local residents. Leisurely strollers walk in small clusters, European-style, chatting amiably while gazing out at the remarkable riverscape and Roosevelt Island. The casual pace is infectious. And the views are particularly breathtaking at night when the river bridges are lit, throwing luminous reflections off the water. Recent re-landscaping of the Axis Garden on the park's southern border and the Hoop Garden, enveloped by the East 86th Street staircase, have made Carl Schurz even more enticing.

There's a children's playground at the south end that can be lively, so for optimum privacy walk north along the promenade past the flagpole to where the footpath narrows and bends to the right. Continue for another 100 feet (if you reach the fire-boat house, you've gone too far) and settle yourself down on a shaded bench against the hillside. You'll know when you've reached the right place by that telltale sound—the sound of silence.

Kayaking on the Hudson River

Address: Pier 40 at Houston St.; Pier 96 at
56th St.; 72nd St. on the river walkway
Hours: Mid-May through mid-October; Saturdays,
Sundays, and holidays, 9 A.M. to 6 P.M.;
weekday evenings at 56th St., 5 P.M. to 7 P.M.
Admission: Free
Getting there: Check website for specific location
● Website: www.downtownboathouse.org

I am a kayak owner. I keep it at a friend's house on the Long Island Sound, so I don't use it as often as I'd like. But every time I slip my body into the cockpit, I know that skimming the water is going to elevate my mood and leave tension in my wake.

That's why I love how easy it has become for New Yorkers to go kayaking. By law, the city has to provide public access to navigable waters from designated pier launches. So they've authorized the volunteer, not-for-profit Downtown Boathouse to offer education and easy access for canoeists and kayakers. Incredibly, it's all free—use of the kayaks, basic instruction, and your time spent on the water.

The Hudson River has tricky currents, strong winds, and floating detritus, but it's still possible to experience this tidal river safely, with profound intimacy, in your kayak. Under the responsible tutelage of dedicated volunteers, you're given a life vest, oar, and kayak, and sent off to paddle the relatively protected waters of the adjacent embayments. The kayaks used here—called "sit-on-tops" because they have no cockpit—are virtually roll-proof and excellent for beginners.

Once you're bobbing on the water—just body, boat, and blade—you experience what veteran "river rats" describe as a transcendent union with your surroundings: expansive water, open sky, the light slapping of water rippling against the boat, the swish of your oar. You see the busyness and the bustle on shore, but you are not there. You are not in the city at all. You are here, immersed in liquid nature.

*Note: If you want to take the kayaking experience to another level, contact the **New York Kayak Company** (40 North River Piers, 800-KAYAK99, www.nykayak.com) for expert instruction and all-day kayaking adventures.*

Lady Mendl's Tea Salon

**Address: The Inn at Irving Place,
56 Irving Pl. at 17th St.**
Phone: 212-533-4466
**Hours: Monday through Friday, 3 P.M. and 5 P.M.
seatings; Saturday and Sunday, 12 P.M.,
2:30 P.M., and 5 P.M. seatings**
Admission: $35 per person, reservations required
Getting there: 4, 5, 6 to 14th St., walk east
Website: www.ladymendls.com

taking afternoon tea began as a fashionable

social tradition in England during the 1830s.

The fancy porcelain settings and parlor ambience

served to give the rite a certain elegance and

sophistication. Afternoon tea made everyone feel

a bit more civilized and a little less harried.

It can have the same effect on today's New Yorker,

especially when served with classic Victorian charm

in the nostalgic parlor of Lady Mendl's Tea Salon.

Situated in a magnificently restored 1834 town

house in Gramercy Park, the salon is tastefully

decorated with upholstered armchairs and antiques

of the era, including period china and silver

tea services. During winter months, the peaceful mood is heightened by the flickering flames from a pair of cozy fireplaces.

The delectable, five-course afternoon tea service—frequently rated the most romantic in the city—includes fresh fruit, finger sandwiches, sweet scones with jam, macaroons, and a final sublime pastry offering. More than 20 fine aromatic teas are available, but you will do well to choose the smoky Formosa Oolong or Fancy Ceylon. After an hour and a half of tea and easy conversation at Lady Mendl's, my guest and I completed our genteel visit to the nineteenth century with a stroll around historic Gramercy Park.

Several upper-crust hotels like **The Carlyle** (35 East 76th St., 212-744-1600) and **The Algonquin** (59 West 44th St., 212-840-6800) offer a fine afternoon tea experience. I also like the casual ambience and very British flavor of **Tea and Sympathy** (108 Greenwich Ave., 212-989-9735) and the stylish setting at the **T Salon in Chelsea Market** (459 W. 15th St., 212-243-0432).

Lighthouse
Park on
Roosevelt Island

Address: Northern tip of Roosevelt Island
Phone: 212-832-4543
Hours: Daily, 24 hours
Admission: Free
Getting there: F to Roosevelt Island; tram departs
from 59th St. and Second Ave.
Website: www.rooseveltislander.blogspot.com

You need to consider a little island hopping whenever the city encroaches on your sanity. Especially when that island is only a five-minute trip from midtown Manhattan.

The beauty of Roosevelt Island is its accessibility as a reliable getaway. No worries about getting over there and being marooned or that the aerial tram will deposit you in the river before landing you safely on the opposite shore. Not only can you get to mellow Lighthouse Park quickly and safely (if you have tram terrors, just take the F train), you can also grab a sandwich, catch a lunchtime half hour of unobstructed rays, and be back at the office before anyone notices you've slipped out

for some island tranquility and a tan.

The four-minute tram ride ($2.25 each way)

offers an expansive dose of urban vistas—you can

see virtually every inch of Manhattan (most of

Queens, too) from 250 feet up on the soaring

Swiss cable cars. Once on this sliver of land, take

the red minibus (a noteworthy bargain at 25 cents)

as far north as it travels, then stroll along the

island's west side until you reach the park. You'll

probably see a few fishermen near the tiny granite

lighthouse and not much else. You'll also find a

wide lawn, inviting picnic tables, and a beautiful

brick-paved promenade for aimless meandering.

For loafers like me, the extent of island activity

involves reclining on a grassy ridge counting barges

as they glide by.

The Lotus Garden

Address: 97th St. bet. Broadway
and West End Ave.
Hours: April to mid-November, Sundays,
1 P.M. to 4 P.M. for the public; accessible
at any time for key holders
Admission: Free on Sundays;
key is $20 for one year
Getting there: 1 to 96th St.
Website: www.thelotusgarden.org

In a city where steel and concrete dominate,
I love to watch nature assert itself in unlikely
places—a dandelion rising from a mound of silt
on a rooftop, an oak sapling poking out from
a crack in the sidewalk.

The clearest evidence of nature's reassuring
determination can be found at the remarkable little
Lotus Garden, sitting twenty feet above 97th Street
atop a busy parking garage. Working with local
developers in 1983, activists Mark Greenwald,
an architect, and Carrie Maher, a horticulturist,
spearheaded the garden's design with other
neighbors. Creating this canopy of fragrant color

over a garage rooftop involved spreading 3.5 feet of topsoil over the entire 7,000-square-foot expanse (about one-sixth of an acre).

There are no actual lotus plants in the garden, but you'll find abundant water lilies thriving in two small goldfish ponds. The garden is artfully subdivided into productive plots tended by 28 families, from which grow peach, apple, and cherry trees, fragrant herbs, and bountiful blooms for all seasons.

Open to the public only on Sundays, you can purchase a key granting you unrestricted, one-year access to this elevated oasis for just $20. During a recent visit to this bountiful green space, I strolled along wood chip–lined pathways, sniffed the blossoms in a dozen flowerbeds, and sat pleasantly alone, listening to a choir of chirping sparrows celebrate the day. If there's a better place for which to hold a key, tell me.

The New York Botanical Garden

Address: 200th St. at Southern Blvd., Bronx
Phone: 718-817-8700
Hours: Tuesday through Sunday,
10 A.M. to 6 P.M.
Admission: $6 for grounds only;
various prices for exhibitions
Getting there: Metro-North (Harlem Line) from
Grand Central to Botanical Garden stop
Website: www.nybg.org

Smell is the most acute of the five senses, a fact that makes a day trip to the New York Botanical Garden one of the most sensual experiences in the city.

Opened in 1902, our nation's largest and oldest botanical garden has 250 paradisiacal acres of blooming, burgeoning, bursting gardens and 30,000 mature trees. Add to that the turn-of-the-century, landmark Haupt Conservatory and you have an all-season olfactory feast. The clever horticulturists here have carefully planned a succession of flowers and foliage that keep the grounds in almost full color and fragrance from spring's first thaw to the onset of winter.

With so many different habitats—woodland,
rock garden, glade, pond, cultivated rose garden—
the staff can be adventurous with its plantings.
And the scents engulf you: sweet and spicy, pungent
and bitter. The air, laden with nature's infinite
perfumes, is a pleasure to breathe.

Let your nose lead you to the heady, organic smells
of the last uncut forest in the city, forty acres of
hemlock, oak, maple, and hickory (some trees
more than 250 years old) crisscrossed with mulch-
covered trails. Follow the woodland path to the old
fieldstone Snuff Mill—a good place to stop and rest
while looking out over the river. There's also a
serene conifer forest; the giant evergreens tower
above an aromatic bed of balsamic pine needles—
perhaps life's most wistful essence.

There are so many pleasurable scents emanating
from the Botanical Garden, it's wise to arrive early
and leave late. That's the best way to fully inhale
New York's most ambrosial experience.

The
New York
Earth Room

**Address: 141 Wooster St.,
a half block south of Houston St.
Phone: 212-473-8072
Hours: Wednesday through Sunday, noon to
6 P.M. (closed from 3 P.M. to 3:30 P.M.);
closed July and August
Admission: Free
Getting there: N, R to Prince St., walk west
Website: www.earthroom.org**

Y ou're going to see lots of dirt here, and you're

going to want to plunge your hands in.

Go ahead, but just remember that this is art,

not agriculture.

The Earthroom is one of New York's most pristine

yet peculiar sanctuaries—a large SoHo loft

filled with 280,000 pounds of topsoil.

It's the creation of artist Walter De Maria, a man of

few words who makes no attempt to explain his

humble earth sculpture. Nevertheless, this inert,

silent scene makes its own powerful statement about

city life—or more correctly, about the absence of pastoral simplicity in our lives.

After exclamations of disbelief, you'll be drawn into the disarming vibrations of this austere space, "empty" except for 3,600 square feet of wall-to-wall soil and a few mushrooms. Hunker down behind the low Plexiglas partition so that the huge expanse of earth is at eye level. Breathe in the sweet smell and cool moisture-laden air emanating from the rich black loam. Let the good earth remind you that it always lies softly underfoot, a healing cushion easily forgotten in a city where an impenetrable concrete crust separates you from nature's own terra firma.

Apart from a few regulars who revive themselves weekly at this fragrant, fallow field (along with one overseas businessman who makes a pilgrimage here on every trip, declaring "it's the quietest place in town"), you can call the Earth Room your own. Just don't complain to me when you realize that the dirt has a better apartment than you do.

New York Public Library and Bryant Park

Address: 42nd St., bet. Fifth and Sixth Aves.
Phone: 212-930-0830
Hours: Monday, Thursday, Friday, Saturday,
10 A.M. to 6 P.M.; Tuesday and Wednesday,
11 A.M. to 7:30 P.M.; Sunday, 1 P.M. to 5 P.M.;
park open daily, 8 A.M. to dusk
Admission: Free
Getting there: 4, 5, 6 to Grand Central, walk west
Website: www.nypl.org

In the main reading room of this massive marble library, there is a muse-worthy ceiling mural of ethereal pink clouds. I've always imagined it was painted here so people could unabashedly have their "heads in the clouds." Honestly, what better place than a library to let the imagination soar, to send creative thoughts skyward?

Built in 1911 by New York's great philanthropists, the library accommodates hundreds of people who come daily for research and refuge. There are more than 630 seats in the Rose Main Reading Room under that mackerel sky, and while they are rarely filled, visitors come to expand their minds and imaginations, not to chat. So the library doubles as a worthy place for rest and renewal.

This is such a magnificent edifice, I'm left a little breathless with every visit. The imposing Beaux Arts detailing and architectural grandeur is a reminder of how much books were revered by Americans at the turn of the twentieth century—a respect that is still evident throughout the vast library. And while the entire space is relatively noise-free despite high usage, you'll find even more seclusion if you can finagle a pass to one of the private study rooms.

Once sufficiently edified inside, go out back to the 9.6-acre makeover masterpiece, **Bryant Park**. The park was transformed in the early nineties from a spooky tangle of hedges infested with drug dealers to a secure, superbly conceived city park. The thick-growing lawn, lovingly maintained perennial borders, and spindly metal café chairs facilitate hours of mindless relaxation. There's free wireless Internet access in the park, too, for bouts of online solitaire in the shade.

Nicholas Roerich
Museum

Address: 319 West 107th St.,
bet. Broadway and Riverside Dr.
Phone: 212-864-7752
Hours: Tuesday through Sunday, 2 P.M. to 5 P.M.,
closed Mondays
Admission: Free (donations encouraged)
Getting there: 1 to 110th St., walk south
Website: www.roerich.org

nicholas Roerich was a man on a mission. He believed that promoting cultural exchange—through art, science, and religion—was the key to achieving global peace, and worked his entire lifetime to reduce belligerence between nations. He was nominated for the Nobel Peace Prize in 1929.

This little-known museum is a tribute to the Russian-born Roerich (1874–1947), a mystic, artist, and author who lived for much of his life in the Himalayas. The converted town house contains more than two hundred of his paintings and is entirely dedicated to his work and spirit. Its casual parlor-style ambience encourages leisurely, deliber-ate viewing of his expansive mountain scenes.

Allow Roerich's luminous landscapes—vibrant with tempera blues, whites, violets, and reds—to lift you up and carry you on a cloud of color to the roof of the world. There is not a disappointing painting on the entire three floors of this blissful brownstone, and most are available as reproductions. But if you really want your soul to fly, one stands out: *Kanchenjunga.* This magnificent image of snow-covered Himalayan peaks will transport you to another realm (I also picked up copies of the transcendent *Star of the Hero* and *Remember* images).

For many spiritual seekers in the West, the search for meaning seems to point East. Some even dream of a trek through the Himalayan foothills as the ultimate spiritual journey. But if neither your schedule nor your budget permits such an expedition, there's a wonderful alternative in New York. At the Nicholas Roerich Museum you'll be as close to God and heaven as you can get with your feet still on the ground. Go in peace.

OM Yoga
Center

Address: 826 Broadway at 12th St.
Phone: 212-254-9642
Hours: Classes daily from 7 A.M. to 8 P.M.
Admission: Classes start at $12
Getting there: 4, 5, 6, N, R to Union Square
Website: www.omyoga.com

Cyndi Lee, the innovative founder of OM, knows where your focus goes when you're lying on your back, practicing yoga asanas—to the ceiling. That observation is what motivated her to paint the ceilings of her four practice studios in a soothing palette of earthy colors (while the walls remained white). It's also the kind of creative detail that prompts yoga aficionados to frequently choose OM—the city's largest independent yoga center—as their top pick.

Those rich, elemental hues, chosen in consultation with a feng shui expert, evoke nature: a tranquil fern green in the Forest studio, an uplifting azure blue for the Sky studio, a hypnotic terra-cotta in the Earth studio, and an invigorating fiery yellow in the

Sun studio. One of the first classes I took at OM was held in the Forest room, where I noticed a prevailing sense of bodily ease and mental stillness as my gaze drifted up to the smooth textures of the dark green canopy.

While this busy yoga center serves as many as 2,500 people a week in more than 100 classes, the 11,500-square-foot space doesn't feel overrun. I have experienced a pleasant community feeling at OM, with a compassionate staff that is knowledgeable and eager to guide me through yoga's transformational possibilities. I bought a mat and take advantage of the gentle, stress-reducing benefits of the vinyasa-style yoga classes on a regular basis. I'm no yogi yet, but at OM they are very patient.

*Yoga Lover's Note: I have also found a soothing atmosphere and sincere, focused instruction at **Laughing Lotus Yoga** (59 W. 19th St., 212-414-2903, www.laughinglotus.com), **Kundalini Yoga** (873 Broadway, 212-982-5959, www.kundaliniyogaeast.com), and the venerable **Integral Yoga** (227 W. 13th St., 212-929-0585, www.iyiny.org).*

Open Center
Meditation Room

Address: 22 E. 30th St., between
Madison and Fifth Aves.
Phone: 212-219-2527
Hours: Daily, 10 A.M. to 10 P.M.
Admission: Free
Getting there: N, R, W to 28th St.; 6 to 28th St.
Website: www.opencenter.org

Silence. It's difficult to find anywhere, almost impossible in New York City. But if it's silence you're looking for, you should know that the Open Center Meditation Room is the single quietest place in this book.

When the center moved from its Spring Street location in 2009, where it had been for more than 25 years, I was concerned that the public meditation room would be eliminated—in this economy, it's valiant for an organization to dedicate valuable square footage to a soul-sustaining, yet nonprofit attraction. To my delight, the meditation room was not only preserved, it's an improvement on its predecessor, a thoroughly supportive and healing environment.

While not an ornate space, the 10-by-12-foot, blue-carpeted room has dozens of meditation pillows and cushions, an altar with candles, bud vase, and Buddha, and nine recessed ceiling lights that can be dimmed to darkness.

But it's the quality of quiet you'll notice immediately, an absence of sound you rarely experience in the city, a stillness that allows you to listen to your own breathing, which in itself can assist meditators deepen their experience.

The New York Open Center claims to be the largest urban holistic learning center in the world, with hundreds of fascinating courses for exploring consciousness, creativity, and spirit. The new location doubles the previous space, and includes a small café. Be sure to stop by the bookstore, too, where you'll find a unique collection of holistic and spiritual books, mind-centering CDs, and accessories for your home altar. And whether you meditate daily, or just need a comforting place to withdraw from a demanding day and pause for a moment's reflection, the Open Center's meditation room is always silent . . . and free.

Paley Park

Address: 53rd St. bet. Fifth and Madison Aves.
Hours: Monday through Saturday, 8 A.M. to
7:45 P.M.; closed January
Admission: Free
Getting there: E or F to Fifth Ave./53rd St.

Sometimes I discover a delightful pocket of city calm and I don't want to share it. I just want to keep it to myself. But Paley Park is such a welcome find in an area of the city where the triple assault of crowds, truck traffic, and noise can feel so overwhelming, it's a spot I suggest you bookmark permanently.

It's more a well-imagined public space than a suburban-style park, but in Midtown Manhattan you take whatever refuge private money is willing to pay for. An almost invisible oasis, Paley Park is situated in a concrete canyon sandwiched between two office buildings, complete with a cascading 25-foot waterfall. Designed so that visitors must step away from the continuity of the street line to enter the park, its offering of serenity is most fully

appreciated as you walk past the potted junipers
and approach the dominating waterfall.

Sitting on the stone steps facing the falls, virtually
all city sounds are muted by the resonant rumbling
of the cascade. Add the visual play of the water and
you have an experience that is both refreshing
and deeply soothing.

The small, lighted niches on each side of the
water curtain offer added seclusion. A cooling mist
bubbles up from the narrow catchment and, for me,
nestling here enhances the sense of ease.

*Note: This happy parklet contains a concession stand
and movable seating, which lures local business
people and their bagged lunches. Between noon and
2 P.M. on nice days, it tends to get crowded, although
not unpleasantly so. Skip those hours and you
can enjoy the full measure of Paley Park's
rejuvenating atmosphere.*

The Paramount Hotel Lobby

Address: 235 West 46th St.,
bet. Broadway and Eighth Ave.
Phone: 212-764-5500
Hours: Daily, 24 hours
Admission: Free
Getting there: A, C, E, 1, N, R to 42nd St.
Website: www.nycparamount.com

technically, hotel lobbies exist for the comfort and service of their guests. But in practice, any veteran of this city can tell you of a favorite hotel lobby where he or she goes to meet friends or business associates, use the "facilities," or cop some quick relief from a city that can get in one's face.

Hotel lobbies often can be quieter and more comfortable than the best public atriums, and easier to find. In lobbies with no bar, you won't be bugged to buy a drink or feel like an interloper. And unless you drag all your worldly possessions around in a laundry cart, security will never toss you to the curb.

For me, the Art Nouveau lobby of one boutique hotel stands above the rest: the Paramount. This fanciful space designed by Philippe Starck is not only cool, but generally calm. I love the boldly styled armchairs and sofas, the gray Venetian walls, the checked rug, the dramatic lighting on the sweeping staircase, and the overhanging mezzanine lounge. The bathroom is always clean and open, too.

I also duck into these other hotel lobbies for refuge frequently, and no one has ever called the gendarmes: the **Affinia Shelburne Hotel**'s intimate yellow- and rust-colored lobby does the tension-dropping trick (37th St. and Lexington Ave., 212-689-5200); the barn-wood detailing and red velour couches of the **Gramercy Park Hotel** soothe and refresh (2 Lexington Ave. at Gramercy Park, 212-920-3300); the Art Deco **Edison Hotel** lobby offers a quick escape from the abyss of Times Square (228 West 47th St., near 8th Ave., 212-840-5000); and the **Grand Hyatt** has those sound-softening water-falls (42nd St. and Lexington Ave., 212-883-1234).

The Pier at Riverside South

Address: Near 68th St. in Riverside Park;
enter at 72nd St.
Phone: 800-201-PARK
Hours: Daily, dawn to dusk
Admission: Free
Getting there: 1 to 72nd St.,
walk five minutes southwest

With the recent openings of several lush, handsomely landscaped Hudson River Pier Parks (see page 42), it's easy to forget one of the first of the ingeniously renovated jetties. This waterside park seemed an inspired idea from the outset. As a West Side commuter, I eagerly anticipated the finished result during the many months crews spent reinforcing the old maritime wharf, capping it with concrete, and laying down the circular shapes and swirling, whimsical brickwork that would form today's recreation-friendly site.

The pier is one of the many highlights of this 21½ acre Riverside South waterfront development that has returned lost and neglected shoreline to the public. Adjacent to the pier is a 50-foot strip of concrete and wood boardwalks swelling with hearty dune grasses. Beach blankets and strollers dot the landscape, and a three-season open-air café offers refreshment.

But I suggest leaving the hard coastline for a walk out on the alluring jetty. Thrusting 150 feet into the river, it seems to place you at the center of the Hudson River shipping lanes. Along the edges of this 40-foot-wide pier you'll find dozens of bolted, wire-mesh stadium seats pleasantly positioned to allow alternating views of the city skyline and unhurried river traffic. The architects showed exceptional sensitivity, an understanding of the romantic promise of the river and the power of whispered sonnets at sunset—most of the seating is in pairs, with plenty of distance between placements. Sweet.

On spring and summer nights, this pier and adjacent esplanade are quintessentially tranquil places to speak softly, share secret longings, and hold hands securely.

Poets
House

**Address: 10 River Terrace at Murray St.,
Battery Park City
Phone: 212-431-7920
Hours: Tuesday through Friday, 11 A.M. to 7 P.M.;
Saturday, 11 A.M. to 6 P.M.; closed Sunday
Admission: Free
Getting there: 1, 2, 3, A or C to Chambers St.,
walk west
Website: www.poetshouse.org**

Word nourishment is a kind of soul food. If we're lucky, it sustains us beginning in childhood with reassuring rhymes read to us at bedtime. Then it follows us into adulthood, revealing its poetic messages in the folds of verse and meter, affirming life by paying homage to our most intimate moments, adding transparency to our deepest feelings.

If you want a generous helping of this subtle nourishment, the new Poets House in Battery Park City is designed for easy intake of meaningful words. After 17 years in a Soho loft, the Poets House moved to a spectacular, block-long, glass-enclosed "green" space on the Hudson River in 2009. Dramatic and yet serene, with expansive park and sunset views, this is the kind of home poetry deserves.

Of course, delivering the power of poetry is nothing new to the people at Poets House. They've been promoting the value and richness of poetry since 1985, when poets Stanley Kunitz and Elizabeth Kray founded the sanctuary for sonnets and refuge for rhyme. It is still one of the most extraordinary public depositories of poetry in the world, with more than 50,000 volumes in its airy, new, 11,000-square-foot center.

Sunlight streaming in through the west-facing windows brings the books to life, and the entire space has colorfully upholstered reading chairs and communal work desks for your quiet comfort. You can come here to read the poetry you love or be inspired to write your own. There is also a full calendar of readings and events for insatiable fans of this form.

Poems are fertile places for quiet self-discoveries, a way to open to our souls on our own terms. The new Poets House makes those terms exceptionally agreeable.

The Quad at Columbia University

Address: 116th St. and Broadway
Hours: Daily, 8 A.M. to 6 P.M.
Admission: Free
Getting there: 1 to 116th St.

Columbia University has a stellar academic reputation, but did you know it's also possible to get an Ivy League education in relaxation on campus? This vital learning happens on the spacious main quad, just steps from the tumult of Broadway, where you can make a quick transfer from the school of urban survival to a restful course on personal revival.

Safely insulated from the busy avenues that surround it, the campus is an epicenter both for academic activity and reclusive repose. There's no need to worry about your age or how you're dressed either—people will assume you're a graduate student or an esteemed university professor strolling to your next class.

Relaxation 101 is self-taught every day in front of the Low Library, where you can nestle against the easternmost corner of that noble 12-foot wall. It's a warm, windless nook excellent for cerebral reading—a popular pastime for all who recline on the broad lawns. You might prefer the smaller, less-frequented quad in front of Uris Hall (look for Clement Meadmore's 1968 *Curl* sculpture of twisted black tubes). Or amble through the maze of century-old buildings until you find your own solitary spot. There are dozens of places on this postcard-perfect campus where you can partake of the scholarly atmosphere undisturbed.

I used to take a bagged lunch on Saturdays to the university quad, where I met a friend for heady discussions on the state of the world. The historic campus was always a quiescent place for intellectual and physical renewal. It still gets my highest grade.

Robert F. Wagner Jr. Park

Address: Battery Pl. and West St.
Phone: 212-416-5300
Hours: Daily, dawn to dusk
Admission: Free
Getting there: R to Battery Park;
6 to Bowling Green; 1 to South Ferry
Website: www.bpcparks.org

good green grass isn't easy to find in New York. I'm talking about the really dense, carpet-thick stuff that's not trampled thin by soccer cleats, littered with cigarette butts, or dotted with dog doo—the kind of lush covering you can lie on, letting your tension seep into the earth.

One of Manhattan's most inviting public expanses of open lawn is in the spectacular Robert Wagner Park, tucked between the expanded Museum of Jewish Heritage and Battery Park in lower Manhattan. A small but masterfully designed wedge of land jutting into the lower harbor, this is an ideal place to watch passing river traffic while comfortably sprawled over soft turf (or if

you prefer observing from on high, climb to
the elevated roof deck).

A team of urban horticulturists has transformed
acres of landfill here into one of the finest display
gardens anywhere in New York. A vibrant palette of
perennials and annuals explodes from dozens of
carefully organized tree pits and planting beds
(in the north and southwest corners), all casting
sweet perfumes across manicured lawns.
Those near-flawless lawns are preserved without
herbicides and pesticides. In fact, they eschew
the use of toxic chemicals here. So feel free
to pluck a blade of grass and nibble on it.

Robert Wagner gets some spillover from Lady
Liberty–bound tourists in nearby Battery Park.
But early on a spring or summer morning, you can
pick a solitary spot on the northern lawn, stare out
at the best harbor views in Manhattan, and let the
blanket of soft blades under your back turn you
warm and wistful. Good green grass—
Mother Earth's natural tranquilizer.

The Rubin
Museum of Art

Address: 150 West 17th St. at Seventh Ave.
Phone: 212-620-5000
Hours: Monday and Thursday, 11 A.M. to 5 P.M.;
Wednesday, 11 A.M. to 7 P.M.; Friday,
11 A.M. to 10 P.M.; Saturday and Sunday,
11 A.M. to 6 P.M.; closed Tuesday
Admission: $10
Getting there: A, C, E to 14th St. and 8th Ave;
1, 2, 3 to 14th St. and 7th Ave.
Website: www.rmanyc.org

The Rubin Museum has a steel-and-marble staircase (famously inherited from the space's former incarnation as the original Barney's store) that spirals up through the seven-story gallery space with dramatic effect. But once this stunning architectural element is absorbed, everything else at the Rubin works to quiet the senses.

There is something palpably slow and peaceful about this intimate museum dedicated to Tibetan and Himalayan art. Much of it—from Bhutan, Tibet, Mongolia, Nepal, India, and China—was created in service to indigenous religions, and the spiritual significance impacts the viewer. Themes like man's suffering, life after death, and the importance of religious devotion are repeated in many of the works on display, but their power is not diminished from one artistic retelling to the next.

Ritual objects, sculptures, scroll paintings, and textiles, many dating from as early as the Second century, carry messages that are often foreign to the Western experience, but nevertheless compelling and thought provoking. The Rubin's high concentration of sacred objects also seems to dramatically uplift the spirit. One recent wall inscription from an esteemed mystic captured the mood precisely: "Flight is within our potential as human beings."

Visit the Rubin and soar for yourself.

Note: There is a modern, handsomely designed café in the lobby here that is a truly quiet and refreshing place to enjoy healthful snacks and fragrant spice teas. I've stepped off the street to relax and imbibe without ever visiting the Rubin's upstairs exhibitions themselves. I trust all those flying mystics and female Buddhas on the floors above are sending their enlightened messages down those spiral steps, washing over my café table.

st. **Luke's Garden**

Address: Hudson St. bet. Barrow and Grove Sts.
Phone: 212-924-0562
Hours: Monday through Friday, 8 A.M. to 7 P.M.;
Saturday and Sunday, 1 P.M. to 4 P.M.
Admission: Free
Getting there: 1 to
Sheridan Square, walk west

for years, I'd peer over the high brick wall on Hudson Street, envious of whoever had access to this private backyard. I'd catch glimpses of colorful climbing roses, sparrows hopping on spindly birch branches, a border flush with variegated plants along a narrow brick walkway. It evoked memories of a suburban childhood, where my backyard was a private place to hide in a daydream or stare at the sky. While I knew a fast-paced world was rushing past my front door, out back life was easy and innocent and fun.

It turns out, all my peering was pointless. You can easily enter this walled treasure by following the footpath running along the parking lot a little west on Barrow Street. The creaky wrought-iron gate on Hudson is often open now, too, permitting easy access.

St. Luke's Garden actually does function as a backyard for several quaint nineteenth-century brownstones that enclose the secret garden on two sides. Splendidly concealed behind that ivy-blanketed brick wall, the two-acre garden feels well removed from street activity, a pocket of calm and quiet that mirrors the slower pace of the surrounding West Village.

The mandalalike design of its stone pathways and the thoughtfully placed magnolia-hidden benches contribute to a sense of "backyard" privacy. The rustic potting shed in the northeast corner adds to the picturesque charm. Be sure to visit this neat retreat in fall and winter, too, when the ancient brick walls radiate heat, and the lingering foliage shimmers in tones of gray, brown, green, and rust.

Shambhala Meditation Center of New York

Address: 118 West 22nd St., 6th Fl.
Phone: 212-675-6544
Hours: Drop-in meditation, Monday through
Friday, 12 P.M. and 5 P.M.; Public sittings,
Monday through Friday, 5:30 to 7 P.M.;
Sunday, 9 A.M. to Noon
Admission: Free for drop-in meditation;
see website for class fees
Getting there: 1, F, V to 23rd St.
Website: www.ny.shambhala.org

Shambhala has been in their current Chelsea location since 1998. Since then, tens of thousands of people have passed through the facility's Main Shrine Room to meditate, sit in silence, practice mindfulness, study Buddhism, and discover the wisdom that lives within.

As I sat alone in the shrine room recently during walk-in meditation hours, propped up on a cushioned mat and navy blue pillow, I wondered if it was possible for four walls to harness the calming energy of countless inhalations and exhalations? Could a physical space resonate with the peaceful, compassionate intentions of an entire meditative community?

These questions arose because on that particular visit I brought a lot of stress with me to Shambhala—a tension that started to ease moments after settling onto my meditation pillow a few feet in front of the ornate altar in this 40-by-60-foot room. I had barely closed my eyes and hadn't started any deep breath work, and yet, I felt calmer. Could the room itself be doing something to me—giving me a head start toward stilling my mind?

These are questions you can answer for yourself because Shambhala makes their three meditation rooms, each with its own unique character and amenities, available to the public. Dedicated to the contemplative traditions of the center's spiritual leaders, founder Chogyam Trungpa Rinpoche and current leader Sakyong Mipham Rinpoche, Shambhala offers a wonderful series of classes and workshops to help individuals cultivate wisdom, compassion, gentleness, and courage through meditation practice and mindful living. Take a look at the website for details.

Sakyong Rinpoche teaches that the natural state of the mind is calm and clear. Sitting at Shambhala, even for a short while, you can start to believe it.

South Cove

Address: South End Ave. at Battery Park City
Hours: Daily, 24 hours
Admission: Free
Getting there: A, C, E to World Trade Center,
walk west
Website: www.bpcparks.org

built in 1987 both as a meditative recess and entrance to a liquid world, South Cove is uniquely situated to immerse you in the sights, sounds, and scents of the New York waterfront.

The vision of environmental artist Mary Miss and landscape architect Susan Child, everything about South Cove—from the boulder-studded boardwalk and bowed bridge to the arching jetty and crownlike observation deck—is designed to get visitors closer to the shoreline. You can sometimes even feel the surge of the river from certain points along the curving architecture of this sheltered recess, as the harmonious sounds of its swirling eddies, pushing into the seawall underfoot, calls you to the water's edge.

The three-acre coastal park overflows with sunny seats, too, like the rail-tie benches against the south-facing wall that stay warm even in winter. An upper terrace, with winding walkways through a dense stand of honey locusts, is dotted with shaded benches overlooking the cove.

While September 11, 2001, changed the landscape of Manhattan's south tip forever, this riverfront refuge remains intact. Even with a massive construction effort underway on the 1 World Trade Center complex nearby, you can find a wealth of waterside peace and quiet here. Keep in mind that the extremely safe, always quiet South Cove reveals its most compelling feature at night, when a series of cobalt blue ship's lanterns turns the nook into a dreamy fantasyland. This is the precious, whispering light of the heart—bring along a friend.

*Note: Walk north along the bench-lined esplanade lined with mini-parks and gardens. You'll be lead to the **World Financial Center Plaza** and its wharf-like mall that acts as a haven for frazzled money managers and passing pedestrians.*

Strawberry
Fields

Address: Central Park West at 72nd St.
Hours: Daily, dawn to dusk
Admission: Free
Getting there: B or C to 72nd St.
Website: www.centralpark.com/pages/attractions/
strawberry-fields.html

he asked us to imagine a world where there was nothing "to kill or die for" and all the people "were living life in peace." Years later he was shot to death in front of The Dakota apartments where he lived, just steps from this bucolic site, a tribute to his life as a singer and peace activist.

In 1981, Strawberry Fields was named a "Garden of Peace" in memory of Beatles icon John Lennon, who enjoyed walking through this favored section of Central Park with his wife Yoko Ono. In the years since, the teardrop-shaped area has lived up to that designation, becoming an essential destination for reverent fans of one of the city's adopted sons.

This free-flowing, two-and-a-half-acre, living
memorial to Lennon seems to be permanently
imbued with the spirit of the sixties. Once you
step over the black-and-white "Imagine" mosaic
embedded in the footpath leading to
Strawberry Fields, you feel just a bit more
hopeful—much like we did back then.

The idyllic setting is always scrupulously cared for,
thanks to private funds earmarked for its upkeep.
Sun-dappled and friendly in every season, the tall
elm trees, planted flowerbeds, and grassy knolls get
daily, almost constant attention. Strawberry Fields
is also marked as a "Quiet Zone," and respect
for Lennon does appear to mute both tourists
and residents who visit.

You won't have any trouble finding breathing space
here, but you can treat yourself to a private moment
by walking to the northernmost end of the
upper lawn where it comes to an abrupt point.
See that lovely redwood tree in front of the hedge
line? Under that tree I fed a sparrow a piece
of bread from my hand. Imagine.

Stuyvesant
Square

Address: Bet. Rutherford Pl. and Second Ave.,
from 15th to 17th Sts.
Hours: Daily, dawn to 11 P.M.
Getting there: 4, 5, 6, N, R to 14th St.,
walk northeast

With more than 1,700 parks in the five boroughs, it would be easy to overlook a relatively small one like Stuyvesant Square. But this is a remarkable neighborhood park, not only encircled by the oldest cast-iron fence in the city (circa 1847), but also acting as front yard for the lovely, landmarked Friends Meeting House (1861).

Actually, there are two sections of the four-acre square straddling Second Avenue. It is the western part that I prefer, having fewer visitors and situated farther away from the foot traffic and passing ambulances of adjacent Beth Israel Hospital. This western section is frequented more by locals, who respect and help protect the lawns, shrubs, and restored flowerbeds that make this slower-paced portion so appealing.

Perhaps because so many features and details of the park are mid-nineteenth-century original, including much of the bluestone walkways, Stuyvesant Square feels like another time and place. There is a wonderful center fountain (1884) that mesmerizes with its cheerful burble. Neighbors relax under the shade of mature English elms and little leaf lindens, reading the paper or talking to old friends. There are always a few moms pushing strollers around the roughly quarter-mile-long walking loop. Birds sing, no one rushes, and Stuyvesant Square prepares for another 160 years of providing simple refuge to New Yorkers who can use it.

Note: This book would not be complete without mentioning an organization that has virtually institutionalized peace and quiet—the Quakers. They gather at the Friends Meeting House (15 Rutherford Place, 212-777-8866), Sunday mornings at 9:30 and 11 a.m. A Quaker meeting is unique, as worshippers wait in silence for God's message to reach assembled "Friends."

Sutton Place Park

Address: Sutton Pl. at 57th St.
Hours: Daily, dawn to dusk
Admission: Free
Getting there: 4, 5, 6 to 59th St., walk east

the most rejuvenating urban parks are those with a distinct feeling of detachment from the noise and turbulence of the city.

The physical design of Sutton Place Park makes it just such a hospitable setting. A three-foot retaining wall and an eight-foot drop from street level completely conceal this park from Sutton Place and 57th Street. But it's there, tucked between a stately brownstone and a tall residential building. Descend the switchback ramp and you'll enter a friendly and protected realm.

At first, your gaze settles on *Porcellino*, the lounging, life-size wild boar (a replica of a beloved seventeenth-century bronze sculpture in Florence), who patiently and imposingly presides over this quiet quadrangle. Next, your eyes are drawn to the movement of the East River—the park's visual focal point. If you stand near the edge of the park and look out, you have the feeling you're suspended over swirling waters. This evokes the pleasant sensation of riding atop the river currents, and lures the mind away from outer-world intrusions.

Extensively renovated several years ago, the park has never been more appealing. New additions include a grid-work surface of bold red brick, a granite-rimmed circular sandbox, four grassy play areas (nannies with toddlers come to see *Porcellino*), and nineteenth-century-style Bishop's Crook lamps. Sutton Place is also one of the city's most exclusive neighborhoods, and as a result, this cribbed quad is well protected. Visitors here are genteel and respectful, the atmosphere is sedate, and you'll ascend the ramp to the real world with renewed equanimity.

The Terrace
at 40th Street

Address: 622 Third Ave. at 40th St.
Hours: Weekdays, April 1 to November 1,
7 A.M. to 8 P.M.; Saturday and Sunday,
9 A.M. to 6 P.M.; Weekdays, Nov. 2 to March 31,
9 A.M. to 6 P.M., closed weekends
Admission: Free
Getting there: 4, 5, 6, 7 to Grand Central Station,
walk southeast

We walk head down, eyes on the sidewalk, maintaining a determined gait as we push to our next appointments. But this beeline betrays us. If we would slow our pace and look up once in a while, we might find an unexpected treasure. Like this hidden rooftop terrace.

Despite initial impressions, this is not a private "patio" for customers of the upscale restaurant below; it's a communal public space designed for your alfresco pleasure. You can enter the airy terrace—hovering 25 feet above the street—from the steep, outdoor staircase on Third Avenue, just north of 40th Street (if your thighs start

burning, there's elevator access in the northwest
corner of the building).

There are no amenities, and nothing particularly
fancy about this unseen setting, just plenty of
fixed, mesh-metal benches and a dozen silver lunch
tables with movable chairs, all nestled among large
concrete planters with tender young birch trees
and dense shrubs for privacy. Two trellises at the
east and west ends of this sunlit space, both covered
with faux grape vines, offer some protection from
the sun at high noon. Good security and very few
people (perhaps thanks to all those stairs)
heighten its "lofty" appeal.

You can enjoy a leisurely, brown-bag lunch here,
or tilt your head back and gaze into the patch of
dizzying sky framed by five office buildings looming
above. This induces a delightful state of reverie.
While sounds from Third Avenue can occasionally
climb up the walls and spill onto the terrace,
I'm still happy to know it's here—an unadorned,
yet always reliable escape from the
thrumming demands of Midtown.

Trinity **Church**

Address: Broadway at Wall St.
Phone: 212-602-0800
Hours: Weekdays, 7 A.M. to 6 P.M.; Saturday,
8 A.M. to 4 P.M.; Sunday, 7 A.M. to 4 P.M.
Admission: Free
Getting there: 4, 5, 2, 3 to Wall St.
Website: www.trinitywallstreet.org

here's a revelation: there are safe, serene, comfortable buildings every few blocks in this city, accessible to the public, open every day, and set aside for nothing more than providing shelter from life's daily storms, a quiet place to be alone, a sanctuary to cultivate some peace of mind.

I'm speaking of churches (or synagogues, or mosques), and they're everywhere. Take advantage of them. I am not in search of spiritual salvation myself, but I rarely miss a chance to slip into the stillness of a nearby church for a few minutes of rest and self-centering.

Trinity Church has always been among my favorites, for three soul-soothing reasons:

the handsome nave of this 1840s, neo-Gothic church offers a surprising core of calm in the busy financial district; the bench-filled churchyard, particularly near the western edge, is a relaxing place to bring a deli lunch year round, while the gravestones keep the superstitious and ghost-wary away; the regular Concerts at One series (which really start at 12:45 P.M.) pampers the senses with a refreshing musical recess.

Trinity Church is too far downtown? You'll find several sanctuaries for the spirit to be equally sustaining. **St. Patrick's Cathedral** (Fifth Ave. bet. 50th and 51st Sts.), despite its many visitors, has the breathtaking stained glass to silence visitors, plus acres of polished wooden pews and always an isolated corner in which to escape. I also recommend **Grace Church** (Broadway and 10th St.), **Marble Collegiate Church** (Fifth Ave. and 29th St.), **Temple Emanu-El** (Fifth Ave. and 65th St.), and the **Cathedral of St. John the Divine** (West 112th St. and Amsterdam Ave.) with its live peacocks on the adjacent Pulpit Lawn.

Tsampa

**Address: 212 East 9th St., bet. Second
and Third Aves.
Phone: 212-614-3226
Hours: Open daily, 5 P.M. to 11:30 P.M.
Admission: $8.95–$12.95 for entrees
Getting there: 6 to Astor Pl.; N, R to 8th St.,
walk east**

t can be a challenge to find a peaceful dining refuge in New York. If it's too quiet, the food is probably below average or, worse, the restaurant is about to shutter its doors. What you're looking for is a place where management is attentive to ambience and consciously creates an environment where easy conversational tones are possible.

I appreciate the effort they make at Tsampa, where reasonably priced, flavorful Tibetan dishes are served under a prayer flag, the overhead lighting is subdued, and soul-soothing Eastern chants or flute music aids digestion. Ask for a table in the back room, where you can eat and talk without straining your vocal chords as you gaze out at a spotlit, well-loved window garden complete with Buddhas, altarpieces, and vibrant growth. Sipping a cup of Tibetan bocha tea while listening to the trickling water fountain brings an agreeable belly-calming stillness to the end of a happy meal.

A diner's right to relaxed conversation is respected at these eateries, too: **The Adore** (17 East 13th St., 212-243-8742) has a rustic upstairs nook best enjoyed over soup on a lazy afternoon; **HanGawi** (12 East 32nd St., 212-213-0077) is a haven for healthy Korean food; **Indigo Indian Bistro** (357 East 50th St., 646-350-3671) serves delicious ethnic fare in a pleasant atmosphere; the intimate **Emilio's Ballato** (55 East Houston St., 212-274-8881) is my downtown favorite; the uplifting **New Leaf Café** (Fort Tryon Park, 212-568-5323) is in a stone house nestled among trees.

Note: I've purposely included only Manhattan restaurants—in the other boroughs, it's much easier to avoid a high-decibel dinner.

Wave Hill

Address: West 249th St. and
Independence Ave., Bronx
Phone: 718-549-3200
Hours: Tuesday through Sunday, 9 A.M. to
5:30 P.M. (4:30 P.M. in winter); closed Monday
Admission: $8 (free Tuesdays and Saturdays,
9 A.M. to noon; also free Tuesdays all day on
off-peak months; check website for details)
Getting there: Check website for directions
with all transportation modes
Website: www.wavehill.org

the first time I saw the Wild Garden at
Wave Hill, with its secluded gazebo and carefully
planned chaos of hillside cultivation, I was relieved.
I knew that I would never have to purchase a
country home or cabin in the woods to achieve
a feeling of getting far away from the city
without ever leaving.

To say Wave Hill is special is to minimize the
impact that 28 acres of award-winning gardens, a
trio of greenhouses, sweeping lawns, huge copper
beech trees, a lily pond, and unspoiled woodlands
on a hilltop facing the 500-foot Palisades can have
on nature-deprived city folk. Currently owned by

the city, the Wave Hill estate in the Riverdale section of the Bronx performs the same function as it did when such famous former residents as Teddy Roosevelt, Mark Twain, and Arturo Toscanini made it their weekend getaway. It offers anyone with an exuberant love of growing things a verdant and ever-changing escape just 20 minutes from Manhattan.

The former mansion contains a cottagelike gift shop and café with outdoor seating, but it's the clean air and open land at Wave Hill, with lots of inviting spots to turn your back on a tight and toxic city, that provides a sensorial feast. Many gravitate toward the Italian pergola framing the river views, or the Marco Polo Stufano Conservatory with its all-season exotic displays.

But it's the ancient elm, sumac, beech, redwood, and maple trees that call to me. If you're as starved for deep roots and soaring limbs as I am, just grab one of the high-backed, signature lawn chairs, slide it under a canopy of protective branches, and let the wonders of Wave Hill's world-class landscape wash over you.

Yelo

**Address: 315 West 57th St., bet. Eighth
and Ninth Aves.**
Phone: 212-245-8235
**Hours: Monday through Friday, 10 A.M. to 9 P.M.;
Saturday, 12 P.M. to 8 P.M.; Sunday,
12 P.M. to 7 P.M.**
**Admission: $15 for 20 minutes, $28 for
40 minutes**
Getting there: N, R to 57th St.; A, E to 59th St.
Website: www.yelonyc.com

Yelo won me over minutes after I entered my sleek "napping pod" and plunked myself down on the cozy, custom recliner. The attendant was describing the features of my private relaxation cabin, but I was barely listening. I felt so drowsy, I wished she'd stop talking so I could surrender to my sinking eyelids and doze off. The weird thing is, it was morning. And I wasn't tired.

And I'm not really a nap person!

What you discover quickly at Yelo is that this is not your kindergarten-variety nap. This is high-tech relaxation therapy based on the latest sleep science, and you'd have to be on a bushel of amphetamines and a bucket of coffee not to succumb.

Owner Nick Ronco knows more about the rejuvenating power of napping than the Sandman. He can quote from reams of scientific evidence about the benefits of daily naps, including increased productivity and mental alertness, reduced stress, and improved overall well-being.

The somnolence begins inside his specially designed YeloCabs—virtually soundproof, honeycomb-shaped sleep pods. A soft recliner surrounds you like a beige leather cocoon, elevating your legs to slow your heart rate. You customize the aromatherapy scent vaporized into the pod and select from a choice of calming music or sedating environmental soundtracks. When your nap is over, you're roused from slumber by a unique LED lighting system that simulates a rising dawn. The overall effect is magical and immediate—like mainlining melatonin with none of the risks.

If you want to maximize the power doze, add a shoulder or foot massage to your sleepy time at Yelo, and watch the zzz's form a thought bubble over your head. That's naptime, New York-style.

More Great Places For Rest, Renewal, and Rejuvenation

AIA Center for Architecture

**Address: 536 LaGuardia Pl.,
just north of Bleecker St.
Phone: 212-683-0023
Website: www.aiany.org**

I like buildings that like people. Buildings designed on a human scale, flooded with natural light so that you're not longing to be outside when you're in. The American Institute of Architecture, an elegant and serene gallery where professionals and the public can immerse themselves in architecture-related events and exhibitions, is exactly this kind of place. Its dramatic 64-foot-wide glass façade is part of an ingenious lighting scheme that ushers luminous, soothing natural light deep into two sub-basement venues. Contributing to the center's tranquil appeal is a conscious attention to sustainability—with renewable cork flooring and wall coverings throughout, plus the first geothermal system in a public building in Manhattan. The result is a pleasing space that lets you shift effortlessly into a lower gear before re-engaging with the city's quickened pulse.

Bike Path on
the Hudson River Greenway

Address: Battery Park to 207th St.

Pedal strokes are like a cadenced meditation to me. Which is why I am grateful to the city for its commitment to building safe, scenic, traffic-free trails for civilized cyclists throughout the boroughs. The Hudson River Greenway is a favorite serpentine stretch, part of an ambitious greenway system that links city neighborhoods through a continuous esplanade. While there are plenty of grassy spots to scoot off the bike path and relax, explore the lovely northernmost portions of the greenway from 140th Street to 207th Street where the cycling crowds thin out dramatically (and sitting on the rocks below the innocent Little Red Lighthouse at 178th Street is a page out of a children's book). Other great routes include the picturesque four miles of the FDR Boardwalk in Staten Island and the amiable bike path that loops lazily around Meadow Lake in Flushing Meadows-Corona Park in Queens. For more pedal points visit www.nycbikemaps.com.

Brooklyn Botanic Garden

Address: 1000 Washington Ave., Brooklyn
Phone: 718-623-7200
Website: www.bbg.org

Except for the Tidal Basin in Washington, D.C., there is no place in the country during cherry blossom season like the BBG. And few places in the city offer such a total package of rest and refreshment as this horticulturally varied, 52-acre palette of ever-changing color and beauty.

Two destinations top my list here. The traditional Japanese Hill-and-Pond Garden is a secluded arcadia, highlighted by a bucolic pond where you can watch the colorful koi loll through still waters. Walk around the pond to the second tier of waterfalls, where small grottos in the rock create a soothing, aural tapestry of overlapping echoes. Over at the Fragrance Garden, you're encouraged to rub the leaves of plants both obscure and familiar. On the tips of your fingers, you'll capture hints of lemon and mint, fennel and lavender—inviting essences that can trigger a lifetime of remembrances.

Central Park
Boating

**Address: Loeb Boathouse, 72nd St.
and Fifth Ave., walk 200 yards north
Phone: 212-517-2233
Website: www.centralpark.com/pages/
attractions/loeb-boathouse.html**

This is one place where I guarantee you won't
be bugged or bothered, badgered or bullied.
Even on busy summer weekends, rowing on the
Central Park Lake is a refreshing, solitary escape.
Wherever you can row, you can go, and with more
than 18 acres of open water and side pools, you can
go far. Pass under the quaint wooden
footbridge, watch flocks of waterbirds take flight,
skim your boat from reed bed to a shallow inlet,
and take in the surrounding cityscape from your
tranquil, midlake vantage point. Bird-watchers
have documented sightings of more than 750
different species near the lake, including long-eared
owls, snow geese, and red-headed woodpeckers.
But whether you're a birder or a boater, this is
an idyllic setting for recalibrating your sanity.

Governor's Island Park

**Address: In the harbor, 800 yards from
Lower Manhattan by ferry**
Phone: 212-825-3045
Website: www.govisland.com

For people who value rest, retreat, and relaxation, Governor's Island has to be viewed as 172-acres of incredible potential. The city just took control of the island from the state in early 2010, so plans for an ambitious 40-acre park (including snoozing cocoons in a hammock forest, wetlands, and man-made hills and meadows) and a 2.2-mile-long circumferential esplanade won't be in full swing until 2012. But as it stands, Governor's Island has its place in this book. While the ferry ride over can get crowded, once on the island it's easy to find solitude along the existing bay-front promenade. The most secluded spot I found was on the eastern edge of the island facing Brooklyn, where visitors inexplicably eschew a number of lovely, tree-shaded park benches and a peaceful new pier. And stay tuned, because Governor's Island will only be getting better.

Housing Works
Used Bookstore Café

**Address: 126 Crosby St., bet. Houston
and Prince Sts.
Phone: 212-334-3324
Website: www.housingworks.org**

Once upon a time, we went to our neighborhood bookstores to bathe in contemplative silence. Preferably that bookstore would have walls lined floor to ceiling with mahogany bookcases; tables overflowing with tempting titles; comfortable chairs nestled in discrete corners; a relaxed atmosphere where the works of great writers could be lingered over, not rushed through. There aren't many of those private literary oases left, but I find this second-hand treasure trove in SoHo (all the titles are donated) to be sweeter than the Strand and more intimate than any Barnes & Noble megastore. The balcony is best, lined on both sides with enticing tomes that turn it into a veritable browser's paradise. Housing Works has a conscience, too: proceeds from sales are used to provide housing, health care, and other services for homeless men and women with AIDS and HIV.

Inwood Hill Park
Riverfront Trail

**Address: Enter through park fence at Dyckman
St. next to Marina and Hudson River
Website: www.nycgovparks.org/
parks/inwoodhillpark**

I have walked down sandy lanes in eastern
Long Island and Martha's Vineyard that were
no more inviting than this one. This little-known,
delightfully secluded, yet safe walking and cycling
trail runs along the Hudson River for more than a
mile, and it is an astonishing find. I stumbled upon
it while mountain biking one spring afternoon, and
followed it to the end as it turns to a single track,
sandwiched between an Amtrak cyclone fence and
a rocky drop off toward the water. Along the way,
there are secondary paths that wind through low
trees, shrubs, and wild grasses onto open spots with
views of the river and the George Washington
Bridge. After an hour on this unhurried,
out-of-the-way Inwood Hill path, you will easily
believe you're hundreds of miles outside of
the city. The Vineyard be damned.

The Jefferson Market Garden

Address: Greenwich Ave. bet. 9th and 10th Sts.
Website: www.jeffersonmarketgarden.org

This is a city that glorifies intensity and excitement, and many New Yorkers are inherent thrill seekers. We like everything bigger, brighter, and more sensational. But a need for equilibrium dwells inside us, too, quietly asking us to consider the city on a smaller scale, and take periodic refuge in a simpler New York. The quaint Jefferson Market Garden sits unobtrusively behind a high wrought-iron fence in the shadow of the Victorian Gothic spires of the Jefferson Market Library. From May through October (every day except Monday), you can sidestep the city and slip into the garden's unhurried charms. This little haven, resplendent with flourishing color in the growing seasons, is designed to stimulate interest in horticulture and the environment. Just follow the red-brick road that snakes through the garden, compose yourself, and appreciate life's gentle wonders.

La Casa Day Spa
Floatation

**Address: 41 East 20th St., bet. Park Ave.
and Broadway
Phone: 212-673-2272
Website: www.lacasaspa.com**

At this detox-oriented day spa, you will find a sterile, state-of-the-art floatation room designed to provide the ultimate in relaxation. All you bring is your over-taxed body. The process is simple. You climb into eight inches of water so infused with Epsom salts that anything (and anyone) will float. Because the water is warmed to precise body temperature, a feeling of weightlessness ensues. Your tightly wound muscles begin to release, as the warm, silky liquid rocks you into a state of suspended tranquility. Within seconds, your buoyant body surrenders to the anti-gravity effects, and a profound mind and body melting begins. Some studies even suggest that a two-hour float can be more restful than a full night's sleep. In any case, soaking in warm water is good for you. Floating weightlessly in your own private sea, tension draining effortlessly from your body . . . that's healing.

Liz Christy Bowery-Houston Garden

**Address: Northeast corner of
Houston and Bowery Sts.
Phone: 212-594-2155
Website: www.lizchristygarden.org**

No matter how many high-rises they throw up around it, this stubborn little community garden insists on hanging in there. And as long as it does, I'll include it on these pages. There are now 700-plus community gardens in the city, but this is the original. In 1973 activist Liz Christy and her resident band of Green Guerillas were the first to successfully reclaim a rubble-strewn lot and return it to a fertile place for growing and gardening. Today volunteers regularly till, weed, and water the 60 beds bursting with vegetables, fruit trees, and fragrant herbs. I am always amazed at how a trio of birch trees and a low ridge of thick wildflowers can buffer the heavy sounds of Houston Street traffic. It's easy to see why locals stop here for quick encounters with nature, whether to gaze at the small pond or pluck grapes from the simple trellis.

Mahayana Buddhist Temple

Address: 133 Canal St. at Manhattan Bridge Plaza
Phone: 212-925-8787
Admission: Free

Chinatown is noisy, crowded, and chaotic. Mahayana Buddhist Temple is here to rescue you. Pass the requisite gold lions at the front door through a passageway with religious souvenirs (for a dollar you can get a tiny scroll with words of wisdom printed on it, mostly phrases from Buddhist scriptures, and fun). A few feet farther on you'll see stall-like altars built along the walls, filled with reverently arranged fruits and offerings. Finally you enter a massive main hall, a colorful red and gold haven with comfortable upholstered benches arranged at the foot of a 20-foot-tall, gilded Buddha. Right hand raised in blessing, the sitting Buddha's quiet eyes are watchful and reassuring. Chants and incense fill the air while locals pray. Take your time. Gather your thoughts. Keep calm. Carry on.

Mount Vernon Hotel Museum and Garden

Address: 421 E 61st St., bet. First and York Aves.
Phone: 212-838-6878
Website: www.mvhm.org

There are few places in the city where you can step into our colonial past, but this charming museum acts as a virtual time machine. Constructed in 1799, the former carriage house is one of only seven surviving eighteenth-century buildings in Manhattan still open to the public. In 1826, it was converted to a fashionable "day hotel" catering to affluent New Yorkers who would escape to the "country" from lower Manhattan for rural walks, fishing, saltwater bathing, and other leisurely pastimes. The museum tour is excellent, but I'm drawn to the backyard garden with its ample dose of colonial-era serenity. Languish on the simple teak benches amidst the precisely planted flora and colorful perennials, or climb the steps in the garden's northwest corner to a peaceful upper terrace, where there's a natural schist outcropping ideal for three-season sunning.

Pier 44 Waterfront Garden

Address: 290 Conover St. at Pier 44, Red Hook, Brooklyn (Note: From Manhattan take $5 ferry at Pier 11)
Website: www.publicgardendesign.com/ projects/red_hook.htm

There are still a few hidden gems in the city, nearly undiscovered and rarely used, but still beautiful, well maintained, and restorative to visitors. This one also happens to be hugging the lapping shores of the New York Harbor, with red-brick, Civil War–era warehouses creating an evocative backdrop. A 50-yard boardwalk and cobblestone-lined pathways meander through beds of wildflowers and native plants, many creating protected niches for the scattered wood benches. This is where landscape painters set up easels and stretch time, capturing the pier's fragrant civility on their colorful canvases. The commerce of the Ikea store and the bustle of the Fairway Market are far enough to the east that few people venture over, but it's a simple five-minute walk along the handsome waterfront esplanade to reach this oasis. The brackish air carried on soothing breezes is just a bonus.

Pure **Yoga**

**Address: Two locations: 204 W. 77th St. at
Amsterdam Ave.; 203 E. 86th St at 3rd Ave.
Phone: (West) 212-877-2025; (East) 212-360-1888
Website: www.pureyoga.com**

Several local magazine polls have identified Pure as
offering the "Best Yoga" in the city, and I don't
argue that; they have thought of everything to
elevate practitioner's experiences. On the West Side,
the location below street level ensures that each of
the seven yoga studios are sedate and grounding.
There are Iyengar, Anusara, Vinyasa Flow,
Ashtanga, and other yoga forms taught here, and
the instruction is at a top level. Both contemporary
locations are impressively spacious, with recessed
lounging nooks so deliciously appointed, you'll
want to curl up with a red pillow and let your office
know you're going to be unavailable for
the afternoon. My one reservation with the dual
Pure studios is that aside from a smattering of
public classes, they are membership based and the
fees won't be affordable for everyone. In that case,
do your down dogs at OM (see page 70).

Riverside Park
Promenade

**Address: Eastern edge of Riverside Park from
100th to 110th Sts.
Website: www.nycgovparks.org/
parks/riversidepark**

Walking at a leisurely pace is an ideal way to shed
that layer of light tension that gathers after an
intense day at the office, a spat at home, or a long
commute. One of the loveliest places to take a walk
in New York City is along the broad promenade
(never do two elbows bump unintentionally) in
Riverside Park that runs north for ten blocks at
100th Street. The 30-foot wide macadam allée
is lined with spectacular old sycamore trees that
form a 50-foot canopy in the sky. Dozens of old-
fashioned park benches (concrete structural frames
with wood slats) face each other along the strip, and
there is always an empty one available for brief rests
or long chapter reading. The classic promenade is
breathtaking and enhanced with Hudson River
overlooks and a seasonal café.

Shakespeare Garden

Nestled into a hillside below the Delacorte Theater
in Central Park, where Shakespearean performances
rule the summer, this shady, texturally enticing
garden plays the role of seductive oasis perfectly.
Its tightly coiled flagstone paths serpentine up a
short hill to a secluded circle of grass favored by
early evening picnickers bound for the theater.
But it's the garden itself—overflowing with more
than 120 plant varieties, some cultivated from
cuttings taken directly from Shakespeare's garden
in Stratford-upon-Avon—that is most enchanting.
There is no way to walk through it quickly because
the placement of the spiraling steps and rustic
benches almost forbids it. But what's your hurry?
Take in the delphiniums, ferns, and delicate
poppies, and leave with Shakespeare on your lips:

"O, beauty, till now I never knew thee!"

(*Henry VIII*).

Staten Island September 11
Memorial

Address: North Shore Waterfront Esplanade, just west of the Staten Island Ferry Terminal

Architect Masayuki Sono's memorial to Staten Island's 270 victims of the September 11th attacks is so striking that no one who lived through the day should miss its soaring glory. Two metaphoric white postcards (a reference to the Twin Towers) stand side by side and peel outward toward the sky, significantly framing lower Manhattan in the distance. In the compressed space between them, Sono placed rows of white granite plaques, bearing the name and a profile image of each victim. The memorial is situated on a broad brick and boardwalk platform surrounded by austere wood slab benches and beautiful plantings. You might find this memorial disquieting or you might find it quieting, but you will not find it lacking in passion. Like 9/11 itself, the installation will stop you in your existential tracks and make you contemplate life, love, and your place in the world.

Tudor City **Greens**

**Address: First Ave. and Tudor City Pl.,
at 42nd St.**

There are days when the energy of Midtown puts a pleasant buzz in my New York bones. At other times, it's just too much—and that's when I climb the 40 steps from 42nd Street, withdrawing to the slower "greens" above. I have a fondness for this pair of modest, gated quadrangles that have been sustaining the Tudor City community since the 1920s and asking little in return. The charming greens straddle both sides of 42nd Street and each has its charms, but I think the best spot is in the north section. Make a right through the gates and take a short stroll toward the small gray apartment building in the northwest corner of the green. There's a bench under a huge rhododendron there that faces a concrete birdbath and is slightly hidden by the wooden potting shed. That's my spot.

But I'll gladly share it.

Washington Mews

**Address: A half block south of 8th St.,
bet. Fifth Ave. and University Pl.**

When you visit this nineteenth-century cobble-stoned alleyway in Greenwich Village, be prepared to walk slowly. As slowly as you'd walk if you were holding the hand of a two-year-old. That's the perfect pace for enjoying its overflowing window boxes and the quaint wooden doorways. I live only two blocks from the Washington Mews and have a chance to amble, snail-like, every morning through this narrow lane, which bisects a block of two-story structures built as stables and carriage houses in the 1830s. Nestled within the campus grid of New York University, the mews is well patrolled and always safe. At one time, at least a half dozen of these private back streets were open to pedestrians who wanted to detour off busier thoroughfares into more peaceful passageways. Now only a few remain unlocked. Get here while you still can and, remember, slow down.

Geographic Index

Where Do You Go for
Peace and Quiet?

Do you know a serene urban sanctuary,
a noise-free New York neighborhood, or a calm
city center that does not appear in this book?
Allan would love to hear from you about quiet
locations you visit in the five boroughs. Please
e-mail him directly at info@tranquilicityapp.com.

About
the Author

Allan Ishac is a former advertising creative director
and also the author of *New York's 50 Best Places to
Take Children* and co-author of *The Guide to Odd
New York.* Allan lives in Manhattan and seeks
serenity (and laughter) through balloon sculpting.
You can communicate with Allan through
his TranquiliCity iPhone app at
info@tranquilicityapp.com.